*Six millionaires each have to spend one month
at a friend's Lake Tahoe lodge. Here's what
happened to the first three…*

Millionaire:
Needed for One
Month

Three powerful romances from three favourite
Mills & Boon auth

D0715551

Millionaire: Needed for One Month

MAUREEN CHILD

CHRISTIE RIDGWAY

SUSAN CROSBY

First published in Great Britain 2012
by Mills & Boon, an imprint of Harlequin (UK) Limited,
Eton House, 18-24 Paradise Road, Richmond, Surrey TW9 1SR

MILLIONAIRE: NEEDED FOR ONE MONTH
© by Harlequin Enterprises II B.V./S.à.r.l 2012

Thirty Day Affair, *His Forbidden Fiancée* and *Bound by the Baby* were first published in Great Britain by Harlequin (UK) Limited in separate, single volumes.

Thirty Day Affair © Maureen Child 2007
His Forbidden Fiancée © Christie Ridgway 2007
Bound by the Baby © Susan Bova Crosby 2007

ISBN: 978 0 263 89677 0

05-0112

Printed and bound in Spain
by Blackprint CPI, Barcelona

THIRTY DAY AFFAIR

BY
MAUREEN CHILD

Maureen Child is a California native who loves to travel. Every chance they get, she and her husband are taking off on another research trip. The author of more than sixty books, Maureen loves a happy ending and still swears that she has the best job in the world. She lives in Southern California with her husband, two children, and a golden retriever with delusions of grandeur. You can contact Maureen via her website: www.maureenchild. com.

To Christie Ridgway, Susan Crosby,
Liz Bevarly, Anna DePalo and Susan Mallery

One

"Hunter," Nathan Barrister muttered as he stared at the mammoth wood-and-stone mansion on the shores of Lake Tahoe, "if you were here right now, I'd kill you for this."

Of course, Hunter Palmer wasn't there and Nathan couldn't kill the man who had once been his first—and best—friend, because he was already dead.

The ice around Nathan's heart thickened a little at the thought, but he used his long years of practice to ignore that tightening twinge. Regrets were a waste of time.

"As big a waste as the next month is going to be." He climbed out of his rental car and stepped into a mound of slush he hadn't even noticed.

With a disgusted sigh, he kicked the dirty snow off the polished toe of his shoe and told himself he should have listened to the clerk at the rental agency. She had tried to tell him that renting a four-wheel-drive car would make more sense than the sports car he preferred.

But who the hell expected snow in March for God's sake?

A wry grin curved his mouth briefly. *He* should have expected it. He'd grown up back east and should have remembered that snow could hit anytime, anywhere. Especially this high up in the mountains. But he'd spent so much time trying to forget his past, was it really surprising that even the *weather* had the ability to sneak up on him?

The air was cold and clean, and the sky was so blue it made his eyes ache. A sharp wind whipped through the surrounding pine trees, rustling the needles and sending patches of snow falling to the ground with muffled *plops*.

Nathan shivered and shrugged deeper into his brown leather jacket. He didn't want to be here at all, let alone for a solid month. He never stayed *anywhere* for more than a few days at a stretch. And being here made him think about things he hadn't allowed himself to remember in years.

Reluctantly, he headed for the front of the house, leaving his bags in the car for the moment. The crunch of his shoes on the ground was the only sound, as if the world were holding its breath. Great. Fifteen minutes here and his brain was already going off on tangents.

He shouldn't be here. He should still be in Tahiti at his family's hotel, going over the books, settling disputes, looking into expansion. And next month, he'd be in Barbados for a week and then Jamaica. Nathan moved fast, never giving himself a chance to settle. Never risking more than a few days in any one place.

Until now.

And if there had been any way at all of getting out of this, Nathan would have taken it. God knows, he'd tried to find a loophole in his friend's will. Something that would have allowed him to keep both his own sense of duty in place and his sanity intact. But even the Barrister family lawyers had assured him that the will was sealed nice and tight. Hunter Palmer had made sure that his friends would have no choice but to honor his wishes.

"You're enjoying this, aren't you?" Nathan whispered to his long-dead friend. And when the wind rattled the pine trees, damned if it didn't sound like laughter.

"Fine. I'm here. And I'll try to make the whole month," he muttered. Once he'd completed Hunter's last request, he hoped to hell his old friend would stop haunting his nightmares.

A long white envelope with his name scrawled across it was stuck to the heavy wood front door. Nathan took the short flight of snow-dusted wooden steps, stopped on the porch and tore the taped envelope free. Opening it, he found a key dangling from an ornate keychain and a single sheet of paper.

Hi, I'm your housekeeper, Meri. I'm very busy, so I'm not here at the moment, and chances are you won't be seeing me during your stay. But here's the key to the house. The kitchen is stocked and the town of Hunter's Landing is only twenty minutes away if you need anything else. I hope you and the others to follow enjoy your time here.

Without thinking, he crumpled the short note in his right hand and squeezed it hard.

The others.

In a flash of memory, Nathan went back ten years. Back to a time when he and his friends had called themselves the Seven Samurai. Foolish. But then, they'd been seniors at Harvard. They'd done four hard years together and come out the other side closer than brothers. They'd had their lives laying out in front of them like golden roads to success. He remembered the raucous evening with just a few too many beers when they'd vowed to build a house together and reunite in ten years. They'd each spend a month there and then gather in the seventh month to toast their inevitable achievements.

Yes, it was all supposed to work out that way. And then...

Nathan shook his head and let the past slide away. Jamming the key into the lock, he opened the door, stepped inside and stopped just inside the foyer. From there, he could see into a great room, with gleaming wood walls, a huge stone fireplace with a fire already ablaze in the hearth and lots of plush, comfortable-looking furniture.

As jail cells went, it was better than most, he supposed. He thought of the housekeeper and the nearby town and hoped to hell he wouldn't be bothered by a lot of people. Bad enough he was stuck here. He didn't need company on top of it.

He wasn't here to make friends. He was here to honor a friend he'd lost long ago.

An hour later, Keira Sanders grabbed the oversized basket off the passenger seat, leaped down from the driver's seat of her truck and slammed the door. Her boots slid around on the slushy ground but she dug in her heels and steadied herself. All she needed was to meet the first of Hunter Palmer's houseguests with dirty snow on her butt.

"Great first impression that would make," she murmured as she looked the house over.

It shone like a jewel in the gathering night. Light spilled from the tall windows to fall on the ground in golden spears. Smoke lifted from the stone chimney and twisted in the icy wind coming off the lake. Snow hugged the slanted roof and clung to the pines and aspens crowding the front yard. Winter tended to stick around this high up on the mountain, and she wouldn't have had it any other way.

There was something about the cold and the quiet hush of snow that had always felt…magical to Keira. In fact, at the moment, she'd like to be back in her cozy place in Hunter's Landing, sitting beside her own fire, with a glass of white wine and a good book.

Instead, she was here to greet the first of six men who would be spending thirty days each in the lakeside mansion. Nerves jumped in the pit of her stomach but Keira fought them down. This was too important—to the town of Hunter's Landing and to her, personally.

Just two weeks ago, she'd received a very legal letter from the estate of a man named Hunter Palmer. In the letter, the late Mr. Palmer's attorney had explained the unusual bequest.

Over the next six months, six different men would be arriving in the town of Hunter's Landing, to spend thirty days in this gorgeous mansion. If each of the men stayed for the entire month, at the end of the six-month period twenty million dollars would be donated to charity—a large chunk of which would belong to Hunter's Landing—and the house itself would be donated to the town as a vacation home for recovering cancer patients.

Keira took another deep breath to settle the last of her nerves. As the mayor of Hunter's Landing, it was her job to make sure each of the six men held to the stipulations of Hunter Palmer's will. She couldn't afford for her small town to miss out on a windfall that would allow them to have a spanking-new clinic and a new jail and courthouse and…

Her head was spinning as she smiled to herself. She tightened her grip on the basket and checked to make sure the lid was latched down. Tugging at the lapels of her black jacket, she straightened her shoulders, plastered a smile on her face and prepared to meet the first of the men who could mean so much to Hunter's Landing.

She was good with people. Always had been. And now, with so much riding on the next six months, she was more determined than ever that everything go right. Not only would she ensure that each of the six men would stay his entire thirty days at the lakeside lodge, she was going to make sure they knew how much this all meant to her hometown.

With that thought firmly in mind, she gulped a deep breath of frosty air and headed for the front door. Her boots crunched in the snow but, when she hit a patch of ice, her feet slid wildly. "Oh, no."

Eyes wide, she held tightly to the basket and swung her arms in a desperate attempt to regain her balance. But her feet couldn't find purchase and as she tipped and swayed, she knew she was going to lose both her balance and her dignity.

"Ow!" she shouted when she hit the ground, landing so hard on her butt that her teeth rattled. The basket tipped to one side and she groaned, hoping that the contents were tightly sealed. "Well, isn't this perfect."

The front door flew open and light spilled over her. She blinked up at the man silhouetted in the doorway. Oh, man. This so wasn't how she'd planned to meet Nathan Barrister.

"Who're you?" he demanded, making no move to come down the steps to help her up.

"I'm fine, thanks for your concern," she said, wincing as icy, wet cold seeped through the seat of her jeans. So much for first impressions. Maybe she should crawl back to her truck and start all over.

"If you're thinking of suing, you should know I don't own this property," he said.

"Wow." For a moment, Keira forgot all about getting up—forgot all about the fact that this man and five others just like him could mean a windfall for Hunter's Landing—and just sat there, staring at him in amazement. "You're really a jerk, aren't you?"

"I beg your pardon?"

"Did I say that out loud?"

"Yes."

"Sorry." And she was. Sort of. For heaven's sake, none of this was going as planned.

"Are you injured?"

"Only my pride," she admitted, though her behind hurt like hell and the melting ice beneath her wasn't helping the situation any. Still, might as well make the best of the situation. She raised one hand and waved it. "A little help here?"

He muttered something she didn't catch and, considering his attitude so far, she considered that a good thing. But he came down the steps carefully, grabbed her hand and pulled her to her feet in one quick motion.

His fingers on hers felt warm and strong and…good. Okay, she hadn't expected that. He dropped her hand as if he'd been burned, and she wondered if he'd felt that small zap of something hot and interesting when they touched.

She brushed off the seat of her pants while she looked up at him. For some reason she'd expected him to be an older man. But he wasn't. Tall and lean, he had broad shoulders, a narrow waist and long legs. Considering how easily he'd plucked her off the ice, he was strong, too. Not that she was heavy or anything, but she certainly wasn't one of those stick-figure types of women that were so popular these days.

Ordinarily, a man like him was more than enough to make her heart go pitty-pat. However, the scowl on his truly gorgeous face was enough to make even Keira rethink her attraction. His black hair was stylishly cut to just above his collar. His blue eyes were narrowed on her suspiciously, and his hard jaw was clenched. And his full mouth was tightened into a grim slash across his face, letting her know without a doubt just how welcome she wasn't.

"Wow. Are you really in a bad mood or is it just me?"

He blew out a breath. "Whoever you are," he said, his voice a low rumble that seemed to dip all the way inside her to start up a slow fire, "I didn't invite you here. And I'm not interested in meeting my neighbors."

"Good," Keira said, grinning at his obvious irritation, "because you don't have any. The nearest house on the lake is a couple miles north."

He frowned at her. "Then who are you?"

"Keira Sanders," she said, holding out one hand and leaving it there until rudimentary good manners forced him to take it in his.

Again, there was the nice little buzz of connection when his skin met hers. Did he feel it? If so, he wasn't real pleased about it. Keira, on the other hand, was enjoying the sensation. It had been a really long time since she'd felt the slightest attraction for anyone. Purposely. "Been there, done that" sort of summed up her feelings about romance.

But she had to admit, it was really nice to feel that sizzle.

Still shaking his hand, she smiled up into his scowl. Gorgeous, but crabby. Well, she'd dealt with irritable people before, and there was just no way she was going to let his bad attitude affect Hunter's Landing's chances at getting money that would be a godsend to the small town. "I'm the mayor of Hunter's Landing and I'm here to welcome you."

"That's not necessary," he said and dropped her hand.

"It's our pleasure," she said, hanging on to her good cheer by her fingernails as she turned to pluck the basket out of the snow. "And," she continued as she walked past him, headed toward the front door, "I've brought you a welcome basket, courtesy of the Hunter's Landing Chamber of Commerce."

"If you don't mind," he countered, following after her quickly.

"Not at all," Keira said, walking into the house and stopping just inside the foyer. "I confess, I've been dying to see the inside of this place ever since they started building it last year."

It took a moment or two, but she heard him come in behind her and close the door with an exasperated sigh. He was not just crabby, but very crabby, apparently.

But that was okay. She'd win him over. She had to. She had to make sure that he and the five others who would come after him here would complete the terms of the will that would so benefit her hometown.

"Ms. Sanders..."

"Call me Keira," she said and turned to give him a quick glance and smile.

"Fine. Keira." He shoved both hands into the pockets of his slacks and rocked back on his heels.

He *really* didn't want her there.

"Don't worry," she said, stepping through the arched doorway into the great room, "I won't stay long. I only wanted to welcome you, let you know that you're not alone here."

"I prefer alone," he said flatly and she stopped halfway across the room and turned to look at him, still standing in the foyer.

"Now, why is that?" she wondered aloud.

His features tightened even further, until he looked as though he'd been carved from stone. Not really a people person, Keira decided, then shrugged.

"Anyway," she said loudly, setting the basket down atop a hand-carved coffee table that probably cost more than her monthly house payment. "I've got a few goodies here to make your stay more comfortable."

"I'm sure I'll be fine."

She ignored him and started rooting through the basket, pulling items out, one after the other, with a brief description of each. "Here's a certificate good for free coffee and freshly made doughnuts every morning at the diner. And a jar of homemade jam—Margie Fontenot, the late mayor's widow, makes the best jam in the state. A bottle of wine from Stan's Liquor Stop, fresh bread from the bakery, a bag of ground Jamaican coffee beans—" she stopped to sniff the bag and sighed at the aroma, then continued "—there's a jar filled with the best marinara you've ever tasted, from Clearwater's restaurant—you really should get over there for dinner while you're here. The outside dining area overlooks the lake and there's no better place to catch a gorgeous sunset—"

"Ms. Sanders…"

"Keira," she reminded him.

"Keira, then. If you don't mind—"

"And," she went on as if he hadn't spoken, "there are a few more goodies in here, but I'll let you discover them on your own."

"Thank you."

"Now," she said, turning to face him from across the room, "is there anything else I can do to help make your stay more interesting?"

"Leave?" he asked.

Keira shook her head at him, as if she were sorely disappointed. Wandering the great room, she ran her fingers along the deeply carved mantel over the fireplace and, just for a second or two, enjoyed the heat pouring from the hearth. Her gaze swept the rest of the room and lingered on the view of the lake out of the floor-to-ceiling windows. The moon was just beginning its climb across the sky, and the water shimmered with a breath of light as if waiting for the show to start.

She gave herself a moment or two to calm the flash of irritation inside her. Wouldn't do to insult the man whose very presence could mean so much to her town. But at the same time, she wondered why he was being so nasty. By the time she'd centered herself and turned her gaze back to him, *still* standing in the foyer as if he could force her to leave by simply not welcoming her in, she was wondering something else.

Why did he intrigue her so much when his rudeness should have put her off immediately?

And how was she going to make this man connect with Hunter's Landing and make a commitment to see this through when he so obviously wanted nothing to do with her or the town?

Two

Nathan had had enough.

He'd been at the lakeside mansion for a little over an hour and already he had an uninvited guest.

Plus, Keira Sanders seemed to be oblivious to insults and clearly didn't care that she was very obviously not wanted.

His gaze swept her up and down more thoroughly than he had when he'd first found her sitting in the snow. Her jeans were faded and hugged her long legs like a second skin. Her long-sleeved black sweater came down to her thighs and, ridiculously enough, made her figure look more exposed than hidden. Maybe it was the way the soft-looking fabric clung to her curves, but whatever the reason, Nathan could appreciate the view even while wishing she were anywhere but there.

Her shoulder-length, reddish-blond hair hung loose in waves that seemed to dance around her animated face whenever she moved—which was often. He'd never seen a more mobile woman. It was as if she couldn't bear standing still. She was wandering the great room, her fingers touching, stroking, everything as she passed and he couldn't help wondering what those fingers would feel like touching *him*.

Yet as soon as that thought hit his clearly fevered brain, he knew he had to get her the hell out of the house. He wasn't interested in a monthlong fling. That was more commitment than he'd given to any woman he'd known in the last ten years.

Best to just get her out of the house now. And if that meant being even ruder than he had been already, fine.

"Thank you for coming," he said, waiting until she gave up examining the bookshelves to look at him again, "but if you don't mind, I'd like you to leave."

There. A man couldn't be any more plainspoken than that.

"Wow," she said softly, her green eyes sparkling in reflected light from the fire, "nobody ever taught you how to treat your guests?"

He swallowed hard and pushed away the thought of just how horrified his grandmother would have been at his blatant rudeness. "You're not a guest," he said tightly, reminding her as well as himself. "You're an intruder."

She actually laughed at him. "But I'm an intruder who brought you gifts!"

Nathan finally left the foyer, since it seemed clear that standing beside the door wasn't going to be enough to convince her to step through it. He'd never met anyone else quite like her. She seemed impervious to rudeness, just rolling right along with a cheerful attitude that must, he thought, really annoy the hell out of people who knew her well.

"Look," Nathan said, walking across the polished floor toward her. "I've tried to be polite."

She blinked at him and her smile widened. "Really? *That* was trying?"

Frowning, he ignored the jab and said, "I appreciate the gifts. Thank you for taking the time to come out here. But I would really prefer to be *alone.*"

"Oh, I'm sure you want to settle in," she said, waving one hand at him, blithely ignoring his attempt to get rid of her. "And I won't stay much longer, I swear."

Hope to cling to.

"I only wanted to let you know that Hunter's Landing is ready to help you and the other men who will be staying here in any way we can." She wandered to the big-screen TV, picked up the remote and studied it for a second or two.

If she turned the damn thing on, she might never leave. Nathan walked to her side, took the remote and set it down on a nearby table. She shrugged, walked to the windows overlooking the lake and stood staring through the glass as if mesmerized.

He watched her and couldn't help feeling a little mesmerized himself. The fall of her hair on her shoulders. The curve of her behind. The defiant tilt to her chin. She turned to look at him and her wide, shining eyes fixed on him with a slam of power he didn't want to think about.

"You'll only be here a month," she said quietly, "and

maybe you don't realize just how important your stay and the others' are to Hunter's Landing."

Nathan sighed and resigned himself to at least a few more minutes of conversation. It seemed plain that Keira Sanders wasn't going to leave until she was good and ready. "I know about what your town stands to inherit from the estate."

"But you can't know what it means to us," she insisted, half turning to lean one shoulder against the cold glass. "With that influx of cash, we can build a new courthouse, expand our clinic..." Her voice trailed off and she smiled as if already seeing the changes that would happen to her town.

"And speaking of the clinic," she said quickly, straightening up and walking toward him. "I want to invite you to the town potluck dinner tomorrow night. We're raising money to get the expansion started and—"

"But you'll have the inheritance—"

"Can't count on that until it's reality, can we?" she pointed out, neatly cutting him off before he could finish his sentence. "Anyway, our clinic is good, but it's not nearly big enough. Of course, there's a terrific hospital in Lake Tahoe, but that's a long drive, especially in the winter snow. We need to be able to take care of our own citizens right here and, with the potluck dinner, all the money collected will go directly into the fund for..."

She was talking so fast Nathan's ears were buzzing. He had no interest in going to her community fundraiser and he suspected that she didn't really want him there, either. What she wanted was a donation. Wasn't that what everyone wanted from him in the end?

With the Barrister family fortune behind him, Nathan

had long ago accepted that he was seen first as a bankbook and second as a man. Which suited him fine. He didn't want friends. Didn't want a lover or a wife. What he wanted was to be left alone.

And he suddenly knew just the way to hurry Keira Sanders out the door: Give her what she wanted. What she'd really come for. While she continued to talk in nearly a stream of consciousness while hardly pausing for breath, he stalked across the room to where he'd dropped his briefcase on one of the overstuffed, burgundy leather chairs. Quickly, he opened it, grabbed his black leather checkbook and flicked his ballpoint pen.

Shaking his head, he wrote a check made out to Hunter's Landing, and then tore it from the pad and walked back to where Keira was still smiling and outlining the plans she had for her little town.

"So you see, it would be a great chance for you to meet everyone in town. Nice for you to see the place you'll be living for the next month and maybe it will help you see how important it is to us that you and your friends complete the stipulations of Mr. Palmer's will." She finally took a breath. "If it's okay with you, I'll pick you up tomorrow about six and drive you to the potluck myself. I can take you on a tour of the lake if you'd like too and—"

"Please," Nathan said, interrupting her when it became obvious it would be the only way to keep her quiet. He held out the check and waited until she'd taken it, a question in her beautiful eyes. "Accept this contribution to your clinic fund."

"Oh," she said, "that's very generous of you but—" She stopped, glanced down at the check and Nathan actually *saw* all the blood drain from her face. She went absolutely white and her hand holding the check trembled. "I…I…you…"

Her mouth opened and closed, she gulped noisily and wheezed in a breath. "Oh. My. God."

"Are you all right?" Nathan reached for her, grabbed her upper arm and felt the tremors that were racing through her body.

She raised her gaze to his, waved the check in a tight fist and swallowed hard a time or two before trying to speak. Apparently, he'd finally found the way to make her speechless.

"Are you *serious* about this?"

"The check?"

"The *amount*," she said harshly, then added, "I've got to sit down."

And she did.

Right there on the floor.

She pulled her arm free of his grasp and folded up on herself. Leaning her head back against the closest chair, she looked up at him in stunned amazement. "I can't believe you—"

"It's just a donation," he said.

"Of *five hundred thousand dollars*," she pointed out.

"If you don't want it…"

"Oh, no!" She folded the check and stretched out her right leg so she could stuff it into her jeans pocket. Then she patted it carefully and gave him a grin. "We want it. And we thank you. I mean, the whole *town* is going to want to thank you. This is just wonderful. Completely generous. I don't know what to say, really—"

"And yet you keep trying," Nathan said, feeling

oddly embarrassed the longer she went on about a simple donation.

"Wow. My head's still spinning. In a good way," she insisted, then raised one hand toward him. "A little help here?"

Nathan sighed, reached for her hand and, in one quick move, pulled her to her feet. She flew off the floor and slammed into his chest with a *whoosh* of air pushed from her lungs. His hands dropped to her waist to steady her and, for a quick moment, he considered kissing her.

Which surprised the hell out of him.

Keira Sanders wasn't the kind of woman who usually attracted him. For one, she was too damn talkative. He liked a woman who appreciated a good silence. And she was short. He liked tall women. And he preferred brunettes. And blue eyes.

Yet, as she looked at him, her green eyes seemed to pull at him, drawing him in, tugging him closer than he wanted to be.

With her breasts smashed up against his broad chest, Keira felt a rush of something hot and needy and completely unexpected. The man was as closed-off as a dead-end road, and yet there was something about him that made her want to reach up, wrap her arms around his neck and pull his head down for a long, lingering kiss.

And it *wasn't* the huge check that was sitting in her pocket like a red-hot coal.

"You're a very surprising man," she finally said when she was pretty sure she could speak without her voice breaking.

His hands dropped from her waist and he stepped back so quickly that her shaky balance made her wobble unsteadily before she found stability again.

"It's just a check."

"It's more than that," she assured him. God, she couldn't wait to show his donation to the town council. Eva Callahan would probably keel over in a dead faint. "You have no idea what this means to our town."

"You're welcome," he said tightly. "Now, if you don't mind, I have some work I have to get to."

"No you don't," she said, smiling.

"I'm sorry?"

"You don't have any work," Keira said, tipping her head to one side to study him, as if getting a different perspective might help understand why such a deliberately solitary man could give away so much money without even pausing to think about it. "You just want me to go."

"Yes." His frown deepened. "I believe I already mentioned that."

"So you did." She patted the check in her pocket, swung her hair back from her face and gave him a smile. "And I'm going to oblige you."

A flicker of something like acceptance shot across his eyes, and Keira wondered about that for a second or two. But then his features evened out into a mask of granite that no amount of staring at would ever decipher.

"Okay then," she said, starting for the front door, only half surprised when he made no move to follow her. He'd seemed so anxious to get rid of her, she'd just assumed that he'd show her out once he had the chance. But when she turned to glance back at him, he was standing where she'd left him.

Alone, in front of the vast windows overlooking the lake. Behind him, the water silvered under the rising moon and the star-swept sky seemed to stretch on forever. Something inside her wanted to go back to him. To somehow make him less *solitary*.

But she knew he wouldn't welcome it.

For whatever reason, Nathan Barrister had become a man so used to solitude he didn't want or expect anything to change.

Well, Keira wasn't going to allow him to get away with an anonymous donation. She was going to make sure the town got the chance to thank him properly for what he had done for them with a click of a pen.

Whether he liked it or not, Keira was going to drag Nathan into the heart of Hunter's Landing.

By the next evening, Keira was running on adrenaline. She'd hardly been able to sleep the night before; memories of Nathan Barrister and the feel of his hands on her had kept her tossing and turning through some pretty detailed fantasies that kept playing through her mind.

Ridiculous, really. She knew the man would be here for only a month. She knew he wasn't interested—he'd made *that* plain enough every time he looked at her. But, for some reason, her body hadn't gotten the message.

She felt hot and itchy and…way more needy than she'd like to admit.

Apparently it had been way too long since she'd had a man in her life. But then, the last man she'd been interested in had made such a mess of her world that she'd pretty much sworn off the Y chromosome.

Then grumpy, rich and gorgeous Nathan Barrister,

rolled into her life and made her start rethinking a few things. Not a good idea.

She spun her straw through her glass of iced tea and watched idly as ice cubes rattled against the sides of the glass. It felt good to sit down. She'd been running all day, first calling an emergency meeting of the town council so she could tell them about Nathan's donation. And, she smiled as she remembered, Eva Callahan had behaved as expected, slumping into a chair and waving a stack of papers at her face to stave off a faint.

Once the meeting was over she'd had to take care of a few other things, like depositing that check, talking to the contractor about the renovations to the clinic, settling a parking dispute between Harry's Hardware and Frannie's Fabrics and finally, coming here to the Lakeside Diner.

Being mayor of a small town was exhausting, and it was really hardly more than an honorary office. Her duties consisted mainly of presiding over town council meetings once a month, playing referee to adults old enough to solve their own problems and trying to raise money for civic projects. And yet, she seemed to always be busy. She didn't have a clue how the mayors of big cities managed to have a life at all.

But then, Keira thought, isn't that the way she wanted it? Keeping busy gave her too little time to think about how her life had turned out so differently from what she'd expected. She picked a French fry off her plate and popped it into her mouth. Chewing, she glanced around the crowded diner and took a deep breath. Here, no matter what else was going on in her life, Keira could find comfort.

The Lakeside Diner was a tiny coffee shop and more or less a touchstone in Keira's life, the one constant she'd always been able to count on. Her parents had owned and operated the diner before her and she herself had started working here, clearing tables, when she was twelve.

Then, when her parents died, Keira had taken over, because there was her younger sister, Kelly, to provide for. Now, she had a manager to take care of the day-to-day running of the diner, but when she needed a place to sit and recharge, she always came here.

The red Naugahyde booths were familiar, as was the gleaming wood counter and the glass covered cake and pie dishes, the records in the jukebox her father had loved hadn't been changed in twenty years. Memories crowded thick in this diner. She closed her eyes and could almost see her dad behind the stove, grinning out at her mom running the cash register.

This diner—like Hunter's Landing—was *home*.

"Hey, Keira. Can I see it?"

She opened her eyes, startled as an older woman slid onto the bench seat opposite her. Sallye Carberry grinned, and held out one hand dotted with silver rings.

"See what?" Keira asked.

"The check, of course," Sallye prompted. "Everyone in town is talking about it. Margie Fontenot told me that she'd never seen anything quite so pretty as all those zeros. I just wanted an up close peek at it."

"Sorry, Sallye," Keira said, taking a sip of her tea. "Already deposited it."

"Well, darn." The older woman slumped back against the seat and huffed out a disappointed breath that waved the curl of bangs on her forehead. "That's a bummer."

Keira laughed.

Sallye waved one beringed hand. "That's okay, I'll settle for meeting the man himself. I hear he's a real looker. He *is* coming to the potluck so we can all get a look at him—I mean thank him—isn't he?"

There was the question.

She knew damn well Nathan wouldn't want anything to do with the town or their potluck dinner. She knew he didn't want their thanks and was pretty sure he wouldn't want to see her again any time soon. So anyone with a grain of sense would keep her distance, right?

The last thing she should do was go back to the lakeside mansion to see a man who wanted nothing to do with her.

And yet…

Keira checked her silver wristwatch, saw she had a couple of hours until six and took one last sip of her tea. Sliding from the booth, she looked down at her late mother's best friend and nodded. "He'll be there," she said firmly.

Three

Nathan felt like a prisoner.

And damn it, he shouldn't.

He *preferred* being alone.

But this kind of alone was too damned quiet.

He stepped out onto the deck overlooking Lake Tahoe and let the cold wind buffet him. His hair lifted in the icy breeze, and he narrowed his eyes as he stared out over a snowy landscape. Silence pounded at him. Even the soft sigh of the lake water slapping against the deck pilings seemed overly loud in the eerie stillness.

The problem was, Nathan thought, he wasn't used to this kind of alone. Other people considered him a recluse but, even in his insular world, there was more…interaction.

He traveled constantly, moving from one of his

family's hotels to the next. And on those trips he dealt with room service personnel, hotel managers, maids, waiters, the occasional guest. No matter how he tried to avoid contact with people, there were always some who he was forced to speak to.

Until now.

The plain truth was he hated being completely alone even more than he hated being in a crowd.

His fists tightened on the varnished wood railing until he wouldn't have been surprised to see the imprint of his fingers digging into the wood. He was used to people jumping when he spoke. To his employees practically doing backflips to accommodate his wishes. He liked dropping in on his favorite casino in Monte Carlo and spending the night with whatever blonde, brunette or redhead was the most convenient. He liked the sounds of champagne bottles popping and crystal clinking, and the muted sound of sophisticated laughter. He was accustomed to picking up a phone and ordering a meal. To calling his pilot to get his jet ready to leave at a moment's notice.

Yet now he knew he couldn't go anywhere.

And that was the real irritant chewing at him. Nathan hadn't stayed in any one place for more than three or four days since he was a kid. Which was exactly how he wanted it. Knowing that he was *trapped* on top of this damned mountain for a damned *month* was enough to make him want to call his pilot now.

Why he didn't was a mystery to him.

"Hunter, you really owe me big time," he said and didn't know whether to look toward heaven or hell as he uttered the words.

Hunter Palmer had been a good guy, but reaching out from beyond the grave to put Nathan through this should have earned him a seat in hell.

"Why did I come here in the first place?" he whispered, asking himself the question and knowing he didn't have an answer.

Old loyalties was not a good enough reason.

It has been ten years since Hunter had died. Ten years since Nathan had even thought of those days, of the friend he'd lost too young. Of the five others who had been such a huge part of his life. He'd moved on. Built his world just the way he wanted it and didn't give a damn what anyone else had to say about it. That pledge the Samurai had made to one another? It seemed to come from another lifetime.

He thought briefly of the framed photos of the Seven Samurai, as they'd called themselves back then, hanging here in the upstairs hall. Every time he passed them, he deliberately looked away. Studying the past was for archaeologists. Not barristers. He didn't owe Hunter or any of the others anything. College friendships were routinely left behind as life continued on. So why in hell was he here?

A bird skimmed the water's surface, its wings stretched wide, its shadow moving on the lake as if it had a life of its own. "And even the damn bird is freer than I am."

Pushing away from the rail, he turned his back on the expansive view of nature's beauty and walked back into what he was already considering his cell.

He glanced at the television, then rejected the idea of turning it on. There were plenty of books to read, and even a state-of-the-art office loft upstairs but he couldn't imagine sitting still long enough to truly accomplish anything, at the moment, all he could do was prowl. He could take a walk, but he might just keep on walking, right down the mountain to the airport where his private Gulfstream waited for him.

"I'm never gonna make the whole damn month," he muttered, shoving one hand through his hair and turning toward the table where his laptop sat open.

He took a seat, hit a few keys and checked his e-mail as soon as the Internet connection came through. Two new letters were there, one each from the managers of the London and Tokyo Barrister hotels.

Once he'd dealt with their questions about his schedule, Nathan was at a loss again. There was only so much work he could do long-distance. After all, if he wasn't there in person, he couldn't scowl at his employees.

When the doorbell rang, he jumped to his feet. This is what he'd come to, then. Grateful for an interruption. For someone—anyone—to interrupt the silence that continued to claw at him. He closed the laptop and stalked across the great room to the front door.

When he opened the door, he said, "I should have guessed it would be you."

Keira grinned, slipped past him into the house and then turned to look at him. "You're going to need a coat."

Nathan closed the door and didn't admit even to himself that he was glad to see her. As annoying as she was, she was, at least, another voice in this damned quiet.

"I'm warm enough, thanks."

"No, I mean, the potluck is outside so you'll really need a coat." She turned again and walked into the great room as if she belonged there. Her voice echoed in the high-ceilinged room and her footsteps sounded like a heartbeat. "We could have held the dinner at the court-house, but it's a little cramped and the band said it would be easier to set up outside."

"The band?"

"Uh-huh," she said, looking around as if she hadn't just seen the place the day before, "it's a local group. Super Leo. They play mostly rock but they'll take requests, too, and they're good guys. They all grew up here."

"Fascinating," Nathan said, moving to the edge of the foyer, leaning one shoulder against the wall and crossing one foot over the other as he watched her move. Damn, the woman looked good.

It was the solitude getting to him. The only explana-tion why he was interested in a short, mouthy redhead when ordinarily, he never would have looked at her twice. The fact that he'd only been "enjoying" this solitude for a day didn't really matter.

"The town council approved new lights for this year, so the square will be bright as day with plenty of room for dancing. When I left they were already setting the food out on the tables and the band was tuning up, so we really should get going if you don't want to miss anything."

"Miss anything?" Nathan shook his head. "I told you yesterday that I had no interest in going to your town party or whatever."

"Well, I didn't think you *meant* it."

"Why not?"

"Who wouldn't want to go to a party?"

"Me." Now, if the party were in St. Tropez, or Gstaad, he'd be right there. But a small-town party in the middle of Nowhere, U.S.A.? No, thanks.

She stared at him as if he'd just grown another

head. Then she shrugged and went on as if he hadn't said a word.

"The town council was incredibly grateful for your donation."

"You told them?" An uncomfortable itch settled between his shoulder blades. He didn't mind donating money. It was simply a part of who he was. But he preferred anonymity. He didn't want gratitude. He just wanted to be left alone.

But even as he thought this, he realized that he'd been complaining about the solitude just a minute before.

"Of course I told them," she said, picking up a throw pillow from the couch and fluffing it before she dropped it back into place. "Who am I, Santa? Dropping money into the town coffers without an explanation? I don't think so. They all want to meet you, to thank you for your generosity."

"Not necessary."

"Oh, but it really is," she said and reached down to straighten a stack of magazines strewn across the coffee table. "If you don't come to the potluck so everyone can meet you…"

"Yeah?"

She shrugged. "Then I guess everyone will just have to come to *you*."

Nathan sighed. She was blackmailing him into attending her damned town function. And doing a pretty good job of it, too. If he didn't go, he had no doubt that she'd lead droves of citizens up the mountain to intrude on the lodge. He'd be hip-deep in people before he knew it.

"Extortion?"

"Let's call it judicial negotiations."

"And if I go to the party, you'll leave me alone."

She held up one hand like a Girl Scout salute and said, "I so solemnly swear."

"I don't believe you."

"Gee, attractive, crabby *and* smart."

A smile twitched at his mouth, but he fought it into submission. No point in encouraging her any.

"Fine. I'll go."

"Wow," she said, patting her hand over her heart, "I'm all excited."

Her green eyes were shining and a smile curved her tantalizing mouth. The gray sweater she wore beneath a black leather jacket outlined the swell of her breasts, and her faded jeans and battered boots made her look too tempting to a man who was going to be trapped on a damn mountaintop for a month.

So Nathan got a grip on his hormonal overdrive and turned to the hall closet. He opened it, snatched out his brown leather jacket and pulled it on over his dark green cashmere sweater.

A few minutes ago, he'd been complaining that he was too alone. Now, he was going to a block party, of all things.

Be careful what you wish for.

Keira sneaked glances at him as she drove down the mountain. His profile was enough to make her heart stutter and when he turned his head to look at her, she almost drove into a tree.

"Whoops." She over-straightened and her snow tires slipped a little on an icy patch of road.

"Was this a ploy to get me on the road long enough to kill me?"

"Everything's fine," she said, tightening her grip on the wheel. "But would you like to take a look around before we head into town?"

"No, thanks." He checked the gold watch on his left wrist. "I can only spare an hour or two."

"Why?"

"Because."

"Ah. Good reason." Keira smiled and followed the curve of the road. There was a steep drop-off beyond the white barrier and Nathan glanced down into the abyss.

"Look," he said, "I'm only coming to this party to avoid the alternative."

"Don't worry, you'll be glad you came."

"Why do you care if I attend this party or not?"

"Why?" She risked another glance at him as soon as the road straightened, then turned her gaze ahead again. "You and the others who'll stay at the lodge after you are doing something tremendous for our town. Why wouldn't we want to thank you for that?"

He shifted uncomfortably on the truck seat. "I can't speak for the others, but I'm not doing this for you or your town."

"Then why?"

His mouth flattened into a grim line. "It's not important."

"But it's important enough for you to come here. To stay for a month?"

Still scowling, he said, "I'm here. As to the month… I don't know."

A small spear of panic jolted through Keira at the thought that he might leave. If he did, then, according to the terms of the will she'd read, the town of Hunter's

Landing would get nothing and the lakeside mansion would be sold.

She couldn't let that happen.

She *had* to convince Nathan Barrister to stay for the whole month. And maybe the best way to do that was to show him the town he and his friends were going to help. To let him see firsthand what a difference a month of his time could make to all of them.

But if he really wanted to go, how could she make him stay?

"But you agreed to the month."

"I did," he said, and she sensed, more than saw, him shrug his broad shoulders. "But I don't know that it's feasible. I have businesses to watch over. Places I'm supposed to be."

Already he was making mental excuses. Giving himself an out. Looking for a way to escape the terms of the will. The panic Keira's heart felt a moment ago jumped into hyperactive life and did a quick two step in the pit of her stomach. Did he believe that by making that incredibly generous donation he didn't have to complete the terms of the will?

"You wouldn't really leave soon, would you?"

He shifted in his seat and the leather creaked as he moved. "If you're looking for guarantees, I can't give them to you."

"But you agreed to the terms."

"Yes."

"So your word's not worth much?"

He frowned at her. "Is insulting me your grand plan to get me to cooperate? If so, it's a bad idea."

"Probably." She sighed and took the final turn down

the mountain road. Just a half mile ahead was Hunter's Landing, where her friends and neighbors were celebrating and planning the changes that would be coming at the end of six months.

She wondered how happy they'd all be to meet Nathan Barrister if they knew just how close he was to ruining those plans.

Pulling the car off to the side of the road, Keira threw the gearshift into park, yanked up the emergency brake and turned in her seat to look at him head-on.

"Problem?" he asked.

"You could say so," she said. In the darkening light, his pale blue eyes shone like chips of ice—and were just as welcoming. "This might not mean much to you," she said, "but your staying here for the entire month can mean a huge difference to the people here."

"I didn't say I was leaving," he pointed out.

"You didn't say you were staying, either," she countered.

"I am for right now," he said.

"That's supposed to make me feel better? Right now?"

"It's all I can give you."

Keira wanted to grab him and shake him, but she knew that wouldn't do any good. He was so closed-off, so shut down from anything other than his own feelings, she'd need a hammer to pound home her point. Tempting, but probably not logical.

"You've been here only one day. Give it a chance. Give *us* a chance."

He looked at her in the waning light and, just for a second, Keira thought those eyes of his warmed a little.

But she was probably mistaken since an instant later, they were cool and distant again.

"If you do," she added, "who knows, you might just like it here."

One dark eyebrow rose. "I'm not expecting to like it."

"Well," she said, smiling as she turned to shift the car into gear again and head into town, "surprises happen every day."

"Whether I stay or go is really none of your business." His tone clearly stated that was the end of the discussion.

Well, Keira wasn't sure who he was used to dealing with, but she wasn't about to back down under that king-to-peasant attitude.

"That's where you're wrong, Nathan." She paused and threw him a smile designed to either put him at ease or worry him half to death. "You don't mind if I call you Nathan, right? Well, Nathan, it *is* my business to see that you stay here. As mayor, I can't let you walk away from something that will mean so much to us."

He studied her for a long minute. She felt his gaze on her and forced herself to keep her own gaze focused on the road ahead of her. As they got closer to town, she heard the still-distant sounds of the band playing and steeled herself for whatever he was going to say next.

"Just so you know, Keira, if I decide to go, there's no way you'll be able to stop me."

She took the last turn in the road and saw Hunter's Landing spilling out ahead of her. Party lights were strung across the street, tiny blazes of white in the gathering darkness. People crowded the whole area, and a few couples had already started dancing.

Her heart swelled with love for the place and the

people she'd grown up with. Determination filled her as she turned to glance at the man beside her. She smiled and said, "Nathan, never issue a challenge like that to me. You'll lose every time."

They were swept into the party the moment she parked the truck, and Keira watched with some amusement as Nathan was dragged unwillingly into the center of things. The man was so stiff, so aloof, he stood out from the crowd like an ostrich in a chicken coop.

With the band's music pouring over them in a continuous wave of sound, Keira stood to one side and watched Nathan's features tighten as a few of the older men gathered around him to give Nathan some advice on fly-fishing.

The devil inside her told Keira to leave him to it. To let him be surrounded by the townspeople she'd so wanted him to meet. But a rational voice in the back of her mind drowned out that little devil by pointing out that if he *hated* it here, he'd have little reason to stay for the month to insure the town's bequest.

So she walked up to the group of men, smiled and said, "Sorry, guys, but I'm going to steal Nathan away for a dance."

"Aw, now, Keira, we're just telling him about the best spots in the Truckee River for fishing," one of them argued.

"And it was fascinating," Nathan said, dropping one arm around Keira's shoulders and dragging her in close to his side, as if afraid she'd change her mind and leave him there for more fishing advice. "But if you'll excuse me, gentlemen, I did promise the lady a dance."

Keira hid her smile and told herself that the warmth of Nathan's arm around her had more to do with body heat than sexual pull. Although she wasn't easily convinced, since parts of her that hadn't been hot in a very long time were suddenly smoking with sizzle and warmth.

When they moved away from the crowd toward the dance floor, Nathan bent his head and muttered, "I don't know whether to thank you for rescuing me or throttle you for bringing me here in the first place."

His voice was nearly lost under the slam of sound, so Keira leaned in closer to make sure he heard her response. "But you looked like you were having so much fun."

"I don't fish," he muttered.

"Maybe not," she pointed out, "but thanks to Sam Dover and the others, you could now if you wanted to."

He stopped and, since his arm was still wrapped around her shoulder, she did a quick stop too and slammed into his side.

"You're enjoying this, aren't you?"

"Would it be wrong to say yes?"

He frowned down at her. "I don't think I've ever met anyone like you before."

"Nathan! A compliment?"

"I'm not sure that's how I meant it."

She grinned. "That's how I'm taking it."

"Big surprise."

Keira wasn't fooled. There was a twitch at the corner of his way-too-kissable mouth that told her he was fighting the urge to smile. In the last day or so, she'd noticed he fought down smiling a lot. And she wondered why.

"So," she asked, "are you really going to dance with me?"

He sighed. "If I don't, are you going to sic the fishermen on me again?"

She lifted her arms into the dance-with-me position and said, "Nothing wrong with a good threat."

Four

The music slowed down into as close as a rock band could get to a romantic ballad, and Nathan reached for Keira. The instant his arm went around her waist, he felt a charge of something that jolted him from the soles of his feet straight up through the top of his head.

She smiled at him and he knew she'd felt it, too.

Her right hand felt small in his and the featherlight weight of her left hand seemed to be branding his shoulder. The air was icy and the street was crowded with people, yet he felt as if he and Keira were alone in the tropics, heat pouring through them with enough intensity to kindle a white-hot flame.

"What're you thinking?" she asked as he steered her around the makeshift dance floor in the middle of town.

"I don't think I'll tell you," he said and deliberately

raised his gaze from the sparkling beauty of her green eyes. "I have a feeling you'd find a way to use it against me."

"Oh, you're a sharp businessman, aren't you?" she asked, and suppressed laughter colored her voice.

He risked a glance down at her and found that the power in her gaze hadn't lessened a bit. "You've already blackmailed me *once*," he reminded her.

"For a good cause," she pointed out.

"I really don't think that's an excuse the legal system would smile on."

"Hey, I'm the mayor. Would I do anything illegal?" She smiled at him again, and damned if Nathan's body didn't do a quick lunge. His arm tightened around her waist, tucking her in even closer, and when she moved in the dance, she did things to him he didn't want to think about.

So he didn't. To distract himself, he let his gaze sweep the town, and it didn't escape him that he could see the whole thing in a matter of seconds. The buildings were old, but well cared for. Fresh paint shone in the lights and sidewalks were swept clean. Flower boxes jutted out from window fronts and he presumed that if spring should ever come to the mountains, those boxes would be full of bright flowers.

A couple hundred people crowded the blocked-off streets, and he saw everyone from old couples sitting quietly holding hands to teenaged lovers gazing at each other so intently, he half expected to see tiny cartoon hearts circling their heads.

Keira fit right in here. She was greeted by hugs, kisses, teasing laughter and shouts, and Nathan wondered briefly what it must be like to so thoroughly belong somewhere. He hadn't known that feeling since he was a kid. And he had, over the years, done everything he could to *keep* from belonging anywhere in particular. Yet he could see that Keira thrived on the very kind of life he'd avoided.

Overhead, the moon peeked through a wisp of clouds and shone down onto the town, bathing it in a silvery glow that made it look almost magical. Which was a ridiculous thought, since Hunter's Landing was clearly no more than a tiny town in between a couple of bigger ones.

If Hunter Palmer hadn't chosen this town—no doubt for the pleasure of building a mansion in a town that shared his name—Nathan would never have known of the place's existence. He wasn't a man to go wandering down unbeaten paths.

He preferred big cities. The anonymity of hotel rooms with an ever-changing sea of faces surrounding him. He had no interest in bonding with a town and people he'd never see again once he got off this mountain.

And yet...

Keira held his hand a little tighter as if she could read his thoughts and was subtly trying to hold him here, to this place.

She felt good in his arms, her curvy little body pressed up close to his, and Nathan could admit, at least to himself, that he wanted her. He hadn't had any intention of making a connection of any sort with the people of this town, but she just wouldn't go the hell away. And was it his fault if his body reacted to hers?

This reaction was chemical, pure and simple.

He'd been so long without a woman sharing his bed
that he was reacting to the first female to get close.

Not that she was close.

But the thought of her in his bed was enough to set
a flash fire racing through his bloodstream.

"Oh," she said, tipping her head back to stare up at
him, "now I *really* have to know what you're thinking.
Your face just got all stiff and your eyes went slitty."

"Slitty?"

"It's a word," she argued.

"Barely."

"You're changing the subject."

"Apparently not successfully," he said, not surprised
at all that she wasn't willing to back down.

"Once you get to know me," she countered, "you'll
know that I don't give up all that easily."

"Trust me," Nathan said, "that much I've already
learned."

"Wow!" Her face lit up and her eyes sparkled in the
overhead lights. "We're really making progress here,
aren't we?"

"Progress?"

"You bet. I know that you get all stiff when you don't
want to talk about something, and you know that I'm a
little stubborn…"

"A little?"

"…we're practically friends already."

"Friends?"

"Nothing wrong with that, is there?" she asked and
came to a stop as the song ended and a new one, one
with a raw, savage beat, started up. "You have so many
friends you can't use another one?"

No, he didn't have friends. Purposely. That need had been satisfied then discarded ten years ago. Now his life was streamlined. Just the way he wanted it.

Nathan let her go gratefully, though he couldn't help but notice just how empty his arms felt without her in them. A warning flag if he'd ever seen one. Keeping a few feet of space between them seemed like the smart move, here. And he'd always been smart enough to protect himself.

"We're not friends, Keira. Friends don't use extortion to get their way."

"Really?" she asked, tipping her head to one side so that her hair fell in a reddish-blond wave to the side of her head, "isn't that what your friend Hunter Palmer did?"

He felt himself stiffen again and couldn't seem to stop it. "Excuse me?"

"Well," she said, linking her arm through his and leading him farther away from the pulsing beat of the song and the jostling crowd on the dance floor, "you clearly don't want to be here, but you're going to stay the month because your old friend asked you to in his will. So, isn't that extortion?"

He supposed it was and hadn't he been thinking pretty much along the same lines earlier today? "You can be extremely annoying."

"I've heard that before."

"Again, not surprising."

"Come on, Nathan," she said, tugging at his arm, "I think it's time I fed you. Maybe your attitude will improve once you've tasted Clearwater's lasagna."

He didn't want to spend more time with her. She had a way of getting into his head that he wasn't entirely comfortable with. So he stopped dead, and Keira jolted back into him.

"Hey, a little warning before a sudden stop might be a good thing."

"Sorry. But I think I've seen enough," he said. "I came to the potluck and now, if you don't mind, I'd like to go back to the house."

"You haven't eaten yet," she said.

"Not hungry."

"Liar."

He shoved his hands into his jacket pockets and gave her a look that had been known to send hotel managers scurrying for cover. "Are you going to take me back or not?"

"You bet. As soon as we eat."

"Damn it, Keira—"

"You have to eat, Nathan. You might as well do it here."

When he didn't budge, she prodded. "You're not scared of us, are you?"

"Us?"

"The town." She spread her arms wide as if encompassing everyone there in a hug. "Hunter's Landing. You a little worried that if you stick around for a while, you just might get to like us?"

"Don't you get it?" he asked, suddenly feeling that, if he wasn't rude, she'd never listen to him. "I'm not here to make friends. I'm here because I have to be. I owe it—" He stopped himself before he gave her more information than he wanted to. "I'm not interested in liking or disliking your town. I just want to put in my time and get back to my life."

"Wow." She blinked up at him. "You did it again."

Nathan sighed and asked the question he knew he shouldn't. "What?"

"Turned on the rude," she said. "It's pretty impressive, really, just how easy it is for you to get all crabby and nasty."

"You don't listen to me otherwise."

"Oh," she said, smiling again like nothing was wrong, "I listen, I just don't pay attention. There's a difference. And whether you want to admit it or not Nathan Barrister, you're hungry. You may not want to be here, but since you *are* here, you might as well eat. Right?"

How was a man supposed to argue with that kind of twisted logic? She grabbed his arm and tugged him toward a long line of tables piled high with what looked like every kind of food imaginable.

Nathan felt like a petulant child and he didn't like it. No point in being stubborn about this, though. There was no way out. He couldn't *walk* back up the mountain. And he wasn't going to ask someone else to drive him up. So he'd wait. He'd eat. And once he got back up the mountain, he'd call his damn pilot and tell him to fire up the engines.

No way was he going to stay for the whole month. A couple of days in Keira Sanders's company was enough to convince him to leave while he still could.

For the next hour, Keira watched him with some amusement.

Nathan probably wouldn't be happy to hear it, but she found it pretty entertaining watching him try to dodge the town's gratitude. Every time someone stepped up to say thank you, Nathan turned into a stone statue. He would nod politely, close down his features and then turn away, only to be met by yet another grateful citizen.

What was it about this man that was so intriguing? She couldn't quite figure it out. But seeing him squirm uncomfortably around her friends and neighbors was just captivating enough that she wanted to know him better. To slip under the walls he'd erected around himself. To get past the arrogant stance and condescending tone to the man who lived within.

Or was she just fooling herself?

Maybe there was no inner Nathan to meet. Maybe he was just who he appeared to be. Rich, aloof, disinterested. But she didn't believe that. She'd seen the quick flash of humor in his eyes before he deliberately stamped it out, and she was willing to put in the time to see if she could reach past his barriers.

Why?

She hadn't figured that out yet.

Oh, sure. She was working double-time to make sure he didn't leave town before his month was up. But this was more personal than insuring a bequest to the town she loved. This was getting to be…interesting.

When her cell phone rang, Keira glanced at the screen, noted the number and got up to walk farther away from Nathan and the crowd to answer it. She threw him a finger-wave as she moved off and smiled to herself at the panic that zipped across his face.

Couldn't really blame him for the panic as Sallye and Margie, the town's two most talkative women, took up position on either side of him. Keira left him to his own devices as she stepped into the doorway of the flower shop and flipped her phone open.

"Hi, Kelly!"

"Hey, big sister, how's it going?" Kelly Sanders sounded like she was down the street instead of calling from her home in London.

Keira didn't even want to think about what kind of charges were going to be adding up on her cell phone. But she was so glad to talk to her younger sister, she wasn't going to worry about it.

"Everything's good," Keira shouted to be heard over the band who, even now, was cranking up the decibels to ear shattering level.

"What's going on?" Kelly demanded, then, after a heartbeat, whined, "It's a block party, isn't it? Everyone's having a good time and I'm not there."

"Yeah, but you're in Europe. Really good times, remember?"

"True," she said wistfully. "Usually I love it here, but I hate knowing life is going on at home without me."

Well, that was typical Kelly. She had always wanted to be in the center of things. Even when she was a little girl, Kelly wasn't satisfied with being in the background. Their mother used to say that Kelly had been born in a hurry and had just never stopped running.

Keira really missed her. They were each other's only family now, and this last year, when Kelly had been living in England, Keira had had a hard time of it.

"I'll tell everyone you said hi," she said and glanced down the street, making sure Nathan hadn't bolted for freedom. Nope, he was still there, sandwiched between the two very nice, very chatty older ladies. Keira grinned, leaned against the shingled wall of the flower shop and said, "So what's going on?"

"Oh, Tony's taking me to Paris for the weekend and I wanted to let you know I wouldn't be home for our Saturday night phone call."

Tony—also known as Stewart Anthony Brookhurst, was CEO of some huge conglomerate based in England and, for the last six months, the main topic of all of Kelly's conversations.

"Paris, very nice," Keira said and tried to keep the sigh of envy from slipping from her soul.

She'd had plenty of plans of her own years ago. She'd wanted to finish college, travel, see the world. But in the blink of an eye, her plans—her world—had changed. Not that she regretted being there for Kelly, for putting her own life plans on hold to see to it that her little sister went to college. She didn't resent the fact that while she had stayed here, in the town she loved, Kelly had gone off on the adventures that Keira had once dreamed of.

And, if she did feel occasional spikes of envy jabbing at her, she'd managed so far to hide them from the sister she loved.

"I know," Kelly said with a laugh. "Who would have thought that I'd be saying stuff like that? *Paris for the weekend.* But you know, K, I really love it here. I mean, I miss home and everybody, you especially, but I love living in London. I even like the rain!"

"I know." She heard that love in Kelly's voice every time they spoke. This was supposed to have been a one-year stint—a year that was almost over—in London, for the international bank that had hired Kelly right out of college. But Keira had been preparing herself for months now, to be ready for the day when Kelly announced that she would be *staying* in Europe.

Kelly loved everything about England and now that she was seriously dating a man who had been born and raised there, the chances of her ever moving back to Hunter's Landing were slimmer than ever.

"So what's going on at home, besides the party I'm not at," she asked.

Keira shook off the gloomy thoughts that had settled over her like some sort of shroud and forced a smile into her voice. "We've got our first guest in the lake lodge."

"Oh my God! You're kidding! What's he like? Did you see the inside of the place? Is it fabulous?"

Keira laughed. God, she missed her little sister. "Not kidding, he seems nice, saw the house, it's amazing."

"C'mon," Kelly whined. "There's gotta be more than that. You've been telling me about that house for a year now. So what's it like?"

"It's so gorgeous, you wouldn't believe it. Awesome views of the lake—built of glass and wood and stone, and there's a fireplace big enough to stand up in."

"Oh, wow."

"I'll say."

"And the guy?"

"What about him?"

"'*He seems nice?*'" Kelly laughed. "Please. Give me more than that."

More? What could she say? That he was arrogant and irritating and altogether too attractive? That she was spending too much time thinking about *him* when she should have been worrying about keeping him in the lodge long enough to fulfill the requirements of the will?

"What's his name, at least," Kelly demanded.

"Nathan." There. That was safe information. "Nathan Barrister."

"*Whoa.* Barrister? Like in the Barrister Hotel Barristers?"

"I don't know," Keira said with a shrug her sister couldn't see. "I…maybe."

"Nathan Barrister was in London a couple of months ago. Had a meeting at my bank. Tell me what yours looks like and I'll tell you if it's him."

"Tall. Dark. Pale blue eyes."

"Snotty twist to his mouth?" Kelly asked.

"Not exactly snotty," Keira argued.

"Woo hoo," Kelly crowed. "It *is* him. And you *like* him."

"Dial it down, Kel," Keira said, knowing it was way too late to put the lid back down on that particular box. Kelly was already enjoying herself.

"I don't believe this. Nathan Barrister in Hunter's Landing? That's too funny."

"Why's it funny?" She stiffened at the amusement in her sister's voice and felt like she should be defending the man for some reason.

"Well, he's just such a *stick*. The man has no sense of humor and one look out of those eyes and you practically freeze over. And I saw my boss's face after his meeting with Barrister. You remember I told you that my boss is mean enough to give the boogeyman nightmares?"

"Yeah…"

"When Barrister left his office, my boss was *pale* and shaking."

"Oh."

"Seriously, K," Kelly said, her voice dropping. It was

a strain to hear her over the crash of the band and the swell of laughter and conversation rising up over Main Street. "If you're thinking about falling for this guy, don't do it."

"Oh, please." Keira sighed, shook her hair back from her face and said, "He's here as part of that will I told you about. If he stays for the month, if the rest of them each stay for a month, the town is going to get a heck of a lot of money that we really need. And that's all there is to it. I just said he was attractive, I didn't say I was going after him."

"You didn't say he was attractive!" Kelly's voice shrieked so high that Keira jerked the phone away from her ear.

"I didn't?"

"No. K, don't do this. Don't let yourself care about this guy. Remember what happened with—"

"Don't go there, okay?" Keira interrupted her quickly, not willing to take a forced march down memory lane. "And let's remember here just which one of us is the *older* sister."

"I know," Kelly said, "it's just that you're so—"

"So *what* exactly?"

"I don't know. Never mind. Just be careful, okay?"

"I'm always careful, Kelly. Trust me. Nothing's going to happen." Even if she wanted something to happen, Nathan had already made it perfectly clear that *he* didn't, so what could happen?

Keira peeked around the edge of the flower shop wall to stare down the street at Nathan again—big mistake. He was watching for her. Even from a distance, his gaze slammed into hers with a punch that was nearly physical. Keira sucked in a gulp of air and reached out blindly with her right hand to slap it against the wall in an effort to balance herself. It didn't help much.

A flicker of heat kicked into life in the pit of her stomach and rolled through her like a storm-pitched wave crashing onto shore. She felt her world rock and had to fight to right it again.

"K?" Kelly's voice was in her ear. "Are you okay?"

"Yeah," she lied, swallowing hard past the knot of need that was lodged firmly in her throat. She couldn't look away from Nathan's eyes. "I'm fine. Don't worry about anything."

"But—"

"Look. Send me a postcard from Paris, okay?"

"Sure, but—"

"Bye, honey, be safe." Keira flipped the phone closed and straightened up just as Nathan headed toward her.

Five

Nathan had had enough.

His ears were ringing and the good manners his grandmother had drummed into him were strained now to the snapping point. He'd excused himself from the two older women who had seemed determined to trap him on Main Street forever, and now he was going to get Keira to take him back to the lodge.

He should have driven himself.

Then he wouldn't be waiting around for anyone. He wasn't a man who liked being dependent on someone else for anything. His insides tightened as people milled past him, laughing, talking, dancing. He wasn't a part of them and never would be. Didn't *want* to be. And the more time he spent with all of them, the more clear that feeling became.

He didn't know why the hell he hadn't left the mountains already. He didn't *have* to honor a promise made in college to a man long-dead. Hell, he could donate the twenty million himself and get out of this mess now.

And with that thought firmly in his mind, his steps quickened toward Keira. Her gaze locked with his and he told himself to pay no attention to the brilliant green of her eyes or the worried twist of her mouth. He refused to notice how the light dazzled the ends of her reddish-blond hair, making it almost glow in a soft halo around her head. And damned if he would remember just how good she felt when her body was pressed against his during their dance.

As he came closer, she shoved her cell phone into the front pocket of her jeans and inhaled deeply enough that her breasts rose and then fell with the rush of her sigh.

If his body tightened suddenly, desperately, he ignored it.

"Hi," she said and, somehow, her voice carried over the other sounds on the street. "Enjoying yourself?"

He frowned at her. "Yeah, it's been great. I've eaten, I've danced and I've listened to enough thank-yous to last me a lifetime, so if you don't mind, I'd like a ride back to the lodge."

"Sure."

"That easy?" He felt one eyebrow quirk. He hadn't expected her to give in without trying to talk him into staying longer.

"Why not?" she asked and looked away from him, shifting her gaze to sweep across the town square. She sighed again and this time her voice was so soft, he almost missed it. "I just wanted you to see Hunter's

Landing. To meet some of the people, so you'd know who you and your friends are helping."

"Thank you." He heard the sarcasm in his own voice but didn't bother to try to take the sting out of it.

"I can take you by the clinic for a quick look on the way back. Then you can see exactly what we're planning."

"Not necessary."

Nathan blew out a frustrated breath. Everything in him was clamoring to be gone from this place. To pick up the threads of his life and get back to living the way he knew best. He didn't do well with other people. Didn't care to. And yet now…

Screw it.

"How about that ride?"

Frowning, she said, "You're just determined not to enjoy yourself, aren't you?"

"Was that a requirement?"

She muttered, "Kelly was right. You really are scary, aren't you?"

"What?"

"Nothing." Reluctantly, she shrugged and said, "Let's go."

He followed her to her truck and when she stumbled over a crack in the road, Nathan lunged forward to grab her before she could fall. Spinning her around, he pulled her in close and she laughed up at him. The woman was so changeable, he could hardly keep up.

"Thanks, didn't see that."

"Weren't looking, you mean."

Her hands were on his upper arms and even through the thick leather of his coat, he felt the heat in her touch and wanted more. Wanted to feel her hands on his bare skin, run his own hands over every curve of her body. Hear her sigh as he buried himself inside her.

The images in his mind were suddenly so clear, so overpowering, he could hardly draw a breath past the hot fist tightening around his lungs.

He willed himself to speak. "It's a wonder you're not covered in bruises the way you stumble around."

"What makes you think I'm not?" she asked, still smiling.

He pulled in another deep breath of cold, mountain air and hoped it would help chill the fire in his blood. "What the hell are you doing to me?" he demanded.

"Depends, Nathan," she said, her smile fading as her brilliant green eyes darkened with a need he recognized. "What do you *want* me to do to you?"

"I'm not interested in a short affair," he said tightly, despite the fact that his body clamored for just that.

"Well, who asked you?" She pulled free of his grasp, straightened up and shook her hair back from her face. "Jeez, save a girl from a fall and then accuse *her* of trying to seduce *you*. Nice. Very nice."

He pushed one hand through his hair and wondered why in the hell he tried talking to her anyway. "Can we just get in the damn truck?"

She dug her keys out of her pocket and bounced them on her palm. "You know, you were the one looking at me like you wanted to gobble me up."

He blew out another breath and glared at her. "Call it temporary insanity."

"Wow, one compliment after another," she said and turned for the truck. "You're really on a roll here, Barrister."

He stood just where he was and watched her open the driver's side door and step up into the cab. "You're an infuriating woman, did you know that?"

She glanced back at him over her shoulder. "Believe it or not, that's been said before."

"My sympathies to the poor bastard, whoever he was."

Her face froze up and her eyes shuttered as effectively as if she'd slapped on a pair of dark glasses. "He doesn't need your sympathy, Nathan. And neither do I. So, you getting in the truck or are you going to walk back up the mountain?"

Over the next week or so, every time Keira drove up the mountain, she was half afraid she'd find Nathan gone. After a *really* quiet ride back from the block party, she had dropped him off at the lodge and had hardly waited for his feet to hit the dirt before she gunned the engine and went home. It still embarrassed her to think about driving off in a huff like that.

She never should have let him get to her—couldn't understand why she had. But that little dig about giving his sympathies to whichever man had last been in her life had come a little too quickly after Kelly had brought up the same damn thing.

It wasn't that Keira was sensitive about her past; she just didn't like being reminded of what an idiot she'd been once upon a time.

But that was the past and this was now. And all that mattered *now* was making sure Nathan didn't leave before his month was up. She was pretty sure he was tired of having her show up on his doorstep every day, but she kept visiting him anyway, because she could practically *see* his need to leave vibrating in the air all around him.

And she wouldn't let that happen.

Parking the truck in the drive, she hopped out, slammed the door and headed for the front door. Dark clouds hung heavy over the mountains and the air felt thick with the promise of more snow. As much as she loved winter in the mountains, she was really ready for spring. Unfortunately, it looked as if nature didn't feel the same way.

She shivered, dug her hands into her jacket pockets and quickened her step, only to stop when she heard Nathan's voice shout, "Back here."

Surprised to find him outside and away from the laptop that he clung to like his last link with civilization, Keira headed down the drive. She saw him at the lake's edge and she wasn't ashamed to admit, at least to herself, that the man was really sigh-worthy.

He wore that dark green cashmere sweater again over jeans that looked worn and comfortable. His brown leather jacket gave him a piratical air, and the wind tossed his hair across his forehead, making him look more free than she could remember seeing him before. Her heart jumped a little and her mouth went dry.

She could be in some serious trouble here. Especially if he started looking at her the way he had the night of the party.

"What're you doing?" she called as her boots crunched on the gravel drive.

He gave her a quick look, then shifted his gaze back to the steel gray surface of the lake. "Just looking. Needed some air."

"Really?" she teased as she walked up to stop beside him. "I thought you were very happy breathing canned air and looking at nature through the beauty of clean glass windows."

He snorted. "Let's just say I'm feeling a little cabin fever."

There it was again. She could see how ready he was to chuck the whole month and escape from what he no doubt considered captivity. So what she had to do was take his mind off it.

"I can cure that."

"How?"

"Take a walk with me." She threaded her arm through the crook of his and smiled up at him.

"It's freezing out here," he reminded her.

"If we keep moving, we won't feel it." She tugged at his arm. "Come on. When's the last time you took a walk along a lake as beautiful as this one?"

His gaze swept out over the wide expanse of water and the pine-tree-studded shoreline before turning back to her. "Never."

"Way too long," she assured him and started walking. His long legs outdistanced hers, and Keira caught herself half running to keep up before she pulled back on his arm and said, "It's not a race, you know. You don't actually get a prize for reaching the other side."

He stopped, smirked a little, then shrugged. "Point taken. But I'm not used to just strolling."

"It's okay," Keira said, enjoying the flash of warmth in his too-cool blue eyes. "You can learn."

They walked in companionable silence for a few

minutes before she said, "The bears will be waking up soon."

"Bears?"

"Oh, yeah. Black ones and brown ones. Mamas and babies. They'll be trolling through backyards and tipping over trash cans looking for food or trouble."

"Bears." He shook his head. "Can't imagine living somewhere I could expect to bump into a bear."

"Funny, huh?" she asked, tipping her face up to the darkening clouds, "I can't imagine living anywhere else."

"You were raised here?"

"Yep. Born in Lake Tahoe, raised here. We didn't have a clinic back then. Now our new moms don't have to take that trek over the mountain for medical help." She grinned and patted his arm with her free hand. "And thanks to you, our clinic's going to be even better than it already is."

"You've thanked me enough."

"Not really," she said, "but I'll let it go."

"Thank you."

"For now."

He snorted.

"What about you?" she asked in the silence, "Where are you from?"

"Everywhere," he said, turning his gaze on the wind-whipped water of the lake again.

"That's not an answer, just so you know."

"I was born in Massachusetts. Grew up on the east coast."

Amazing how the man could give information and still make it seem like so little. But Keira wasn't a woman to be dissuaded easily. She dug a little deeper.

"Your family still there?"

"No family," he said shortly, and his gorgeous blue eyes squinted into the wind racing past them.

"I'm sorry."

"No reason to be. You couldn't know."

"Well, I am, anyway," she said and squeezed his arm companionably. "My folks died when I was in college," she said, thinking that maybe if she gave a little, he'd be willing to give a little, too. "They went skiing. Got caught in an avalanche."

His gaze shifted to hers. "Now I'm sorry."

She looked up at him and smiled. "Thank you. It was really hard. I still miss them so much."

"I was ten," he said. "Car accident."

A few words, but said so tightly, Keira could feel the old pain still welling inside him. At least she'd been grown when she lost her parents. She couldn't even imagine how lonely and terrifying it would have been to be a child and lose the safety of your own little world.

"God, Nathan, that's terrible."

"A long time ago," he reminded her. "Had my grand-mother. Dad's mom. She took me in."

"That couldn't have been easy for her," Keira said, then stumbled on a piece of wood jutting up into the rocky trail.

Nathan caught her by tightening his grip on her arm and keeping her steady. "It wasn't much of a hardship. She sent me to boarding school, and I was only home for a month every summer."

"She *what?*"

He blinked at her, clearly surprised by her reaction. What kind of people farmed out ten-year-old kids to boarding schools? What kind of grandparent couldn't see that the child left in her care was in pain and needed more than the impersonal attention of someone *paid* to watch over him?

"It was a very good school," he said.

"Oh, I'm sure." A spurt of anger shot through Keira on behalf of a child who no longer existed. "No brothers or sisters?"

"Nope. You?"

God, he had been all alone with a grandmother too busy to give him what he must have craved. A sense of belonging. A sense of safety. Keira couldn't even imagine what that must have been like for him, and a part of her warmed up to his frosty nature a little more. After all, if he'd been so cut off as a child, how could she possibly expect the man to be open to possibilities?

He was watching her, waiting for her to answer his question, and so she gave him a smile that didn't let him in on the fact that she was really feeling sorry for the boy he'd once been.

"I have a sister. Kelly. She's younger than me and was still in high school when our folks were killed. So, I came home from school, watched over her and started running the family diner."

He frowned. "The coffee shop in town?"

"You noticed it? Yep. The Lakeside was my dad's baby. It's small, but it's been good to us. Made it possible for me to get Kelly into college—well, the diner and a few good loans."

"What about you?" he asked. "You didn't go back to school?"

"No," she said, still irritated with his grandmother for some bizarre reason. "I meant to, I really did. But then

Kelly was in college, and no way could we afford for both of us to go. And when she graduated, I'd already hired a manager for the diner and was running for mayor, so…" She shrugged.

"Your sister should have taken her turn in town to give you a chance to go to school."

Keira shook her head. "No, she got a tremendous job offer right out of school and there was no way she could not take it."

He was silent, but the quiet held a lot of disapproval.

"You could go back to college now," he pointed out.

"Oh, yeah," Keira said, laughing shortly. "Just what I want to do. Go to school with a bunch of kids. Sounds like a great time."

"What's your sister doing now?"

"She's living in London," Keira said, defensive of a little sister who didn't need defending. "She loves England," she added with a wistful sigh. "She sends me pictures that make me want to pack my bags and go there for myself."

"Why don't you?"

"I can't just leave because I *want* to. I have responsibilities to this town."

He sighed, frowned and turned slitted eyes on her. "Is that a not so subtle hint?"

"I wasn't going for subtle," she admitted, smiling up at him despite the glower in his eyes. "Just for a reminder about the responsibilities *you* and the others have to Hunter's Landing."

"I'd never heard of your town until a month ago," he reminded her, "and a month from now, I will have forgotten it."

"Well, don't we feel special," she mused.

"It's nothing personal," he said. "It's just…"

"None of that really matters, does it? You agreed to the terms of the will and—" The toe of her boot caught under a root and she would have gone sprawling if Nathan hadn't steadied her again.

"You're dangerous," he snapped. "Why don't you pay more attention to where you're walking?"

"Hey, I have you here to catch me."

"Don't count on that."

"I am, though," Keira said, blocking his way by stepping in front of him before she stopped dead. "We're all counting on you. You and your friends."

The wind sliced in off the lake and cut at them like a knife straight out of a freezer. Keira's hair swept across her eyes and she plucked it free so she could look at Nathan.

He didn't look happy, but what was new about that? His gaze was locked with hers and his mouth was tightened into a grim slash that told her exactly what he was thinking.

"I know you don't want to hear it," Keira said and reached out to put both hands on his forearms. And even through the icy brown leather jacket, she felt the strength of him, tightly leashed. "But it's true. I can't even tell you how important it is to all of us that you stay for the month."

"Keira—"

"I know, I know," she said, lifting both hands in a mock surrender. "You don't want to hear about this anymore."

"The night of the town party," he admitted quietly, "I had every intention of calling my pilot and flying out of here."

"But you didn't," she said lightly, despite the quick tightening around her insides.

"That doesn't mean I won't," he pointed out. "I don't want you—or anyone—counting on me. For anything."

"That's a hard way to live," she said.

"It's my way."

"It doesn't have to be," Keira said, her voice a whisper that was nearly lost in the swirl of the wind. Why was she doing this? Why did she care how Nathan Barrister lived his life?

He laughed shortly, and the sound was so surprising that Keira blinked at him.

"I *like* my life just the way it is," he said. "I'm not interested in changing it."

"Just like you're not interested in a one-month affair."

His jaw clenched.

Oops.

She didn't know why she'd said that. But now that it was back out in the open between them, she wasn't sure how to *un*-say it, either.

"Keira…"

A puff of white danced on the wind and flew between them as if trying to end their conversation.

"Was that…?" he asked.

"Snow," she said.

And in that split second, several more flakes of snow whipped around them, carried on the wind that snapped and rattled at the pine trees. The temperature dropped what felt like twenty degrees and the lowering clouds looked black and threatening.

"Of course it's snow. For God's sake, does spring *ever* get here?" He inhaled sharply, deeply, and looked at her as if there was something more he wanted to say.

The look in his eyes was nearly electric. Despite the

snowflakes just beginning to flurry around them, she felt heat arcing between them.

Her heartbeat was jittering in her chest, her blood was pumping hot and thick in her veins, and she had the most overpowering urge to reach up and smooth his hair back from his forehead.

Instead, she curled her fingers into her palms and took a deep breath. "It's coming down harder. We should start back."

Six

By the time they reached the lodge, snow had dusted their hair and shoulders and was thick enough in the air that every breath tasted like ice.

When Keira would have turned down the driveway to head for her truck, Nathan caught her elbow and tugged her up the back steps to the house by the lake.

"Nathan…"

He stopped on the top step, looked down into her soft green eyes and said, "You might as well wait out the storm here."

She hunched deeper into her jacket, swung her snow-dusted hair out of her eyes and said, "It might not stop for a few hours."

Glad to hear it, he almost said and was glad he'd managed to clamp his jaw shut. But the truth was, he didn't want to go back into that too-damned-quiet lodge. It was bad enough to be trapped there in the silence when the sun was shining. He had a feeling that being alone with the falling snow and lowering clouds would make him feel as though he were buried alive in a dark cave. Not something he really wanted to experience.

"And it might stop in a few minutes," he pointed out, but, as if to prove that prediction false, the wind kicked up and the snow flew in frenzied flurries.

"If I was home right now," Keira said, "I'd make myself some hot chocolate."

"I can probably handle that," he said. "Or, there's some excellent brandy."

She climbed up a step, coming that much closer to him, and the depths in her green eyes called to him, reached for him. "Brandy would be good, too. Got anything to eat?"

He held out one hand and waited for her to take it. When she did, his fingers folded tightly around hers. "There's plenty of stuff in the fridge."

She took the last step that brought her beside him and gave him a smile that warmed him through, despite the icy wind and the snow sneaking beneath the collar of his jacket. "Then why are we still standing in the storm?"

They walked across the covered deck, stepped into the mudroom and pulled off their jackets and boots. Then, together, they went into the kitchen. The room was cavernous, with built in niches for the stainless steel appliances and a mile of granite counter. The walls were painted to give them an antiqued finish, and the colors were warm cream and brown, making the kitchen seem cozy even in the midst of a storm.

"Let's get that brandy first, worry about food later," Nathan said, and led the way from the kitchen to the great room.

"Good plan," she said and shivered a little as she followed him down the hall.

A fire was blazing in the hearth and Keira moved straight toward it as Nathan walked to the wet bar. He poured them each a drink, then walked to join her by the fire. Handing her one of the crystal snifters, he watched the amber liquid swirl in the bottom of his glass for a long moment before he took a sip.

He swallowed and felt the alcohol fueled fire rush through him as he shifted his gaze to Keira. Firelight played on her skin and danced in her eyes. The ends of her hair shone with a nearly incandescent light and when she lifted her glass to her lips, everything inside him tightened.

After taking a sip, she blew out a breath, smiled and looked up at him. "Wow. Well, that warms you up fast, doesn't it?"

Nathan ground his teeth together and then took a sip of his own brandy. The heat it produced was nothing like the *other* kind of heat swamping him. Just looking at Keira made him burn.

For more than a week now, he had tried not to think about her, to put this insane attraction out of his mind. But he hadn't been able to manage it. When he closed his eyes, he saw her. When he dreamed, he touched her. When he thought he would go out of his mind from the silence in this place, she arrived and he nearly went out of his mind for different reasons entirely.

She sat down on the stone hearth, the fire at her back,

and looked up at him as she cradled the brandy snifter between her palms. "So, Nathan, are you the Barrister Hotel guy?"

One eyebrow rose and he took another sip of his brandy, welcoming the steady fire. "Hotel guy? Yeah. I suppose I am. How'd you know?"

She smiled. "Just a guess. Hunter's Landing isn't exactly on the moon. We get newspapers and magazines here, too. Which one of your hotels is your favorite?"

He shrugged carelessly. "I don't really have a favorite, they're all top-of-the-line establishments, each of them with their own unique pluses and minuses."

"Boy, feel the enthusiasm."

"I'm sorry?"

"Well, come on, Nathan, you own four-star hotels—"

"Five-star," he amended automatically.

"Right. In beautiful, exotic places all over the world. You talk about them as if they're nothing special. As if they're no different from any other exclusive hotels. Is that really what you think?"

Nathan frowned, sat down beside her and instantly appreciated the heat of the fire warming his back. "It's the family business, Keira. They're valuable properties with impeccable reputations that I work hard to maintain."

"Uh-huh," she said and nudged his upper arm with her shoulder. "And do you ever drop in on one in say…Paris, or Dublin…just for fun?"

"No," he said and wondered why he cared that she looked disappointed at his statement. "I have a rigorous schedule I adhere to. The managers of the hotels know when I'm coming, know to have everything ready for my inspection and—"

She sighed.

"What?"

"Do they salute? Click their heels together when you walk into a room?"

He scowled at her. "I'm not a general or something."

"Could have fooled me," she muttered, and took another sip of brandy. "Seriously, do you scare all the people who work for you? I bet you do."

"Certainly not," Nathan said and wondered why he suddenly sounded so damn pompous, even to himself.

"You know," she said, lifting her brandy glass to peer at the room through the amber liquid, "if you changed up your *schedule* once in a while, you might actually catch people unaware. Find out what life in your hotels is really like."

He stared at her, but she wasn't looking at him. Her words, though, were running through his brain as if they'd been etched in neon. Funny, but he'd never thought to do something like that. He was a man who lived his life as efficiently as possible. And to do that, he required a schedule. But...

"You mean, I should show up when they're not expecting me?"

"Why not?" she mused. "They're *your* hotels, aren't they?"

"Yes, but a schedule is necessary to maintain some kind of order."

"And if the kids know that daddy's coming home, they're on their best behavior."

Frowning, Nathan kept staring at her until she finally turned and looked at him, her eyes wide.

"What?" she asked.

"I can't believe I never thought of that."

"Me, neither," she said, smiling. "For heaven's sake, Nathan, do you *ever* do something that you don't have scheduled? Do you ever take a little time out for yourself? You're wound so tight, it gives *me* a headache."

He sighed and shrugged. "In my world, there's no time for relaxing."

"You should make time." She turned on the hearth, laid one hand on his forearm and asked, "For instance, when you're at one of your fabulous, oh-so-exclusive hotels, do you ever take a swim? Get a massage? Sightsee?"

"No. I'm not there for pleasure—"

"Why not?"

"Because…"

"People all over the world want to go to your hotels to experience something amazing. I've seen some of them on TV. And in magazines. God, the one in London, I would actually kill to stay in."

He smiled, picturing the stately stone entrance of the London Barrister with its sweeping marble floors and Old World chandeliers in the lobby.

"It is beautiful," he mused, surprised that he hadn't really appreciated the place until seeing it through Keira's enthusiasm.

"It's amazing," she said with a sigh. "Some rock star held an interview in the penthouse suite and the news covered it—there was an incredible view of London."

"The view from the owner's suite is even more impressive," he told her, picturing it vividly now in his mind. "You can see Big Ben in the distance and the Millennium Wheel."

"The huge Ferris wheel!" she cried and grabbed his

arm hard. "Have you ridden it?" She paused, and said, "Of course you haven't. Honestly, Nathan, don't you ever have any *fun?*"

A little insulted, he said, "Sure I do."

"Prove it. Name one thing you've done just for fun in the last month," she challenged.

"I sat on a stone hearth letting a beautiful woman insult me."

She tipped her head to one side, gave him a smile that made his heart jitter in his chest and repeated, *"Beautiful?"*

"Figures that's the part you heard."

Her smile brightened into a grin. "Well, *duh.*"

He really enjoyed the flash of humor in her eyes. And for the first time in way too long, he realized there wasn't a steel band wrapped around his middle. There was no pressure pounding through him. No hurry to get work done. To check his e-mail. To leave the lodge.

Because suddenly and completely, there was simply nowhere else on earth he'd rather be.

The quiet between them stretched on for another minute or two, the only sound in the room, the snap and hiss of the fire behind them. Shadows stretched across the room and, outside, dots of white swirled in ever changing patterns driven by the wind.

"I envy you," she said quietly. "All the places you've seen."

"You like traveling?"

"Never really traveled much, but yeah, I think I would." She folded her legs up beneath her on the stone, her white socks standing out brilliantly against her dark denim jeans. "I had big plans," she admitted. "When I was a teenager, I went to bookstores and bought street maps of foreign cities. If you had dropped me into the middle of Paris, I could have found my way around blindfolded, I studied those maps so often. London, Dublin, Barcelona, Rome, oh…*Venice.*" Her voice took on a dreamy quality that tugged at something deep inside him. "I wanted to drink wine while riding in a gondola. And see the windmills in Holland, and the Swiss Alps…"

"But…"

"But," she said, giving him a dazzling smile and lifting her glass for another sip of brandy, "life happened. I had to take care of Kelly, and then I got busy with the town and…"

"You stopped reading your maps?"

"Oh, no," she said, "I've still got them all and I still pore over them and plan trips and, one of these days, I'll get away." She looked down into her glass and asked, "What about you? When the month is up, where do you go next?"

"Barbados for a couple of weeks, then Madrid."

She sighed. "It sounds wonderful."

"Barbados or Madrid?"

"Both. But Barbados first. A tropical island." She sighed again.

"A beautiful one," he agreed.

She leaned her head against his shoulder and said, "Show me."

"Can't. Don't have any pictures of it."

"No," she said softly, "Draw me a picture with words. Show it to me through your memories of the place."

Nathan frowned down at the top of her head and tried to give her what she wanted. He thought about the

Barbados Barrister for a long moment, bringing it up in his mind, then slowly said, "It's our newest hotel. Only been open a few months. It sits right on the beach, stretches out almost a block. It has five stories for guest rooms and the sixth floor is the owner's suite." His voice warmed as his memories thickened and the ease of sharing them became more comfortable. "The views stretch on forever. The ocean is so blue you're not sure if you're looking at the sea or the sky."

"Keep going," she said.

He smiled. "There are palm trees and sand so white it hurts to look at it. Green-and-white striped umbrellas surround an infinity pool, and waiters dressed in green shirts and white pants carry trays of drinks to the people lounging poolside."

"More," she said, nestling in closer.

The feel of her leaning into him, the heat of the fire behind them and the quiet of the house all made for a feeling of intimacy that Nathan hadn't allowed himself to feel in years.

"Inside the hotel," he continued, "the wood is pale, almost gold. The windows are always open, and the sea wind sweeps through the lobby where pots of flowers and trailing vines make it seem almost like a jungle." He rested his head on top of hers. "There are deck chairs on a wide, white porch that stretches the length of the first floor, and people sit out there, sometimes all day, just to watch the ocean. And the restaurant has an outside deck where you can dine and watch the sunset."

"Sounds wonderful."

"Actually," he said, not a little surprised himself, "it really is."

She raised her head and smiled up at him. "I'm going to buy a map of Barbados," she said, "and I'm putting that hotel on my list."

He smoothed her hair back from her face, his finger-tips lingering on the softness of her skin. She closed her eyes at his touch and shivered a little as his fingers slid down to her jaw.

"I'll put your name on the VIP list," he whispered, threading his fingers through her silky hair again just to enjoy the sensation.

"Nathan?"

"Keira…"

"The storm's still blowing," she said softly, her gaze locked with his. "What will we do while we wait it out?"

"We could eat," he offered.

"True," she said. "Or you could tell me about another of your hotels."

"Or play chess."

"Watch a movie."

"Read."

She nodded and reached up to catch his hand with hers and hold it against her cheek. "All good ideas. But, I have a better idea."

Nathan bit back a groan as she leaned in close to him. His body was hard and tight and every breath now was a victory. If he didn't have her in the next few minutes, he was going to explode. "Yeah?" he asked. "What's that?"

"I think you know," she said and took one more sip of brandy before setting her glass down on the hearth.

Nathan tipped his head back and tossed the last of his brandy down his throat before setting his glass down beside hers.

"Possibly," he said, though a voice in his brain was telling him to stop now before it was too late. But damn it, he wanted her. Keira's image had been haunting him for days—she'd gotten to him more than any other woman he'd ever known. He wasn't used to waiting for something he wanted. Usually, he simply *took* what most women were more than willing to offer. Keira was different. "Why don't you tell me, and I'll let you know if we're on the same page."

"Why don't I show you?" she whispered, and then pressed her mouth to his.

Air.

He probably needed air, because the edges of his vision were blurring and his brain felt as if it had been short-circuited. But breathing didn't seem as important as kissing her—harder, deeper—did.

Nathan groaned, pulled her in tightly to him and opened her mouth with a sweep of his tongue. She sighed into him as he tasted her, tangling their tongues together in a wild, frantic dance of need and promise.

He felt her hands tighten on his shoulders, her fingers digging into the soft fabric of his sweater to brand his skin with match-head dots of flame. Electricity hummed between them and Nathan surrendered to the sensations coursing through him.

He needed her.

Now.

He pulled her into his arms and settled her on his lap. His hands swept up and down her back, defining her curves through the soft knit of her sweater. She sighed heavily, pressed herself more firmly to him and rubbed her body against his.

Nathan's mouth moved over hers like a dying man seeking the only sustenance left in the world. He shared his breath with her and she gave it back to him. Their tongues and lips melded, savored, enjoyed. Nathan slipped both hands beneath the hem of her sweater and his palms slid across her back, his fingertips smoothing over her satiny skin.

She tore her mouth free, let her head fall back and sighed at his touch. "Nathan…"

He lowered his head, kissing her jaw, her neck, following the line of her throat with his lips and teeth and tongue. She shivered in his grasp and fed the need pulsing inside him.

Lifting his head, Nathan looked down at her as his hands, sliding beneath her sweater, swept around her body to find the front clasp on her bra. Deftly, he undid the tiny plastic clip, then pushed her bra free and cupped her breasts in his palms. His thumbs caressed her hardened nipples as his fingers kneaded her soft flesh.

Her hands clutched at his shoulders as he held her tightly to his lap, letting her feel the hard length of him.

Need roared and crashed through Nathan until he could hardly draw breath. He couldn't remember *ever* wanting like this before. He couldn't remember another woman in his life who had pushed him to the razor's edge of rationality. All he could think of was Keira.

All he wanted was Keira.

He didn't care what it might mean.

What it might cost him.

Didn't want to examine every feeling, every ache.

He only wanted to lose himself in her. For this one moment in time, he wanted nothing more than the feel of her beneath his hands and the sensation of burying his body within the hot, tight channel of hers.

"I've got to have you," he whispered, hearing the raw throb in his own voice.

"Me, too," she said, opening her eyes and pulling herself upright, leaning into him. "Oh, Nathan, me, too. Now, okay?"

"Right now." He pulled his hands free of her body, not even thinking about how empty he felt without the warmth of her pouring into him. Then he stood up, set her on her feet and led her across the great room toward the foyer and the majestic staircase that led to the second floor and the master bedroom. With their boots off, their sock feet made almost no noise at all in their rush for the stairs.

She stumbled behind him, kicked an end table and letting go of his hand, hopped ungainly for a minute, whimpering. "Ow, ow…"

Nathan turned, swept her up into his arms and said thickly, "Okay, I'm carrying you from here. I'm not taking any chances with a tumble down the stairs."

"Right, right," she said and leaned in to nibble at his throat as his long legs took the steep stairs two at a time.

He hissed in a breath, took a sharp turn at the head of the stairs and headed for the only bedroom in the place that had been furnished.

Keira looked around quickly as Nathan carried her into the master bedroom. The log walls were pale and the honey-colored floorboards gleamed from a thick coat of polish. A stone hearth, much like the one in the great room, boasted a fire that warmed the room and made it feel, for all its size, cozy. A bank of windows overlooked the lake and the forest and showcased the snow falling steadily.

But Keira didn't really care about the storm or the decor. All she was interested in now was the feel of Nathan's arms around her as he walked toward the huge, dark sleigh bed tucked against the far wall. Her heartbeat thundered in her chest as Nathan set her on her feet, grabbed a corner of the old-fashioned quilt and tossed it to the foot of the bed.

Then he grabbed her again and Keira stopped thinking in favor of *feeling*.

His mouth claimed hers again and her brain sizzled. Every nerve ending she possessed hummed with an awareness she'd never experienced before. His lips and tongue tasted her, tormented her, and she gave as good as she got.

Holding on to his shoulders, she pushed her body against his and rubbed her aching nipples across his chest. She needed him. And that thought was enough to make her splintered brain try to work for a second or two. She knew she should stop. Think about what she was doing.

But a heartbeat later, when Nathan pulled her sweater up and over her head, and bent to take one hardened nipple into his mouth, Keira silently told the cautionary voice in her mind to shut up.

Seven

Keira groaned gently as his mouth closed over first one nipple, then the next. His lips, tongue and teeth teased her already aching flesh until her whole body felt as though it were on full alert. She felt his touch in every cell. Her blood pumped thick and hot through her veins and when she closed her eyes and tipped her head back, she could have sworn she actually saw fireworks bursting in electric flashes of heat and color.

She held his head to her, half afraid that he might stop what he was doing. Her fingers speared through his thick, soft, black hair and when he sighed against her flesh, she felt the heat of his breath brush her skin in an ethereal caress.

He dropped his hands to the waistband of her jeans and, in just moments, he had the button and zipper undone and was sliding them, along with her pale ivory panties, down the length of her legs. She helped as much as she could, stepping out of her jeans and lifting first one foot, then the other, so he could pull her socks off.

The air in the room felt cool against her skin, despite the fire in the hearth. She listened to the snap and hiss of the flames on logs and let the sound fill her mind until all that remained was the music of the fire and Nathan's breath against her body.

She smiled up at him and tugged at the hem of his sweater, fingers curling into the soft fabric. "Someone here is overdressed."

"Not for long," he promised and quickly got rid of his own clothing before laying her back on the cool, soft sheets.

He looked down at her for a long minute, and Keira arched her back from the bed and stretched both hands back and over her head, enjoying the power of his gaze on her. She saw the passion in his eyes and responded, moving sinuously over the bed, sweeping her own hands down her body, pausing at her breasts, stroking her own nipples as she watched his eyes darken and his jaw clench. Finally, when she lifted both hands toward him in open invitation, Nathan groaned and leaned over her.

"No bruises," he said quietly as he studied her.

She smiled and stroked his cheek with her fingertips. "It's been a good week for me. You were always around to rescue me from a fall."

"You're making me nuts. You know that, right?"

She reached up and cupped his face between her palms. Drawing his head down to hers, she kissed him once, twice and again. "Of course I know. The question is, what're you going to do about it?"

"Return the favor," he assured her.

He kissed her, hard and long and deep, until her body was quivering and her breath was hissing from her lungs. And when she tried to hold onto him, to pull him closer, Nathan slipped from her grasp and Keira could only watch as he moved along her body, sliding his flesh across hers, kissing every inch of her skin as he moved down the length of her.

She trembled, her breath caught and she bit into her bottom lip as she moved, twisting into him, arching into his movements, trying to keep their bodies connected, their flesh burning into each other's.

But Nathan had other ideas; he continued his slow, torturous assault on her nerve endings by stroking his tongue across her abdomen and nibbling at her skin until she was whispering his name in a broken hush. He smiled against her body, and kept moving, lower and lower still until finally he had backed off the mattress.

And kneeling beside the bed, he grabbed her legs and pulled her close, until her legs hung free and she was balanced precariously on the edge of the bed. He lifted her legs, laying them across his shoulders and Keira watched him as he smiled knowingly.

"Your turn," he whispered and scooped his hands under her behind before lifting her to meet his questing mouth.

Keira sucked in a gulp of air and held it, afraid to let it out because if she did, she might not be able to draw another, and she was pretty sure she was going to need to breathe.

His mouth claimed her, and Keira pushed herself up

onto her elbows to watch him take her more intimately than anyone ever had before. Her eyes widened and locked on him, as aroused by the sight of him taking her as she was by the incredible sensations coursing through her.

Keira had never known anything like it. His tongue swept a caress across her inner folds and dipped within her body to tempt her with even more.

She was really grateful for that lungful of air, because now she had forgotten how to breathe. Her world centered on this one man and what he was doing to her body.

Again and again, he stroked and nibbled and caressed. His tongue touched a tiny bud of sensitized flesh and—" Nathan!"

She felt him smiling, and then lost herself in the wonder of what he was able to do to her. He suckled and teased and stroked until the ball of need in the pit of her stomach bubbled into a fiery cauldron that tipped and spilled an unbelievable heat throughout her body. Keira rocked her hips, reached down to cup the back of his head to hold him to her and couldn't seem to look away.

Her heels dug into his back as he slipped one finger, then two inside her body and quickened the intensity of her experience in a heartbeat. There was so much, too much. Her mind couldn't capture it all, so she quit trying and surrendered to the incredible wash of anticipation building within.

"Nathan, if you stop," she whispered through dry lips, "I'll have to kill you."

He chuckled and then closed his mouth over that one most sensitive spot. Keira cried out his name as her body shuddered with the force of the climax ripping through her. She held onto him as the only stable point in the universe and as the tremors rocking her slowly faded, like far-reaching ripples in a pond, Nathan moved, easing her legs from his shoulders, shifting her further back onto the bed and then covering her body with his own.

"I can't...I mean..." She blew out a breath and laughed shortly. "I think I may be paralyzed."

"Not yet you're not," he murmured, dipping his head to taste one of her pale-pink nipples.

Instantly, need rebuilt at the feel of his body pressing her down into the so-soft mattress. She stroked his skin, running her hands up and down his back, kissing the underside of his jaw, his neck.

"That was..." she said.

"Only the beginning," he said and kissed her, his tongue plunging into her mouth, tangling with hers, stealing what breath she had left, then giving her his own to replace it.

Keira's body lit up again with fresh need and she lifted both legs to wrap them around his waist. "I want you inside me, Nathan."

"Just where I want to be, Keira," he whispered and lifted his head so he could watch her face as he entered her.

She tipped her head back on the bed, but kept her gaze locked with his. He pushed himself home with one long, deep stroke, and Keira gasped as she rocked her hips, taking even more of him within.

Outside, the storm raged, and inside, a different kind of storm swept the two of them into a world of mindless passion. Where all that mattered was the next touch, the next kiss, the next stroke of heat to heat. Their bodies moved in an ancient dance with a rhythm that seemed as old as time and as new as her next breath.

His body moved with hers, invaded hers, claimed hers, and Keira gave him all she had to give. Her hands smoothed over his back and around to stroke down his chest, her thumbnails flicking at his flat, brown nipples until he was gritting his teeth to hold back a shout.

She liked knowing that he was as lost to sensation as she was. That his body was screaming for release as loudly as her own. That she could shatter Nathan's rigid sense of control.

Arching into him again and again, she urged him deeper, faster, harder. Her fingers clawed at his back while the pressure within tightened ferociously, demanding release.

"Now, Nathan," she groaned, moving with him at a fever pitch that couldn't be sustained without the two of them bursting into flames, "please *now*."

He pushed himself up on his hands, stared down at her face and whispered, "You first, Keira. You first and I'll follow."

He slid one hand down the length of her body, across her flat abdomen, down to where their bodies were joined. His fingers dipped into the joining and stroked her damp heat as he continued to move inside her.

"Nathan!" Keira shrieked his name, clutched at his shoulders and bucked beneath him as an overwhelming wave of pleasure swept through her on what felt like an endless tide of mind-shattering explosions rattling just beneath her skin.

"Now," he groaned and plunged deep inside her, his

body shaking as he fell into the same tidal wave that had captured Keira and let it carry them both away.

An hour…or, for all Keira knew, a *week* later, she forced her eyelids open and stared up at the ceiling. Fire-cast shadows leaped and danced across the beams in hypnotic pulses.

"You okay?" Nathan murmured from close to her ear.

"Not sure yet," she admitted, turning her head on the pillow to smile at him. Reaching out, she smoothed his hair back from his forehead with her fingertips. "Hey, I can move my hand, so…good sign!"

Pushing himself up on one elbow, he stared down at her for a long minute or two, his eyes unreadable. A curl of unease opened inside Keira as she studied him, searching for a shadow of the passionate man he'd been so short a time ago. But the Nathan watching her now was more like the closed-off man she'd met his first day at the lodge.

"What?" she finally asked, unable to stand the silence any longer.

"I was just thinking."

"About?" she coaxed.

He looked as if he were about to say something, then thought better of it. Shaking his head, he said only, "Nothing. Never mind."

He rolled off the bed and walked naked across the room to a door that he opened to reveal a gigantic closet. It was practically empty from what Keira could see, since he'd brought only enough clothes for a month. But he stepped inside and when he came back out, he was wearing a thick black robe and carrying a dark green one that he tossed onto the foot of the bed. "I brought my own robe, but this green one was hanging in the closet when I got here."

"Thanks," she said, reaching for it and shoving both arms into the sleeves before slipping off the bed and tying the belt of the robe at her waist.

His features were tight, closed off as if he were carefully preventing whatever he was thinking from showing on his face. Which only served to really irritate Keira. A few minutes ago, they'd shared something truly amazing. They'd been as close as two people could get. Yet now…he was looking at her as if she were a stranger.

A really unwelcome stranger.

"Nathan, what's going on?"

"Not a thing," he said and started for the bedroom door and the stairs beyond. "But I promised you food, didn't I? I'll check out the kitchen. See what I can find."

Very nice, Keira thought. He'd shut her out so politely, so neatly, she had to wonder if maybe his hideous grandmother, who'd shipped him off to boarding school with hardly a wave goodbye, had taught him how to do that? How to push people away without even breaking a sweat.

Well, she wasn't going anywhere. Not until the storm stopped. And to be honest, even if the storm stopped right this minute, she wouldn't have been going anywhere. Not until she found out what the hell had happened to send Nathan from orgasmic to crabby in no time at all.

She followed him down the stairs, keeping one hand on the banister to make sure she didn't fall down the damn stairs and break her neck before she got some answers. She made a sharp right at the bottom of the stairs just in time to see his black robe disappear into the distant kitchen.

Well, if he thought she was that easy to get rid of, he really didn't know her well at all. Walking quickly, her bare feet hardly making a sound on the area rugs tossed across the gleaming wood floors, Keira got to the swinging door to the kitchen, slapped her palm against it and sent it crashing open.

He was at the fridge and raised his head to look at her when she stepped into the room. Then he dismissed her coolly, reached into the freezer and pulled out a long, flat aluminum tray.

"The housekeeper fills the freezer for me once a week. I think this is…" He read the label. "Fettuccine Alfredo with grilled garlic chicken. It's from the Clearwater, the restaurant you seem so fond of."

"Their fettuccine is great," Keira said, walking toward the granite counter and one of the stools pulled up beneath it. She sat down and tucked her bare feet up to get them off the cold floor.

"Glad you approve," he said, and turned to quickly take off the lid, turn on the oven and pop the tray inside. "Shouldn't take too long," he said, and walked to the wine cooler along the wall. "Would you like a glass of wine?"

"Sure," Keira said, trying to figure out a way to get past the wall he'd erected around himself so quickly and so completely. "Nathan, is everything all right?"

"Why wouldn't it be?"

"You're just acting a little…weird."

One black eyebrow rose as he set a bottle of white wine on the countertop. He opened a drawer, took out a corkscrew and then tore off the foil top from the bottle. Keira shivered a little and he said, "Cold?"

"A bit."

There was another fireplace in the kitchen, but this one was cold and dark. Beyond the windows leading to the covered deck, the world was a whirl of white. Light faded from the sky, the heavy clouds dropped even lower, and the flurries of snow were thick enough that it looked as though someone had hung a sheet from the edge of the patio cover.

"There's extra firewood on the deck. I'll get some."

"Okay, fine," Keira said as Nathan walked to the back door, "but first, tell me what you were going to say upstairs. When you were looking at me so funny. When you said, 'oh, it's nothing, never mind.'"

"Keira," he said with a sigh, "just let it go."

"Oh no," she assured him, shaking her head at the sheer folly of the man. "That's never gonna happen. So it'll be quicker and easier on both of us if you'll just spit it out."

"It's nothing."

"Then *say* it," she insisted.

One hand on the doorknob, he stared at her for a long moment, as if trying to decide whether to speak or not. At last, though, he nodded and said, "Fine. I was thinking about the sex. And I wondered just how far you were willing to go to get me to stay here for the whole month."

Keira felt the slap of his words like a physical blow. Stung, humiliated and furious, she glared at him with enough heat that, if there were any justice at all, he would have been a pillar of fire. "Are you serious?"

"You asked what I was going to say," he said and watched her through narrowed eyes.

"I didn't know you were going to say *that!*"

"Don't sound so offended." Nathan looked at her for a long minute. "It's not like I'm surprised."

"Is that right?"

"For God's sake, Keira, you think this is the first time a woman's used her body to get me to do something for her? We're both adults. You wanted something from me and you used sex to get it."

Fury whipped through Keira. "You…you…"

He shrugged and headed for the back door. "It was good for both of us. We each got what we wanted. No point now in trying to make it something it wasn't."

He opened the back door to a gust of icy wind and said, "Look, let's just forget it, all right?"

"Sure," she whispered as she watched him hurry barefoot across the icy deck toward the neatly stacked pile of firewood. As he gathered up a few logs and some kindling, the wind whipping the edges of his robe around his calves, Keira jumped off her stool, crossed the floor and quietly closed and locked the back door.

Instantly he straightened up, whirled around and shocked, stared at her through the glass. He crossed to the door and gave the knob a turn and a shake. "Keira, open the damn door."

"I don't think so," she said, folding her arms over her chest and tapping one bare foot against the cold wood floor.

She'd never been so mad in her whole life. *Or* so humiliated. For God's sake, she'd let him do things to her no one had ever done before, only because she'd felt a connection to him somehow. Some minuscule, apparently clearly one-sided, *feeling*. How could he ever think that she would have slept with him just to make him stay?

Did she really give off such a slutty vibe?

And what the hell kind of people was he so used to dealing with that would make him assume she was so coldblooded?

He shivered, clutched the firewood tighter to his chest and gave her a glare she was sure sent his employees scuttling for cover.

Keira, however, remained unmoved.

"Damn it, Keira, it's snowing out here!"

"You're under the porch roof."

"It's freezing."

"Start a fire."

"On the *deck?*"

"Frankly, I don't care if you freeze solid to the spot. I'll put up a small but tasteful plaque, something like Here Stands An American Moron."

"This is *not* funny!" he shouted, and hunched deeper into his way-too-thin-for-snow robe.

"No kidding!" Keira walked closer to the glass so she could burn her stare into his eyes. "I cannot believe you. You actually think I'd *prostitute* myself to get you to stay here?"

"I didn't say *that*," he reasoned.

"Oh, yes you did, you pompous, self important, miserable son of a bitch."

"Look, I was *wrong*, okay?"

"You're just saying that so I'll open the door," she snapped.

"Damn straight."

"Well, forget it! You deserve to freeze, but you

probably won't. You're so damn cold already, I don't see how you could possibly get any colder!"

"Can you let me the hell in the house and *then* yell at me?"

"Why should I let you in?" she demanded, so furious she was seeing red at the edges of her vision. Amazing. You really *did* see red if you were angry enough.

"Because…because…"

"See? Even *you* can't think of a reason!" Keira shouted.

"Hah!" Nathan raised one hand in the air, dropped some kindling on his foot and hopped in place. "Because if I die out here, I won't be able to stay the damn month and your town won't get the money you want so badly."

"Funny," she said, thoughtfully tapping one finger against her chin, "but I don't remember it saying anywhere in the will that you had to be *alive* and here for a month. It'd probably be okay if we just prop you up out there on the deck."

"You are the most infuriating woman I have ever met."

"You've got a heck of a lot of nerve, Nathan Barrister. You call me a *ho,* and I'm the one who's infuriating?"

He flicked a glance behind him when the wind shifted and a flurry of snow rushed at him from the lake. Turning his gaze back to hers, he said tightly, "Keira, open this damn door and let me inside."

"And if I don't?"

"Then I'll break the glass with one of these logs and we'll *both* be freezing our asses off."

Hmm. Good point. Well, she hadn't really planned on letting him become an ice sculpture on the deck. Though the idea was all too tempting at the moment.

"Fine." She reached out, unlocked the door and then stomped across the room so she was as far from Nathan as she could get and still be able to give him dirty looks.

He rushed into the room, dropped the firewood into the hearth, then pounded his bare feet against the floor and slapped his hands at his arms, trying to get his blood moving.

"Cold?" she asked sweetly.

"Funny," he snapped, snarling at her.

"As cold as that tiny little marble in your chest? You know, the one you call your *heart?*"

Still shivering, he turned his back on her, started a fire in the hearth and huddled next to the flames as they sputtered, caught and licked at the dry wood. Finally, he turned a look on her. "My heart's got nothing to do with any of this."

"Since it probably gets very little use, I'm willing to bet you're right," Keira hissed.

"You tried to freeze me to death!" His voice ricocheted off the high beamed ceiling and Keira didn't even flinch.

"Don't be such a baby."

"A *baby?*" Astonishment flashed across his features and she waved one hand at him dismissively.

"You're lucky I let you back in."

There was a long moment of silence before he finally said, "Yeah. You're just crazy enough to have left me out there, so I guess I am lucky. And frostbitten."

"That was a nasty thing to think about me," she said, ignoring his complaint, "and even nastier to say."

"You wouldn't leave it alone. You had to know what I was thinking," he pointed out, raising his hands high in amazement. "What is it about women, anyway? They poke and prod at a man to tell them what he's thinking and when he does, they lock him outside in a damn snowstorm!"

"Is it our fault that what you're really thinking is so ridiculously insulting that we aren't prepared?" Keira slapped the granite counter. "We want to know what you're thinking, because, silly us, we actually think your minds *aren't* twisted little black holes."

"No, you expect us to be like you," Nathan said tightly, still scowling, still stamping his feet on the floor trying to get his circulation moving again. "All warm and fuzzy, wanting kids and a dog and a white picket fence and—"

"Are you *delusional?*" Keira interrupted his rant. "Who said anything about a picket fence?"

"You don't have to say it," he challenged, stabbing one finger in the air, pointed at her. "It's who you are. You're Ms. Roots herself. Well, I don't have roots. Don't want any and if I found some I'd rip 'em out of the ground."

Keira stomped across the room until she was right in front of him. His blue eyes were wild and hot, and the set of his jaw told her he was every bit as furious as she was. Well, good. No point in being mad all by yourself. And besides, he'd probably *never* lost his temper. Not the ever-polite, always distant Nathan Barrister. So, she'd let him rant and rave. Maybe it'd do him some good. God knows it was doing wonders for *her.*

"Your perfect little town has nothing I want or need. As soon as possible, I'll be on my jet, heading for the opposite end of the world."

"Good. Nobody's asking you to settle down in

Hunter's Landing, *Mr. Wonderful*." Keira stabbed her finger at him, poking him several times dead center of the chest until he grabbed her finger in self defense. She shook him off a second later. "*I'm* certainly not laying out traps for you—"

"Oh, no?" Nathan countered quickly, apparently enjoying interrupting her for a change. "No traps, huh? Did it happen to escape your notice that we didn't use any protection?"

Keira blanched for a second. Damn it, it *had* escaped her attention. Then his words hit home. *A trap?* "First I'm a slut and now I'm trying to trap you and your golden sperm? Aren't I the busy little bee?"

"You're deliberately avoiding the point," he said. "We didn't use anything and—"

"Well, jeez," she said, interrupting him neatly for the umpteenth time, "color me *human*. You know, I don't actually travel with condoms in my jeans on the off chance that some spoiled, snotty rich guy will want to have sex with me and then insult me!"

He grabbed two fists full of his own hair and yanked. Hard. Then, his voice rumbled through the kitchen at a level just below howling. "For God's sake, I just told you I could have made you pregnant and you take *that* as an insult, too?"

"I'm not pregnant," she snapped. "Just so you know, I'm on the Pill, so no worries there, Mr. Barrister. Your personal fortune is safe from this particular gold digger."

"I never said you were a—"

"But as long as we're on the subject," she continued, her voice rolling right over his, "how about you?"

He grimaced. "I'm not on the Pill."

"Not the best time to develop a sense of humor, just so you know."

He raised his hands in mock surrender. "Fine. Fine. I'm healthy. No worries there. You?"

"Contrary to certain people's opinion, I am *not* a slut and, therefore, I, too, am very healthy." She crossed her fingers over her heart. "Of course, I'll be happy to get you a letter from my doctor to alleviate any further concern…"

"Damn it, Keira, I'm not calling you a slut for doing whatever you have to do to get what you want. That's how the world works. The real world, that is, not your own personal little Xanadu here."

"Believe it or not," she shouted, "I did *not* have sex with you to keep you here for the month!"

"You keep telling yourself that," he said tightly.

"Jeez," Keira muttered, shaking her head. "Are you really so far out of touch with humanity? Does *everything* in your world carry a price tag?"

"There are price tags everywhere in the world. Wake up and maybe you'll notice them."

"You lead an ugly life," she whispered.

"At least I live with my eyes open," he countered. "I know that people are mostly out for themselves and willing to do just about anything to take care of number one."

"So I slept with you to get what I want?"

"Wouldn't be the first time it's happened."

Keira flinched at the coldness in his eyes. He really did believe that anyone getting close to him was out for his money. His lifestyle. How sad. How unbearably empty his world must be. And the saddest part was, he didn't even realize it.

"And so, because you've surrounded yourself with

sycophants and users, you naturally assumed that I was one, too."

He gritted his teeth and a muscle in his jaw twitched. "And you're telling me you're not."

"Yeah," she said, "I am. And what's more, you know it. Somewhere in that cavernous emptiness you call a heart, you know it. And you insulted me on purpose."

He glared at her. "You are the most—" He caught himself, dragged in a gulp of air and then fired his gaze into hers. "Okay, yeah. I did."

"Finally!" Keira shouted and scooted a little closer to the kitchen fire, nudging Nathan out of her way. "The question is *why?*"

"Why?"

"Why did you want to insult me, Nathan?" She tipped her head to one side, stared up at him and asked, "If you wanted me to leave, all you had to do was say so."

"I didn't want you to leave," he admitted, though it was clear he wasn't happy about the confession.

"Then why?"

"I honestly don't know," he said and pulled her up close against him. When she tried to push herself free, he simply tightened his hold on her middle, pinning her body to his until Keira could feel his need building again.

Was he so unused to people wanting to be with him just to be with him? Was his world so insulated that the only people he ever saw were the ones who worked for him or wanted something from him?

Slightly mollified, Keira stared up into his eyes and saw questions still lingering in those pale blue depths. The man did things to her she had never expected. He had a way of touching her heart at the oddest moments and she was more than a little confused about that.

She could continue the fight, which, let's face it, she was enjoying. She could give him answers to his questions. She could even make him wonder about lots of other things.

Or, she could do what she most wanted to do.

Tugging the lapels of his thick, cashmere robe aside, Keira stroked his bare chest with the flat of her palms and watched his eyes narrow into slits and his jaw clench as he hissed in a long, slow breath.

Deliberately, she teased him, spreading his robe open, baring his body to her touch. She slid her hands over his still cold skin and felt heat bubble beneath the surface at her touch. Then she tugged the belt of the robe free and swept one hand down to capture his hard length in a soft, firm grip.

"You know, Nathan," she said, smoothing her fingers up and down his erection with slow caresses, "the simple truth is, I've wanted you almost from the moment I first saw you. That's why I stayed. That's why I want you again now."

He groaned as she slipped her free hand down to cup him. "Works for me."

Eight

The rich scent of Alfredo sauce was beginning to fill the kitchen, but Keira was hungry for something other than food. Strange, but even fighting with Nathan was stimulating.

Her body was quickening as his hands moved to tug her robe open and pull it down off her shoulders to let it pool on the floor at her feet. The air in the kitchen was still icy from the wind that had whooshed inside when the door was opened. Yet she didn't really mind it. Instead, that sensation added to the others already coursing through her body, mingling together, causing a ripple effect of near turmoil in her system.

His hands swept up and down her body, his long, talented fingers exploring every curve as she ran her own hands over him. His broad, muscular chest was clearly defined, sculpted and tanned, making him look as though he were carved from the same kind of honey-toned wood that graced the lodge.

But he was warm and ready, and his body was already pressing into hers, letting her know that he felt the same blood pounding need she did.

"Why do I want you so much?" he whispered, his fingers stroking, sliding down her body to caress the heat between her thighs.

Keira sighed and swayed unsteadily on her feet as a rush of something delicious began to build within. "Why do you ask so many questions?" she answered.

He smiled, and her heart flipped in her chest. A weird sensation, but a shockingly good one.

"You're the one with all the questions," he murmured, dipping his head to kiss the curve of her neck, to nibble at the base of her throat.

Her hands moved to his shoulders and she clung to him desperately as he continued to smooth his fingers over her damp heat. Instinctively, he found that one most-sensitive bud and concentrated his attentions on it, thumb and forefinger gliding, stroking until Keira's blood felt as if it were boiling just beneath her skin.

"No questions," she said, licking dry lips and trying to catch her breath. "Not now, anyway."

He slid one hand up to hold the back of her neck while his other hand continued to gently torture her with anticipation. His blue eyes caught hers and Keira wished she knew what he was thinking now. Now, when passion simmered in pale eyes gone dark with desire.

She wanted to give him what he was giving her, so she slid one hand down his body until she could encircle his length with her fingers again. He swallowed a great gulp of air before lowering his head to take her mouth with his. His tongue plunged into her mouth, claiming her fiercely, desperately, as if he couldn't wait another moment to taste her.

And Keira matched his need with her own. She shifted position, sliding her hands around his waist to splay them against his back. She felt his heart pounding and knew her own was in sync that wild rhythm.

His fingers dipped into her center, first one, then two, diving in and out of her heat, touching her deeply, but not deep enough. Not as deeply as she wanted him. Needed him.

When he tore his mouth from hers, he stared down at her and whispered, "We'll never make it back up to the bedroom."

"Not a chance," she agreed, already so hungry for him, her arms and legs were trembling.

"Here then," he said and, moving quickly, he picked her up, carried her to the counter and plopped her down onto it.

"Yikes!" The cold granite bit into her heated skin and sent a chill slicing right through her.

He grinned wickedly. "Cold?"

She narrowed her eyes on him. "You enjoyed that. Payback for locking you outside?"

"Just a little," he admitted, then leaned in and bit her bottom lip gently, swiping his tongue along the crease in her mouth. "But I'm willing to warm you up again, too."

She reached for him, sliding her arms around his neck, pulling him in closer. "A generous man," she said with a sigh as his mouth came down on hers.

As he kissed her, he parted her thighs, moved in close and entered her body on a rush of sensation that poured through the two of them, linking them in a way that neither had experienced or expected.

Keira arched into him, moving her hips on the hard granite in a desperate attempt to get closer, to take him more fully within. She closed her eyes and saw swirls of vibrant color as her body leaped into life. Her being soared, and something deep within her unexpectedly awoke. Her eyes opened again as that thought sang through her mind. She watched him and felt new feelings stir within. New emotions. New and incredibly fragile threads of connection.

Nathan's hands dropped to her hips and he held her still, trapped within his steely grip as he plunged in and out of her depths in a ferocious rhythm designed to drive them both quickly over the edge.

The world dropped away and it was just the two of them. Nothing beyond existed anymore. Passion swelled and trapped them in a silky web of desire. Keira held on to him, and lost herself in his strength, surrendering to the twist of anticipation curling inside her.

Her body tightened, her mouth mated with his and she hooked her legs around Nathan's waist, pulling him in harder, deeper. She felt his body's invasion of hers all the way to her soul and knew she would never get enough of him. Knew that this man was touching more than her body. He'd already laid claim to a piece of her heart.

Whether she wanted it or not, she cared for him. More than she wanted to think about. More than she dared to admit.

She pulled free of his kiss so she could watch his

eyes as he claimed her. His beautiful blue gaze locked with hers, as though he understood her silent plea and felt the same way.

Her body quickened, anticipation exploded and a climax stronger than anything she'd ever known before shattered inside her, splintering itself into brilliant colors that tore through her heart and spilled into her bones.

Nathan kept his gaze fixed on hers and when she cried out his name, he gave himself up to the release clamoring inside him and followed her over the ragged edge of control, into oblivion.

By morning, Nathan was rethinking the whole situation.

The night before, he'd thought it a great idea having Keira stay with him. They'd come together often during the night and each time had been more incredible than the first. He felt as though each time he touched her, he felt something more, something different. And he'd reveled in their time together, knowing that in the morning, she would be going home.

At least, that's what he had thought.

He gritted his teeth and stared out the bank of windows in the kitchen. Outside the lodge, the world was a wash of white. Snow piled on the sides of the deck and blew in under the overhang to coat the wood planks with a layer of snow at least a foot deep. And that was under the porch roof. It was much deeper everywhere else, and it was still falling.

He'd never seen anything like it.

"It's mid-March and it looks like Siberia in December out there," he muttered.

Keira came up behind him, threaded her arms around his waist and rested her cheek against his back. "Welcome to the high Sierras."

"I tried the phone," he said. "No dial tone."

"Uh-oh."

"What's that mean?" He turned his head to look at her.

"It means," she said, "that with the phone lines down this early in the storm, it's a big one."

Nathan glowered at her. "Which translates into…?"

She shrugged. "If the roads aren't completely blocked already, they soon will be."

"Surely you have crews to take care of that."

"Of course we do," Keira said, smiling up at him. "But they can't roll till the heavy snows are over, and even when they do…"

He didn't like the look on her face. The look that said *he's not going to like this.*

"What?"

"They take care of the town first and then the main stretches of highway. Those are priorities for obvious reasons."

"And…?"

"And," she said with another shrug, "the roads up here probably won't be cleared for a few days."

"A few *days?*"

"Maybe sooner," she said, he suspected simply to placate him. "But the private roads and the roads leading to them are pretty much a lower priority. Unless there's an emergency or something. If the road crews get a call like that, they'll come right away."

"The phones are out." He paused, then said, "Wait. I've got my satellite phone."

"But no one else around here has one."

"Right." Nathan shook his head.

She pulled her arms from around his waist, shoved her hands into the pockets of her robe and said, "Look, we do the best we can. And people generally privately contract to get their roads cleared, so that takes care of a lot of problems."

"And does the lodge have a private contract?"

"I don't know."

"Perfect." Nathan blew out a breath. This month was turning into a real trial. "How long is this going to keep up?" He shook his head as he shifted his gaze across the lake, watching snow slide in sideways, riding a wind that was rattling the windows.

"Well," she said, giving him a brilliant smile, "if it keeps up, at least it won't be coming down anymore."

He glanced at her. "Oh, very humorous."

She moved to stand in front of him, leaning both palms against an icy window to get as good a view as she could of the blustering storm outside. "I always laughed when my dad said it." She glanced at him over her shoulder. "Of course, I was ten."

Nathan wasn't amused. Nor was he charmed. He'd wanted her here last night—and he'd enjoyed every minute of his time with her. But that didn't mean he wanted her at the lodge for freaking *ever*. Scowling, he saw the wind spit snow at the windows and knew that she wouldn't be going anywhere. At least not today.

As if she was reading his mind, Keira turned around, leaned back against the floor-to-ceiling windows and tipped her head to one side, staring up at him. "So, what'll we do while we're stuck inside?"

He knew that gleam in her eye. Hell, he'd seen it most of the night. He was willing to bet they hadn't had more than a couple of hours' sleep. Yet even thinking about being inside her, touching her, holding her, tasting her, made him hard and eager again.

Which was clearly unacceptable.

He wasn't a kid to be led around by his groin. And damned if he'd let himself get any more tangled up with Keira than he already was. Just because she was here, with him, didn't mean she had to be *with* him.

"Uh-oh," she said, tugging the edges of her robe more firmly together over her chest. "It suddenly got very cold in here."

He nodded. "I'll turn up the thermostat."

"That's not what I meant."

"What're you talking about?" he asked as he walked to the coffee pot on the kitchen counter.

God.

The counter.

How was he ever supposed to walk through this kitchen again without remembering her sitting naked on that counter? Without thinking about how she'd taken him so deep inside her he'd thought he might never find his way out again?

Crap.

Now he had a headache.

Rubbing his temple, he asked, "Coffee?"

"Sure. I'll have a cup of coffee, black, with answers."

"Huh?" He half turned to look at her as she walked slowly across the kitchen. Did her hips always sway like that, he wondered, or was she doing it purposely now?

"I said I'd like some answers."

"To what?" He was stalling. He knew it. He poured two cups of coffee, handed her one, then stalled again by taking a long sip of his own.

"To why your eyes suddenly looked even colder than this stormy day outside."

"Keira," he said tightly, "you're making too much of nothing."

"So you're *happy* I'm here," she coaxed, taking a drink of her coffee and moving in closer to him.

"Delirious," he assured her.

"Liar."

"Why do you do that? Accuse me of lying at every opportunity?"

"A better question is why am I always right?"

He set his coffee cup down, tugged at the belt of his robe and said, "You're not right. Women always say that to win an argument, but it's never true."

"Of course it is," Keira said, sipping her coffee. "Women are right because we *see* everything and we *remember* everything."

"Sure."

"Just like I can see that you're trying to start a fight so you won't have to answer my question."

He sighed. This woman got to him like no one else ever had. And he was forced to admit that part of the reason why was because she never took any of his crap. She always called him on everything.

"Fine," he said tightly and met her gaze with a hard look designed to put some distance between them. "I was thinking that it would be more comfortable if you could have gone home this morning. Happy?"

"Delirious," she said, throwing his own word back at

him. Then she turned around and pulled a chair out from under the kitchen table. Curling one leg under herself, she plopped down, propped her elbow on the table and took another sip of coffee before saying, "Was that so hard?"

Nathan just blinked at her. Any other woman would have been insulted, giving him all kinds of frosty attitude right now. Figured Keira would react differently. She had to everything else.

"You're not mad."

"Nope, sorry to disappoint." She took long drink of her coffee, then set the cup onto the table. "Nathan, I know you don't really want me here, and that's okay. I mean, I hadn't planned on staying forever, you know."

"Yeah, I know."

"But it's really storming out there, so I'm stuck here and you're stuck with me. We might as well make the best of it, don't you think?"

A constant surprise. Keira Sanders never failed to bewilder him with her reactions to things. He couldn't depend on what she'd do next, because she never responded to *anything* the way he expected her to. How was a man supposed to find his emotional footing if a woman kept changing on him?

"I suppose that's logical."

"Excellent," she said. "I've got a few ideas on what we could do today." She hopped off her chair, stumbled over her own foot and slammed into his chest. She grabbed him in self-preservation and spilled his coffee down the front of his robe. Grinning up at him, she said, "Maybe we should do some laundry first."

* * *

Cold fettuccine Alfredo for breakfast, a load of wash done and in the dryer, and the snow was still blowing outside.

Keira wandered through the lodge, peeking into closets and exploring rooms that were still standing empty waiting for the decorator. From every room, the view was outstanding and displayed the growing storm to its advantage.

She chewed at her bottom lip and wondered how the town was doing, then reminded herself that the people of Hunter's Landing dealt with snowstorms every year. The only difference with this storm was that she wasn't there. She couldn't see for herself that everyone was fine, hunkered down to wait out the snow.

She couldn't even *call* anyone to check on them. The phone lines were still down. Remembering the look on Nathan's face when he'd tried the phone again an hour ago made her smile.

Leaving one of the bedrooms, she wandered back into the upper hall, passed the master bedroom and paused for a moment, remembering everything she and Nathan had done together the night before. Her heart filled, her body ached with tired satisfaction and the small smile on her face faded slowly. She knew that today, he was regretting their time together.

He probably wasn't used to facing his nighttime bed partner the next day. Well, this was pretty new for Keira, too. But at least she was trying to make the best of it. Unlike Nathan, who'd buried himself in busywork on his laptop. The man had avoided talking to her for hours now and the quiet—except for his fingers hitting the keyboard—was starting to really bother her.

The wind howled around the corners of the house, sounding as though it was looking for a way in. Shivering, Keira headed for the stairs. She held onto the banister, and started down, her bare feet making no sound at all on the dark carpet runner that covered the wood planks.

Walking into the great room, she headed for the fire crackling in the hearth, turned her back to it and stared at Nathan, just a few feet away. He hadn't even looked up when she entered the room.

"Ignoring me doesn't make me invisible," she said abruptly.

"Huh? What?" He raised his head, turned to look at her and asked, "What did you say?"

"I said, are you going to be sitting in front of that computer all day?"

"I have work to do."

"That you can't send anywhere because the phone lines are down."

"It's not e-mail, it's work," he said.

"Fine." She blew out a breath, walked toward him, then squatted beside him until they were eye to eye. "My point is, does *everything* have to be done *today?*"

"Keira…"

She hopped up, plopped onto the couch beside him and leaned in, staring at the computer screen. "Okay, okay. So you have to work. Tell me about it. Talk to me."

He sighed in resignation, and Keira hid a smile. "I'm working up a new schedule for impromptu visits to my hotels."

She looked at him, stupefied for a second, then burst out laughing.

"What's so funny?"

She waved one hand, shook her head and fought for breath. Laughter spilled from her throat, bubbled into the room and crashed down around them as she wrapped her arms around his shoulders and gave him a fast hug. "Nathan, you're really something," she said when she finally got control of her giggles.

"I'm so happy I can entertain you."

"Don't you get it?" she asked, grinning. "You're making a *schedule* for *impromptu* visits. The whole point of impromptu is *no* schedule."

Nathan scowled at her, then at the computer screen. He felt like an idiot. But in his own defense, he'd only been making busy work anyway. Anything to keep his mind off the fact that Keira was here and way too accessible.

He had no intention of getting in any deeper with her. And the best way to keep from doing that was to keep his hands to himself. Yet…everytime he heard her breathe, or caught a whiff of her scent, all he wanted to do was carry her back upstairs and bury himself inside her.

He wanted to experience again that incredible warmth that he'd only found with her. But it wouldn't be right. He wanted to enjoy her, enjoy their time together and still be able to walk away. Because he *would* be leaving. Nothing would stop him.

She reached out and closed the computer, then clambered onto his lap. Threading her arms around his neck, she looked into his eyes and asked, "What do you do when you're not working?"

He didn't have an answer. Strange, but he'd never really thought about it. "I'm always working."

"Well, let's see what we can do about that."

Nine

An hour later, Nathan rolled out of bed, his body replete, his mind racing. He glanced at Keira languidly stretching on the mattress and had to fight down an urge to lay back down and gather her up close. And because that thought was uppermost in his brain, he took a step or two away from the bed just for good measure.

"Now," she said, sweeping her hair up to lay across the pillow like a red-gold banner, "wasn't that more fun than planning schedules?"

He grabbed his robe from the end of the bed, slipped it on, then stood up to look down at her. "If we spend the next few days like this," he said with a smile he couldn't quite prevent curving his mouth, "by the time the storm ends, we'll be dead."

"I can think of worse ways to go."

So could he. That was one of his problems. Always before, Nathan's relationships with women had been un-complicated and straightforward. Before he took a woman to bed, he made sure she felt as he did about affairs—that they should be undemanding, easily slipped in and out of, with no hard feelings, no promises made, so no promises broken.

Ordinarily, he never would have become involved with a woman like Keira. She had "complications" written all over her. And yet, at this moment, he couldn't really bring himself to regret what he'd found with her.

Regrets would come later. Once he was gone and safely wrapped up in his normal world. Once he was far enough away from her eyes that they didn't haunt him every damn minute.

"You're an unusual woman."

She sat up, completely comfortable with her own nudity, and swung her hair back from her face. "Thanks."

"You're welcome," he said, his gaze dipping to the swell of her breasts, then back to her fathomless green eyes. She was tempting. More tempting than anyone he'd ever known before. He was walking through unfa-miliar territory here and he felt as though he were trying to negotiate his way through quicksand.

What he needed was a little space. A little time to himself to gather his defenses and shore up the inner walls she seemed so determine to shatter.

Decision made, he said, "I'm going downstairs to get some work done."

She looked at him for a long second or two, shook her head, then flopped back onto the bed, dragged the quilt up to cover herself and muttered, "Of course you are."

* * *

A few hours later, Nathan was hunched determinedly over his computer, doing an excellent job of pretending Keira wasn't in the room.

Tossing the book she'd been trying to read for the last half hour onto the sofa cushion beside her, she frowned at the back of his head and said pointedly, "What're you doing?"

"Working."

"*Again,* you mean. Well, I can see that, Mr. Chatty. Working on what? Still trying to find a way to schedule spontaneity?"

"No." He shook his head, turned back to the computer and typed something else.

"Then what?"

"You're not going to give me any peace at all, are you?"

"Probably not," she said.

"Fine." He leaned back into the couch, winced and re-trieved the book she'd dropped out from behind his back and set it on the coffee table. When he was settled again, he glanced at her and said, "I'm making some notes on how to confront the manager of the Gstaad Barrister."

"Switzerland," she said with a sigh. Then she asked, "Confront? About what?"

"I gave him specific instructions last time on how I wanted him to deal with the housekeeping staff, and they haven't been implemented."

"Why not?"

He looked at her. "How the hell do I know?"

She curled her legs up under her, propped her elbow on the back of the sofa and leaned in. "What's wrong with the way *he's* handling things, then?"

Nathan sighed. "He's very…relaxed in his position. He allows the employees too much leeway in their work."

"Does it all get done?"

"Yes, but—"

"So maybe," Keira said, "he knows his people better than you do?"

"Maybe, but—"

She smiled. "So if you weren't stomping around bellowing orders like a bully, maybe you'd get more cooperation out of him?"

"I do *not* bellow," Nathan said and sat up straight.

"But you *do* bully."

He blew out a disgusted breath. "You don't understand. There's a right way and a wrong way to run a business, Keira."

"Oh, I understand," she said, reaching out to pat his shoulder, then letting her fingertips linger there just a moment or two. "Believe me, as mayor, I have to deal with people all the time. And it's just not logical to assume you can use the same strategy when dealing with different types of people."

"It's always worked before," he pointed out, scowling at her.

Keira scooted closer, leaned down and looked him dead in the eye. This she knew about. He might own all of the gorgeous hotels in the world, but Nathan Barrister was *not* a people person.

"But the thing is, Nathan, you don't know if it might work better doing things differently."

"The company's policy has been in effect since my grandfather started the first hotel."

"Jeez," she said softly. "No wonder it's out-of-date."

"I didn't say it was out-of-date."

"Nope. I did." Turning around, she sat back beside Nathan, tucked her hand through the crook of his arm and cuddled in. "Like, for instance, when Donna—she owns the pottery shop on the outskirts of town—wanted to increase her number of parking spaces in front of her shop, I went to bat for her with the town council. After all, her shop is out of the way, it wouldn't infringe on anyone else's parking. Why not?"

"Okay…"

"But, when the Clearwater wanted the same deal, I had to tell them no. Because they're in the middle of town, lakeside, and we just couldn't afford to lose tourist parking slots to make more room for their customers. Different situations, different rules."

"Ah," he said, smiling at her, "but the situations in my hotels are all the same. Each one is a Barrister. So the rules should apply evenly."

She nudged his shoulder and laughed shortly. "The hotels are all in different places. Different traditions, different employees."

"But—"

"Would you decorate your Barbados hotel the same way you decorated the one in say, D.C.?"

"No…"

"So, same thing applies." Leaning her head against his shoulder, she added, "Cut your managers a little slack, Nathan. Trust them to know their people and their hotels. Lighten up a little and you might be surprised by the results you get."

He frowned thoughtfully and shifted his gaze to the screen of his laptop, where his carefully written-up notes were marked with bullet points. "You couldn't have made your point an hour ago? Before I started working on this stupid list?"

Keira laughed and Nathan took a heartbeat of time to simply enjoy the sound as it swirled around him. She was cuddled in close and he liked the feel of her pressed against him. He liked knowing she was sitting beside him reading quietly—or that she was in the kitchen making grilled cheese sandwiches—or tripping over a rug on her way down the hall.

He just liked knowing she was here. Outside, the storm was still blowing and Nathan was willing to admit, at least to himself, that if he had been here, trapped by himself, he would have been half crazy by now.

But having her here made for a different sort of crazy. Keira was becoming too much a part of his world. He hated knowing that he was beginning to count on hearing her move through the house. That he was looking forward to their next argument. That he wanted her even more now than he had the first time they were together.

Somehow, she was worming her way right into the heart of him. And Nathan wasn't sure how to keep her at a distance anymore. Or even if he wanted to. Which worried him more than a little.

He hadn't thought about anything but business for years. Now, his life was on hold and he was in a situation where the rules had all changed on him. He was in a place where there was too little work to do and too few distractions to keep him from having too much time to think. To wonder. To ask himself a few fundamental questions. Like what his life might have been like if he'd taken a different path.

He supposed most men wondered those things from time to time, but he never had. He'd never had any doubts about his life or how he lived it.

Until now.

Until Keira.

"What're you thinking?" she asked.

"No way," he said. "I'm not playing that game again. I'm in no mood to get frostbite, thanks."

Keira laughed, gave him a punch on the arm and said, "Fine, coward. Can I use your satellite phone?"

He turned and looked at her, curiosity taking small, annoying bites of him. "Who're you going to call? The lines are all down, remember?"

"My sister," Keira said. "I know, it's really long distance, you know, to London and all. But I won't stay on long and I'll pay for the call."

Something inside him eased back and he really didn't want to explore what that might mean. Instead, he rummaged through the briefcase beside him on the floor, came up with the phone and handed it over. "Talk as long as you want. My treat."

"Wow. You'll do *anything* to get me to leave you alone, huh?"

The answer to that question should have been yes. Since he wasn't sure anymore if it was or not, he said nothing, just turned back to his computer and began to delete his well-thought-out letter.

Keira punched in her sister's number as she walked into the kitchen and poured herself a cup of coffee.

While she waited for Kelly to pick up, she took a sip and leaned back against the kitchen counter.

"Hello?"

"Hey, Kel," Keira said, pushing away from the counter and walking toward the bank of windows. Her gaze fixed on the storm still blowing like crazy out there, she listened to Kelly's excited yelp and settled in for a good talk.

"Where have you *been?*" Kelly demanded. "I've been trying to get you forever but the phone at home's out of order and, by the way, how are you calling me and whose phone is it? I didn't recognize the number."

Keira laughed, took another sip of hot coffee and said, "Big storm blew in yesterday. Phone lines are down."

"Then how—"

"It's a satellite phone," Keira said quickly. "Nathan let me borrow it."

"*Nathan*, is it?" Kelly whistled a little, then asked, "what's he doing at the house?"

"He's not at the house, *Mom*—I'm at his place."

"You mean the lodge?"

"That's the one." Keira grinned and watched her reflection smile back at her.

"So this storm. How bad is it?"

"Phone lines down, remember?"

"Which means the roads are blocked, which means you're stranded in that big lodge with Nathan Barrister?"

Keira laughed. "All that college wasn't a waste after all. You're really quick."

"Very funny. How did this happen? Oh, K. You slept with him, didn't you?"

"Kelly…" Keira glanced back over her shoulder, as if Nathan could hear her sister's voice.

"You did. I can *so* hear it in your tone. It's that, *this is none of your business, butt out, Kelly,* tone. I know it well."

"And yet," Keira said through gritted teeth, "you always seem to ignore it."

"I'm sorry. No, wait. I'm not. Honest to God, Keira, are you nuts? This is Nathan Barrister, for God's sake. He is sooooooo not your type."

A quick jolt of anger shot through Keira but she managed to squelch it before she could shout. "What exactly *is* my type then, Kel? You tell me."

"Someone remotely normal? As in, not some damn recluse? Someone who isn't one of the richest men on the planet? Someone who isn't *renowned* for strings of one night stands?"

Well, Keira thought bitterly, she'd had to ask. "You're really making me sorry I called," she muttered and took another drink of coffee, appreciating the scalding heat as it sang down her throat.

"It's not like I don't want you to find somebody," Kelly said, her voice a lot softer now, as if carrying an apology she wouldn't actually say, "it's just. Keira, you've been down this road before, remember? Remember how hurt you were?"

"Trust me," Keira said tightly. "I remember."

How in the hell could she forget? Three years ago, she'd fallen madly, wildly in love with an Olympic skier who was in town training over the winter. Max had been exciting and funny and sexy and he had seemed to care for her as much as she had for him.

In a few short months, they had gotten so close that Keira was mentally making plans for a life together.

They spent every night locked in each other's arms. And Keira had never been so happy.

She'd never seen him for what he really was. Never suspected that he didn't feel the same way she did.

Until the day his fiancée rolled into town.

And Max, smooth, gorgeous Max, had turned and introduced Keira to the woman he was going to marry—as a *"good friend."*

The pain of that humiliation was going to be with her forever. Seeing the sympathetic understanding in the other woman's eyes when they met had told Keira that she wasn't the first woman he'd cheated with. Wasn't the first woman he'd lied to.

But that information had done little to heal a broken heart.

So, when the aching misery had finally faded along with her memories, Keira had made herself a promise. To protect herself, she wasn't going to fall for anyone again. Wouldn't believe more pretty lies. Wouldn't let a man get so deep inside her that she couldn't shake him loose any time she wanted to.

And her plan had worked pretty well. Until Nathan Barrister had walked into her life. Now she knew that her sister was right to worry. Because Keira was falling for him.

Despite knowing better, despite knowing that there was no future for them, her heart hadn't learned its lesson.

"I know you remember," Kelly said softly. "And I don't want to hurt you. It's just…I don't want to see you get all torn up again."

"Kelly…"

"Keira, why don't you come to London? Right now.

Well, okay, when the storm stops. Hop on a plane and come see me. It'll give you some distance. Some time to think. And you've been promising for a year you'd come anyway."

"I can't," Keira said, leaning her forehead against the window, allowing the icy cold to sweep through her. "I can't just pack up and go. You know that."

"I know that the town would be just fine without you for a month. Or two."

Chuckling in spite of the heaviness in her heart, Keira said, "Two months? Oh, I'm sure Tony would love to have your big sister around for that long. Great idea, Kel."

"Omigod!"

"What?" Keira's heart jolted. "What is it?"

"Tony. I can't believe I forgot."

"Is he okay?" Keira asked, though she couldn't imagine that her little sister would have had time to lecture her about her love life if her own man were in danger.

"Oh, he's way better than okay," Kelly said, then without even taking a breath, continued in a rush. "Remember I told you he was taking me to Paris for the weekend?"

"Yes."

"Well, we stayed a little longer than we planned, or I would have called you sooner and then, when I did try to call, the lines were down, so just keep in mind that I *did* try to get hold of you and—"

"Will you just say it?" Keira demanded.

"He asked me to marry him," Kelly said, with a sigh that told Keira her little sister was no doubt staring at her engagement ring and getting all misty-eyed.

"He did?"

"Yes. I'm engaged."

"That's—" Keira didn't know what to say, so she said nothing at all. Her heart took a small ping of something she really didn't want to call envy, but there didn't seem to be any other name for it. Oh, God, Kelly was getting married. She was living in Europe and marrying a man who was crazy about her.

And Keira was standing still.

Not that she didn't like her life—she did.

But…she'd had so many plans once upon a time and none of them had come true. And now, despite being happy for her little sister, there was a small, whimpering voice in the back of her mind, wishing that things were different for her, too.

"I have the most beautiful ring you've ever seen, it's so amazing. We're getting married this summer. At his parents' estate in Sussex. Oh, Keira, it's going to be so gorgeous. So perfect. And Tony's so great. I really love him so much and everything is so wonderful."

No one but Kelly could cram that many *so's* into a single paragraph. Her palpable excitement hummed through the phone like a live electrical wire.

"That's great, honey," Keira said and she really meant it. She was glad for Kelly. Glad she'd found someone to love and to love her back. Glad that she was building a life she was happy with.

Really.

"So will you come?"

"To the wedding?" Keira asked, dumbfounded. "Of course I'll come to the wedding! I'm completely expecting to be in the wedding."

"You're my maid of honor, Keira," Kelly said, clearly

exasperated now. "But I'm not talking about you coming to the wedding. I want you to come see me now. Please, Keira. Come and see me. Get away for a while."

"This is about Nathan, isn't it?" Keira whispered, not wanting him to overhear her.

"Well, yeah," Kelly said. "I don't want you getting attached to somebody like him. I know you, Keira. And I'm afraid you're gonna set yourself up for another fall."

"Hcy. Who's the big sister here? You or me?"

"What? Because I'm younger I can't be right?"

Keira glanced over her shoulder again to make sure Nathan was still in the great room where she'd left him, then she closed her eyes, took a deep breath and said, "Even if you're right, Kel, getting away wouldn't change anything."

"Oh, God," Kelly said with a sigh. "It really is too late, isn't it? I can hear it in your voice. You already love him."

Did she? Instantly, images of Nathan flashed through her mind. The day they met, that night at the town party, dancing with him under the stars, the panicked look in his eyes everytime someone in town tried to thank him for his donation.

Memories raced through her mind now, one after another, almost too fast to separate one from the other. She remembered his rarely seen smile and the stunned look on his features whenever she made him think beyond what he'd always done. The gleam in his eyes as his body moved within hers. The stillness of the coming storm as they took their walk around the lake.

Making love in front of the fire, shouting at him as he stood on the snow-covered deck, furious with her for locking him out. His carrying her up the stairs and catching her whenever she stumbled because she wasn't paying attention.

He was arrogant and abrasive and annoying.

And God help her, she was crazy about him.

Leaning her head against the icy glass again, she whispered, "Oh, Kelly. You're right. I *am* in love with him."

Ten

"No way this is happening," Keira whispered frantically. "I've known him only a couple of weeks."

"Uh-huh," Kelly muttered. "And just what is the time frame for falling in love? A month? Six?"

"This can't be happening." Keira thunked her head against the windowpane and welcomed the hard jolt. What an idiot she was. She'd been so busy spending time with Nathan so he wouldn't split, she hadn't noticed that she was falling in love with the man.

"Run," Kelly said. "Run fast, run far."

"I can't," Keira snapped. "Snowed in. Remember? Besides, it's too late for that."

Kelly sighed. "I know. What're you gonna do?"

"Well, I'm not telling him, that's for damn sure," she said. She might be an idiot, but she knew enough to know Nathan wouldn't want to hear her declaration of love any more than Max had.

No, thank you. She wasn't going to set herself up for another kick in the teeth. She'd made the mistake of falling in love with the wrong man. Again. But that didn't mean she had to let anyone else know.

"Probably a good plan," Kelly said, then added, "but if you want my advice…"

"I really don't."

"Well, that's nice."

"Kel, I'm sorry. But this one I'm going to have to take care of on my own."

"Fine. Just—watch yourself, okay?"

"Yeah." Keira inhaled sharply, blew the air out in a rush and said, "I've gotta go. I've got some thinking to do."

"Okay, but call me this weekend."

When she hung up, Keira didn't move. She just stood there, rooted in the kitchen, staring out at the storm and, for the first time in her life, she hated the snow. Hated the storm that was trapping her there with a man who didn't want her. Hated that she couldn't get away. Hated that she'd set herself up for more pain.

And mostly, she hated herself for being jealous of her little sister.

"Why is it that when Kelly falls in love, everything works out great?"

"Who you talking to?"

She spun around to see Nathan standing in the doorway, watching her. A flush of heat swept over her and she hoped to hell he hadn't overheard any of her conversation with Kelly. "No one. How long have you been there?"

"About ten seconds. Did you get hold of your sister?"

"Yes," Keira said, plastering a brilliant smile on her face. "She's terrific. Better than terrific, really. She's engaged."

"That's nice."

"Yeah," she said, shifting her gaze to the phone she still held in her hand, "it is."

"And you sound really excited for her."

"Oh, I am."

"Well, now I'm convinced," he said, walking over to the counter to pour himself another cup of coffee. "What's wrong, don't you like the guy?"

"Never met him, actually. Talked to him a couple of times, but they live in England, so…"

"Why don't you go visit?"

Keira looked up at him as he leaned casually against the kitchen counter, taking a sip of his coffee. "I believe we already covered that. I have responsibilities here."

One dark eyebrow rose. "So mayors don't get vacations?"

"Why do you care if I visit my sister or not?" she snapped.

"Whoa. Don't care. Just asked."

Keira held up one hand, crossed the room and gave him back his phone. "Sorry, sorry. That wasn't about you. That was about me."

He looked at her for a long minute or two and Keira stared up into those pale blue eyes of his. How could she not have realized that she was falling in love with him? And when had it happened?

When he told her about his awful grandmother? When he actually listened to her advice? When they took a walk beside the lake? When he touched her and made her body sing?

Oh, God.

Why couldn't she have fallen for the right guy this time?

"What's wrong?" he asked and his voice was so quiet, she nearly missed the words.

"I don't know," she said, because she couldn't tell him the truth. Turning her back on him, she walked to the windows and stared out at the storm that had become an enemy.

She heard his footsteps behind her, but didn't turn to watch him approach. Instead, she watched his reflection in the dark glass and, when his hands came down on her shoulders, she managed to suppress a sigh of satisfaction at his touch.

"Tell me," he said softly.

Keira shook her head and said, "I'm evil."

He laughed shortly. "Yeah? Evil how?"

"My sister tells me she's engaged and I'm envious. How evil is that?"

He dropped his hands from her shoulders and Keira thought he couldn't have made it any clearer just how he felt. He didn't move away, though. Just stood there behind her, his body sending waves of heat her way.

"You want to get married?"

Now *she* laughed a little. At the situation. At herself. At the raw panic in the reflection of his eyes.

"I always planned to," she said. "Just like I planned to travel. But things don't seem to work out the way you think they will."

"Maybe that's for the best."

She turned around to look up at him. "For the best?"

He shrugged. "Who cares what your old plans were? Thought you liked your life the way it is."

"I do," she admitted, "It's just…different from what I expected it to be. My mom used to say that life is what happens while you're making plans. And I guess that's true."

As she talked, Keira knew she was trying to convince not only Nathan, but herself, that her life was just the way she wanted it. That she would be fine when he left. That it didn't matter to her that he didn't love her. That he would be leaving without a backward glance.

She would be all right because she still had her home. Her place in the world. If it wasn't the place she'd always planned on, did that make it any less important? No.

"I mean," she said, pulling a chair out from under the kitchen table and plopping into it, "I love Hunter's Landing. I love belonging and being a part of the town's life. So, plan or no plan, I like my life. Don't get me wrong, I'd still like to travel, but this will always be home. I'll always come back here."

He looked down at her and shook his head, taking another sip of his coffee. "I don't understand tying yourself to a place."

Keira's heart felt another twinge, but she managed to avoid showing it. "The word *home* isn't synonymous with *prison*."

"Might as well be," he said. "The best way to live is to just keep moving."

Which is just what he'd be doing in a couple of weeks. He'd be moving on so fast that he probably wouldn't even bother to say goodbye. It hurt her to know that she'd remember him long after he'd forgotten her *and* Hunter's Landing. "Because if you keep moving, you make sure you never have time to care about anyone or anything, huh?"

His gaze narrowed on her. "You like sitting still. I like moving. Who's to say which way is best?"

"Me."

"Ah," he said, setting his coffee cup down onto the kitchen table. Shoving both hands into his pockets, he said irritably, "Ms. Roots speaks. Hearth and home and everything that goes with it, right? Well, not all of us are looking to get stuck in a rut so deep you can't see over the top of it."

"Who said anything about a rut?" she demanded, standing up so she was more on an even keel with him. It hadn't taken long for the two of them to start an argument. And maybe it was better this way, she thought. Maybe if they kept fighting, then it wouldn't hurt so much when he left.

But, even as she thought it, Keira knew it for a lie. She *liked* fighting with Nathan. So this would be just one more thing to miss.

"Please. Your rut is so comfortable, you've hung curtains and had it carpeted."

"Excuse me?"

"Come on, Keira. Admit it. You're stuck here in this little town, and the only reason you keep talking about how wonderful it is, is to keep yourself from feeling cheated out of the life you wanted."

"Is that right?" Incensed, she poked him in the chest with her index finger and seriously thought about kicking him. But she wasn't wearing shoes so she'd probably break her toe. "Just so you know, Mr. Fabulous World Traveler, I do *not* feel cheated. If I wanted my life to change, I'd change it. I'm not the one who's too afraid to try something new."

"Afraid?" He snorted a laugh. "Is that supposed to mean that *I'm* afraid of something?"

She blinked at him. "Duh."

"This should be good." He folded his arms over his chest, tipped his head to one side and waited, a smirking half smile on his face. "Fine. Tell me. What am I so afraid of?"

"I don't know," Keira admitted, wishing she did. Because then, maybe she'd have half a chance to fight through the walls he'd built around himself so many years ago.

"Hah!"

"But *you* know," she added quickly. "You might not admit it to me, but deep down inside, you know damn well there's a reason you're constantly moving on."

"Yeah," he said. "I like it."

"Liar."

He blew out a disgusted breath.

"You spend your whole life running so fast that nobody can catch up," Keira said, more thoughtful now as the temper that had spiked within her slowly drained away. "The question is what're you running from, Nathan?"

"I'm not running from anything."

"Well," she mused. "I guess you've said that often enough that even you believe it now."

She walked around him, careful not to brush against

him as she headed for the doorway leading back to the great room. When she reached it, she paused and looked back at him, standing alone in an elegant kitchen. This is how she'd remember him best, she thought. Stubbornly aloof. Alone.

Her heart ached, almost in preparation for the coming pain, but she held it inside as she said, "Someday, I hope you figure it out, Nathan. Before it's too late to stop and let somebody catch up to you."

She avoided him for the rest of the day and Nathan told himself he didn't care. He appreciated having some quiet time to work uninterrupted. God knew, since he'd met Keira, he'd had little enough peace and quiet.

And after an afternoon of it, he was going quietly insane.

He kept looking for her, expecting her to run into the room and trip over a table or something. He kept listening for the sound of her voice. But there was nothing. The big lodge fairly echoed with a stillness that was starting to really grate on him. Disgusted with himself, he finally realized that his satellite phone could connect him with more people than the citizens of Hunter's Landing.

Grabbing it, he hit the speed dial and called the one person on earth he knew would understand exactly what he was going through.

"Barton."

Nathan smiled at the sound of his old friend's voice. They hadn't really seen each other since college, but Luke Barton was one of the Seven Samurai he'd managed to keep in touch with, however loosely.

"Barrister here," he said and stalked to the wide

windows overlooking the white stillness covering the front yard of the lodge.

"Hell, Nathan." Luke laughed. "Good to hear your voice. How's life in the wild?"

"Not as wild as we might like," he grumbled and turned his back on the view of Mother Nature. "Glad to say my month is almost up and yours is coming."

"That bad?" Luke asked, dread clear in his voice.

"Small-town America at its coziest."

"Jeez. Sounds horrifying."

Nathan laughed and felt better. Good to know he wasn't the only person in the world who preferred big cities to quiet reflection. "Exactly. I got your e-mail last week," he said. "How the hell did Matthias convince you to switch months at the cabin with him? Are you two speaking again?"

"Not likely," Luke admitted.

The Barton twins had been at war for years, ever since their father had cooked up a competition between the two of them for the right to run the family business. Matthias won, but Luke was always sure his twin had somehow cheated him. Not that Luke was starving or anything. He'd built his own fortune—one to rival the legacy that Matthias had inherited—by starting up Eagle Wireless, a tech company that had pretty much taken over the world.

Still, old rivalries would never die.

"So, how'd Matt get you to switch?"

"Bastard couldn't do his month—some business emergency or other. Not sure, really. His assistant talked to my assistant." Luke blew out a disgusted breath. "The only reason I agreed to the damn switch was so Hunter's last request wouldn't be ruined."

Nathan wandered the great room while he listened. The house was crouched in quiet, and he was as cut off from the outside world as neatly as he would have been if he'd been on Mars. Talking to Luke took the edge off, and he wondered why the hell they didn't talk to each other more often.

"How bad is it?" Luke asked. "Have you at least been to Tahoe? Stateline?"

"No," Nathan answered. "I can see the lights from the casinos in the distance though—when it isn't snowing."

"Snowing?" Luke echoed. "It's March, for God's sake."

"And I'm talking to you from the middle of a blizzard."

"God, if Hunter wasn't gone, I'd kill him myself."

Nathan laughed again and dropped onto the couch. "Just what I was thinking when I first got here."

"But not now?"

"Don't get me wrong," Nathan said, "I can't wait to shake this place. Get the jet fired up and leave Hunter's Landing in the dust."

"But…"

"No but."

"I heard an implied but."

Frowning, Nathan said, "But there's a woman."

"Isn't there always? Who was that last one? Some Hollywood babe who wanted you to produce her next movie?"

He smiled, then frowned again. Maybe he was too used to people using him. "This one's different."

"This must be a sign of the Apocalypse," Luke said. "Nathan Barrister in love?"

"Who the hell said anything about love?" Nathan countered and jumped off the couch like he'd been set on fire.

"Okay then, I stand reassured," Luke said, then covered the receiver with one hand and muttered something Nathan couldn't catch. "Nathan," he said a moment later, "I've got to run. I have a meeting with some new Japanese clients and want to get this deal sewn up before I have to take my place in the cottage at the end of the world."

"Right. Well, hurry the hell up and get me out of this place, all right?"

"Not a chance, pal. You finish out your damn month. I've got my own to worry about."

After he'd hung up, Nathan stood in the middle of the great room and listened to the quiet. He should be glad Keira was giving him some space. It wasn't like he needed to be around her, for God's sake. But the quiet nagged at him and, when he finally couldn't stand it anymore, he went looking for her, sure that he'd find her sitting in a corner somewhere, pissed off and thinking of ways to make him suffer.

But she wasn't anywhere in the house.

Scowling, he grabbed his jacket from the hook in the mudroom, walked outside into the slap of an icy wind and squinted into the lamp-lit darkness. Even the night seemed deeper here. More black. More all-encompassing.

The moon was hidden behind clouds that showed no sign of leaving and snow was *still* falling, though in lighter flurries than before. He walked across the deck, grabbed the railing and leaned out, scanning the area for her.

"Surely she wouldn't have gone on one of her *walks* in the snow," he muttered. And as he considered that, he imagined her lying on the ground, unconscious from hitting her head when she fell because *he* hadn't been there to catch her. She could freeze to death out there and no one would find her until the spring thaw—if spring ever really came to the high Sierras.

Ridiculous. He tried to dismiss the worry. She'd managed to survive without his help for thirty years; he was sure she'd be fine tonight, too. "But she could have told me where she was going," he said softly.

An explosion of icy wet hit the side of his head and Nathan jerked upright like he'd been shot. Almost before he realized that he'd been hit with a snowball, he heard her laugh and turned toward the sound.

Keira stood beneath the deck, her breath puffing out in white clouds in front of her. Her smile stretched across her face and her laughter rose up in the air like music.

"Got ya!"

"Are you out of your mind?" he shouted to be heard over her wild whoop of renewed amusement.

"What's the matter, Nathan?" she taunted. "Afraid of a little snow?" Then she bent down, scooped up more of the icy stuff, patted it into a ball and let it go.

This time he saw it coming and ducked. And while he was bent down low, he scooped up some snow of his own, packed a mean snowball and let it fly while she was bent over gathering new ammunition. He hit her on the back of the head and she went down on one knee.

Instantly, he worried that he'd actually hurt her. A second later though, she raised her gaze to his and said, "You realize this means war."

He'd never get used to her, he thought. While he had been expecting to find her sulking and nursing a temper—as most other women he'd ever known would have been doing—she had been outside waiting for the opportunity to execute a surprise attack.

She wasn't angry. She was laughing. And the joy in that sound touched something inside Nathan that had been locked away for more years than he could count. He didn't examine it too closely. Instead, he gave himself up to the moment. He forgot about work. Forgot about keeping a safe distance from a woman who too easily found her way around his defenses. He forgot everything in the moment that was *now.*

"You're gonna pay for this," he shouted.

"Talk is cheap," she taunted.

Setting one hand on the railing, he vaulted over the edge and landed five feet down in the snow, bending his knees to absorb the jolt.

Her eyes went wide, and stunned surprise kept her frozen just long enough to give Nathan time to form another snowball and let her have it. She shrieked when the snow hit her face and did a funny little dance as some of the cold wet stuff slinked beneath the collar of her jacket.

But she didn't let it slow her down. In seconds the war was raging and the two of them were running around the snowy yard like a couple of ten-year-olds. Nathan hadn't had so much fun in years. He couldn't remember the last time he'd done anything like this and he was loving it. Their shouts echoed off the mountain and snow flew from half-frozen hands like white bullets.

Lamplight gleamed golden and shone in her hair as Nathan circled her, waiting for an opening. When he got it, he charged her, grabbing her around the waist and carrying them both to the snowy cushion atop the cold ground. He hit the ground first, taking the brunt of the fall, keeping her on top of him until he rolled over her, pinning her in place.

"I win," he said, grinning at her.

"No fair," she countered. "I didn't know we were playing tackle snow war."

"All's fair," he said—then caught himself before he could utter the rest of the old cliché.

She smiled up at him and the warmth in her gaze started a fire inside him that burned away every icy edge he had ever carried. He felt…different somehow and, later, when he thought about this moment, he might do some worrying. But right now, all he wanted to think about was her. What she did to him with a smile. How she could constantly surprise him and jolt him out of the ordinary.

And just how much he wanted her.

Bending his head to hers, he kissed her and the cold of her lips met his, eagerly, hungrily. When he finally broke free, he said, "How about we finish this inside?"

Eleven

Two days later, the lodge phone rang and Keira nearly jumped out of her skin. Nathan grabbed it and, after a second or two, handed it over to her. A brief conversation later, she hung up, looked at Nathan and said, "Phone lines are working again."

His mouth quirked and she felt a tug in the pit of her stomach. Something like the beginnings of loneliness. Their time together was over and it was time to go back to the real world. The world where Nathan wasn't a part of her life.

"I got that. How about the roads?" he asked.

Keira raised her chin and gave him a bright smile. "Your prayers are answered. That was Bill Hambleton, the deputy mayor. He was calling to let me know the crews were out and the road to the lodge should be clear by late afternoon."

"Bill, huh?" Nathan nodded, picked up the remote and turned the TV off in the middle of the movie they had been watching. "How'd he know you were here?"

"His wife, Patti, knew I was coming here the day the storm hit." She shrugged. "Guess she just figured when she didn't see me in town that I had gotten stuck here."

"His wife," he mused.

"Yeah." Keira cocked her head and smiled at his expression. Was it possible he had been—even momentarily—jealous?

"So you'll be leaving."

"Time to go home."

"For some of us."

"You're the one who said you didn't have a home," she reminded him.

"Touché," he acknowledged with a nod. "I guess I meant that one of us will be leaving."

"So, you'll definitely stay for the rest of the month?"

Nodding, he leaned back into the couch. "Yeah. I'll stay."

"Thanks," she whispered and resisted the urge to reach out and smooth his hair back from his forehead.

"It's okay." He propped his feet up on the coffee table and said, "It's only two weeks. And, hell," he added quietly, more to himself than to her, "guess I owe it to Hunter."

Keira leaned into the couch too, curling her legs up under her. "Tell me about him."

"What?"

"Hunter Palmer," she urged. "Tell me about him. I mean, all I know is that, for some reason, he chose our town to build his lodge in—and he's arranged for some amazingly generous donations to charity."

Nathan looked at her briefly, then shifted his gaze so that he was staring at the fire burning in the hearth. As if mesmerized by the flames, he began talking slowly, as if unsure just where to start. "My guess is Hunter chose your town because its name was the same as his. Probably thought it was a good joke. Anyway, we went to college together. Hunter, me, and the other guys who'll be coming here."

"Where?"

"Harvard," he said easily, and she wondered if he knew he was smiling. "After our first year, we rented a house off campus together."

"Just you and Hunter?"

"No, all seven of us. Back then we called ourselves the Seven Samurai." He shot her an amused look. "Not real clever, but…" He shrugged and let it go. "We were all as close as brothers back then."

"I was looking at the framed photos of all of you in the upstairs hall yesterday," Keira said. "Your hair was a lot longer then."

He chuckled at that, and she thought he looked a little surprised. "Don't remind me."

"Oh, I don't know. I sort of like a man in a ponytail."

His smile slowly faded as he shook his head. Firelight shimmered in the room, and Keira watched as memories swarmed in the depths of his eyes. "We were different then. All of us," he said, his voice soft and far away. "We were so certain how life would turn out for us. That night we promised to build this lodge together, it never crossed our minds that we wouldn't all be there to see it." He paused. "Hunter got sick our senior year. Skin cancer. By the time they found it, it was way too late. He died by inches."

"Oh, Nathan."

He let his head fall to the back of the sofa and stared up at the ceiling. "I watched him sliding away and finally one night I couldn't take it anymore. I went to a bar near the campus, got blind drunk and picked a fight." A quirk of his mouth appeared and disappeared again a moment later. "Naturally, I picked the wrong guy to mess with and got my ass kicked. I ended up in the hospital."

Keira's heart ached listening to him, but she knew she had to let him finish. She had the distinct impression that he'd never said any of this before.

He turned his head to look at her. "I woke up three days later and found out Hunter had died and was already buried."

"I'm sorry."

A closed door snapped into place over his eyes and his voice lost the memory-tinged softness. "It was a long time ago."

"It was yesterday."

He turned and speared her with a look. "What's that supposed to mean?"

"Nathan, I can see it in your face," she said gently. "The pain of it is still with you."

"You're wrong," he said and pushed himself to his feet. Shoving his hands into his pockets, he walked around the room like a caged tiger looking for a way through the bars. "It was ten years ago, Keira. I'm over it."

"I wish that was true," she said softly. "But it's not." Shaking her head, she got up from the couch, crossed the room and stopped right in front of him. Reaching up, she cupped his face between her palms. "Whether you can admit it or not, you're punishing yourself for a single mistake you made when you were in pain. Don't you see that Hunter wouldn't want you to be so alone? Still suffering over something you never meant to do?"

"Oh, for God's sake," he said, pulling away from her touch, "I'm not a wounded animal, Keira. Or a child. I don't want or need your sympathy."

"Well, you have it anyway," she said.

Shaking his head, he choked out a strangled laugh. "God. I don't know how you got me talking about this, but don't think I'm looking to be *cured.* I'm not carrying around a burden of guilt for being a stupid kid. I'm not hiding myself away from people so that I never have to worry about letting someone down when they need me again."

"I didn't say that's why you're alone so much," she pointed out quietly, "but it's interesting that it's the first thing that came to you."

"This is great," he snapped, pushing one hand through his hair and looking like he'd rather be anywhere but where he was at the moment. "A mayor who's a part-time psychiatrist. Lucky for me you were here."

"Nathan…"

"Forget it, Keira. I'm not interested in being analyzed."

"I wasn't—"

"Yes, you were. Well, don't bother. I'm not 'punishing' myself," he said, his voice as grim as the bleak shine in his eyes. "I'm just living."

"Are you?" she asked. "Really?"

He laughed sourly and shook his head. "You're seeing things that aren't there, Keira. Quit fooling yourself. I'm not the man you think I am," he said. "I'm not looking to be saved. I'm not looking for roots. My life is just the way I want it. I'm happy going from Monte Carlo to Venice to London. I have friends, I go to parties, I come and go as I please and I live exactly the way I want to live. Not all of us want to be buried alive in a small town on top of a mountain."

Her heart twisted in her chest as she looked up at him and watched him emotionally pull further away from her than he'd ever been. "Nathan…"

He took a long step backward. "Just leave it alone, okay? Today you go back to your life. I go back to mine. And it's probably best if we just don't see each other again while I'm here."

There it was—the pain she'd been waiting for since the moment she realized she was in love with him. God. She hadn't expected it to be so sharp. So devastating. When Max had betrayed her, she'd thought herself wounded. But now, knowing that she was losing Nathan, Keira finally understood what real misery was. What real heartbreak was.

Instantly, her imagination played out in her mind, showing her the coming years. The long, lonely years when she would be wondering if he ever thought of her. If he missed her. If he ever wished he had stayed in Hunter's Landing.

And in the next moment, Keira had to ask herself if she would come to regret never telling him that she loved him. If she didn't, she'd never know if there might have been a chance for them. Besides, if she kept quiet about her feelings, hiding behind her fear, wouldn't that make her as big a coward as Nathan—hiding from possible pain?

That thought was enough to spur her into action. She

would take a chance because that's who she was. Who she had always been. And if he didn't want her, then she would know. If he didn't love her, she'd never have to wonder. She would only have to mourn what might have been.

"Maybe you're right," she said after taking a moment to steady herself. "Maybe we shouldn't see each other anymore. But before I leave, I want you to know something."

His jaw clenched and his pale blue eyes shone with wariness. "I really think we've said enough already."

"I don't," she countered quickly, before she could talk herself out of this. "You may not want to hear this, but I'm going to say it because if I don't, I know I'll regret it and, damn it, there are enough regrets in the world already."

"Keira…"

"I love you," she said, the words dropping into a sudden silence like stones into a well. When he didn't say anything, Keira pushed on, knowing that if she didn't get it all said now, she might never have another chance. "I didn't expect to, but I do. I really love you, Nathan."

Suspicion glittered in his eyes now, and she knew she was fighting in a battle already lost. He'd closed himself off so tightly, she could barely see a shadow of the man she'd spent the last four days with. But still, she'd come this far; she would say the rest, too.

"I'm not expecting you to say anything, and hey," she forced a short laugh she didn't feel "good thing. And I don't want anything from you, either. I just…wanted you to know that somebody loves you. That *I* love you."

She couldn't reach him. She could see it as plain as anything. He had withdrawn so far from her, it was as if she was alone in the room.

The silence screamed at her. The snap and hiss of the fire sounded as loud as gunshots. While she watched him, Keira remembered everything they'd shared here during the storm. The wild, passionate lovemaking, the snowball fight, the arguments and the laughter.

She recalled turning to him in the middle of the night and feeling his arms slide around her middle, pinning her to him as they slept, and she wondered how she would ever sleep through the night again without him. How was she going to face every day, knowing she wouldn't see him? Would never talk to him again?

A soul-deep ache washed over her and Keira wanted to moan at the swell of looming emptiness inside. But she didn't. If this was the last time she was going to see him, then she wanted him to remember her smiling. And maybe someday, when it was much too late for either of them, he would think back to this moment and wish he'd had the courage to accept the love she had offered him.

"Well," she said briskly, giving him her brightest smile and hoping it was enough to ease the shadows she knew were in her eyes, "I guess that's it. The road should be clear in a couple of hours, so I'll just stay out of your hair until then."

He nodded so stiffly, it was a wonder his neck didn't snap.

Keira walked up to him, went up on her toes and planted a quick, fierce kiss on his unyielding mouth. Then she stepped back, looked into his eyes and whispered, "Goodbye, Nathan Barrister."

Then she left him, and the only sounds in the room were the fire and her quick steps as she ran up the staircase to get her things.

* * *

Several hours later, Keira was gone and the big house on the lake echoed with emptiness. Nathan wandered from room to room, too restless to sit still, too wired to work. Instead, his mind continued to taunt him by replaying those last few moments with Keira.

She loved him.

He should have said something, but damned if he knew what. She'd caught him completely off balance and that wasn't something that happened to Nathan Barrister. He was a man who always knew where he stood. What to do. What to expect. He'd made a habit of being prepared for any eventuality.

She loved him.

He took the stairs two steps at a time, listening to the sound of his own footsteps thump like a jittering heartbeat in the big house. When he hit the upper landing, he headed for the bedroom. But, instead of averting his gaze from the old photos on the wall, he stopped to look at them all for the first time.

Echoes of the past reached out for him as his gaze moved from one familiar face to the next. There was Hunter, of course, laughing into the camera without a care in the world. And Nathan smiled at the photo of Luke and Matt Barton, back in the days when they were still speaking, holding Ryan Sperling in a friendly headlock, while Devlin Campbell and Jack Howington poured bottles of beer over them all.

His friends. More than friends, they'd been brothers—the only real family Nathan had known after his parents' death. And he'd let them all slip mostly away from him.

When Hunter died, the rest of the group had splintered, as if its heart had been removed and there was no way to keep the rest of the whole together. Nathan reached out and touched the glass covering a photo of the Seven Samurai and he realized just how much he missed them all. How he missed what they had been back then!

And he wondered what kind of man he might have been if things had been different.

Would he have known how to accept Keira's love? Would he have believed her when she said she wanted nothing from him? Shaking his head, he stepped back from the images of his past and walked on, into the master bedroom.

No. How could he believe her? *Everyone* wanted something from him, he thought as he laid down, fully clothed across the bed. Why should she be any different?

One day bled into the next and that one into another until a week had crawled past.

And Nathan hadn't gotten a damn thing done.

No lists. No memos. No e-mails to hotel managers setting up meetings. Instead, he was restless. Couldn't think. Couldn't sleep. Couldn't keep his mind from turning to thoughts of Keira, damn it.

She was everywhere in the lodge. He couldn't take a step without remembering something she had said. He couldn't lay in bed without recalling the feel of her body pressed to his. He couldn't walk into the kitchen without seeing her naked on the counter. He stepped outside and was whisked back to the night of their snowball fight. He went for firewood and remembered her locking him outside and shouting at him through the glass.

He walked down the stairs and remembered catching her as she fell—and, damn it, he was worried about who was going to catch her when he wasn't around.

"Not my problem," he grumbled into the silence. "If the damn woman is too busy to watch where she's going, she'll just have to fall. Probably break her damn neck one of these days."

The quiet mocked him as his own voice faded into the stillness crouched in the big, empty lodge. One week to go and then he could leave. He had to stick it out now; he'd promised Keira, and a Barrister never went back on his word. No matter the temptation.

Scowling, he told himself that Keira was probably worried that he was going to leave anyway. Probably hadn't believed him when he'd promised. Well, he could just go into town and assure her that he would be right where he said he would be. That he was staying until the end of the month and then he was going to leave this town and *her* behind him as fast as he was able.

But, even as he thought that, something else occurred to him. Something he hadn't considered before and, frankly, at the moment, he couldn't figure out why not. It made sense. It fit the situation and would give both he and Keira what they wanted.

Damned if he wasn't a genius.

A week with no word from Nathan, and Keira was forced to admit that he just wasn't interested in what she felt for him. Of course, she hadn't really expected him to do an about-face, shout *I love you, too!* and carry her off to his castle—er, favorite hotel.

"But damn it, he doesn't have to completely ignore

me, either." She kicked her living room couch and limped into the kitchen for yet another cup of coffee. "It's my own fault," she muttered before taking a sip. "I knew who he was and how he felt, and I went ahead and fell in love with him anyway."

If she could have figured out exactly how to do it, she would have kicked her own ass.

"Idiot." She cupped both hands around her coffee mug and hoped that the heat would wipe away the chill sweeping through her. But it didn't help. Nothing would and she knew it. She was going to carry this icy loneliness around with her for the rest of her life. All because of one stubborn, miserable, selfish son of a bitch who didn't have the decency to accept an offer of love freely given.

"There. That's better," she whispered. "Be mad, not sad."

But the sad went too deep and the mad wasn't nearly enough to bury it.

When the doorbell rang, she set her coffee down and went to answer it. With any luck, there was some town crisis she could lose herself in. She threw the door open and stared up at Nathan, way too shocked to think of anything to say.

He smiled, and Keira swallowed hard. "What're you doing here?"

Stepping past her, he walked into her house, looked around, then turned to look at her, a wide smile brightening his features. "I have a surprise for you."

Intrigued and, damn it all, a little hopeful, Keira closed the door, shoved her hands into her jeans pockets and said, "A surprise?"

"Yes." He looked so pleased with himself, Keira

didn't know what to think. "I took care of everything this morning. You don't have to do a thing."

Worry began to nibble at her. He was taking care of everything? Taking care of what, exactly? "What is this great surprise then?"

He walked toward her, took hold of her shoulders and held on as he looked down into her eyes. "You know I'm leaving for Barbados at the end of the month."

"Yeah…" That sinking sensation in the pit of her stomach simply refused to go away.

"You're going with me."

Keira staggered and probably would have fallen down if his grip on her shoulders hadn't tightened perceptibly. "I'm what?"

He grinned, apparently taking her shock for pleasure. "I talked to your deputy mayor—Hambleton?"

"Bill, yes." She was struggling for air. Her chest felt tight and her whole body was tingling with nerves that were pushing her to do *something*.

"Right," he said. He released her, then walked into the living room and spun around, folding his arms across his chest, looking like a king who had finally figured out how to please the peasants. "I told Bill you'd be leaving with me and we didn't know how long we'd be gone. He's fine with it. He can handle whatever happens here—" He shrugged. "Town this size, running it can't be too difficult anyway."

"Is that right?" Cold. She felt cold all the way through. How weird. For the last week, she'd alternated between fury and grief, and now all she could feel was this body-numbing iciness.

"I called the hotel in Barbados," he was saying. "Told

them I would have a companion accompanying me and arranged for a personal shopper for you the moment we land. You don't even have to pack for the trip. While I'm working, you'll have the run of the shops—unlimited expense account, of course—and we'll have every night to ourselves."

"I see." She really did and she was hurt in more ways than she could count.

"From Barbados," he said, hurrying on to fill the silence growing between them, "we'll head to London. Maybe visit your sister. Or even better, we'll go to Venice—I'll send for your sister, make all the arrangements. You can have her with you as long as you want."

"How nice for me—you can arrange Kelly's life, too."

He frowned briefly, shoved one hand through his hair and said, "If you don't want to go to Venice, we'll go somewhere else."

"Oh," Keira said, walking past him now, into the kitchen where she picked up her coffee cup. "I get a vote?"

"What?"

She took a breath, hoping to steady the swell of fury rising up to choke her. "And if I tell you I can't afford to take off work? To go and travel around the world with you?"

"I didn't ask you to pay for anything," he said, frowning. "I've taken care of it. I told you that."

"Right. Silly me. So *you* decide what I do and where I go. *You* pay for me and I'm supposed to just be grateful to be taken care of."

"Is there something wrong with that?"

He was looking at her like she was speaking Greek. Could he really be this clueless?

"You really don't see it, do you?" Keira felt like her head was exploding. How could she ever make him see who she really was if he was convinced his bank account would fix any problem?

"I'm offering you the travel and excitement you always dreamed of and that makes me a bad guy?"

"You didn't even *ask* me, Nathan. You just order me here or there, and I'm supposed to come trotting along behind you fluttering with gratitude?"

"I'm confused," he admitted and stopped in the doorway between the kitchen and the living room. "You said you wanted to travel."

"Yeah, I did."

"You want to visit your sister. See Venice."

"All correct," she admitted, and took a sip of coffee that she didn't even taste. Heck, she was half amazed that she could force the liquid down past the knot in her throat.

"Then what's the problem? Why the hell aren't you happy?" He was shouting now, and that at least made her feel a little better. She'd finally cracked through his wall of blasé.

"Because you *told* me what I was going to do," she countered, slapping her cup down onto the counter with enough force to slosh coffee over the edge. "You didn't ask. You just arranged everything the way you wanted it to be. God, you went to Bill and told him we'd be traveling together. That's just fabulous."

"You said you loved me," he said tightly. "I naturally assumed you would want to be with me."

Keira choked out a laugh. "And because I love you I would want to be your 'companion'? How many times have your hotel employees been told to prepare for your current 'guest'? What number am I in line? Is there a salary that goes with the position? How much does your own private whore make? Am I paid by the hour? Or is my new wardrobe my payment?"

"For God's sake, that's not how I meant—"

"You're unbelievable," Keira said, striding across the kitchen to slap both hands against his chest. "You go behind my back to *arrange* my life. Oh, and you don't even stop there. You think you can arrange my *sister's* life—she has a job, you know? And a fiancé. She can't just entertain me when it's convenient for you."

"This is not the way I expected this conversation to go," he said.

"Well, maybe you should have written out a script for me."

"Damn it, that's not what I meant. I thought you'd be happy. I thought you wanted to travel. To see the world. That's what you said."

"I said a lot of things. Some of them you obviously ignored. I *love* my home. I don't want to leave it forever, and I can't just walk away from my responsibilities here because you say so."

He inhaled sharply, deeply, and blew the air out in a long rush of exasperation. Well, now she knew just how he felt. She loved the man and now she knew all too well that he would never love her back.

"I didn't tell you I loved you so that you would *do* something for me, Nathan," she said, and all of her anger drained away in the wash of despair swamping her. "My love doesn't come with a price tag. You don't have to throw presents at me to try to even the playing field. I didn't ask for anything from you. I offered you my love, free and clear. No strings attached."

"Keira—"

"You know what? I think you should go, Nathan," she said, moving past him to the front door, locking her knees so that she wouldn't slump to the floor until long after he left. "You just don't understand me and you never will."

He stopped beside her and looked down into her eyes for one brief moment. "You're right," he said. "I don't understand you. I offered you everything you ever wanted and you turned it all down."

"Not everything, Nathan," she said, and quietly closed the door behind him.

Twelve

Keira smiled and tried to focus on her friend standing in front of her. It wasn't easy. For a week now she'd been moving in a fog. She couldn't get Nathan out of her mind and she wondered if she'd spend the rest of her life like this—only half aware of the world going on around her.

She'd had to tell several people that she wasn't actually leaving with Nathan at the end of the month. And she'd had to put up with their knowing smiles and nods of sympathy for a love affair gone bad. Damn Nathan anyway. By trying to run her life, he'd made it that much more complicated.

"The contractor says he's ready to start on the clinic next week," Mike McDonald was saying, and Keira made an effort to concentrate.

"He wants to start before the thaw?"

Mike, an older man with long gray hair that he kept in a neat ponytail, shrugged and said, "He says he wants to start on the inside and then, by the time the snows are gone, his crew will be ready to begin the structural changes."

"Okay," she said, nodding as she shifted her gaze to the clinic that was going to become so much more, thanks to Nathan's contribution and the promise of Hunter Palmer's legacy. "I'll tell the town council and you can give the contractor the go ahead."

"Great," Mike said, adding, "and you're gonna be here, right?"

She sighed. "Yes, Mike. I'll be here. I live here. Where else would I be?"

He clucked his tongue and patted her shoulder before heading off down the sidewalk.

Alone, Keira turned and took in all of Hunter's Landing in a single glance. A sad smile curved her mouth as she realized what an idiot she had been to think that a man like Nathan would want to give up his travels to exotic cities and countries in favor of settling down in a tiny town like this one.

Kelly had been right. Nathan was *so* not the right man for Keira. He'd proven that himself only two days ago when he'd tried to hijack her life. "Unfortunately," she whispered, her heart as heavy as it had been the last time she'd seen him, "he's the only one I want."

"Talking to yourself, Mayor?" Francine Hogan called from the doorway of the post office.

Jolted, Keira forced a smile. "Nobody understands me better than me," she joked.

Just as Keira had hoped, Francine laughed and went

about her business. Stuffing her hands into her pockets, Keira walked down the street, nodding and smiling at the people she'd known her whole life.

The sun was shining and the temperature was finally starting to climb. Maybe spring was actually going to arrive at last. Just in time for Nathan to shake off the dust of Hunter's Landing and move on to Barbados. Without her. She felt a twinge around her heart and knew that it was something she was just going to have to get used to.

Then she stopped and blinked. Okay, she was worse off than she'd thought. If she didn't know better, she would swear that Nathan Barrister was standing outside the grocery store, chatting with Sallye Carberry. Oh, Keira thought, she was really losing it.

Putting one hand up to shield her eyes, she took a better look and could hardly believe what she was seeing. It *was* Nathan. Smiling and talking as if he and the older woman were the best of friends. As she stood, rooted to the spot, she watched him say goodbye to Sallye, then move along the walk on the opposite side of the street, stopping now and then to greet someone else he'd met at the block party three weeks before. For a man so determined to be alone, he had already made connections with some of these people, whether he realized it or not.

"What is he doing?" she murmured, then followed that up with, "and why do I care?"

It was no business of hers what Nathan did. He had promised to stay in town through the end of the month and that was all that mattered now. And, since their last fight two days ago, she knew that any chance they might have had together was gone. Still, her heartbeat quick-

ened and her mouth went dry just watching him walk.
Oh, she really didn't want him to see her.

So, to minimize the risk of that happening, Keira
hurried her steps, heading to the diner. She needed
coffee and some comfort food, and the diner was the
best place to find both.

Several days later, Nathan sat, having a solitary drink
on the Clearwater restaurant's deck. He'd been in town
every day now for nearly a week and he hadn't seen
Keira once. Everywhere he went, people told him he'd
just missed her. How was that possible in a town this
size? Was she deliberately avoiding him? All because
he'd wanted her with him? What in the hell did the
woman want, anyway?

He stared out over the lake and watched the first deep,
rich colors of sunset stain the sky. Around him, families
laughed and talked together; waiters moved through the
crowd with expert agility and, directly across from
Nathan, a young couple sat so lost in each other they
might as well have been alone on a deserted island.

A ping of envy rattled Nathan enough that he took a
long drink of his Scotch and shifted his gaze back to the
lake. Rose and gold streaks lay across the surface of the
water and the cool evening breeze was so different from
the icy wind that had held the mountain in a tight grip
just the week before, it amazed him.

"Your usual, Mr. Barrister?" The waiter was standing
beside his table, smiling.

"Yes, Jake. Thanks." As the young man moved off to
get his dinner, Nathan surprised himself by smiling. He
had, over the last few days, become a regular at the

Clearwater. The waiters knew his name and his favorite meal—the chicken Alfredo, no surprise there—and always greeted him like family.

But then, he'd been experiencing the same feelings all over town. The shop owners smiled, people stopped to talk with him and he had begun to feel as if he actually *belonged* in Hunter's Landing. A strange feeling for a man who had spent most of his life on the move. Even stranger…he liked it.

In a couple of days, his month would be over and he would be leaving. And the truth of it was, he'd never been less interested in moving on—alone. But Keira wouldn't come with him and he didn't know *how* to stay. Didn't know how to become a part of something greater than himself.

Didn't know how to love someone like Keira—and the thought of somehow screwing up what they had so briefly had together…making her sorry she'd ever said she loved him, was enough to make him see that leaving was really his only option.

He finished his drink and ordered another.

An hour later, Keira took her sandwich into the living room, dropped onto the couch and flipped on the television. She used to love sitting in the quiet, letting her mind rest after listening to people chatter all day long. But these days, she needed the noise. The distraction.

Because, in the quiet, her brain was too free to wander—and inevitably, it went straight to thoughts of Nathan. She took a bite of her grilled cheese sandwich, blindly stared at the game show playing out on the screen and thought about how Nathan had looked that afternoon.

She'd hidden inside the diner and watched him laughing with Bill Hambleton. The man who had fought so hard against staying in Hunter's Landing now seemed perfectly at home here. She'd been ducking him for days, not wanting to get close enough to be hurt again, but somehow needing to see him while she could.

"Pitiful. A thirty-year-old sixth grader," she muttered, setting her sandwich down on the coffee table. "That's what you are now, Keira. Aren't you proud?"

She flopped back into the couch cushions and pulled a pillow onto her chest. Wrapping her arms around it tightly, she hugged it to her, stared at the blasted TV and tried to concentrate on the inane game show host who was trying to be funny.

But how could she focus on anything but the fact that Nathan would be leaving in a few days? She thought about calling him now, telling him she'd changed her mind and would go with him, but she couldn't. She couldn't let him think that what she felt for him was temporary. Or that she was just another woman in a long line of impermanent lovers. But how could she let him go without talking to him again? And how could she face him without wanting to kiss him? Or kick him?

"God. I'm an idiot."

A knock on the door sounded out and she rolled to her feet, reluctantly pulling herself up and out of her own misery. As much as she wanted a distraction from her own thoughts, she was in no mood for company. She walked across the room, pulled the door open and said, "Nathan?"

He looked so good, it made her heart hurt. Why was he here?

"Keira," he said, shoving one hand through his hair, as his heated gaze raked her up and down. "I had to see you."

Hope leaped up into her chest and nearly strangled her. Was he here to admit that he cared? To tell her he wanted her as much as she wanted him? Her mouth went dry and her stomach did a weird pitch-and-roll that made her reach out and slap one hand to the doorjamb to keep herself upright. "What is it?"

He stepped past her into the house, not waiting for an invitation. When she closed the door and turned around to look at him, he was looking around her house. "I didn't say anything the other day, but this is a nice place."

"Thanks," she said, glancing at him over her shoulder as she moved past him into the living room. "Smaller than the lodge, but I like it."

Her knee caught the edge of a chair and Nathan reached out to steady her. His hand on her elbow sent bolts of heat rocketing through her body like frenzied lightning strikes in the middle of a summer storm. God, she'd missed that sensation.

"Still tripping, I see," he whispered, then let her go.

In a few days, there'd be no one around to catch her when she stumbled. She'd have dozens of small aches and bruises competing with the giant ache in her heart. She rubbed her elbow as if she could ease away the hum he'd created, and looked up at him. "Why are you here, Nathan?"

"I'm sorry we ended things the way we did," he said tightly.

"But not sorry we ended," she whispered, feeling a quick stab of fresh pain. So he wasn't here to grovel and beg her to take him back. When would she stop being an idiot?

He scrubbed one hand over his face, then reached into his jacket pocket. "I wanted to see you in person again. To give you this."

He handed her a folded slip of paper. Keira knew what it was before she opened it. Hadn't he given her one before? A personal check. Made out to Hunter's Landing. Only this check was for *one million dollars*.

"I want the town to have that," he was saying, and she could barely hear him over the roaring in her ears. "The clinic can become a first-class hospital and I want—"

"What?" Keira ground the word out as she tore her eyes from the check to meet his gaze. "You want what exactly? To be a hero? To be remembered? Well, the money isn't necessary, Nathan. I'll remember you just fine without it."

"Keira…"

"No," she snapped, fury rising up to swamp her pain, "you already made a huge donation, and I don't need you to throw more money at me because you're feeling guilty."

"Guilty?" he repeated.

"You're unbelievable," Keira said, riding that anger gratefully, because rage was so much easier to handle than pain. "I offered you *love* and you offer to make me your mistress. And when I turn that lovely offer down, you offer me cash."

"Damn it, Keira, this is all I *can* do. All I know how to do."

"Bull," she said and angrily swiped at the one stray tear that coursed down her cheek as she faced him down. "I can see in your eyes that you want to stay. I've watched you with everyone these last few days. I've seen you in town and you *like* it here, Nathan. I know that you want to be more, have more in your life. But you're too scared to try. Too caught up in your own careful world to take a risk—even if it means cheating yourself out of a real life."

He stalked away from her, whirled around to face her again and said, "I offered to take you with me."

"As your 'companion.'"

"I wanted you with me, I don't care what you call it," he said. "I never promised you anything, Keira. I made it clear right from the first that I wasn't the kind of man you needed."

"How the hell do you know what kind of man I need?" she argued. "Nathan, look at you. You've completely forgotten how to give *yourself* because giving money is so much easier. You hand out checks so you don't have to get involved. It lets you stay in the shadows, safe at a distance."

He didn't say anything though she waited a moment or two, desperately hoping he'd argue with her, tell her she was wrong and he *did* want a life. With her. When the words didn't come, Keira shook her head, crumpled his check in one tight fist and then shoved it into his jacket pocket.

"You already donated money for the clinic," she said, pride coloring her tone now as much as fury. "And the town will get its share of Hunter Palmer's bequest when the six months is up. We don't need more from you."

"Keira—"

"Go away, Nathan," she said, sorrow filling her voice and staining the words until she was sure she could see the pain she was feeling actually coloring the air. "Just leave. Go back to your travels. Go to Barbados. Find some woman who'll want your money so you'll know what to do with her. Move from hotel to hotel, making sure to never speak to anyone. Keep your insulated life because I don't want you *or* your money."

Nathan couldn't breathe. He looked into her stormy green eyes, heard her order him out of her house and knew that if he left, he was a dead man. He'd come here telling himself he only wanted to give her money for the town she loved. Telling himself he only wanted to see her one last time.

When she'd turned down his offer to travel with him, he'd been lost. He had been so sure she'd accept. He'd never had anyone turn him down before. Never had anyone tell him that what he could buy for them wasn't enough. He'd been so damned sure that she'd throw her own life away to follow him. And he hadn't even admitted to himself how important it had been that she come with him. He hadn't wanted to see just how much she meant to him.

When she told him to leave, he'd felt more alone than he ever had before. He couldn't see the coming years without Keira in them. He couldn't see himself without her in his life.

She was right. He was a damn liar.

Panic clawing at him, he reached out, grabbed hold of her and yanked her up against him. Wrapping his arms tight around her waist, he bent his head to the curve of her neck and inhaled her scent, drawing his first easy breath since the day she'd walked out of the lodge and out of his life.

"Keira, don't," he whispered, his words muffled against her skin. "Don't ask me to leave again. I'll do anything in the world for you but that."

She pulled her head back to look up at him, and it tore at him to see tears swimming in those brilliant green depths. This is what he'd brought her to. He'd reduced an incredibly strong woman to tears. He felt like the biggest jackass in the world.

"Nathan, I can't do this anymore," she said, shaking her head and squirming in his arms, trying to get free.

"Keira," he said quickly, holding her as if his life depended on it—because it did. "Don't cry," he said, bending his head to kiss away her tears before saying, "I'm so sorry. I tried to tell myself I could go back to my old life. Tried to believe it. Tried to convince myself that nothing had changed and that my life could continue along as usual. Hell, I tried to drag you into my old life, thinking that having you temporarily would ease the need I feel for you."

"Nathan—"

He moved his hands to cup her face, to stroke the pads of his thumbs across her cheeks. "But the truth is, nothing is the same for me anymore, Keira. You changed everything. I *love* you."

She sucked in a gulp of air and hope lit her eyes. Nathan smiled, finally feeling hope himself. Maybe it wasn't too late for them. Maybe he hadn't already completely screwed it all up.

"I need you, Keira. Can't imagine my life without you in it." He kissed her hard, quick. "We'll live here on the mountain if you want. Build our own place however you want it. I'll still have to travel, but I want you to go with me—only when you want to," he added. "It's up to you. I won't try to make plans without talking to you again. Won't tell you what to do—"

She laughed at his pained expression.

"Fine, I'll probably *still* tell you what to do. It's who I am. But you'll fight me on it because that's who you are. And it'll be good. Damn it, Keira, it'll be *great*. We'll be great. I need you so much. I want to show you the world. I want to give you everything you've ever wanted."

He paused for breath, gave her a half smile, swallowed what was left of his pride and admitted at last, "I'm just not sure how to do it without messing it all up. I've never loved anyone before, Keira. And I don't want to hurt you."

"I don't know what to say," she whispered, her voice breaking.

"Say you'll forgive me. Say you still love me," he urged before kissing her again, this time long and hard and deep. "Say you'll marry me, Keira."

"Nathan..." She laughed, reached up and grabbed hold of his hands, still on her face. "I can't believe you're here. Can't believe you're saying all of this. And I *do* love you. So much. Of course I'll marry you."

"Thank God," he said with a rush of breath. Grinning now, Nathan pulled her in close for a hug that nearly cracked her ribs. "It's your own fault, you know," he said, kissing her hair, resting his head atop hers. "You're the one who wouldn't let me stay on the outside. Now, you're just going to have to find a way to deal with having me on the *inside*."

She hugged him back, nestling in close, tucking her head beneath his chin. "I think I can handle that."

When he pulled back and held her at arm's length, he said, "I don't have a ring to give you, yet. We can go now—wait. Damn it, the lodge thing. I can't leave for a few more days."

She laughed. It sounded wonderful to him, the sweetest music Nathan could ever remember hearing.

"I don't need a ring right this minute," she said.

"I *need* you to have one," he told her, grinning as he suddenly saw the rest of his life stretch out in front of him, bright and beautiful. "The biggest damn diamond we can find. No, wait. Not one. Two diamonds. Or three or four. We'll look."

She laughed even harder and leaned into him to wrap her arms tightly around him, and Nathan sighed, completely content to stand here with her pressed against him forever. Just feeling her heart beat in tandem with his made him feel that his life was finally the way it should be.

Whispering now, he said, "I promise you, Keira, I will spend the rest of my life loving you and I will do everything I can to make you happy."

"I'm happier now than I've ever been, Nathan," she said, cuddling closer, holding him. "I will love you forever, and we'll make each other happy. I know we will. And I swear, you'll never be on the outside again. Neither of us will be."

He kissed her, feeling the magic, the rightness of it, and knew that for the first time in his life, Nathan Barrister had finally found home.

At the end of the month, Keira was practically dancing in place, impatient to board Nathan's private jet for their trip to Barbados—after a quick stop in London to visit Kelly. Before hoisting their bags, Nathan taped a note to the wall in the foyer of the lodge where his life had changed forever.

> Luke,
> It's been a hell of a month. Turns out, the middle of nowhere isn't exactly the black hole I thought it was. I hope you get as much out of your time here as I have.
> Nathan

Then he left his past behind and hurried out to keep his future from breaking her leg in a fall.

* * * * *

HIS FORBIDDEN FIANCÉE

BY
CHRISTIE RIDGWAY

Christie Ridgway is a *USA TODAY* bestselling author who has been writing contemporary romance for over a decade. Her love of romances began when she spent all her babysitting money on novels, and she's still happiest when reading a story with a guaranteed happy-ever-after.

A native Californian, she has a busy family life (husband, two sons, yellow labrador, two turtles, a tortoise, four parakeets, two crawdads, two bearded dragon lizards and assorted fish) and lives in the 'corner house,' which is a natural gathering place for the neighborhood kids (all boys). She loves the chaos—that is, until the feeder-crickets escape captivity. Then her office is her retreat, and her stories are her escape.

For Elizabeth Bevarly, Maureen Child,
Susan Crosby, Anna DePalo and Susan Mallery.
Thanks for making this project so much fun!

One

The only thing the first-class-all-the-way log house lacked was a sexy female in the master bedroom's quilt-covered sleigh bed. Make that a naked sexy female. Blond. Curvy.

Make that lots of curves.

Coat hangers with legs didn't interest Luke Barton. He liked his women built for pleasure. His pleasure.

"Did you say something, Mr. Barton?"

He started, then tore his gaze from the decadent bed to frown at the caretaker who was showing him through the home that was his for the next month. Had he been talking out loud? Luke shoved his hands in his pockets and tried out a noncommittal smile before trailing the woman toward the adjoining bathroom.

She was attractive enough, he supposed, and somewhere in her twenties as well as sort of blondish, but it wasn't her who had sparked his imagination. It was that luxurious bed, he decided, glancing back at it over his shoulder. That quilt-covered bed with a mattress wide enough to rival the sizable slice of Lake Tahoe that he could see through the room's tall windows.

There was a stone fireplace near the bed's carved footboard with wood neatly laid inside and Luke could imagine the logs burning brightly, licking golden color along the naked, fair flesh of his fantasy woman. He'd follow suit with his tongue, tasting her warm—

"Mr. Barton?"

His attention jolted to the caretaker again and he realized he was standing, frozen, in the middle of the room. "Call me Luke," he said.

"What?" The caretaker frowned. "We were expecting Matthias Barton this month."

Perplexed, Luke stared at her for a moment. Matthias?

Oh. *Matthias*. Matt. That luxurious decadent bed was making him forget everything. It wasn't often that Luke Barton forgot his bastard of a twin brother, Matt. And it was never that he did his bastard of a brother a favor.

Except for now.

Damn Matt.

When his assistant had called Luke's assistant he'd wished like hell he could have turned the cheating, thieving SOB down flat. *"Your brother has to take care of some unexpected business and he wants to know if you'll switch months with him,"* Elaine had imparted, as if it wasn't damn strange that identical siblings refused to speak to each other.

But for once, Luke had been unable to refuse his brother's request.

"I'm sorry. I meant to mention it right away," Luke told the caretaker. Apparently she hadn't noticed the cryptic note Nathan left behind had been addressed to him. "Something came up and my brother and I had to trade months." The ol' twin switcheroo.

"Oh, I suppose that's all right," the woman replied, then gestured him forward. "So, as I was saying, Luke, you must spend the next month in the lodge in order to fulfill the requirements of Hunter's will. Your friend Nathan was here last month and your brother Matthias will then take your place in the fifth month."

Luke knew all that. A while back, letters had been received by each of the remaining "Seven Samurai" as they'd called themselves in college. The six had lost touch after the death of Hunter Palmer and graduation, but with the arrival of those letters they'd been reminded of the promise they'd once made to one another as they closed in on getting their diplomas. Though they were from families of distinction and wealth, they'd been determined to each make their own mark on the world. In ten years, they'd vowed.

Over a table filled with empty beer bottles they'd pledged to build a lodge on the shores of Lake Tahoe and in ten years, each of them would take the place for a month. At the end of the seventh month, the plan had been that they'd all come together for a celebration of their friendship and the successes they'd achieved.

But after Hunter's illness and subsequent death, that dream had died with him.

Though apparently not for Hunter. Even aware he wouldn't be there to share it with them, he'd made arrangements for a lodge to be built at the lake. The letters he'd written to each of the friends said that he expected them to honor the vow they'd taken all those years ago.

The caretaker stepped aside as they reached another arched doorway. "And here's the master bathroom."

As Luke stepped inside, the fantasy blond popped back into his thoughts. The light of a fire was tracing her skin again, all that pretty, pretty skin, as she lowered herself into the deep porcelain tub that was surrounded by slate and butted up against yet another fireplace. The ends of her hair darkened as they swished against her wet shoulders. Bubbles played peekaboo with her rosy nipples.

"Do you think you'll be comfortable here?"

Sidetracked again by his enticing little vision, Luke was jolted once more by the sound of the caretaker's voice.

Damn! What was the matter with him? he wondered, firmly banishing the distracting beauty splashing in his suddenly sex-obsessed brain.

"I'll be just fine here, thank you." Even though he was going to be "just fine" three months early, all for the sake of his brother.

He must have been scowling at the thought, because the woman's eyebrows rose. "Is something wrong?"

"No. Not at all." There was no reason to expose the family laundry to a stranger. "I guess I'm just thinking of...of Hunter."

The woman's gaze dropped. "I'm sorry." The toe of

her sensible black shoe appeared to fascinate her. "I think…I think he intended this as a nice gesture."

"Hunter Palmer was a very nice man." The best of the seven of them. The very best. Luke let himself remember Hunter's wide grin, his infectious laugh, the way he could rally their group to do anything from nailing all the furniture in the freshman-dorm rec room to the ceiling to organizing a charity three-man basketball tournament senior year.

Hunter had been part of Luke's squad. They'd won the whole shebang, too. What a team they'd made, Hunter and Luke…and Matt.

In those days, like never before and never since, Luke and Matt had played on the same side.

But it was Hunter who Luke had been thinking of when he'd agreed to take his brother's place for the next month. Their dead friend's last request had been for the six other men to spend time at the lodge he'd built. If they fulfilled his request, then twenty million dollars and the lodge itself would be turned over to the town of Hunter's Landing, here on the shores of Lake Tahoe.

Luke wasn't going to be the reason that didn't happen, no matter how he felt about his brother.

So he followed the caretaker through the rest of the rooms, keeping his mind off the fantasy blond by thinking of the twin switcheroo and how he was replacing Matt Barton, #1 bastard. He spent little time looking on the framed Samurai photos mounted in the second-floor hallway. If he were really playing the part of Matt, Luke thought, it would mean keeping his tie knotted tight, his smiles as cold as Sierra snow, and his mind open to how he could take advantage of any situation without regard to kith, kin or even common decency.

That was how his brother operated.

Finally the caretaker gave him the ornate keychain that contained the house key and departed, leaving Luke alone inside the big house with only his grim thoughts for company. The place was quiet and absent of any signs of Nathan Barrister—who had been staying here the month before—unless you counted the hastily written note Luke had found from him. But Nathan hadn't gone far. He'd fallen for the mayor of Hunter's Landing, Keira Sanders, and now they were flitting between the Tahoe town and sun-filled Barbados, where his old friend was presumably mixing business with pleasure.

Jacket and tie discarded, Luke found a beer in the overstocked fridge and settled himself by the window of the great room. Through the trees was another spectacular view of the lake. It wasn't its famous clear-blue at the moment, not only because it was settling into evening, but also because gray clouds were gathering overhead.

Dark clouds that reflected Luke's mood.

What the hell was he going to do with himself for a month?

Nathan had done okay here, apparently. His note said it wasn't "exactly the black hole I thought" and he'd occupied himself by jumping into a full-on love affair. Luke didn't wish that potential quagmire on himself, though a visit from that blond sweetheart of his imagination might make the month pass just a little bit faster. It was too damn bad she couldn't stroll out of his fantasies and straight into this room.

Yes, that would make the thirty days more interesting.

Except it wasn't going to happen unless Matt had invited someone to join him here. And even if that were the case, blond sweethearts just weren't Matt's type. Being identical twins didn't mean they had identical taste when it came to women.

Luke hooked his heels around a nearby ottoman and dragged it closer as the first drops of what appeared to be a heavy spring rain started to hit the windows and roll down like tears. Yeah, he'd be crying, too, if the vision from his daydream showed up on his doorstep looking for Matt.

Though he shouldn't rule that out, come to think of it. His brother might set up just such a thing to shake Luke's cage. Matt ruined Luke's life any chance he got.

To be fair—unlike his brother—Luke had to admit that it was their father, Samuel Sullivan Barton, who had sowed the seeds of their ugly rivalry. He'd run their childhood like an endless season of *The Apprentice,* with himself playing Donald Trump, constantly orchestrating cutthroat competitions between his two sons.

Their enmity had abated in college. But after Hunter had died, so had their father, and he'd left behind one last contest that rekindled his sons' competitive fire. Whichever twin made a million dollars first would win the family holdings. Both of them had separately gone to work on developing wireless technology—Luke doing it hands-on, using his engineering degree, while Matt tapped into his undeniable business acumen to hire someone to work with him.

When it came to any kind of gadgetry, his brother

was all thumbs. But when it came to building a successful team, Matt was a master.

Of course, that time he'd ensured his mastery by
bribing a supplier and knocking Luke right out of the
running. Matt had made the first mil and won all the
family assets, to boot.

Luke hadn't spoken to his brother since, though he'd
gone on to do a damn fine job with his own company—
a meaner and leaner version of what Matt continued to
build upon with the Barton family wealth behind him.
That was Luke in a nutshell these days: a leaner—
okay, maybe by only a pound or two—but definitely
meaner version of his brother Matt.

Working his ass off had a way of doing that to a
man, Luke thought. And maybe bitterness, too. He
couldn't deny it.

The rain was really coming down now, and the
house took on a chill. He got up and lit the fire laid in
the great room's massive fireplace—it took up one
huge stone wall—and the flames set him thinking
about his blond again.

When he got back to his own condo in the San
Francisco Bay Area he was going to have to make a
few phone calls, apparently. This fantasy woman was
a new fixation for him. Work usually was his only ob-
session—work and finding some way to pay back his
brother at some future date—so his sex life was more
sporadic than people believed. It looked as if he
needed to be paying more attention to his bodily
needs, though.

Or maybe the blame rested on this house, he
thought. Or the fireplaces. *That bed.*

The blond continued insinuating herself into his thoughts. He could practically smell her now. Her scent was like rain—clean, cool rain—and he'd sip the drops off her mouth, her neck, her collarbone.

Closing his eyes, he rested his head against the back of the chair. As his fantasy played on, his heart started to hammer.

Except that it wasn't his heart.

His eyes popped open. He stared out the windows, trying to determine if the pouring rain or the waving trees were causing the loud drumming.

He decided it was neither one.

Luke set his beer down and rose, following the noise to the front door. Who the hell would be here now and in this spring deluge?

He jerked open the door. As he took in the dark shadow of a figure on the porch, a chilly blast of wind and a spray of rain wafted over him. Suppressing a shiver, he fumbled for the light switches. Brightness blazed over the porch and in the foyer.

The shadowy figure became a woman.

Her white blouse was plastered to her body. Wet denim clung to her thighs.

She raised a hand to her hair and tried fluffing the drenched stuff. A few locks gamely sprung from straight strands into bedraggled curls that hinted at gold.

Luke looked back at her clothes again.

More accurately, he looked at the curves cupped by all that wet cloth.

Her nipples were hard buds topping spectacular breasts.

Even from the front he could surmise she had a round backside, too, just the way he liked it.

She was exactly how he liked it.

Bemused, he continued to stare at her as he tried figuring out what combination of beer, rain and rampant fantasy had brought such a sight to his front door.

Could she possibly be real? And if so, whom did he have to thank for such a surprising gift?

She frowned at him. Her lips were generously pillowed, too. "Matthias, aren't you going to invite your fiancée in?"

Fiancée? Matthias?

Luke spent a few more long moments staring at the wet blonde on his doorstep. When another cold blast of air and rain slapped him, he blinked and finally stepped back to let his brother's fiancée inside.

As she moved forward, questions circled in his mind. Was this some joke? That trick he hadn't put past his brother? Or could Matt really be engaged? If so, it was news to Luke. He'd thought his brother was the same kind of workaholic confirmed bachelor he was. And when had Matt's taste turned to blondes?

Inside, with the door shut behind her, the young woman wrapped her arms around herself and licked her bottom lip in what seemed a nervous gesture. "I, um, know you weren't expecting me. It was sort of an—an impulse."

"Oh?"

"Yes. I jumped in my car and before long I was almost here. Then it started pouring rain and now…" Her voice drifted off and she shrugged, her gaze going to her feet. "And now I'm dripping all over this beautiful carpet."

She was right. She was as wet as his bathtub fantasy, and probably cold, too. He gestured up the stairs toward the great room and its crackling fire. "Let's get you warmed up and dried off."

He tried to be a gentleman and keep his gaze above her neck as she preceded him into the other room but, hell, he knew he was no gentleman. So he confirmed what he'd already suspected by running his gaze from her nape to her heels. She was just his type.

Except she was his brother's fiancée. Or was she? It could still be a trick…

Stopping in front of the roaring fire, she faced him again. Another rush of words spilled out, giving him the idea that she chattered when she was anxious. "My mother would kill me if she knew I came up here. 'Lauren,' she'd say in that disapproving tone of hers, 'is this another one of your Bad Ideas?' That's just how she says it, with capitals. Capital *B,* Bad. Capital *I,* Ideas. 'Another one of Lauren's Bad Ideas.'" A nervous laugh escaped before her hands came up to try to suppress it.

Lauren. Her name was Lauren. It didn't ring any bells, but Luke didn't keep tabs on Matt's social life. Maybe he should, if his brother was really going around snatching up just the sort of women that Luke liked. For God's sake, Matt shouldn't be allowed to have everything Luke wanted.

She shivered and he spotted a wool throw draped over a nearby chair. He grabbed for it then brought it to her. As she took it from his hand, she looked up at him, all big, blue eyes. Her pink tongue darted out to wet that pouty lower lip.

"You've got to be wondering why I'm here, Matthias."

"I'm not—" Matthias. But something made him hold that last word back. He ran his hand through his hair, buying himself some time. "I guess I am a little surprised to see you."

She gave another small laugh and then turned toward the fire. "This whole engagement thing has been a little surprising, don't you agree?"

"Yeah." He could be honest about that, anyway. "I suppose so."

She continued to study the fire. "I mean, we don't know each other that well, right? You've worked with my father and Conover Industries for years, of course…"

Hell, Luke thought. She was Conover's kid. Ralph Conover's daughter. Ralph Conover, who'd been the first to cozy up to Matt after he'd cheated Luke out of his fair chance to win the Barton family holdings.

"…but there's the fact that we haven't talked that much or ever really been…um, alone together."

What? Luke stared at the back of her head and the gold curls that were starting to spring up there. His brother was engaged to marry a woman he'd never been alone with? Luke had a guess to what that was code for and, if he was right, it meant Matt *hadn't* suddenly developed a yen for cute curvy blondes.

Instead, it meant Matt had developed a yen to more tightly cement his relationship with Conover Industries. Luke's mind raced ahead as he imagined all the implications this could have for Eagle Wireless, his own smaller company. With Conover Industries and Barton Limited "married," Eagle could find its own perch in the wireless world very precarious.

God. Damn. It.

Lauren turned toward him again, clutching the throw at her chest. "You haven't said what you think about that, Matthias."

Because Luke hadn't had enough time to think it through completely. He cleared his throat. "I suppose some people would find it a bit odd that we haven't…" Since he didn't know precisely what Matt and Lauren had or hadn't, he let the sentence hang.

"Touched?" she conveniently supplied. "Even kissed, really?" Then color reddened her cheeks. "And we certainly haven't made love."

Staring into her big, blue eyes, suddenly Luke could picture—in vivid detail—doing just that very thing with her. He saw it on his mind's high-def big screen, the two of them making love in that big bathtub upstairs, Lauren's soft, wet thighs wrapped around his hips. Or on that quilt-covered bed, her blond curls spread out against the pillowcase.

Her eyes darkened and he heard a tiny gasp as her breath suddenly caught. Was she reading his thoughts?

Or did she feel that same sharp tug of attraction that he did?

Could she possibly share the images dealing out like X-rated playing cards in his mind?

Blond, curvy Lauren, and Luke, the mean twin.

The cheated twin.

He lifted his hand and trailed one knuckle along the

downy softness of her cheek, wondering if she would taste as sweet as she looked. His fingertip touched the center of her bottom lip and he saw her eyes widen.

Oh, yeah, the message in them made it clear that she felt the attraction, too. And the bit of confusion he could read as well told him she hadn't felt it for Matt.

Luke ran his thumb over her bottom lip this time, moving inside just a little so that he grazed the damp inner surface. She stood frozen before him, trapped between the fire and his touch. In the sudden heavy silence of the room he could hear the light, fast pants of her breath. Color ran high on her cheeks.

God, she was beautiful.

And we certainly haven't made love.

She'd said that, and that's where Luke's brother had slipped up. If she were Luke's, he wouldn't have wasted any time before taking their engagement—even one motivated by business reasons—to a more serious level.

Okay, be honest. He wouldn't have been able to stop himself.

The pulse along her throat was racing, begging him to touch it with his mouth. And now that her hair was starting to dry, he could smell her shampoo, something flowery, but not cloying. It was a fresh smell and he wanted to rub himself against it. He wanted to smell her on his own skin.

Really, it came down to one very simple thing. He wanted his brother's bride-to-be.

"M-Matthias?" she whispered.

Luke didn't flinch at the wrong name. Instead, he tucked a damp curl behind her ear. At the sight of the goose bumps that raced down her neck in response, he smiled, careful to keep the wolfishness out of it.

But he felt wolfish.

Smug, satisfied and ready to eat Goldilocks up in one big bite.

And then he'd want to do it again, this time taking his time to savor every taste.

His hand lingered near her shell of an ear. He'd mixed up his fairy tales, hadn't he? The wolf was Little Red Ridinghood's nemesis, wasn't he? But no matter. Lauren was most certainly Goldilocks and Luke hadn't felt this predatory in a long, long while.

Catching her gaze with his, he grazed his thumb along her velvety cheek.

She released her grip on the wool throw. It fell at her feet as she circled his wrist to pull his hand away from her face. "What do you think you're doing?"

Goldilocks wasn't quite so ready to test out feather mattresses as he'd thought. But that was okay. He needed some time to process all this himself. "Nothing you don't want," he reassured her, stepping back and trying on another smile.

She shivered again.

Frowning, he ran his gaze over her, noting that her wet clothes still clung. He shoved his hands in his pockets to disguise the effect her curves had on him and cleared his throat. "Why don't you take a hot shower? Warm up."

So he could cool down. Think things through. Decide what to do with all the sexual dynamite in the room, especially when they were standing so close to the fire.

Especially when the woman who had walked out of his fantasies was his brother's bride-to-be.

"Take a shower *here?*" She was already shaking her head. "No, no, no. I only came to talk and then—"

"What?" Luke interrupted. "Go back out in that?" He gestured toward the windows and the full-on storm and wilderness-level darkness beyond them. "Now *that* would definitely be a Bad Idea, Lauren."

She made a face. "Oh, thanks for reminding me."

He allowed himself a little grin. "Fair warning, kid. Never show me your weakness. I'll use it against you."

"Kid." She made the face again, though he could see the appellation relaxed her. "I'm twenty-six years old."

"Be a grown-up then. Go upstairs and take a hot shower. Then we'll put your clothes in the dryer, I'll rustle us up some dinner and after that we'll reassess."

Her eyes narrowed. "Reassess what?"

She was a suspicious little thing, but God knows that was sensible of her. He shrugged. "We'll reassess whatever occurs to us." Like whether he should let her know who he really was. Like whether he could let her drive away from him tonight.

After another swift glance at the scene outside the windows, she appeared to make up her mind. "All right." She bent to retrieve the throw.

As she handed it to him on her way toward the stairs, he used it to reel her closer.

"What?" she said, startled. Round blue eyes. Quivering curls.

"We haven't had our hello kiss," he murmured.

Then, curious as to what it might be like, he placed his mouth on top of hers.

At contact, his heart kicked hard inside his chest. Heat flashed across his flesh, burning from scalp to groin.

Lauren had the softest, most pillowy lips he'd ever encountered in thirty-one years of living. Eighteen years of kissing. His biceps were tight as he lifted his hands to cradle her face.

He took a breath in preparation, then touched the tip of his tongue to hers.

Pow.

They both leaped away from the sweet, hot explosion.

She regained her breath first. "I'll…I'll just take that shower," she said, her gaze glued to his face as if she were afraid to turn her back on him.

"Sure, fine, go on up," he managed to get out, when he should have said, *"Run, Goldilocks. Run as far and as fast as you can."*

As if he wouldn't run right after her if she tried.

TWO

Lauren Conover stared at her bedraggled reflection in the bathroom mirror, looking for any evidence of the backbone she'd thought she'd found this morning before driving to Lake Tahoe. Instead, all she saw was a wet woman with reddened lips and a confused expression in her eyes.

"You were supposed to walk in and break it off with him immediately," she whispered fiercely to that dazed-looking creature staring back at her. "Nowhere in the plan were you supposed to find him attractive."

But she had! That was the crazy, spine-melting trouble. When the door to the magnificent log house had opened, there stood Matthias Barton, looking as he always had on those few occasions they'd been together. Dark hair, dark eyes, a lean face that she couldn't deny was handsome—and yet, never before had it drawn her.

Then he'd invited her inside and when she'd been looking up at him with the fire at her back she'd felt fire at her front, too. A man-woman kind of fire that made her skin prickle and her heart beat fast.

The kind of fire that a woman might be persuaded to marry for.

And she'd come all this way to tell him it wasn't going to happen.

And it wasn't!

When her mother had plopped a stack of bridal magazines onto the breakfast table that morning, Lauren had looked at them and then at her thirteen-year-old sister's face. Her tough-as-nails tomboy sister who had been giving Lauren grief since the engagement had been announced two weeks before.

"You'd better do something quick," Kaitlyn had said, backing away from the glossy magazines as if they were a tangle of hissing snakes. "Or the next thing you know, Mom will have me in some horrid junior bridesmaid's dress that I'll never, ever forgive you for."

Lauren had known Kaitlyn was right. Her mother's steamroller qualities were exactly why she'd found herself engaged to a man she barely knew in the first place. That is, her mother's steamroller qualities combined with her father's heavy-handed hints about this marriage being good for the family business he always claimed was faltering. As well as Lauren's own embarrassment over her three previous attempts to make it down the aisle.

She'd picked those men herself and the engagements had each ended in disaster.

So it had been hard to disagree with her mother and father that their choice couldn't be any worse, despite Kaitlyn's teenage disgust.

But the sight of those pages and pages of bridal gowns had woken Lauren from the stupor that she'd been suffering since returning home from Paris six months before. Hanging a third now-never-to-be-worn wedding dress in the back of her family's cedar-lined luggage closet had sent her to a colorless, emotionless place where she'd slept too much, watched TV too much and responded almost robot-like to her parents' commands.

Until glimpsing that tulled and tiara-ed bride on the front cover of *Matrimonial*, that is. The sight had hit her like a wake-up slap to the face. What was she thinking? She couldn't marry Matthias Barton. She couldn't marry a man for the same cold, cutthroat reasons her father picked a new business partner.

So she'd grabbed her keys and gathered her self-confidence and driven straight to where Matthias had mentioned he'd be staying for the next month, determined to get him out of her life.

Now she couldn't get him out of her mind.

Sighing, she turned away from the mirror and adjusted the spray in the shower. She'd found the master bedroom right off—my God, that luxurious bed had almost made her swoon!—but spun a quick about-face and entered a smaller guest bed and bath instead.

The hot water felt heavenly and some of her uneasiness went down the drain with it. All she had to do was walk back out there and tell that gorgeous hunk of a man that she wasn't marrying him. He'd probably be as relieved as she was. After that she'd drive home, face the certain-to-be-discordant music chez Conover and get on with the rest of her life.

The rest of her life that wouldn't include any more engagements to wrong men.

A few minutes later, wrapped in an oversized terry robe she'd found hanging on the bathroom door and carrying her damp clothes in hand, Lauren made her way to the staircase. Some framed photos lined the walls but she didn't give them but a cursory glance as she was more concerned with getting away from the house than anything. She could tell it was still raining and even from the second-floor landing the downstairs fire looked cozy and inviting, but she straightened her shoulders and mentally fused her vertebrae together.

Break it off, Lauren, she ordered herself as she descended the steps. *At once. Then get in your car and drive home.* Who cared about not waiting to dry the wet clothes? The robe covered her up just fine.

She could see Matthias standing by the fireplace now. He looked up…and somehow made her feel as if she wasn't wearing anything at all.

A flush heated all the skin under the suddenly scratchy terry cloth. Lauren's nipples hardened—though she wasn't the least bit cold, oh no sir—and she knew they were poking at the thick fabric. Would he notice? Could he tell?

Would he care?

Trying to pretend nothing was the least amiss, she made herself continue downward. But, man-oh-man,

was he something to look at. He'd rolled up the sleeves
of his dress shirt and unfastened a second button at the
throat. The vee of undershirt she could see was blinding
white and contrasted with the dark, past-five-o'clock
stubble on his chin and around his mouth.

His mouth made her think of his kiss again. It was
just a regular man's mouth, she supposed, but she liked
the wideness of it and the deep etch of his upper lip.
She really liked how it had felt on hers and, then, when
his tongue had touched—

"Don't look at me like that," he suddenly said.

She was two steps from the bottom and the rasp in
his voice made her grab for the railing. "I'm sorry," she
said, unable to move, hardly able to speak. "What?"

"You look at me like that and I forget all about my
intentions."

Her mouth went dry. "What intentions?" Maybe
they were bad intentions...yet why did the idea of that
sound so very good?

Matthias glanced over his shoulder. "My intention
to feed you before anything else. Didn't I promise to
rustle up dinner?"

Behind him she could see he'd set two places on the
coffee table pulled up before a wide, soft-cushioned
couch. Something was steaming—she could smell it,
beef bourguignonne?—on two plates and ruby-colored
liquid filled two wineglasses. Candles flickered in low
votives.

Had she mentioned she was a sucker for candlelight?

She took another whiff of that delicious-smelling
food. "Are you a good cook?"

He smiled and she liked that, too. His teeth were as white as his undershirt and they sent another wave of hot prickles across her flesh. "Maybe. Probably. But I've never tried."

She had to laugh at that. "Are you usually so confident? Even if you haven't attempted something you just expect you'll excel at it?"

"Of course. 'Assume success, deny failure.' My father taught us that."

"Yikes." And Lauren thought *her* cold-blooded *père* knew how to apply the screws. "That's a little harsh."

"You think so?" Matthias walked over to take her wet clothes in one hand and her free hand in the other.

He insinuated his long fingers between hers and the heat of his palm against hers shot toward her shoulder. "I think…I think…" Lauren couldn't remember what she was about to say. "Never mind."

He was smiling at her again, as if he understood her distraction. He led her toward the couch. "Let me put your clothes in the dryer, then we'll eat."

She stared after his retreating form for a moment, then started back to awareness. She was supposed to take the wet clothes home! Right after she told him the engagement was over! Right before walking out the door without dinner, without anything but her car keys and the comforting thought that she'd done the right thing.

But now he was coming toward her again, that small smile on his face and that appreciative light in his eyes. He brought that attraction between them back into the room, too—all that twitching, pulsing heat that drew her heart to her throat and her blood to several lower locations.

Tell him it's over! Her good sense shouted.

Tell him later, her sexuality purred, with a languid little stretch.

"Sit down," Matthias said, reaching out to touch her cheek.

Her knees gave way.

Merely postponing the inevitable. Lauren assured herself that she'd take care of what she came for and leave. Soon.

Except, an excellent dinner later, she was feeling a bit fuzzy from more merlot than she was used to. As well as a lot charmed by the man who had taken their dishes into the kitchen and was now sitting back on the cushions beside her, dangling the stem of his wineglass between his fingers.

Over the meal he'd entertained her with stories that all revolved around his adventures in take-out dining. If she needed any further evidence that he was a business-obsessed workaholic like her father—and why else would Papa Conover have pushed so hard for her to marry Matthias?—now she had it. The man couldn't remember the last time he'd eaten food prepared in a home.

"Even this doesn't qualify, I'm afraid," he said, gesturing to where their plates had been. "The cartons were printed with the name of some gourmet catering place in town."

"Hunter's Landing, right?" Lauren asked. "Though it's not named after your friend from college? The one who built this house?"

Matthias shook his head. "No. Just a little joke on his part, I guess. He had a wild sense of humor."

The suddenly hoarse note in his voice made her throat tighten. He missed his friend, that was certain. Swallowing a sigh, she closed her eyes. This wasn't the way it was supposed to be. This wasn't the way *he* was supposed to be. She didn't want her parent-picked fiancé to be sexy or charming or vulnerable and, for God's sake, certainly not all three. It only made it that much harder to break it off with him.

She was always such a nitwit when it came to men. There was a reason she'd been engaged three times before now. There was a reason she'd picked the wrong men and then stuck with them until the humiliating end—until they walked out on her.

"So," Matthias said, breaking into her morose thoughts. "Enough about me. Tell me all about Lauren."

All about Lauren? Her eyes popped open and her spirits picked up. Was this the answer? If she told Mr. Assume-Success-Deny-Failure Barton all about Lauren, he might break it off between them himself! Because the truth was, when it came to romance, she was all about failure. And obviously more accustomed to getting dumped than the other way around.

Drawing her legs onto the couch, she turned on her side to face him.

Except his face was directed at her legs, bared by the edges of the terry robe that had opened with her movement. Heat rushing over her face, she yanked the fabric over her pale skin. She wasn't trying to come on to him. She was trying to get him to see that a marriage between the two of them would never work.

When she cleared her throat, he looked up, without a hint of shame on his face. "Great legs."

The compliment only served to discombobulate her further. The heat found its way to the back of her neck and she blurted out, "You know, you're fiancé number four."

He stared. "Number four?"

Ha. That had him. Now he'd turn off the charm and dam up that oozing sex appeal. She nodded. "I've been engaged before. Three other times."

He gave a small smile. "Optimistic little thing, aren't you?"

She frowned, bothered that he seemed more amused than appalled by her confession. Maybe he didn't believe her. Maybe he thought she was joking. Holding up her hand, she ticked them off. "Trevor, Joe and Jean-Paul."

"All right." He drained the remainder of his wine and set the glass on the table, as if ready for business. "Give me the down and dirty."

He still seemed amused. And charming. And sexy. Blast him.

Lauren took a breath. "I almost married Trevor when we were nineteen. It was going to be a sunset ceremony on the beach, followed by a honeymoon—one that I'd planned and paid for—that would hit all the best surfing spots in Costa Rica. On my wedding day, I was supposed to wear a white bandeau top, a grass skirt I found in a secondhand shop in Santa Cruz, and a crown of plumeria blossoms straight from Hawaii."

"Sounds fetching," he said, "though I don't see you as a surfer."

"That's probably the biggest reason Trevor ran off without me. He cashed in our first class tickets for coach ones and took his best surfing buddy to Central America instead. I haven't heard from him since."

Lauren experienced a little pang thinking of the bleached-blond she would always consider her first love. He'd driven her parents nuts, she recalled with a reminiscent smile. He'd been the perfect anti-Conover.

"Okay. That's number one. But why aren't you now Mrs. Joe…?"

"Rutkowski. His name is Joe Rutkowski."

Matthias bit his lip. "You're kidding."

"No. Joe Rutkowski was—well, *is*—my father's mechanic. If you find a good car-man, you don't break up with him—even if he breaks up with your daughter. That's what my father says, anyway."

"So what gave good ol' Joe second thoughts?"

"His pregnant other girlfriend."

"Oh."

"Little Jolene was born on my birthday, which also happened to be our proposed wedding date."

"Tell me you sent a baby gift. Little coveralls? A tiny timing light?"

Lauren narrowed her eyes at him. He didn't seem to be getting her point. "My heart was broken. My mother sent a certificate for a month of diaper service and signed my name." It still annoyed her that she'd lost the opportunity to watch her hoity-toity parents introduce the town's best Mercedes mechanic as their new son-in-law.

"But your broken heart recovered enough to find yourself in the arms of—what did you say his name was?—Jacques Cousteau?"

"Very funny. Jean-Paul Gagnon." Her father hated

Frenchmen. "I met him in Paris. We were going to get married on top of the Eiffel Tower. I had a tailored white linen suit with a long skirt that went to my ankles and was so tight that I couldn't run after the nasty little urchin who stole my purse on the way to the ceremony."

"I hope you're going to tell me that Jean-Paul took after the urchin himself."

"He did. But when he came back with my purse he told me that it had given him time to think about what he was doing. And marrying me was not what he wanted to do, after all." She gazed off into the distance, remembering her disappointment at not being able to shock her parents with the groom she brought home from Europe. "I really *liked* Jean-Paul."

"In the morning, I'll find some place that will feed you crepes."

In the morning? Lauren jerked her head toward him. "Have you been listening to a thing I said?"

"Of course I have." He moved closer and wrapped his hands around her wrists. "I just haven't figured out what the hell it has to do with you and me."

Lauren swallowed. Here was the opening she'd been waiting for. Now was the time to say, "There is no you and me, Matthias. There never really was."

Except the words wouldn't come out. They were stuck in her tight throat—and all it could handle was breathing, a task that seemed to be so much more complex when he was touching her.

"This is a lot harder than I thought," she whispered.

A ghost of a smile quirked one corner of his handsome mouth as he slid his fingers between hers. "You're telling me."

Despite her breathlessness, she found she could still laugh. "Are you being bad?"

"Not yet. But the night's still young."

Night? Good Lord, she'd completely lost track of time. It had been early evening just a minute ago. She checked her watch. "I've got to leave." Scooting back, she tried yanking her hands from his.

He merely held her tighter. "Not now, honey."

"But Matthias was…"

Something flickered in his eyes, but he didn't let go. "I may be an SOB, but I'm not completely black-hearted. It's too late, too dark, too stormy for me to let you leave tonight. It wouldn't be safe."

She looked out the windows and could tell he was right. The rain hadn't let up in the hours she'd been at the house and it was still coming down in torrents. Oh, great. She was stuck with the man she couldn't bring herself to break up with and her heart was thrumming so fast and he was so gorgeous she worried that if she didn't get away from him soon she'd… "I'm not so sure it's safe here, either."

"Will anyone be worrying about you? Do you need to make a call?"

Registering that he hadn't addressed the safety issue, she shook her head. "I had planned to stay with a friend in San Francisco for a few days on my way back. She said she'd expect me when she saw me."

"So here we are." He dropped her right hand so he could toy with one of her curls instead. "All alone on a dark and stormy night."

"So here we are," she echoed. "All alone." Oh, but her mother definitely could have called this one.

Coming up here was truly another of Lauren's Bad Ideas.

"How do you propose we entertain ourselves?" Matthias asked, twining a lock of her hair around his forefinger.

Lauren pretended not to notice. "Swap ghost stories? That sounds appropriate."

"But then we might be too scared to sleep."

Oh God. Her heart jumped and her gaze locked on his face. He was wearing that little smile again, as if he knew that mentioning the words *we* and *sleep* in the same sentence had her thinking of the two of them together, in a bed, doing everything *but* sleeping.

What the heck was going on? In the last few months, she'd chitchatted with Matthias at parties, danced with him a couple of times at charity events, pretended to be interested during family dinners while he talked shop with her father. Not once had she felt the slightest shiver of sexual attraction and now it was all she could do not to squirm in her seat.

Or squirm all over him.

"How come you weren't like this before?" she demanded.

His teeth flashed white. "I suppose I'll take that as a compliment."

"Seriously. Matthias—"

He put his hand over her mouth. "Shh. Don't talk."

She reached up to pull his fingers away. "If I don't talk I'm afraid I'll—"

And then he stopped that sentence, too, by swooping forward to kiss her for a second time. "Sorry," he said against her mouth. "I just can't help myself."

But *she* was helping him already by spearing her fingers through the crisp hair at the back of his head. He angled one way, she angled another and then they were *really* kissing, lips opening, tongues touching, tasting, their breaths and the sweet tang of merlot mingling.

Goose bumps rolled in a wave from the top of her scalp to the tickly skin behind her knees. She scooted closer to him, bumping the outside of his legs. Without breaking the connection of their mouths, he gathered her and the voluminous terry cloth onto his lap. In the move, the robe's hem rode up and she found herself settling onto him with nothing between her bare behind and his hard slacks-covered thighs.

Yanking her mouth from his, she glanced down, relieved to see that her front was covered decently enough and that the robe was draping her legs modestly, too. Still… "We shouldn't be doing this," she said, taking her hands from his hair.

"What?" His voice was hoarse.

Where to start? The engagement? The kiss? The lap? Or the bare skin which only felt barer because it was against the soft fabric that was clothing all those male muscles? "You know exactly what I'm talking about."

His eyelashes were spiky and dark, as masculine as the rest of him. "So you're holding out for the wedding night?"

The edge in his voice didn't surprise her. She felt edgy, too, torn between what her head was advising and what her body was demanding.

"We hardly know each other," she said. "So all this… this…"

"Hankering for hanky-panky?"

She narrowed her eyes at him. "…is a product of the rain, the wine, the—"

"The stone cold truth that we turn each other on hard and fast, Goldilocks, no explanations, no apologies. And to be honest, I'm as floored by it as you are."

"You are?" Not that she figured he considered her an ogre or anything, but the idea that this kind of "hankering for hanky-panky" wasn't standard for him, either, was a fascinating notion.

He laughed. "You look awfully pleased with yourself about it."

"Hey, in the past few years, I've been rejected on a regular basis, so forgive my dented ego for giving a little cheer." The merlot had seriously loosened her tongue.

"Fiancés one through four were idiots."

"*You're* number four," she reminded him.

"I'm trying to forget that." At the frown on her face, he shook his head and pinched her chin. "Goldilocks, I'm suggesting we try to forget everything but the fact that it's a dark and stormy night and we're alone together with our hankering. What do you say? Why not see where it takes us?"

She stared at him. "That's male reasoning."

He raised a dark eyebrow. "Cogent? To the point?"

"Shortsighted and all about sex."

"And your point is?"

Oh, he was making her laugh again. And *that* made her wiggle against his lap. And that made him groan and she was so…well, captivated by the powerful feeling the sound gave her that she leaned in to buss him on the mouth.

Which he turned into a real kiss.

Next thing she knew their tongues were twining and her hands were buried in his hair again. Heat was pouring off of him and his skin tasted a tiny bit salty as she kissed the corner of his mouth. "I want to bottle up this feeling," she told him, awed by its strength. Sexual chemistry, who knew? "We could market it and make a kabillion dollars."

"A kabillion is a lot," he murmured, then turned his attention to her left ear.

Goose bumps sprinted across every inch of her skin as his tongue feathered over the rim to tickle the lobe. "A kabillion-ten," she corrected herself. "In the first year."

He traveled back to her mouth, then took his time there, leisurely playing with all the surfaces. Her breath backed up in her lungs when he sucked her bottom lip into his mouth. Her fingers tightened on his scalp when he slid the tip of his tongue along the damp skin inside her upper lip. She moaned when he thrust inside her mouth, filling her with his purpose and male demand.

And all the while she was excruciatingly aware of her nakedness under the robe. Of her bareness resting against his pant legs. The soft wool scratched at her skin now, sensitized as it was by the kisses that never let up and the hands that never wandered beyond her hair and her face.

She was fast losing all the reasons why she should be happy about that. In the face of this "hankering" as he called it, she'd been unable to stand up against the kissing. It wasn't such a bad thing, though, was it? For goodness sake, she *was* engaged to the man.

Still.

A little voice somewhere in the dim recesses of her mind reminded her she was here to put an end to that engagement, but she shushed the crabby killjoy. Because this man could *kiss*, and there was no reason to deny herself the pleasure.

Except that kissing was quickly becoming not quite enough.

To ease the growing ache, she squeezed her thighs together and wiggled her naked behind. Matthias tore his lips from hers to gaze at her with serious eyes. "You're making me crazy." His mouth was wet.

She dried it with the edge of her thumb. "What'd you say?" She stroked her thumb the other way and he caught it between his teeth. Nipped.

Lauren shivered once and then again when his tongue swiped over her fingertip. The inside of his mouth was hot and wet and she leaned forward to taste it again.

He caught her shoulders, keeping her a breath away. "Lauren, maybe you were right…"

"Just one more." She pushed at his hands and, as they fell, they took the robe with them. It dropped to her waist.

Leaving her naked from her belly button up.

And frozen between caution and desire.

His gaze stayed on her face, but when she made no move to cover herself, he let it wander southward. Slowly.

Like a caress, she felt it move across her features, from her nose, to her mouth, over her chin and then down the column of her neck.

It traced the edges of her collarbone and her breath caught, held, as he finally stared at her breasts. Under the weight of his gaze, her nipples went from tight to tighter. She glanced down, noticing how hard and darker they looked against the pale skin of her swollen breasts.

Without thinking, she moved her arms up to cover herself.

"Don't." He caught her wrists. "Don't keep them from me."

Hot chills tumbled down her naked spine. She didn't want to keep them from him. She didn't want to keep any part of herself from him.

In a blur of movement, he stood, lifting her in his arms. "Wh—?" she began.

"Shh," he said. "Don't talk." He strode for the staircase, rushing up the steps as if she weighed nothing.

She felt weightless, too, as if she were floating on a cloud of desire. And a cloud of impossible dreams. Good God, could her parents have been right? Had they picked the right man for her after all?

He didn't hesitate at the top of the stairs, but headed straight for the master bedroom. At the foot of the enormous sleigh bed, he hesitated.

Lauren rested her head against his chest, his heart beating hard and fast in her ear. There was nothing she wanted more than to get naked, completely naked, with him. She smiled up at his face, seductively, she thought. "Matthias? Aren't you going to make love to me?"

Three

Lauren stirred, stretched, came awake to the knowledge that she was in a strange bed in a strange room, wearing a near-stranger's T-shirt and nothing else. A trio of emotions washed through her. Relief. Embarrassment. Annoyance that her parent-picked fiancé proved to be more cautious and in control of his libido than she was of hers.

Last night, when she'd said, "Matthias? Aren't you going to make love to me?" he'd gone still and silent. Further prodding, "Matthias? Matthias?" had caused him to close his eyes as if in pain. Then he'd taken a long deep breath and replied, "No."

In less than forty-five seconds he'd left her in the guest bedroom with one of his shirts and a kiss on the nose.

You had to hate that kind of self-control in a man.

But now it was morning and from the quiet sound of it, the rain had stopped, so she was free to take herself and her humiliation out of his house. She'd give herself a pass on breaking off the engagement in person. When she got a safe one-hundred miles or so away, she'd give him a call. Better yet, she'd send an e-mail from an anonymous account. Or perhaps a note by slow-flying carrier pigeon.

She wasn't going to face him again, even if it meant driving home in a knee-length T-shirt and nothing else.

A woman who wasn't yet thirty and yet who'd been rejected at both the altar and in the bedroom didn't need to eat any more humble pie, thank you very much.

However, she wasn't destined for near-naked driving that day. When she inched open the bedroom door, she found a neat pile of her dried clothing. Once she'd pulled it on, she crossed to the door again, listened to the quiet for a moment, then tiptoed along the hall and down the stairs on the first leg of her furtive escape.

Only to find her host was watching her take those exaggerated silent footsteps over the rim of a coffee cup.

"Oh, uh, hi." She tried tacking on a casual expression to convince him that strutting like a soundless rooster was one of her normal morning activities. "I didn't, um, see you there."

Seeing him was the problem! Seeing him reminded her of what he'd looked like last night, smiling at her, touching her hair, her face, coming close-up for kisses that were burned into her mind. Crossing her arms over her chest, she tried banishing the memories of his dark gaze on her naked breasts.

How *much* she'd wanted him to touch her.

In an abrupt move, he half turned away, the liquid in his cup sloshing dangerously close to the edge. "Are you ready for that breakfast I promised?"

"Breakfast?" She sounded stupid, but she felt stupid that even *sans* merlot, cozy firelight and distant drumming of the rain, her attraction to him was alive and quite, quite well.

Her attraction to the man who'd been able to deny everything she'd offered him last night.

"I said I'd feed you." He turned back. "And if I don't get some decent caffeine I might start gnawing on table legs. I freely admit to being a coffee snob and this stuff isn't up to my usual standards. This stuff is instant. There isn't anything else in the house."

"Oh. Well. Then." She would have liked nothing better than to grab her keys and get out of there, but she was suddenly rediscovering that spine of hers. And her pride. Instead of running off like a cowardly ninny, she'd spend another hour with him.

Then she'd hide off someplace where she could rent a pigeon.

An hour without making a further fool of herself. That shouldn't be so hard, should it?

She chalked up the silence of the car ride into the tiny town of Hunter's Landing to his need for quality caffeine. For herself, she managed to clamp down on her usual nervous babble by digging her fingernails into her palms whenever she felt compelled to volley a conversational gambit.

She was afraid a neutral comment intended to sound like "Beautiful morning, isn't it?" might come out as a plaintive "Why didn't you go to bed with me last night?"

So she created some half-moon marks in her hands and applied herself to observing the view outside his SUV's windows. It *was* a beautiful morning. The road was narrow and windy, taking them through heavy woods with pine boughs that still held raindrops winking like crystals in the sunlight. Every once in a while she'd catch a glimpse of the lake, its deep blue a match of the spring sky overhead.

As they neared the town, there was a slow-moving parade of "traffic"—actually a short line of cars in both directions that were pulling into or out of parking lots of small stores and cafés. Matthias glanced over at her. "Have you been to the lake before?"

She nodded. "But only during ski season."

"You downhill? Cross-country? Snowboard?"

"Truth? I'm best at hot chocolate and stoking the fire."

He grinned. "A woman after my own heart."

Ha. After last night, they both knew that wasn't true. "What, you don't like snow activities that much either?"

"No, I like all sorts of snow activities. But when I'm done playing, I like a warm beverage, a warm fire and a warm woman waiting."

She curled her lip at him. "That's an incredibly sexist thing to say."

He steered the car into a parking space outside a restaurant called Clearwater's. "Hey, I didn't say I expected it to be that way, only that I liked it. Since you do, too, I don't see the problem."

What did he mean by that? Did he mean he didn't see the problem that she had with his comment or that, given their natural proclivities, he didn't think they'd have a problem with their marriage during ski season?

Except they weren't getting married. And she wasn't going to bother making that point in case he really was only referring to the comment and he'd think her assumption about thinking he was referring to their marriage incredibly presumptuous. Oh, God. Now she was babbling to herself.

Get out of the car, Lauren. Get out. Eat breakfast and don't make a fool of yourself for a single, simple hour.

They were shown to a table by the window, overlooking a spectacular view of the lake. Boats of all shapes and sizes were already on the water and Lauren shivered, thinking how chilly it must be out in the wind. Matthias had given her a sweater of his before they left the house and she was grateful for the soft warmth.

And the delicious smell of him that clung to it.

She shivered again.

Matthias looked over his open menu. "You all right?"

"Sure." She looked down at the offerings to avoid gazing at his face. Unlike last night, he was close-shaven now, and she itched to run her fingers along the smooth line of his jaw. *Don't do something dumb, Lauren.*

"Sorry about this, but I don't see crepes."

She glanced up. "Crepes?"

"Remember? I was going to get them for you as a way of making up for Gaston's absence in your life."

"*Gagnon*. Jean-Paul Gagnon. Gaston is from Disney's *Beauty and the Beast*. You know, the ego-inflated villain."

"See? I was right after all."

She found herself smiling at him.

He reached out and brushed her bottom lip. "I like that. You've been very serious this morning."

Her gaze dropped back to her menu while her lip throbbed in reaction to his light touch. "I need my caffeine, too."

"Amazing how compatible we are," he murmured.

She pretended not to hear him. Compatibility made her think of marriage again and made her wonder if *he* was thinking of marriage, and also made her wonder if he was really seriously considering putting a wedding band on her finger or if was he going to dump her like all her other fiancés had.

No, wait. See how confused he made her? She was going to be dumping *him*.

The waitress came by, served up the gourmet caffeine, then took their order. They sipped coffee until the food arrived—the whole nine yards for him, oatmeal and fruit for her—and she had a mouthful of the brown-sugary stuff when he spoke again.

"You know, I just realized I'm not completely clear on why you came to the house last night."

To give herself thinking time, she pointed to her full mouth and did the whole pantomime that translated to "just a second, let me chew and swallow." Once the spoonful was on its way to her stomach, however, the best she could come up with was misdirection.

"Well, you know, I'm not completely clear on why

you're at that beautiful house in the first place." She held her breath, hoping he'd fall for her ruse.

"I didn't mention it?"

"Nope. Not exactly why you're living there. My father was the one who gave me the address. I only know that it has something to do with your college friend Hunter."

He cleared his throat. "Hunter Palmer."

"I think my family knows some Palmers. Palm Springs? Bel-Air?"

Luke nodded. "That's his family. Pharmaceuticals and personal-care products. We met in college. There was a group of us, we called ourselves the Seven Samurai."

Lauren smiled. "And you males think *The Sisterhood of the Traveling Pants* sounds silly."

He sipped at his coffee. "Ours was a special friendship, I'll give you that."

"Tell me about them."

"We were all privileged sons of prestigious families. But what brought us together was that we weren't content to merely suck from straws stuck in family trust funds. We wanted to make our own ways, our own marks. And we did. We have."

The conviction in his voice made him only more interesting. "How does that relate to a Lake Tahoe log house?"

The quick flash of a grin. "Oh, well, that's a bit less noble. I think it was the beer talking. No, it was definitely the beer talking."

She laughed. "Thank you for showing the statues' feet of clay."

"I won't mention the aching heads the next morning."

"Oh, come on. Tell."

He pulled his coffee cup closer and stared into the black liquid as if it was a screen on the past. A small smile quirked the edges of his lips. "After a little too much partying one night, we made a pact that in ten years, we'd build a house on Lake Tahoe. Then we'd live there in successive months, meeting after the last one to celebrate all that we were certain we would have accomplished."

The smile deepened and he looked up to meet her gaze. "I'll say it for you. Arrogant brats."

She put her elbow on the table and rested her chin on her hand. "I don't know. You said that you arrogant brats had done what you set out to do."

"Guess so." He shrugged. "Besides me, there's Nathan Barrister, who continues making money hand-over-fist for his family's hotel chain; Ryan Matheson, who has his own pockets full of cable companies; Devlin Campbell, über-banker; and Jack Howington, our adventurer."

"That's only five," she pointed out.

"You know that Hunter died. Right before graduation." His gaze returned to his coffee. "I still miss him."

Lauren's heart squeezed, but she could still count. "That makes six."

His coffee appeared to fascinate him. "And then there's my brother."

She'd wondered if he'd be able to bring himself to mention his twin. Though she was aware of their estrangement, she didn't know the particulars. It seemed a shame—but then she'd never met Luke Barton. Maybe he really was enemy number one.

"Let's not talk about him," Matthias said.

The sudden strain in his voice and the tension in his expression made Lauren want to, though.

"Let's talk about you instead," he continued.

Lauren started. Uh-oh. Not her. Talk about her could lead to trouble. The kind where she ended up humiliated again.

"I already know about the fiancés in your past. But I don't know much about your work—"

"You know I'm a freelance translator." Okay. Work was a safe topic. She could talk about work. "It pays well, even though my father was sure my dual degrees in French and Spanish would never amount to anything."

"That's why you were in Paris?"

She nodded. "A long-term project. Unfortunately, I had to give up my apartment before I left the States, so now I'm back with Mom and Dad until—"

"The convenient merger of the Bartons and the Conovers," he inserted, a new, hard edge to his voice.

A shiver rippled down Lauren's back, not a sexy shiver, but a what's-going-on-here warning. Her expression must have betrayed her dismay, because he reached over for her hand.

"Sorry," he said, squeezing her fingers. "Don't mind me."

The fact that the marriage would be good for both family businesses had been hammered home to her by her father. Wrapped up in the cotton wool of what she had to acknowledge now was likely a depression, she'd barely felt a prick of worry over it. And she'd assumed Matthias was happy about that part of the deal. He didn't look happy now.

"Look…" she started.

"Shh." He lifted her hand and kissed her knuckles.

There was that other shiver. The one she was now familiar with when she was around him. It tickled up her arm and trailed down her back.

Without breaking her gaze, he ran his thumb across her knuckles. "I'm a bastard."

"I thought something similar myself last night," Lauren heard herself say—then wished it back with all her might. Dang it. Dang it! *Humiliation, here I come.*

Matthias's hand tightened on hers. "I—"

"Don't bother coming up with an excuse," she said hastily. "You were right. That was smart. We barely know each other and the bedroom isn't the best way to rectify that. Cooler heads prevailed. Give the man first prize."

"Lauren…"

She knew her face must be red because she felt heat from her neck on up. And she was babbling like she always did when she was uncomfortable, but it was too late to alter a lifetime's bad habit now. "I should thank you. I do. Thank you. Thank you very much. I appreciate your restraint and your…uh…uh…disinterest."

"Disinterest?" He was staring at her as if she'd grown another head. She wanted to take the single one she did have and bang it against the tabletop.

"Did you say *disinterest*?"

She tried to pull her hand from his. "Maybe. No. Yes. Whatever you think you heard I probably said."

"Hell!" He threw his napkin onto the table. "That's

it. We're done." He stood up, threw some bills on the table, then pulled her from her chair. Her napkin fell to the floor but he didn't give her time to pick it up. Instead, he hustled her out of the restaurant then started walking, dragging her along beside him.

There was a pretty footpath along the lake, but she didn't get much chance to appreciate the view because his long strides made her nearly run to keep up. When they reached a small covered lookout, he yanked her inside and then dropped onto the wooden bench. She was tugged down beside him.

"For the record, I was *not* disinterested last night," he said. "How could you even think that?"

"Uh, guest room? Long T-shirt? The way you practically ran away?"

"I was trying to be a good guy, you know that."

"Bet that's what my three previous fiancés told themselves, too."

He groaned. "Lauren."

Maybe she was being a tad unreasonable. Remember, she'd been grateful this morning that he'd showed restraint last night.

Oh, who was she kidding? She'd been mostly irritated that he'd been all dazzle but no follow-through. And she'd been hurt. And in serious doubt about her particular powers to ever really capture and keep the interest of a man.

"I've been going through a bad stretch, okay?" she said. "And there I was, practically begging, and you backed away. It's…"

Mortifying. And, oh, now even more so, as she felt the sting of tears at the corners of her eyes. She jerked her face away from his and toward the lake. "My, this wind is brisk, isn't it?"

He groaned again. "Lauren. Lauren, please." His fingers grasped her chin and he brought her face back to his. "Damn it. Last night, this morning, right now, I've been frustrated in four thousand different ways. My good intentions are running on empty, Goldilocks, and—oh, forget it."

Then he kissed her again.

Finally.

It tasted wonderful…and perhaps a touch angry.

"It's just so good," she whispered against his mouth.

He buried one hand in her hair as he deepened the kiss. The other hand slipped under his own oversized sweater to mold her breast. Her nipple contracted to a hard, desperate point. His thumb grazed over it.

As payback, Lauren ran her hand up his lean thigh to cup the hard bulge in his jeans. He jerked against her palm and his thumb moved over her nipple again. Harder.

She moaned. *It's just so good.*

So good that bells were ringing.

Matthias yanked his mouth from hers. "Hell." His hand left her, too, as he stood and dug in his front pocket.

The bells were still ringing. No, the *cell phone* was still ringing. Matthias's BlackBerry. He looked at the screen, muttered another curse, then pointed a finger at her. "Stay there," he barked, then ducked out of the little shelter.

Boneless, she fell back against the bench's seat. Now that she'd come clean about her feelings, she wasn't going anywhere. It hadn't been so humiliating after all. It had felt a lot more like heaven.

The call was from Luke's Eagle Wireless office. He ran his hand through his hair, trying to cool himself down before answering. Lauren had walked straight out of his fantasies to wreak havoc on his self-control and it didn't help that the sexual attraction ran so fast and hot both ways. Last night he'd come too close to letting sex take over his common sense.

He needed to get her out of the log house and away from him. She needed to go back to where she belonged. Back to her life.

Back to his brother.

That last thought took a vicious bite of him and he took it out on his assistant as he answered the call. "What do you want?"

"Good morning to you, too, Mary Sunshine."

He ignored her sarcastic rejoinder, then forgot it completely when she told him the reason she'd rung. She wanted to patch a call through from his brother.

"You know I don't talk to him." They hadn't spoken in seven years. Seven, like the Seven Samurai. Something about that stabbed like an ice pick to the chest, but he rubbed the useless feeling away. "Tell him to go to hell."

"He thought you'd say that. He told me to inform you he's in Germany, so you know he's already been there."

Luke almost laughed. Matt hated to travel overseas. Foreign flights, foreign food, foreign beds, they all put his brother off eating and sleeping. So why was his twin in Europe? Luke's mind raced through the possibilities, then locked on one that made the hair on the back of his neck rise. *Germany*. Anger burned like fire up his spine.

"Patch him through, Elaine."

And then there was Matt's voice. Tired, a little hoarse, but so damn familiar. "Yo, brother."

So damn familiar and so damn traitorous.

"Why are you in Germany?" Luke demanded.

"Is that any way to talk to the man who is calling to see how things are going at Hunter's house? I know you did this as a favor and—"

"I didn't do this as a favor to *you,* you bastard, and you know it. I agreed so that your 'last-minute business trip' wouldn't screw up Hunter's last wishes and now it looks as if you're screwing me over."

"I don't know what you're talking about."

"You're in Stuttgart, aren't you?" Stuttgart, the home base of a supplier Luke had been wooing for the last eight months. The deal he'd been nurturing would double his domestic profits. Triple the money he could make in China. He'd heard rumors that Conover Industries had been sniffing around, but Ralph Conover couldn't put together the kind of package that Luke could. Neither could Matt—not unless he got into bed with Conover.

Or Conover's daughter.

Damn them. Damn all of them.

"You're not going to cheat me this time, Matt," he ground out.

"I didn't cheat you *any* time, lunkhead."

Lunkhead. It was the name Matt had coined for him when they were kids. When they'd hated each other as much as they hated each other now. Only in college, those brief years when they'd really felt like brothers, had the nickname been said with affection.

"I don't have anything more to say to you." He flipped off the phone.

Shoving it in his pocket, he stared out at the lake, trying to get himself under control. That thieving bastard had tricked Luke into taking his place at Hunter's house so that he could head off to Germany undeterred and take over the deal that belonged to Eagle Wireless. Maybe Ernst would be loyal to what he'd already started with Luke. Maybe not.

Hell, probably not.

Loyalty wasn't something Luke had much faith in.

What he wouldn't give to screw over his brother as Matt had screwed over him! Just once, just once, Luke would like to take something that was his brother's. Then Matt would see what it was like to feel that sharp stab in the back from the one person who was supposed to be *watching* his back.

Luke turned to head back to his car and his gaze caught on the wooden lookout. Lauren. Hell, he'd nearly forgotten her.

Even as angry as he was, a little grin broke over his face. If he'd left her there she would have his liver for dinner. Sweet Lauren, who had thought he'd left her alone last night because he was disinterested! Sexy Lauren, who could be the model for the co-star in every hot dream he'd ever had.

He jogged over to the shelter and grabbed her hand to pull her up. "Let's go."

"Where?" She smiled.

Lauren smiled. Lauren who was engaged to his brother. Lauren who was Ralph Conover's daughter.

An idea, an oh-so-fitting idea, started creeping from a dark corner of his mind. And Luke let it. Then he pulled her against him and dropped a kiss on her bottom lip.

She looked up at him. Sweet. Sexy. Trusting.

"We never cleared up why you showed up at the house last night," Luke said.

Her eyes rounded. Her tongue darted out to wet her lower lip.

"No," she answered slowly.

Thinking back to all the things she'd said and the others she'd hinted at, Luke thought maybe she'd come to break the engagement. And if she *had* decided to give Matt the old heave-ho, then Luke would let her go. But after this month was up, if he still couldn't get her out of his head, he'd contact her and see if she felt the same way. He'd make it clear that Luke Barton was only after fun and games, but if she wanted to play, he was ready for a round or two.

However, if she was actually serious about this business-deal merger-marriage with Matt…

He had to find out for sure.

"So why'd you come, Lauren?"

"Ummm…"

He could hear the wheels turning in her head. "It's a simple question, Goldilocks." His fingers brushed back the hair from her forehead and a flush rose on her cheeks.

"I came to…umm…"

Her hair blew across her eyes and he caught it, then tucked it behind her ear. She shivered at his touch.

"Goldilocks?"

"I came to get to know you better," she blurted out. Her flush deepened. "We *are* barely acquainted and we *are* engaged, after all, and engaged people should know each other, don't you think? Because really…"

She continued chattering away, but he had stopped listening. He already had his answer. She hadn't come here to break it off with Matt.

Meaning Luke had in his hands right now, this minute, something that cheating, thieving Matt Barton wanted.

Oh, it was going to be sweet, sweet revenge when Matt discovered Luke had set out to seduce his brother's bride.

Luke wasn't going to feel bad about it.

Certainly not on Matt's behalf.

And not on Lauren's, either.

Because, after all, it was up to her whether or not he succeeded.

Four

Matthias pulled Lauren in the direction of the restaurant. "Let's go back to the house," he said.

She swallowed and tried hanging back. "Um. Uh. Right now?"

"You said you wanted to get to know me better."

Lauren's pulse quickened. Yes, yes, she'd said that, but there was a new, predatory gleam in her fiancé's eyes and maybe it was time to take a few deep breaths.

Back at the house there would be that decadent, quilt-covered bed, but would there be air?

"I was thinking it might be fun to explore the town," she said, slipping out of Matthias's hold. "You know. Look around." Which would give her time to consider her options and decide whether she should stay or whether she should go.

Matthias slid his hands in his pockets. "I don't know what there is to see," he said, sounding impatient.

"That's the whole point," Lauren replied. "Finding out what there is to see."

He paused a moment, then gave a little shrug followed by a small smile. She got the feeling he'd diagnosed her stall tactic and was indulging it…for the moment.

"Fine," he said, taking off at a pace so fast that his long legs ate up the path that would take them back toward the restaurant and, from there, to the rest of the little town of Hunter's Landing.

Lauren had to jog to catch up with him and her pace was still hurried as they traversed the streets of the small town, passing small shops, businesses and cafés. At the end of what Lauren supposed the residents called "downtown" sat the post office and Matthias paused beside the American flag that was flapping in the brisk breeze.

The wind fluttered his dark hair and tousled it over his forehead. The cool air or the sun or both had washed a tinge of ruddy color over the rise of his cheekbones and reddened his lips. Lauren stared at them, remembering the kisses from last night, how the burr of his evening beard had burned the tender edges of her mouth, rendering each caress hotter than the one before. She pressed the back of her hand over her own lips and shivered at the memory.

His eyes narrowed. "You're cold," he said. "And you've seen the whole of Hunter's Landing. Ready to go back now?"

Ready to go back? She shook her head. Not when

just the thought of kissing him continued to be so distracting. She needed more time.

"We've done the town," Matthias said, frowning. "What more do you want?"

That was easy. She wanted an un-befuddled head, one that wasn't affected by these inexplicable hormone rushes. She cleared her throat. "We haven't done the town, we rushed through it. Haven't you heard of strolling? Of enjoying the fresh air and the beautiful day?"

"To what end?"

She blinked. To what end? Must there always be an end? Obviously, the man needed to learn to relax. But he was already jiggling the change in his pocket, ready for action, so she gazed around her and hit upon inspiration.

"There. Coffee," she said, pointing across and down the street. A small shop called Java & More. "Didn't you say the house needs a fancier blend? I'll bet we can get some freshly ground at that store."

It worked. Sort of. Matthias set off in the direction she'd indicated, but first he slid his arm around her shoulders. And then, when she shivered in reaction, he drew her close against the side of his body.

"I'll keep you warm," he said, hugging her close as they crossed the street.

Too warm. Oh, much too warm.

Her hip bumped against him with each step. His fingers were five hot brands on the curve of her shoulder. He was near enough that she could feel the heat of his breath against her temple and the sensation made her skin jitter in reaction. His hand slid to the nape of her neck and gave a little squeeze. She glanced up.

Their eyes met and there it was again, an almost audible sexual snap, and it had her stumbling on the sidewalk. Matthias's hand tightened once more to keep her upright and she found herself leaning against him, her heart fluttering like that flag across the street, her nipples tightening as if they could feel the cold instead of all this delicious heat. With his free hand, he tilted her chin higher.

Tilting her mouth to his, he brushed his thumb across her bottom lip.

Heat tumbled from that point, rushing like a fall of water over her breasts and toward her womb. Lauren clutched his hard side as support for her rubbery knees.

His thumb feathered over her lip a second time. "Come back to the house," he whispered.

She watched his mouth descend.

"Come back to the house right now." He murmured it against her lips.

His kiss tasted like coffee and maple syrup and seduction.

It was a gentle press of mouth-to-mouth and she softened instantly, without thinking anything beyond how right it felt to be kissing this man. He angled his head to take it deeper and she opened her lips for him, but he did nothing more than breathe inside her mouth.

She wanted the thrust of his tongue!

He wasn't giving it up.

He was waiting for her.

Lauren felt heat again, flushing over all her skin. Matthias was waiting for *her* to make the next move. Waiting for her to make a decision. But before she could, a car honked.

The sudden noise caused her to jerk back. Matthias didn't move, though, instead remaining close and watching her with that same hungry light in his eyes she'd noticed after he'd returned from his phone call. It scared her.

Liar, it called to her.

Here was a man, not a boy-surfer, not a two-timing mechanic, not an intellectual yet indecisive cosmopolitan. Here was a one-hundred-percent red-blooded, single-minded American male animal who knew exactly what he wanted.

Her.

And she *did* want to get to know him better. She wanted to get to know *everything* about him. Her blood felt thick in her veins, and her heart beat harder inside her chest to move it through her body.

"Matthias." Her voice came out so hoarse that she had to clear her throat and start again. "Matthias. I'm ready to go back to the house."

He smiled. The fingers holding her chin slid down to caress the soft skin beneath and then to stroke along her neck. His thumb found the notch of her collarbone and rested there a moment. "A kabillion one hundred," he said.

The value of their bottled sexual chemistry had just gone up.

Taking her hand in his, Matthias turned them both back in the direction of the car and took off again at his brisk pace.

"We can still make a quick stop for the coffee," she said as they passed the shop.

He paused, and just then another couple exited the

door of Java & More. They weren't looking at them, they weren't looking at anything but each other, yet something about the two galvanized Matthias. Murmuring an indecipherable phrase beneath his breath, he quickly pushed her forward and then through the door of the neighboring business.

Lauren looked around the dim confines and found herself in teen paradise—a place stuffed with videogame and pinball machines, Skee-Ball ramps, an air-hockey table and a counter with a bored guy presumably able to provide change if only he'd look up from his magazine. Matthias shot a look out the streaky front window and guided Lauren farther inside.

"No pool table?" he murmured. "Hell, fine then." His fingers on the small of her back proceeded her toward an air-hockey table. He fished in his pocket for those coins that had been jangling earlier.

"You play?" he said, glancing out the front window once more. "Let's play. First to seven points wins."

Since her little sister Kaitlyn had walked all over her at a similar table not long before, Lauren released a sigh, but didn't try to talk him out of it. She might be an altar reject, but she wasn't completely clueless. For some reason Matthias wanted to avoid that other couple. They'd looked harmless enough to her—a man about Matthias's age and a woman about her own, in love, but she didn't have more time to ponder the situation because already Matthias was flinging that air-hockey puck in her direction.

Her hand grabbed her mallet to make an instinctive defensive move.

And her instincts—as was obvious by the three

previous broken engagements—weren't worth an anthill of beans. She lost the first game seven-zip. And the game after that. And the game after that.

A crowd of teens gathered around the table. She couldn't understand exactly why until Matthias barked something to one of them and she realized they were checking out her backside. Apparently the place—not to mention the young men—was sorely lacking from a dearth of the female gender. It did smell like a gym after an afternoon of six-man dodgeball. On a rainy day.

Following her three losses she conceded defeat, hoping they could go on their way, but when she stepped back from the table, a stringy-bodied, stringy-haired teenager stepped up in her place and slammed his quarters on the edge of the table. Lauren gathered it was some sort of challenge and, like a scene out of an old Western, Matthias's eyes took on a new gleam and he slammed his quarters down in return.

The competition was on.

And on.

Without a word being spoken about it, as Matthias defeated each challenger, another came to stand in his place. He met each one with the same ruthless intensity as the contender before: his sleeves pushed up to his elbows, his face a mask of concentration, his stance wide and aggressive. At first Lauren was amused and then a bit admiring—the muscles of his forearm flexed in a purely masculine manner—and then…and then she was alarmed by the obvious ferocity of his desire to win.

After a while it was clear he wasn't aware that she was there or aware of where he was or aware of anything but slamming that puck into the goal, over and over and over.

"Matthias…" she ventured.

He didn't flick her a glance as another player stepped in to replace the one he'd defeated.

"Matthias."

No response.

"Matthias!"

He started, then his head swiveled toward her. She saw him blink as if coming out of a fog.

"Assume success, deny failure?" she asked.

He frowned. "What?"

"Is that what this is all about? Victory at all costs, no matter what?" She tried to make light of it, but the way he looked when he played wasn't funny. The way he was looking at her now wasn't funny either.

"What's wrong with wanting to win?" His voice was puzzled. "What's wrong with hating to fail?"

Nothing, unless that was *all* you'd been taught. If you'd never learned that it was okay to fall down sometimes and how to pick yourself up if you did. Lauren thought of her three unsuccessful attempts at marriage.

Losing was something she wished she didn't know so much about.

She cleared her throat and changed the subject. "I thought we were going back to the house."

"There's a competitor…" His voice trailed off as he looked across the table at the scruffy boy who was no more than four feet tall. "It's a kid."

"Matthias, they've all been kids."

He looked around at the faces ringing the table. Then with a half-smile that was more a grimace, he stepped back from the table. "Um, all done for today. Thanks for the games."

He took Lauren's arm and started for the front door. "Okay. I admit it. I got a bit carried away."

Outside the place—named The Game Palace, she now saw—they both paused, adjusting to the bright sunshine. "I thought you'd forgotten all about me," Lauren said, her tone light. "I guess I'll need to take air-hockey lessons to keep some of your attention."

She was teasing, of course, but when he turned to face her, she could see that he was serious again. "Sweetheart, after last night, I know you don't need lessons in the kind of thing that will keep *all* of my attention."

The flush moved up her body this time, a warm wash that surely covered her face to the roots of her hair. "Matthias…"

"Lauren…" His voice echoed hers as he drew a fingertip from her earlobe to the corner of her mouth. "Let's go back now. Let's take the time to learn everything we can about each other."

"Does that mean you're going to tell me all your secrets?"

His finger paused in its wandering. "That might take a while."

She had a while. She had a lifetime, if he was the right man. And suddenly she realized that she was stronger than she'd first thought. Yes, he was sexy, charming and vulnerable in a way that tugged at her from many different directions, but she wasn't going to let those qualities tumble her immediately into his bed.

"Let's go back to the house," she said. "But once we're there, we need to discuss some rules."

"I don't like rules," Matthias cautioned, slanting her a glance from his corner of the living-room couch.

Lauren grimaced. After their return from Hunter's Landing, she'd managed to keep her fiancé distracted for a while by exploring the grounds and then the interior of the luxurious log-and-stone house. It had been built under the auspices of the Hunter Palmer Foundation and, once all of the Seven Samurai had completed their month-long stays, the place would be turned into an R&R retreat for recovering cancer patients—something Hunter himself had understood the need for, presumably, as he'd died of melanoma.

While a couple of the bedroom suites were decorated, as well as most of the living spaces, it was obvious that there was some decorating yet to be done. Still, the whole setup was incredible and it didn't surprise her that her business-oriented fiancé had been drawn to the state-of-the-art office that occupied the loft on the third floor. When she'd made noises about wanting to relax and read for a bit, he'd immediately headed up the stairs with his laptop and didn't come down until the hands of the grandfather clock in the foyer announced it was five o'clock.

After a brief stop in the kitchen, he'd found her in the great room. He'd handed over one of the glasses of wine he was carrying before taking his seat, from which he made that *un*surprising announcement: *I don't like rules.*

Lauren inspected herself for any imaginary lint as

she debated how to answer. While he was mired in work, she'd finally recollected and then retrieved from her car the small weekender bag she'd packed in anticipation of visiting her former college roommate in San Francisco. Now she wore a fresh pair of jeans and a cream-colored cashmere sweater she'd bought in Paris.

"My little sister Kaitlyn has rules that govern just about everything."

"You have a sister?"

Lauren looked up at him in surprise. "You've met her a couple of times, remember? Thirteen? Braces?"

"Of course." Matthias's gaze shifted from her face to the window. "I wasn't thinking…"

Lauren took a breath. "That's where I want to do things differently, Matthias. I want to think before I leap."

"You're doubting that the fourth time's a charm?"

Her face heated at his reference to her three botched engagements. "I'm talking about this…this attraction between us. I'm doubting whether it's smart to act on it and tumble into a sexual relationship so quickly. Aren't you willing to applaud my caution? After all, it's your marriage, too."

Matthias's gaze shifted away again. "Tell me about Kaitlyn and her rules."

Lauren smiled. "Besides the old standbys about avoiding sidewalk cracks and lines, these days she approaches her mirror backward, only whirling around when she's ready to see herself. According to Kaitlyn, true beauty only comes upon you by surprise, so…" Her hands rose.

"If she looks anything like her sister, the question of beauty isn't any question at all."

"Thank you." The compliment pleased her more than she wanted it to. "You've seen Kaitlyn for yourself. No matter how pretty we tell her she is, she's at that hyper-self-critical age. You remember thirteen, right?"

"Yeah." He took a swallow from his glass. "Come to think of it, when my brother and I hit thirteen our father laid a whole list of rules on us."

This was the kind of thing she wanted to know! That his kiss was divine, that he smelled like heaven, that his hands on her was something she desired more with each passing minute—that kind of knowledge was pleasing, but it certainly didn't promise a happy marriage.

She circled her forefinger along the rim of her glass. "What sort of rules?"

"We had chores, everything from the upkeep of our rooms to taking care of our bikes, then later our cars. At our weekly 'academic accounting' meeting with dear-old-Dad, the twin with the highest GPA was declared that week's winner. The loser had to take care of all the combined chores by himself, with the winner supervising. Then Dad supervised *him,* so that if he didn't come down hard enough on the working twin, he was punished."

Lauren stared. Matthias had said his spiel without emotion, but she could barely hold hers back. It formed a lump of appalled sympathy in her throat that was thick enough to bring tears to her eyes. "I—I don't know what to say," she finally managed to choke out.

"We were forced into competition over sports, too. At our weekly meetings he would tally up who had scored the most points in soccer, basketball, lacrosse, whatever the particular sport of the season was. Whichever one of us had done the most for the team that week got a free pass."

She swallowed, hard. "From?"

"A three-page, single-spaced book report. The loser had to read from a selection of nonfiction titles— Machiavelli's *The Prince, The Art of War* by Sun-Tzu, current books penned by the superachieving CEOs of the day—and then sum it up in three pages that would pass the muster of our Donald Trump of a dad. After, of course, being graded on the essay by the higher-scoring twin."

Lauren could only state the obvious. "I suppose that didn't foster much brotherly love."

His response was flat. Cool. "After our mother died, the Barton house was devoid of love."

Okay. Wow. There was the getting-to-know-you-better chat and then there was the really getting-to-know-you-better chat. What her fiancé had just told her went a long way to explaining not only his workaholic ways, but his strained relationship with his twin. They'd been raised as warriors in opposing armies instead of brothers who could rely on each other for support.

When was the last time the man sitting two feet away had felt as if someone was on his side?

Without thinking, she scooted along the couch so that she could touch him. She couldn't help herself from wanting to make contact with him, skin to skin. Her hand found his strong forearm and she laid her fingers on it and stroked down toward his wrist, trying to tell him through touch what she wasn't sure she could—or should—say.

I'm here for you. We can be allies, not enemies.

Matthias looked down to her caressing fingers, then back up to her face. "Not that I'm complaining, mind you, but are you by any chance breaking one of your rules already, Lauren?"

She froze, then backed away from him. She was already breaking her rules! She was! How could she have forgotten so quickly how she wanted to limit their physical contact?

Matthias gave her a wry smile, as if he could read her mind. "Don't worry, sweetheart. As to where we're taking the attraction…well, that's all in your hands now, Lauren. As a matter of fact, 'hands' is the operative word here. I promise I won't lay one of mine on you unless you ask."

Oh, terrific, she thought, looking at the beautiful man who had just bared a part of himself to her. He wasn't going to lay one of his hands on her unless she asked.

Just what she was afraid of.

Five

An hour later, Luke still didn't know what had possessed him to spill about what had passed for "childhood" in the cutthroat Barton household. Uncomfortable with his own revelations, he'd jumped up from the couch as soon as he could and strode toward the kitchen.

"There's plenty of food in the freezer and fridge for dinner options," he'd called to Lauren, who'd stayed behind on the great room's couch. "I'll let you know when it's ready."

When he was ready to face her again.

Maybe she'd figured that out herself, because she left him alone to microwave another gourmet meal from Clearwater's, only venturing as far as the dining area to set their places. Smart girl, he thought, as he

exited the kitchen with a plate in each hand. She'd put
them at the two heads of the long table, leaving a safe
distance between them.

He needed that space so that he could keep his mind
on what he was doing here with her. He hadn't wanted
to jeopardize it when they'd nearly bumped into Nathan
and his mayor on the street that morning—he'd had to
call his old friend with excuses that afternoon. He
didn't want to jeopardize it now.

Their time together wasn't about Luke discussing
his ruthless father's way of raising children. It wasn't
about exploring the chemistry that she was so intent on
making rules about. No, he'd encouraged her to stick
around because this was about Matt. It was about how
Luke could use this chance encounter with Lauren to get
retribution for what Matt had done to him seven years
before and for what he seemed to be preparing to do
now.

As they finished the last bites of their meal, Luke
looked down the length of the dining room table to
study his dinner companion. What did Lauren know
about what her father and Matt were planning? And
what would it take for him to get it out of her?

"So," he said, pushing his plate away from the edge
of the table. "How about a soak in the hot tub on the
deck?"

Her gaze flew to his. "Um…"

"Warm water. Relaxing bubbles." The perfect
location for him to worm from her the combined
Conover-Barton intentions.

"I don't…a hot tub…"

From the alarmed expression on her face, he might

as well have suggested doing something X-rated in the middle of Main Street.

He shook his head, smiling a little. "I told you, everything—or anything—physical between us is up to you, Lauren. You can trust me."

"Well—"

"Or at least you can take this opportunity to find out exactly how trustworthy I am."

A smile twitched the corners of her lips. "Not a bad idea, but I didn't bring a bathing suit with me."

He shrugged. "Me neither. We'll skinny dip."

"I'm—"

"Chicken? There isn't any reason to be, you know. I won't turn the deck or hot tub lights on. We can slip outside in towels and slip into the water when the other person's eyes are closed."

"But—"

"You were all set to marry a Frenchman on the top of the Eiffel Tower but now you won't get into a Tahoe hot tub with your fiancé? Where's your sense of adventure, Lauren?"

She scowled at him, and for some reason it made him laugh. "You make it hard for a woman to say no," she complained.

He laughed again. "I take it that's a yes?"

And it was, though half an hour later he doubted his powers of persuasion. Not that she didn't scurry out to the deck wrapped in nothing more than a striped beach towel, but he was doubting the wisdom of what he'd persuaded her into in the first place. As promised, he'd left off the lights but, even with forested darkness surrounding the house, thanks to the moon her bare shoulders gleamed like the surface of a pearl and her blond hair stood out—a pale flame in the night.

He remembered her body beneath the robe, how it was as if it had been constructed to his exact specifications. Curvy breasts, curvy behind—dangerous, dangerous curves.

"Close your eyes," she ordered, approaching the side of the redwood tub.

It didn't matter that he was obedient. Even with his eyes screwed shut, he could imagine everything as he heard the soft plop of her towel dropping to the deck. She'd be naked now. And then he heard the quiet swish of the water and felt the way it lapped higher on his chest as she lowered herself inside the hot tub—calves, knees, thighs, hips, rosy nipples now disappearing from his fantasy view.

His body responded accordingly, part of him rising up as he imagined her dropping down into the wet, silky heat. Even though he knew the night would cover his reaction, he edged away from her on the hot-tub bench.

She exhaled a relaxed little sigh. "You can open your eyes now."

Maybe he shouldn't. Maybe he should keep them closed so he could concentrate on the information he hoped to get from her. *Don't think about her body!* he reminded himself. *Don't think about her wet, naked, curvy body!*

Think instead of saving Eagle Wireless.

And of retribution.

He cleared his throat and slipped a little deeper into the water as if he were unwinding, too. "So," he said, pretending the question was just an idle musing, "how involved are you in your father's company?"

"You mean Conover Industries?"

"Does he have more than one?"

"No." She released a wry laugh. "He needs to have a single company, I guess, if he's going to be as single-minded as he is about business."

"Mmm." Luke tried again for that idle-musing tone. "Does he talk about work at home? You know, about how the company's doing, possible new ventures, that sort of thing?"

"I don't listen when he does."

What? "Not ever?"

"If you think listening to my father drone on to the point of talking over everyone else—including his teenage daughter who wants to share about the new play she's in, or her new teacher, or her new passion for Web site design—is suitable or enjoyable, then you need to eat more meals with the Conover family."

"Ah… Well…"

"You see, in my opinion, the dinner conversation *chez* Conover is pretty much as appropriate as talking about my father and his company on a beautiful spring night in a heated hot tub instead of simply being quiet and appreciating the incredible stars overhead and the inky shadows of the trees around us."

Luke blinked.

If he wasn't wrong, she'd just told him to shut up.

To shut up and relax.

Then he remembered her remark during their exploration of Hunter's Landing that morning. *Haven't you heard of strolling?*

Apparently he was supposed to be "strolling" through this evening as well. Fine. Willing his legs not to fidget, he shook out his arms and raised his gaze. Okay. There were those stars she'd mentioned. That moon.

What the hell is my brother doing right now?

The question popped into his head and he saw spreadsheets instead of sky. He breathed in fire instead of fresh air.

Despite the heat of the water, his muscles went rigid. *If Matt ruins my Germany deal, I'm ruined.*

Luke jumped to his feet. Lauren let out a little shriek. Startled, he fell back to the bench. "God," he said. "You just scared the life out of me. What is it?"

"You. *You* scared *me.*"

"Huh?"

She made a vague gesture in his direction. "All of a sudden you stood up and you were, um, wet."

Wet and naked. Hell, he hadn't been thinking about his state of undress. He'd been thinking about his damn twin and then he'd been on his way to his cell phone and a plane ticket to Germany where he would wring Matt's neck.

But he couldn't do that. For the rest of the month, Luke couldn't leave this house, not when it was Hunter's last request.

Swallowing his frustrated groan, he tipped the back of his head against the rim of the tub and tried uncoiling the tension in his neck, his spine, the back of his legs. *Take it easy, Luke. Relax.*

"Are you all right?" Lauren asked.

"No." He grimaced at the clipped sound of his voice.

"Look, I know I invited you out here, but the truth is, I'm not so good at this relaxing stuff. I don't nap, I don't meditate. As far as I know, I don't even take deep breaths."

She laughed. "Is there anything I can do?"

He rolled his head toward her. The starlight caught in her eyes and they gleamed. *So pretty.* "Talk to me, Lauren. Otherwise, I think the silence might make me nuts."

"You just need to get used to it."

This time he didn't hold back his groan.

She laughed again. "All right, all right. What should I talk about? My father, or—"

"Kaitlyn," he said, surprising himself. "Tell me about your sister."

"Ah. Kaitlyn." Lauren wiggled on the bench, sliding a bit lower into the tub. She must have stretched out her legs, because the water feathered against his foot, letting him know she was only a toe or two away. "My infuriating, adorable and genius-IQ baby sister."

"Genius IQ?"

"Mensa genius IQ and then some." Lauren shifted again and this time he felt the brush of the bottom of her foot against the top of his.

He pretended not to notice.

"Kaitlyn terrifies my mother and father."

"But not you?"

"Oh, me, too, but when she points out their foibles and flaws, my parents can manage only to sputter and spit."

As he slid his heel along the slick bottom of the tub, his toes found the little bump of her ankle bone. He gave it a small nudge. "And what does Lauren do?"

"I humbly acknowledge she's right and promise to do better next time."

She went silent, so Luke nudged her again. "Don't leave me in suspense. What's her latest critique of your character?"

"Let's just say she's not fond of junior bridesmaid dresses."

Little sister Kaitlyn thought Lauren's marriage to him was a bad idea.

No. Her marriage to *Matt*.

The reminder annoyed him. "Maybe if the Conovers and the Bartons merge, I'll have to be listening to Kaitlyn myself. Does she have ambitions regarding your father's company?"

"She has ambitions to take over the world. Global peace for the masses and Justin Timberlake for all teenage girls." Her leg moved again and a silky swipe of calf met his own hair-roughened one. "But seriously, I can see her being the CEO of Conover in the not-so-distant future."

He stretched a little more in order to hook his foot around her delicate ankle. They were twined together, now, but it didn't appear to bother her. "What about you?"

"What about me what?"

Did she sound a little breathless? "Do you have any interest in getting involved in the family business?"

Her laugh was short. "You're kidding, right? My father wouldn't find use in Conover Industries for my skills in French and Spanish."

But what about German? Could she speak that, too? Luke remembered he was supposed to be digging for anything he could find about his brother's business instead of finding her sleek leg in the warm wetness. "Lauren—"

"You can't be surprised. I'm sure my father made it clear. The first and only time he's ever approved of me or anything I've done was when I agreed to marry Matthias Barton."

Lauren wished she'd never mentioned the word *marry*. It had sent Matthias catapulting from the hot tub with only a curt "Close your eyes" warning. While wrapping a towel around his hips—of course she'd watched through her eyelashes!—he'd mumbled something about bringing them back some wine before disappearing into the house.

She'd spooked him with the wedding talk, which was weird, because she'd come to the Hunter's Landing house spooked by the idea herself. Yet now…now the idea of being with him gave her an odd feeling of rightness. Odd, because she'd never sensed it on those other occasions when she'd been with him. But the feeling itself was familiar.

The day she'd met her freshman roommate in college, she'd known they were going to be friends for life.

Her senior year, within an hour of interning at the publishing company she still translated for, she'd understood at some cellular level that she'd found her place.

Did it work like that with the man one married?

And if it did—then why hadn't she known when she'd danced with Matthias at the Jewel Ball or when she'd passed him the basket of dinner rolls at her family's table?

Maybe it was her glimpses of all his wet muscles

that had turned the tide. Face it, both sides of his body were spectacular. He might be a workaholic, but some of those long hours must be spent working out. While the wide set of his shoulders might be genetic, it took effort to create the sleek round of muscles supporting them. And then there were his pecs—she'd never considered herself a connoisseur of a particular male body part, but she might have to change her own opinion of herself. Could be she was a chest girl after all.

Yes. After looking at those defined, yet not overdone plates of pectoral muscle gleaming with water in the moonlight, she'd definitely discovered their allure.

And she'd peeked at his butt as he was wrapping that towel around his hips. *Bad Lauren!* But she'd merely been checking out his shoulders from behind and then her gaze had coasted down all that wet skin toward his waist and from there it was just a little *whee!* of a slide to his cute, contoured backside.

So maybe that was it. Maybe her marriage *no* had been transformed into a marriage *maybe* by something as shallow as the way her fiancé looked wearing nothing but H_2O.

Except that didn't explain why she'd felt so drawn to him last night. How much she'd enjoyed breakfast and their walk that morning, even counting the way he'd exposed his hypercompetitive streak at The Game Palace. He'd laughed at himself about it and that kind of humorous self-deprecation held as much charm for her as his smile, as his interest in Kaitlyn, as his understanding that she didn't want to fall right into his bed without getting to know him better, engagement or no.

No engagement. That's what she'd wanted, but now

she didn't want to make *that* mistake either. Now she wanted to be with him.

And so where was he? Surely a simple bottle of wine wouldn't take this long?

A niggle of unease tickling her spine, she scrambled out of the hot tub and swiped up her towel. When he still didn't appear, she took herself and her terry cloth-wrapped body through the French doors. "Matthias?" she called out. "Everything okay?"

Their stemmed glasses were on the countertop in the kitchen along with a bottle opener. But no wine and no man. Recalling the location of the wine cellar from her earlier tour, Lauren headed in that direction.

Her bare feet were silent on the carpeted steps that descended to the lower level. A right turn took her into the small room lined with shelves stocked with bottles. A small table stood in the middle of the room and what looked like a merlot rested on one corner. It was clear that Matthias had forgotten all about it, his attention now focused on dozens of photographs fanned across the wooden surface.

She thought of the framed photos in the hallway upstairs. She hadn't done much more than glance at them enough to gather they were various shots of scruffy young men whom she presumed were the Samurai. She suspected these were more of the same.

Gripping the doorjamb, Lauren called softly in order not to startle him. "Matthias?"

Her fiancé didn't turn around. "He's right here," he said, tapping a photo.

"Hmm?" She ventured farther into the room. "That's a picture of you, you mean?"

He froze, then whirled around, his hands going wide as if he was trying to hide what he'd been inspecting. "Oh. Sorry. I left you out there, didn't I?"

Curious, of course, she drew closer to the table. "That's all right. What're you looking at?"

For a second he didn't move and she wondered why he was so protective of what lay on the table.

"What?" she said, trying to peer around him. "I didn't uncover you admiring your stash of secret black-mail material, did I?"

A ghost of a smile broke over his face. "Close. More college photos of the Seven Samurai. I stubbed my toe on the box."

It was beneath the table now, the white cardboard neatly labeled "Hunter-Samurai." She shifted her gaze to the top of the table. "May I look?"

She had the distinct feeling he wanted to refuse, but then he sidestepped to give her access.

"I'm not going to be shocked, am I?" she asked as she moved in.

He shrugged. "You tell me."

Even with his earlier admission about not doing well with relaxing, there was no missing the new, tighter tension in his body, just as there was no missing the lack of reason for it—at least from her first, cursory in-spection of the photos. "Hmm," she said, peeping at Matthias through the corner of her lashes. "If I had to guess I would say you seven majored in beer, basket-ball and busty co-eds."

Truly, though, there was nothing she could see that would put him on edge. There were plenty of grins, some boozy, on the faces of young-faced college boys who posed with their buddies and some long-legged girls—was every female long-legged at the age of twenty?—in various combinations.

Matthias was in many of them, most often with a sandy-haired, good-looking boy with a buzz cut and a laugh in his eyes. His charisma came through paper, space and time. Lauren lifted a close-up of the smiling face. "Let me guess. Hunter?"

"Yeah." A corner of his mouth hitching up, Matthias took the photo from her hand. He ran his thumb along the edge. "Hunter. He could make an all-night study session an adventure. He'd set an alarm for every hour and when it went off he'd announce some crazy item we'd have to scavenge for in ten minutes or less. The quick break combined with the adrenaline rush would hone our focus for the next fifty minutes of studying."

The easy way he talked about the other young man told Lauren it wasn't memories of Hunter that had agitated him. She looked back at the photos, pushing some aside with her finger to reveal another, larger one, beneath.

And then it struck her, something she hadn't thought through during her cursory view of the photos upstairs. On the table were plenty of shots of a younger Matthias but, looking at this particular picture, she realized they might not all have really been of him. Because this photo showed two faces mugging for the camera. *Two identical faces.*

Of course he had a twin, Luke. But until this moment she hadn't thought to determine how closely they resembled each other. And now she knew. Picking up the photo to hold it closer, she confirmed her first thought. They looked exactly alike.

And in this picture, at least, they looked pleased to be in each other's company. From the corner of her eye, she noted Matthias was studying her face instead of the photo she held. She turned it his way. "Which one is you?"

He shrugged without looking at it. "Doesn't matter."

She shrugged, too. "I guess not. You both look equally…"

"Drunk?"

Her gaze shifted back. "I don't think so. There's a basketball in your hands and it appears you've just finished a hard game."

He nodded. "Hunter likely took that one then. We were a team in a huge three-man basketball tournament. We came out on top."

"You and your brother were a team?"

"With Hunter."

She pressed. "You and your brother were on the same side?"

"We seemed to be in college."

For those years, they'd somehow left behind that sick competition their father had fostered during their childhood. Had it been Hunter's influence, or just a natural brotherly love allowed to find the sunshine away from their father's presence?

"What happened after college?"

"You don't want to know about all that."

Like heck she didn't, particularly because her sudden shiver underscored the new cool tone in his voice. This was exactly the kind of thing she wanted to know all about.

"You're chilled," he said. "Let's go back to the hot tub."

She was chilled *and* naked. He was still just in a towel, too, and there was quite a bit of male muscle to admire. But it didn't stir her even one iota at the moment, not when the sort of nakedness she was interested in right now was the emotional kind—the kind a man shared with the woman who had promised to become his wife.

"What happened between you and your brother, Matthias?"

"Matthias," he muttered under his breath. "Damn. Matthias and Luke. Luke and Matthias. It might as well be Cain and Abel."

"Matthias—"

"Forget it, okay?"

"No. I—"

"I said, leave it alone." He strode toward the doorway. In a moment he would be gone.

The moment would be gone.

"Wait, wait. Just answer me this."

He paused in the doorway, his back still to her. "What?"

"Why? Why do you hate your brother?"

He didn't turn around to face her. But she didn't need to see his expression because she could hear the frigid anger in his voice. "It's because, God help me, he so often has what I want. Now leave it alone."

With that, he left *her* alone in the wine cellar. Alone and with one sure thought. She'd wanted to get to know him better and now she did. Now she knew that talk of his twin was off-limits.

With a sigh, Lauren left the wine and the photographs scattered on the table. Unfortunately, she suspected it was his relationship with his brother that her man needed to open up about most.

At 2:45 a.m., Lauren gave up on sleep. Her lightweight cotton-knit travel robe lay across the end of the bed and she slipped it over the matching nightgown and barefooted it downstairs. The house was silent and dark, but her fingers managed to find the kitchen light switch to flip it on.

"Huh!" A startled male grunt and a liquidy thud told her she wasn't alone. It took her a moment to blink past the fluorescent dazzle of the overhead fixture, but then she saw that Matthias stood at the sink, an empty glass in one hand. A half-gallon carton of milk had landed in the sink, but enough of it had geysered from the open top upon being dropped that there was a big puddle on floor at his feet.

"I'm sorry!" Lauren hurried forward. "Don't move or you'll track the milk all over the place."

With a wad of paper towels in hand, she knelt to soak up the liquid on the floor. "You didn't hurt yourself, did you?" she asked.

"I'll survive a milk bath," Matthias grumbled. "You surprised me, that's all."

"I'm sorry about that, too." She rose with the dripping paper towels and dropped them in the sink. "I couldn't sleep."

"Me neither."

What was the cause of *his* insomnia? "I'm sorry—"

"That's not your fault either," he answered, wiping off the sides of the carton with a wet sponge.

Reaching around him, Lauren wet clean towels then kneeled again to wipe the floor. As much as she regretted being the cause of the mess, she was glad for the opportunity to talk to him again after what had happened earlier. She didn't want the awkwardness of it lingering between them.

A swipe of dry cloths later, the floor was once again pristine. The used towels went in the garbage. "You're free to move now," she said to his back.

He turned to face her.

"Oh." She tore another towel off the roll. "Not quite done after all." Her arm reached out to wipe away the drops of milk that were sprinkled over his chest.

His bare chest. Revealed in all its lovely male perfection thanks to the low-slung pair of pajama pants he was wearing as his only sleep attire. The pants were really cute—a soft olive cotton with all-business pinstripes. All-business pinstripes that didn't appear the least bit Brooks Brothers when they were slung so low they were doing that whole mouth-drying, hormone-heating, hanging-by-the-hipbones thing.

Lauren realized she was standing there, staring.

And that he was staring at her staring.

And that the temperature in the room had turned so warm that the milk on his miles of bare chest had to be in danger of evaporating into latte steam. Clearing her throat, she reached farther to dab at his chest with the paper towel. At the touch, goose bumps broke out across his collarbone and she saw the centers of his copper-colored nipples tighten into hard points.

She swallowed her squeaky moan and tried breaking the sudden sexual tension with her usual MO—babbling.

"I really am sorry about surprising you in here, Matthias," she said, as she continued stroking spots on his skin. "And that you're having trouble sleeping. And then there's the milk that went on the floor, not to mention all over these gorgeous muscles on your hunky chest…"

Her voice petered out as the sound of her own words reached her brain. Her hand froze and her gaze dropped to their bare feet. "Oh, tell me I didn't just say out loud what I think I said out loud."

She felt his laugh through her fingers. "Lauren, Lauren, Lauren." His hand came up to cover hers and then he guided it lower so the towel bumped over the sculpted muscles of his abdomen.

Her fingers opened. The paper wad dropped to the floor. The tips of her fingers absorbed the heat of his skin and he drew them lower, lower. Now she felt the soft fur of the hair below his navel. Now her fingers grazed the waistband of his PJs.

His free hand at her chin, now he tipped up her mouth and looked into her eyes. More heat. And need.

And then that undeniable, oh-so-puzzling but oh-so-welcome feeling of rightness.

"Lauren," he said again, his thumb brushing over her bottom lip. "Didn't anyone ever tell you not to cry over spilled milk?"

•

Six

Didn't anyone ever tell you not to cry over spilled milk?

The words echoed in Lauren's mind as she looked up into her fiancé's face. Did that mean she shouldn't cry over broken rules, either?

In particular, the one regarding not falling into bed with Matthias until she got to know him better?

Spilled milk. Broken rules. The parallel between the two didn't make real sense, she could admit that, but nothing was making sense lately. Not the strength of this attraction she had to him and not the way it had suddenly come upon her the moment he'd opened the door to her on that rainy night.

"Oh, boy," she whispered, knowing she was in trouble. Her fingers curled, her nails scratching at his bare belly skin. She felt his muscles flinch and his cheeks hollowed as he sucked in a sudden breath. "Oh, boy."

"Oh, man," he corrected, with a faint smile. The hand he'd cupped over hers guided her palm a tad lower until she wrapped his rigid flesh. It twitched at her touch. "Oh, *man*."

Her mouth curved as his lips lowered. She couldn't help but smile into his kiss.

But it turned serious the instant her mouth parted and the tips of their tongues met. Heat rushed across the surface of her skin and she went on tiptoe to press harder against him. His wide hands splayed against her back and drew her nearer.

Her head fell back as she surrendered to his deepening kiss. His tongue plunged inside her mouth and she echoed the motion by sliding her hand down his shaft. His whole body stiffened in reaction and, after a pause, he withdrew his tongue in a slow, deliberate movement.

She mimicked the action by gliding her hand high again. He thrust inside her mouth, she stroked down. He groaned and, loving the sound, Lauren palmed his erection in a seductive caress.

On another sound of need, he tore his mouth from hers. "Witch," he whispered, his eyes glittering. "Beautiful witch."

Hauling in much-needed air, Lauren wondered if the oxygen would bring back her common sense—or at least her sense of caution. But both seemed to have fled for good—or at least for the night. She wanted this man. She wanted, wanted, wanted him.

His head bent again to kiss her cheek, the side of her neck, and then he tongued the whorls of her ear, making her shiver. "Beautiful witch, are you going to let me have you?"

More shivers trickled down her neck. Have her? Would she let herself be had?

She'd wanted to know him better before acting on her desire and the truth was, she did understand him more. Though she didn't know how deep they went, she was at least aware of some of his wounds. And then there was the fact that she was hurt, too. Three times she'd been rejected as she stood on the curb of lifelong commitment and she knew those rejections had affected her confidence in herself, in her femininity and her own appeal as a sexual being.

By giving in to this man who made her heart beat so fast and her blood run so hot, to this man whose own desire for her she was holding in the palm of her hand, wouldn't she be getting so much else back?

And it still felt so right.

If nothing else, Lauren decided, she could regard going to bed with Matthias as a test. Perhaps the "rightness" was just a trick of the mind to pretty up something as simple as lust. And when the lust was sated, then the "rightness" would disappear and she'd no longer be fooling herself about it being something so much more… Something maybe even worth marrying for.

He caught the lobe of her ear between his teeth. Her fingers flexed on his shaft. They both groaned.

His mouth found hers again. He parted her lips and plunged inside and she twined his tongue with hers and crowded against his body, rubbing his erection, rubbing her aching nipples against the hot, naked flesh of his chest.

One of his hands slid from her back to cover her breast. He squeezed and the pressure felt so sweet— oh, fine, *so right*—that she had to bury her face against his neck and ride out the tremors of reaction. Kissing her temple, her cheek, any place he could reach, he continued molding the soft flesh in his palm and used his other hand to pull away the fingers she had around his own straining flesh.

"Can't take it right now, honey," he said, placing her palm on the bare skin of his torso. "It's too early for the fireworks."

She lifted her face and linked her hands around his neck to draw down his mouth. "I'm seeing sparklers everywhere."

They shot into wild arcs of heat and light as they kissed again, a wet, deep kiss that was a whole Fourth of July show unto itself. She lost herself in it, lost herself in his taste and his strength, until his thumb grazed her nipple.

Then flames shot up around her. Her body jerked in his arms and he slid his other hand to the curve of her bottom while his fingers found that tight bud and made maddening circles around it. She jerked again, her hips butting up against his erection, tilting to make a place for it as desire caused a liquid rush between her thighs in preparation for him.

He pushed back, nudging against the notch of her body with the head of his penis. With only thin layers of cotton between them, he was able to insinuate himself between the petals of her sex, the tip of him discovering her sensitive kernel of nerves. She cried out, unable to hold back the sound, and he responded by rubbing there again.

"You like that, sweetheart?" he murmured, looking down into her eyes.

She could hardly breathe and her nerves were humming like a tuning fork. "I—I like you."

He smiled and then the hand on her bottom started drawing up the material of her robe and nightgown together. Cool air washed over the back of her knees and then the back of her thighs and she shivered again, overloaded with sensation. When he had the hem of her clothing in his fingers, he drew up his hand and held his fist at the small of her back.

That cool air now found her naked bottom.

Wet heat rushed between her legs again.

Then in a quick movement he dropped the robe and nightgown—his hand now beneath them. His big male palm now covering her round, bare bottom cheek. Goose bumps prickled over her skin.

"You ready for me, sweetheart?" he whispered.

Ready? How could that be a question? She drew his head down for another kiss. His hand reached between her legs and just as his tongue plunged into her mouth, a long finger slid into her body.

Lauren gasped, then softened against him, opening to his intrusion by hooking her ankle around the back of his calf.

"You *are* ready for me," he murmured against her mouth and there was no way to deny it, no reason to deny it, when he was stroking in and out of her wetness with his clever, clever finger.

Then two fingers. She shivered, sucking on his tongue because she loved the feeling of fullness. Of being open then filled by this beautiful, beautiful man.

It still felt so right.

He lifted his head, his gaze narrowed, a pronounced flush on his cheekbones. "Counter or comforter?"

His fingers were deep inside her body. The tip of his erection was pressed tight against the pulsing ache at the top of her sex. She had no idea what he was talking about and couldn't care less.

"You have to decide, Goldilocks," he said.

She shook her head. She'd decided minutes ago, hadn't she? It was time to ease her lust, to test that sense of rightness, to get over those three rejections that had battered her heart.

"On my bed or on the breakfast bar?"

His question startled a laugh out of her which turned into a tiny groan as it shifted her body against the sweet invasion of his fingers. "You don't have to make the choice sound so romantic," she said, smiling to let him know she was teasing.

"And you don't have to make me so crazy with wanting you that I'd cover you out in the cold, lonely rain if that was the only way I could have you."

That's when she realized the weather had turned again. She could hear the sound of raindrops pattering down and she shivered a little, remembering how frozen she'd been last night. "By a fire," Lauren said. "Take me by a fire."

"Then wait here," he replied, removing his touch so that she wanted to cry with the loss of it. "Wait here until I tell you that it's time for me to have you."

Have you. Cover you. Take me.

As she waited alone in the kitchen, trembling with wanting and anticipation, the phrases ran in a loop through her mind. *Have you. Cover you. Take me.*

Primal, man-woman words of possession.

And she was possessed by the idea of having him, too. Of having him in her body. Of having sex with this particular man who might be the last man in her life if they survived the test.

His voice reached her in the kitchen. "Lauren, come upstairs."

She didn't remember the journey from the hardwood floor to the carpeted steps. She didn't remember mounting them or how she knew to go into the master bedroom with its half-closed door.

It was as if she heard Matthias's voice and then she was in his bedroom—that decadent bedroom, now made even more decadent with the light from a fire burning in the fireplace and casting yellow, orange and red tongues of light across the rumpled bed.

He stood to one side, still in his low-slung pajama bottoms. Lauren felt the heat of his gaze and the heat of the fire and the heat from wearing too many clothes when all she wanted between the two of them was the palpable desire that filled the room.

Her gaze on his face, she loosened the tie of the sash of her robe. She shrugged and the material fell to her feet. As she stepped away from it, her hands rose to the spaghetti straps of her gown. She pushed them aside and stepped forward again after the nightwear shimmied down her naked skin.

And then she stood before her fiancé, offering him all she had.

The poleaxed look on his face made her smile.

Have you. Cover you. Take me.

That could work both ways and it surely seemed as if it was up to her to jumpstart the rest of the event, now that her man appeared lust-stunned by the sight of her. At least she thought he was lust-stunned...

Uncertainty licked a cold line down her spine. Maybe what had been feeling so right to her wasn't mutual. "Is there...is there something wrong with...with..."

"With what?" Matthias said, a frown flickering over his face.

And the word popped out, driven by anxiety. *"Me?"*

He laughed, low and sexy, and her uncertainty and anxiety were chased off by the seductive sound. "The only thing wrong with you is that you're too far away, sweetheart."

His arms reached out and swept her up against him. The contact of their naked torsos made her gasp, but then he muffled the sound with his mouth, taking her into a kiss that turned up the heat all over again.

He backed up and when he fell onto the bed, she fell onto his chest, breaking their joined mouths. She sucked in a breath. "Are you okay?"

Sifting his fingers through her hair to push it away from her forehead, he laughed again. "I'm the most okay I've been in years."

She smiled, but then it died as Matt circled her waist with his hands and lifted her up his body so that he could nuzzle the valley between her breasts. Her palms slid across his crisp dark hair and her fingernails bit into his scalp as he turned his head to catch her nipple in his mouth.

Her back arched into the delicious sensation. He curled his tongue against her, gentle and tender, then sucked hard with a raw, male sound of need coming from deep inside his throat. His sound of pleasure only added to the agony of almost unbearable pleasure that arrowed from her breast to her core.

His head shifted and he plucked at the wet nipple with his fingers as he gave her other breast that arousing attention with his mouth. Lauren could hear her shallow breathing and even when she closed her eyes she could still see the shadows and firelight in the room.

It was like the two of them, that darkness and those flames. Though there were still things they didn't know about each other in the shadowed corners of their souls, that didn't stop the fire from burning between them, from consuming her doubts, from lighting the way to a future that felt so…so…right.

Always so right.

Matthias flipped their positions. Suddenly she felt the sheets at her back and on top the hardness that was his sinew and muscle and bone. She spread her legs to make a place for him, but he ignored the invitation to draw back and stand beside the bed.

With half-closed eyes, she watched his hands go to the drawstring at his waist and she let her gaze drop down to the erection straining behind the cotton.

"So pretty," Matt said, his voice almost harsh.

Her gaze shifted to his face, its angles made even more stark and beautiful by the flicker of the light. He was studying her, his eyes tracking over her breasts and down her parted legs.

Instinct caused her to bring them together again.

"Don't," he said softly. "Don't hide anything from me. Please."

And because she wanted that, too, she slid her heels along the smooth cotton and held out her arms in her own plea. "Come to me."

He shucked his pants in one swift move, then reached into the drawer of the bedside table for a condom. She had the brief impression of thick strength and then he was off his feet and in her arms, his shaft nudging at her entrance even as he took her mouth in yet another devastating kiss.

Lauren twined her arms around his neck and tilted her hips, asking for all of him, and he leaned more of his weight into her, taking her body one inch at a time. She stretched around him in degrees, going from breathtakingly tight to deliciously full.

He lifted his head as he joined them that last little bit. Her eyes closed with the goodness of the completion.

"Don't," Matthias whispered to her. "Don't shut me out like that either."

Smiling, she lifted her lashes. "Doesn't it feel good?"

He rocked a little into the cradle of her body. "What do you think?"

"I think it feels…feels…"

"Just right, Goldilocks," he said. "Not too hot, not too cold, not too hard, not too soft. Just right."

And of course those were her exact thoughts. And of course to hear them from his lips, in his husky heavy-with-desire voice, only made her more certain that she was in the right place with the right man.

Finally.

She tilted her hips to take him deeper, and he groaned, his head falling back. Then he drew away from her, almost to the brink, before sliding forward again. Her muscles tightened to hold him there, it felt so wonderful, but he pulled back again before another slow glide of penetration.

It was a rhythm she tried to fight and yet didn't want to fight. It felt so good to be filled by him and yet she had to let him go for him to come back to her. Her legs wrapped around his strong hips and he found a different angle that made goose bumps break across her skin.

"Oooh," she moaned, as he dropped his head to place openmouthed kisses against her neck. "Please."

"Please what?" he whispered against her ear. "Please what?"

As he continued to stroke in and out of her body, Lauren couldn't think of what she wanted more than this, just this, the play of reflected flames on his wide, powerful chest, the gleam of fire in his eyes, the blissful joining as the two people that were Lauren and Matthias became a single, indivisible whole.

His mouth found one of her nipples again and her body responded by tightening on his. He groaned, and the rhythm altered as both their bodies drove harder toward climax.

"I'm afraid I don't deserve this," he whispered against her mouth.

"I do," she returned.

He half laughed, half groaned and then his hand crept between their bodies and he touched her there, right at the spot that pulsed like another heart.

Gasping, Lauren lifted into the touch and his fingers grazed her again. And again.

"Let me have you," he whispered. "Go over, Goldilocks. Go."

Let me have you.

And she did, shuddering against him, around him, taking his own climax into her body. *Take me.*

As the last of the tremors wracked both their bodies he collapsed over her, heart to heart. *Cover me.*

And oh, Lauren thought. Oh, yes. It still felt so right.

It was hard to regret a nanosecond of what had just occurred, Luke decided, with Lauren's cheek resting on his chest and her blond curls drifting across his shoulder.

Who was he kidding?

It was *impossible* to regret the way her curves had looked, lapped by the light from the fire. It was impossible to regret the way her kisses had burned, the way her breasts had felt cupped in his palms, the sweet little noises she'd made when he'd taken their hard peaks into his mouth.

Hell, even as sated as he was, just remembering that made his blood run south again.

He pressed his mouth against her temple. "Lauren, are you all right?"

"Mmm." She snuggled closer against his side. He smiled at the contented noise, surprised to realize that he felt exactly the same way as she sounded.

But the guilt should be stabbing at him, right?

"Are *you* okay, Matthias?"

Ah, there was that guilt, he thought, wincing. Matthias. She'd gone to bed with him, thinking he was Matt.

He stroked his palm over her soft curls, wondering if he would be able to look at himself in the mirror come morning. "I didn't plan this. I didn't mean for us to end up here tonight."

"I know."

The two words didn't absolve him, though. He finger-combed her hair away from her temple. "I intended to honor my word to you."

"You did honor your word. You promised that whatever happened between us would be up to me, and as you'll recall, I walked in here of my own free will."

There was a hint of annoyance in her voice and he smiled. "You took off your clothes of your own free will, too. I particularly liked that part."

She let out a soft snicker. "You should have seen your face. You looked like a cartoon character after being hit by a frying pan."

"Are you laughing at me?" He reached down to pinch her curvy little butt.

She yelped. "Yes." Then laughed as he pinched her again. "Ouch! That hurts."

Without feeling an ounce of contrition, he rubbed at the spot, reveling not only in the satiny sensation of her skin, but in the relaxing, intimate laughter. Had he ever before found this combination of humor and sex? Before Lauren, he wasn't even sure he remembered the last time he'd laughed with anyone about anything.

At the thought, the guilt-knife stabbed again. Deep. She'd given him herself, laughter, this unfamiliar sense of contentment, while he'd been pretending to be her fiancé.

"Still, Lauren, I can't help but think this shouldn't

have happened. You aren't sure about the engagement, and—"

Her warm fingers pressed against his mouth. "Let me tell you something, okay? Something important."

He nodded, and she drew her hand away from his lips.

"When I was a little girl, I remember asking my mother how I would know the man I should marry."

"And she said…"

"She said I shouldn't worry about it. That she and Daddy would know and then tell me when they found him."

Luke had a sudden flash of insight. "For some reason I'm thinking that Mom and Dad weren't the ones to single out the surfer, the mechanic or even Jacques Cousteau."

"Jean-Paul," she corrected, then sighed. "But yes, you're right. You're my first family-picked fiancé, and you'd also be right if you guessed that I'm not entirely comfortable with the idea, either."

"So…"

She shifted to stack her hands on his chest. Resting her chin on them, she gazed straight into his eyes. Her pale hair frothed wildly around her face, the fire lending it the colors of sunrise and sunset.

"So I'd like to take the engagement off the table for the moment, okay? Instead, can we just be two people enjoying each other's company and nothing more? Can we do that?"

"Yeah," he said slowly, aware he couldn't have asked for anything more, though he likely deserved so very much less. "We can do that."

"Good."

He couldn't help but smile at the new, carefree sound of her voice. He couldn't help but feel carefree himself—once again, so unfamiliar but so damn wonderful. With a twist, Luke took her under him again. "So why don't you let me start enjoying you again, Goldilocks, right this minute."

Seven

Lauren left her lover sleeping in the rumpled covers of his bed. She tiptoed back to her own room, showered, then dressed and tiptoed again, this time heading downstairs to make coffee as quietly as she could. Something told her that Matthias didn't often let himself sleep late and she wanted to give him the opportunity.

Even as she worried about wanting to give him too much.

As she measured out grounds and water, she noted the new look of her bare left hand. Before taking her shower, she'd removed her engagement ring and she intended to keep it off. Last night, once he'd started making guilty noises about breaking his promise to her, she'd needed to say something to get him off that track. But once she'd made her proposition—that their engagement was now off the table—it actually had made sense to her, as well. As right as things were still feeling between them—last night neither that nor lust had been burned out—it was way better to proceed with caution.

She wasn't going to think of Matthias and marriage in the same sentence for the rest of her stay.

As she poured herself a cup of coffee, from her purse sitting on the corner of the counter came the sound of her cell phone ringing. Upon flipping open the phone, she grinned at the tiny screen, then held the piece of equipment to her ear. "What's up, Katy can-do?"

Her little sister got right to the point. "Connie called. You're not in San Francisco. Is everything okay?"

"Oh." Lauren made a little face at the mention of her former college roommate. Though she'd been hazy about her arrival time at her best friend's condo, she should have called to say she was postponing the visit. "I'll phone and tell her I'm staying here in Tahoe for a while."

"With Matthias?"

Lauren hesitated. "Promise you won't say anything to Mom and Dad."

The Mensa-moppet let out a deep groan. "Nooooo. That doesn't sound good. You said you were going there to break things off with him."

"I know." Lauren worried her bottom lip. "Look, Katy, you've been very eager for me to end this. Do you think...do you really think he's a bad guy?"

God, she sounded like *she* was in junior high, but who else could she speak to about him? Her parents were prejudiced, obviously, and Connie hadn't met the man. And to be fair, aside from her fixation on Justin Timberlake, her little sister happened to be a good judge of character.

"I never said he's a bad guy," Kaitlyn said with a little giggle. "I think he's funny. Have you ever watched him trying to work his BlackBerry?"

Lauren frowned. As a matter of fact, she'd seen him take a call on it when they were walking beside the lake the day before. She didn't remember anything remarkable. "I don't get it."

Her sister giggled again. "It was ringing one time when he was over at our house and he didn't know what to do. He had the most befuddled expression on his face and his fingers kept punching buttons until he'd set the alarm so it was both buzzing and ringing at the same time. I thought he was going to throw it into the deep end of the pool until I grabbed it away."

"Well you must have been a good teacher, because he doesn't appear to have any trouble with it now."

"Really? He didn't seem like a very good pupil and he told me he relies on his assistant to work all things technical."

Though that wasn't consistent with what Lauren had observed herself, she shrugged it away and pressed her sister again. "But despite that, you truly like him?" she asked.

"As a husband for you?"

"No, no, no." Remember? She wasn't supposed to be thinking of Matthias and marriage in the same sentence. "Just as a…as a person."

"I told you what I think. Yes, I like him. But wait a

minute." Kaitlyn's voice lowered. "Lauren, are you having sex with him?"

"What?" Her voice rose and she tried to soften it as she strode out of the kitchen and farther away from the man sleeping upstairs. "That is none of your business."

"Why?"

Lauren shot a glance up the stairs to the second floor and scurried down the other set of steps that led to the lower level. In the wine cellar, she closed the door and leaned her shoulders against it. "Why what?"

"Why won't you tell me if you're having sex with Matthias?"

Her fingers pinched the bridge of her nose. "Hasn't Mom taught you not to ask questions of that kind?"

"Yes, but after your stay in Paris, I thought you might have lost some of your American puritanism."

Lauren closed her eyes. "It is not puritanical to refuse to discuss sex with one's thirteen-year-old little sister."

"Then how am I supposed to learn anything about it?"

"Like the rest of us," Lauren retorted. "When you're much, much older."

"Puritan," Katy muttered under her breath.

Lauren pinched the bridge of her nose again. Not that she was going to discuss this with her sister, but last night pretty much proved she was not, in any way, shape or form, a puritan. Sex with Matthias had been pretty spectacular, if she did say so herself, and her heart gave a little jump-skip thinking about indulging in those kind of fireworks for a lifetime. Imagine—

No. She wasn't supposed to be thinking of lifetimes with him.

"So does this mean I'm going to have to wear one of those grody junior bridesmaid dresses after all? Mom found this one that I could *maybe* live with. It's pale blue with a darker blue satin sash…"

Lauren's mind spun away. Kaitlyn would look so pretty in blue. She could see it now, her little sister in a tea-length dress. Lauren herself in something simple and white, with a low, scooped back that would look demure from the front but would give Matthias that same hit-by-a-frying-pan face when he—

With a silent groan, she pushed away from the door. She walked over to the table in the middle of the wine cellar, idly picking up a photo in order to replace in her mind that prohibited matrimonial image. It was the shot of the twins she'd studied last night and, in looking at those two identical faces, she was struck by a new resolve.

"I've got to go now, Katy," she said, already starting to sort the pictures into two piles. There was something she had to do.

The truth was, with or without the engagement ring, with or without her declaration that their wedding was off the table, there was no way she was going to be able to get the idea of marriage and the man upstairs separated in her mind. But she wasn't going to take the notion seriously yet, either. At least not until she understood more about the two so-similar men smiling at her from the stack of photographs in her hand.

* * *

From the angle of the sun in the room, Luke knew he'd slept past his usual 6 a.m. start. Turning his head, he inhaled Lauren's flowery scent on the empty pillow beside his and smiled. He didn't stretch, he didn't even move, he just lay against the soft sheets and let himself wallow in the unfamiliar combination of satiation and relaxation.

Contentment. Yeah, that's what it was called.

And he intended to hold on to it with both hands.

Luke closed his eyes and conjured up Hunter's laughing face and mischievous eyes. *Thanks*. Without his late friend's will, he wouldn't be here in this house.

With this woman.

Thinking of Lauren again got him up and out of bed and into the shower. Once dressed, he found himself whistling as he made his way downstairs.

He *whistled?* Who knew?

Grinning at his own surprise, he helped himself to coffee in the deserted kitchen and took a few moments to gaze out the window and into the verdant forest surrounding the house. He couldn't whistle and swallow coffee at the same time, but his lighthearted mood didn't die.

No wonder. A guilt-free night of great sex with a great woman.

Lauren had given him a free pass on the engagement issue, which in turn gave him freedom from the identity problem. *Can we just be two people enjoying each other's company and nothing more?* she'd asked. *Can we do that?*

Yeah, they could do that.

Luke topped off his mug and then went in search of the woman he very much enjoyed enjoying. But she wasn't in any of that level's living spaces and he knew she wasn't in any of the bedrooms. He wandered downstairs and didn't find her in the wine cellar or using the equipment in the home gym.

Worry took a small bite out of his good mood as he trotted back up the stairs. Pulling open the front door, he saw her car still sitting in the drive. All right, he thought, his disquiet abating.

She hadn't found him out. Surely if she'd discovered who he really was she would have either left him or left him for dead.

But Lauren was still here and he was still alive.

He was certain of that when he finally found her standing in the loft-level office space, her back to him. His heart gave a weird clunk in his chest as his gaze ran from the springy denseness of her blond curls to the heels of the suede boots on her feet. It took him only four silent strides to reach her, it took only a breath to set down his mug on the desk in front of her, it seemed only right to sweep away her hair and press his mouth against the scented skin at the back of her neck.

She gasped, then relaxed as his hands cupped her upper arms. When he lifted his mouth, she turned her head to smile at him over her shoulder. "Good morning."

He returned her sunny smile and caressed her with a stroke of his thumbs. "I woke up alone," he said, trying on a mock ferocious frown. "Maybe I should have tied you to the bed."

"Then who would have made the coffee?" she asked, nodding at the steaming mug he'd slid on the desk.

"There's that." He reached around her body for the hot beverage then held it to her lips as she turned to face him. "Want some?"

"Mmm." Her hands cupped his as she tilted it for a sip.

Luke found himself staring at the way her pretty lips parted and then at the glimpse of wet, pink tongue he saw between them. Her gaze jumped to his over the rim of the mug and he felt the tug on that thread of sexual tension that was, as usual, running between them.

It added a spicy little kick to the warm contentment still oozing through his veins. Maybe it was time they went back to bed. "Lauren. Sweetheart…" He smiled again and let her see the wicked intent in his eyes.

Her pupils flared and she edged back, knocking something off the desk. He bent to retrieve it, then froze as he glanced down at what was in his hand.

One of those college pictures. Matt and Luke, looking… His fingers tightened, crumpling the photo. Looking happy, the way he'd been feeling until two seconds ago.

"Why the hell do you have this up here?" he demanded, his voice harsh.

Lauren snatched the snapshot away from his brutal grip. "Look what you've done," she scolded, placing the photo facedown against her jean-covered thigh, trying to smooth it out from the back.

"You didn't answer the question."

She gestured behind her. "I thought I'd make a collage on the corkboard of some of the college photos. There are several in the hallway but I like these, too."

His gaze followed her gesture. The long desk sat

facing the wall and on that wall was a rectangle made of corkboard tiles already peppered with pushpins, convenient for holding a calendar, take-out menus, or a montage of pictures that were at least ten years old. And that were mostly of Luke and his brother.

Staring at them, he felt anger surge through his system, flushing away that whistle-inspiring happiness that had been inside him only minutes before.

Lauren touched the side of his face. "Don't look like that. I'm sorry if seeing them bothers you, but I thought…"

"You thought what?"

She linked her fingers with his. "I've told you about the bad exes. I thought maybe you could tell me about…about…"

He couldn't seem to wrench his gaze from yet another photo of him and his twin, this one freezing forever a moment with Matt balanced on Luke's shoulders, ready for some ridiculous dorm-wide chicken fight. They'd laughed their asses off…and together taken on all comers and won.

Lauren squeezed his hand. "Matthias?"

Luke started at the sound of his brother's name on her lips. He wanted to get away from those photos and from the damn memories. He wanted her to be in his arms and take all the old anger and frustration away. Drawing her closer against him, he slid his cheek down the side of her face. "What do you say we leave the past up here and find a more pleasant way to spend our present?"

Kissing her neck beneath her ear, he felt her shiver. As she pressed herself against him, the warmth of his previous mood returned, along with a quick spike of sexual heat when her mouth rose to kiss his.

"What happened between the two of you?" she said against his mouth.

Closing his eyes, he pushed her away from him and took a couple of steps back. "Don't."

"Matthias." Her voice was full of disappointment. "*Matthias*."

That other name jabbed at him like a sharpened stick. "Lauren—"

"Please, Matthias."

"All right, all right." He shoved both hands through his hair. "You're not going to leave it alone, are you? You're not going to leave *me* alone."

He crossed to the room's small sofa and dropped onto it. Maybe if he told her then they could go back to that quilt-covered bed and forget everything but each other. His fingers combed through his hair again.

"My father's will went like this…" he started, and then he told her about Samuel Sullivan Barton's last contest. About how whoever made a million dollars first inherited all the family holdings. About how Matt had won everything and left Luke with nothing.

"You mean you," Lauren said, her hand rubbing against his thigh. Somewhere during the telling, she had found her way beside him on the couch.

Shaking his head, he looked into her concerned, sympathetic face. "What did you say?"

"You said that you were left with nothing. But it was Luke who lost that last competition and you, Matthias, who won."

"Right." He nodded. "That's the way it was. Matt

won. Luke lost." Looking away from her face, his gaze found those damn photos again. Basketball. Chicken fights. There'd been a short time when the Barton brothers had been an unstoppable team.

To avoid the thought, he jumped to his feet. "Let's get out of here," he said, pulling her up. "We'll do anything you want. Lady's choice, I promise, as long as it involves the bathtub or the bed."

But she wasn't looking at him in a sexy or steamy way. There was a frown between her eyebrows and more questions on the tip of her tongue. To stymie them, he leaned down and kissed her, thrusting deep inside her mouth until she moaned and clung to his shoulders.

Yeah. That contentment was just around the corner.

But then she broke away from him and stepped back. "Matthias…"

Always damn Matt. "What?"

"There's one thing I don't understand. If you received all the family wealth thanks to the terms of your father's will, why are you and your brother still estranged?"

"What do you mean by that?"

"Once you took over the Barton holdings, didn't you offer your brother half?"

He stared at her. "That's not the way my father wanted it."

"So?" She crossed her arms over her chest. "Are you saying you *didn't* ask him to join you in running everything together?"

Damn it, why was she pressing him on this point! "Yes. Yes, I offered him half of everything. I offered him joint authority and…and he refused." Luke would never forget how angry he'd been at Matt that day. To think that his twin could act so generous by offering to share what he'd actually stolen from him!

"He refused?"

Damn right, Luke had refused. "Yes." He grabbed her hand and started drawing her toward the door. "How about I find us some soap bubbles?"

She dug in her heels. "The story still doesn't make sense. If you made the offer and he refused, why are the two of you still not on speaking terms? Surely you both realize that it was your father who put you into that competition and not each other?"

Luke dropped her hand and stalked to the window. He stared out through the trees at that beautiful blue lake, but no matter how stupendous the view, it couldn't make over the truth. "We don't speak because Luke thinks I cheated in order to become the winner. He...he believes I bribed a supplier to favor me instead of him."

There was a moment of stunned silence. "You wouldn't do such a thing!"

His head whipped toward her. "What makes you so sure?"

"It's obvious. Your father raised you brothers to win, and neither of you would be satisfied to achieve victory through some sort of dirty trick."

For a moment, a weird emotion churned inside Luke's belly. Doubt? *Neither of you would be satisfied to achieve victory through some sort of dirty trick.*

But she didn't know Matt as well as she thought. And she didn't know the details of the events that had occurred seven years before. Luke knew. Luke knew what his brother had done to him. Didn't he?

Neither of you would be satisfied to achieve victory through some sort of dirty trick.

The words looped through his head again. And then again.

Staring at Lauren's big, blue eyes and flushed-with-righteousness face, he couldn't forget how she'd leaped to the—correct—conclusion that Matt had offered up half his winnings. He couldn't forget how she'd instantly assumed Matt wasn't a cheater as well.

Luke couldn't help but remember that he was bamboozling her right now, by pretending to be the very man whom she was so eager to defend.

Images of the night before scattered like more snapshots in his mind. Lauren's eyes, wide and darkening, as she lifted her hand to daub the milk from his chest.

The look of her kiss-swollen mouth as she laughed when he demanded she decide between the bed and the breakfast bar.

Her perfect body, all pale curves, rosy nipples, blond curls as she let her nightgown drop to her feet.

Later, when she'd let him look his fill, taking in all the female enticement of her petaled sex between her splayed, satiny thighs. She'd blushed, but she'd opened to his gaze and opened to his body.

Luke's body, but she hadn't known that.

Maybe he should tell her. Explain. Reveal the whole ruse before it went any further. As Luke, he could woo her now. Win her this time as himself. Then there would be nothing to threaten the contentment he could find in her arms.

"Lauren…" He crossed the room to cup her cheek in the palm of his hand. She edged closer and nuzzled into his touch and her trust struck him like a blow. His voice lowered. "Sweet Lauren…"

At his hip, his BlackBerry buzzed. He grimaced at Lauren, who let go a little laugh.

"Is that a bumblebee," she said, making it obvious she could sense the vibration, "or would someone be happy to reach you?"

His hand was reluctant to let her go, but business instincts ran deep and when he checked the screen he knew he would have to take the call. "Excuse me," he said, stepping back. Then he brought the device to his ear and acknowledged his assistant. "Elaine? What do you need?"

"I've been talking to Ernst in Stuttgart."

The supplier Eagle Wireless had been in talks with. And if those talks were successful, they'd take Eagle a nest or two up in the world. If not… Muting the phone, he looked over at Lauren. "I'm going to take this call downstairs, okay? Will you excuse me for a few minutes?"

She shook her head. "You stay here. I'm going to the kitchen to see what I can do about breakfast."

"Did I mention I don't deserve you?"

On tiptoe, Lauren pressed her lips against the corner of his mouth. "Just what I like. A man with a debt to pay."

He watched her sashay out the door, then returned his attention to the phone call. "Elaine? What's up with Ernst?"

"He's chilly."

The European had never been a particularly cheerful sort. "Any idea why?"

"If I had to guess, I'd say he has a second suitor for those components we've been talking to him about."

His hand tightened on his BlackBerry. "Do you know who?"

"I have my guesses."

"Yeah," Luke said. "Me, too." Matt. Matt was in Germany. Luke had suspected it before and now it didn't take a huge leap to deduce that Matt was his rival in the deal with Ernst. Damn Matt.

Luke's eyes closed as tension tightened like a vise around his head. See? Lauren was wrong for leaping to his brother's defense. And though that was no surprise, it shocked the hell out of him how his brother's betrayal could still hurt. He didn't have to open his eyes to see those college photos once again. Remembering each one opened yet another old wound.

For a short time they'd been so close. Together with Matt, Luke had felt as if nothing could vanquish him. How he missed that.

Opening his eyes, he strode to his laptop, closed on one corner of the desk. Seating himself in the nearby leather chair, he rolled it under the desk at the same time that he pulled the computer toward him. "I'm going to book a flight to Germany."

"I thought you had to stay in the house."

Luke's fingers froze on the keys. "I'll think of something." He was going to have to say goodbye to Tahoe and goodbye to Lauren, too, but it couldn't be helped. "Business comes first."

"Unfortunately for both of us," Elaine said, "and I say 'both of us' because I know what kind of mood you'll be in when I tell you this and that my poor, tender ears will be forced to bear the brunt of your outrage and I'll have to go home to my loving family, deaf in my right ear and thus unable to fulfill my motherly and wifely duties because—"

"Spit it out." Luke braced, because Elaine was nearly as ambitious as he was, and if she said "unfortunate" then it truly was.

"Ernst is going to be incommunicado for the next week. He's attending a big family wedding in the north and will not be available to talk business or do business until he gets back."

Luke blew out a long breath. "Hell. A week?"

"A week."

A week for him to stew over how he was going to save the deal. A week for him to nurture his rage at his brother over the way he was trying to pull the rug out from under the feet of Eagle Wireless.

A week to be with Lauren.

As Matt, damn it. As Matt.

He wasn't going to renege on the revenge he was plotting on his brother, though. No way. Not now. If Matt wanted to be Luke's rival on the Ernst deal, then Luke would continue wooing Lauren just as he had been doing. In Matt's name.

She'd taken off her engagement ring, hadn't she? They were "just two people," not two engaged people any longer.

With that thought in mind, he could still be content with making her happy in bed while waiting for the even happier day when he could watch his brother's face as he learned Luke had had his fiancée first.

It wasn't so despicable, was it? He made her as satisfied in bed as she made him, he was sure of it.

And Lauren had said, after all, she liked a man with a debt to pay.

Luke had a hell of a disbursement to lay on Matt.

Eight

Days passed, and Lauren didn't manage to coax Matthias into talking about Luke again—and to be honest, she didn't try very hard, suspecting it would ruin what they'd found. Together, they'd created their own little world within the environs of the log-and-stone house and the tiny town of Hunter's Landing; she didn't want anything to pierce the bubble of what they'd made together. Anyway, they talked about nearly everything else. The places they'd traveled to, the places they wanted to travel to, the interesting characters they'd met in their lives.

Nothing occurred to change Lauren's opinion that Matthias was a workaholic who needed to learn to relax, though, and the forced vacation at Hunter's lodge was the perfect opportunity for him to take his pace down a notch or two or ten. While he complained about feeling lazy, they slept in every morning. And because he seemed to have never taken the time off in the last few years to see even the most popular movies, she managed to persuade him into slow, cozy afternoons and evenings in front of the plasma TV, making headway through the extensive DVD collection they'd discovered.

Shivering, laughing or tearing up at a Hollywood offering was all the sweeter from the warmth of her man's arms. He'd squeeze her tighter when she'd bury her face in his neck as the knife-wielding villain approached the unsuspecting hero. His eyes sparkled when a particular comedy tickled her funny bone. As he'd thumbed away her tears during the denouement of an excruciatingly tragic love story, her stomach had flipped at the expression of tenderness on his face.

"Sweetheart, it's just a movie," he'd said, wiping away yet another tear.

She'd sniffed. "Great love isn't 'just' anything."

Amusement had joined the affection in his gaze as he'd shaken his head. "I'll take your word for it, I guess, but I'm thinking the hero might feel better if he went back to work or at least went out for a couple of beers instead of moping around with his dead lover's moldy nightgowns."

"Back to work. Out for beers. Moldy nightgowns." She'd tried pushing him away, but he'd lifted her like a rag doll and placed her on top of his body so there was nothing for her to do but accept his kiss.

And wonder if she should worry that he didn't appear to believe in love.

Maybe he'd sensed her mood, because then he'd distracted her by issuing a challenge to yet another of their air-hockey rematches. They were quite the regulars at The Game Palace now. She liked the sense of fun the place was now giving Matthias and something of his competitive spirit had begun to rub off on her.

She was the current champion in the twelve-and-under age bracket. It was a feat she was embarrassingly proud of, even though she'd been allowed to compete against players less than half her age only because the younger contenders had stated with a pithy pity bordering on scorn that they would let her play against them because she was "only a girl."

Ha! Now the preteen set had reason to rue the day they'd said those words and she continued to take each and every opportunity she was offered to hone her skills in preparation for beating the big, bad champion of them all—Matthias.

Now, from across the air-hockey table in The Game Palace, he paused, mallet in hand. "I don't like that ruthless gleam in your eye. You used to play with this don't-hurt-me-because-I'm-cute look on your face. Now that's changed."

She wiggled her brows, then gave him her best gunslinger glare. "I don't have to settle for that namby-pamby passive-aggressive stuff any longer. I'm going to start doing things your way—straight up."

A funny expression crossed his face. "I take it you mean you're out to win?"

"Loser buys the lattes."

She was crowing thirty minutes later as they waited in line at Java & More. "I did it. I did it," she started, then paused. "You didn't let me win, did you? Promise you didn't let me win."

He shook his head. "I didn't let you win. Fair and square, you beat me, Goldilocks."

She bounced on her heels, thrilled at the idea. Maybe some would see it as a silly accomplishment, but there was a deeper meaning to it. There was. Her usual response to the kind of aggressive attitude Matt showed toward air hockey was to either find a less-than-straightforward way to fight or to back away altogether. This time, though, she'd held up her head and kept her gaze directly on the prize.

From the corner of her eye, she sent a sidelong glance at Matthias. It had helped that he'd seemed distracted during the game. Though she could admit that, too, it didn't change the fact that she'd learned something from the win. And from him.

Spinning his way, she put her hand on his arm. "Hey."

He looked down at her, his gaze quizzical. "Hey, what?"

"You're good for me."

His muscles went rigid under her hand. "Lauren—"

"What can I get you?" the person at the counter asked.

They both looked up, startled to find themselves at the head of the line. "A medium coffee for me," Matthias answered, "and for Lauren…"

"Lauren?" The man on the other side of the counter blinked, then his gaze switched from Matt to her. He had sun-bleached blond ringlets that hung raggedly to his shoulders and bright blue eyes in a walnut-tan face. "Is that you, Lauren Conover?"

As she looked, really looked at the barista, heat flooded her face and she felt a distinct, needle-like poke. Ouch, Lauren thought, wincing. Ouch and damn. Her happy little bubble had just been pricked.

Beside her, Matthias cleared his throat.

Okay, that was her cue. She should say something. Do something.

Make introductions? Haul off and slap the guy who was supposed to be making their coffees? Curl up and die due to sudden onset of old humiliation?

As the silence stretched longer, Matthias's left hand curled around the back of her neck. His right stretched across the counter. "Matthias Barton, Lauren's…fiancé."

The barista shuffled his feet even as he shook hands. "Uh, Trevor Clark, Lauren's…first fiancé."

The shame of rejection flamed through her again, as hot as it had on the day she'd discovered he'd left on their honeymoon trip without her. She'd been in her bedroom when his note arrived, trying on her grass skirt which rustled every time she moved like the sound of a rodent running through weeds. Knowing it was going to make her mother nuts, she'd been smiling at her reflection in the mirror as Kaitlyn came in to deliver the sheet of paper bearing Trevor's nearly indecipherable scrawl.

For a few moments Lauren had thought he was suggesting they streak at their wedding ceremony. After squinting and making allowances for spelling errors, it became clear he was breaking it off. She could still feel the texture of the paper against her fingers. She could still remember the gossipy whisper of her skirt's grass fronds as she'd dropped to her bed. The guest list had been small, but gifts had already arrived and she could still remember each burning tear spilled as she'd repackaged for return every ten-speed blender and every gleaming set of chef's knives.

Alone.

Unwanted.

Unloved.

Now Trevor turned away to get the drinks and, mortification still coursing through her, Lauren couldn't think what to do next. She tried pretending she wasn't in the shop. Would that work? Was it possible to make believe she and Matthias were back at the house on the couch, in their just-the-two-of-us little world and that this embarrassing encounter wasn't happening?

Except the other half of "just-the-two-of-us" was squeezing her neck and bending close to peer into her eyes. "Are you all right?" His voice was quiet. Kind. Concerned.

She wasn't all right. Not only was it more-than-awkward to come face-to-face with the first man to dump her, but…but… Though a few days ago she'd wanted Matthias to know all about her failed engagements to make it clear what a bad bet she was when it came to marriage, things had changed since then. Now she definitely didn't want fiancé number four contemplating for even two seconds why she hadn't been able to please even a shaggy-haired coffee counter-person.

The only halfway decent option was to get the two

of them out of Java & More and back to the bubble ASAP. When Trevor returned with the drinks, she made to snatch them out of his hands. Who would guess that he'd choose to hold on to them when he hadn't been inclined to keep her all those years ago?

The grim set to his mouth was as tenacious as his grip on the coffees. "Look. I really should explain…" Trevor started.

"No need." On her end, Lauren tugged on the drinks, hard enough to burp a froth of foam from the sippy hole on the plastic top of her latte. Maybe if she pulled harder it would spew enough hot coffee to force Trevor into letting go. Her fingers tightened.

Another set of hands took over the paper cups. A warm chest pressed against her back. "I've got them, Goldilocks," Matthias said. "Let go, baby."

Baby. He'd never called her that before. It sounded sexy. Like a name a man would use for a woman who pleased him in bed. It sounded intimate. Like the way a man would talk to the woman he wouldn't mind keeping around for the rest of his life. Some of her humiliation leached away as her fingers loosened and then her hands dropped to her sides. Matt remained a warm presence behind her.

"Now—Trevor, was it?" he said. "What did you have to say to my wife-to-be?"

At the question, Lauren wanted to duck away, or at least close her eyes and again try that pretend-she-wasn't-in-the-room technique, but with Matthias at her back, she had nowhere to go. Make-believe wasn't working, either. The only consolation she had was that

Trevor looked more miserable than she felt. His gaze flicked to Matthias, then back to her.

"Lauren, I—I've felt guilty about it for years." He pushed his corkscrew curls over his shoulders. "I shouldn't have run off on you like that. With such a lame note and—"

"And with those trip tickets that Lauren had paid for herself?" Matthias sounded so polite.

Still, Trevor's face flushed an unbecoming red against the streaky-blond of his hair. "I'll pay you back someday, I swear. I don't make all that much right now, but I did okay as a ski instructor last winter. Maybe if I get the kayaking job this summer."

As he continued talking, his promises sounded as lame as that note he'd left behind and Lauren didn't know how to respond. Once upon a time Trevor had been the love of her life, and now he just seemed sort of…

"Pathetic," Matthias remarked as they finally exited Java & More. "My God. If this is an example of the kind of man you wanted to marry I'm starting to wonder if all your previous choices were simply a way of rebelling against parents. You certainly weren't thinking with your head. What did you ever see in that goofy, overgrown Peter Pan?"

"I loved him!" Lauren heard herself snap back. "He…he was a free spirit."

"Freeloader, you mean. Did you catch on to the part where he's living with some girl whose daddy owns a local resort?"

"Yes." Her voice sounded glum.

There was a moment of tense silence, then he

wrapped his hand around her arm and swung her to face him. "Tell me you're not still in love with him."

In love with Trevor? Lauren stared off into the distance. Of course she'd been in love with Trevor once, but it was hard to exactly recapture the feeling. It was much easier to remember the grass skirt, the embarrassment of rejection and how relieved her parents had been that she wasn't marrying a man—a boy—with such a distinct lack of prospects and ambition.

Now she looked up at *this* fiancé, noting the expression of irritation on his face. Because he was mad at her first fiancé *for* her, she realized. He'd given Trevor the icy poke about cashing in on the honeymoon, even as he'd stood behind her, a warm and solid presence.

Warm and solid. That described Matthias to a *T*, except it didn't take into account hot and sexy. And sweet and fun, she added, remembering all the sweet kisses as they lay laughing together on the couch and all the sweet moments she'd spent watching his face relaxed, finally, in sleep.

All at once, that bubble they'd been living in—the one she'd thought seeing Trevor had popped—was back. It seemed to invade her chest now, though, filling her so full that her heart crowded toward her throat and her stomach was flattened like a pancake. But then she realized the bubble *was* her heart and it was growing, taking up every inch of space it could find inside of her, because…because love took up a lot of room.

Love.

Swallowing hard, she gazed, helpless, into the dark eyes of the man her parents had picked for her.

"Well?" he demanded.

She swallowed again. Was there a question on the table? "Well what?" It came out a squeaky whisper, her voice box compressed by that unstoppable emotion getting bigger inside of her.

"Do you still love Trevor?"

"No!" Not him. There wasn't room for any other man in her mind, body or heart but Matthias. Yes, there was no doubt she was in love with him. This man.

The one whose ring she'd removed from her finger.

During the past few days, Luke had become accustomed to Lauren's moods. He knew what made her laugh and what made her sigh. He knew what she wanted when their eyes would suddenly meet across a table, a room, the mattress of the bed they'd been sharing.

He liked her moods. Her playfulness amused and distracted him during this period of forced inactivity. When he started stewing over his brother's machinations or when he experienced a resurgence of guilt over playing Matt, they faded away under his new preoccupation with the expressive curve of her lips or the wink of the dimple in her left cheek when she laughed. He found her sentimental side to be excessively girlie, sure, but a romantic movie could make her melt in his arms and who could find fault in that?

She'd become a damn good air-hockey player. Which would have been only a more amusing distraction if she hadn't spooked the hell out of him after their latest match by saying, *You're good for me.*

Good God. *You're good for me,* she'd declared.

He knew that wasn't true.

Luke wasn't any better for her than that loser Trevor who'd left her at the altar.

But she didn't know that, though he couldn't figure out another reason why she'd so suddenly be giving him the silent treatment. All the way back to the house from Java & More, she'd been like a ghost beside him in the passenger seat. Ghost wasn't one of Lauren's regular moods.

He unlocked the front door and she drifted in ahead of him, still surrounded by that unusual quiet.

Why?

She'd claimed to no longer be in love with Trevor, but…

"Lauren." His voice sounded harsh to his own ears.

"Hmm?" She kept drifting ahead of him.

It made him nuts; just as he thought he understood her, now he couldn't read what was going on inside her blond head. And his frustration with that only made him more nuts.

When it came to relationships, he never looked deep. He never cared too much.

Yet now he couldn't help thinking about which wheels were turning in Lauren's mind.

Yet now he couldn't help worrying about how this was all going to end up.

Yet now he couldn't help wondering why the hell he'd gotten himself into such a predicament.

She turned her head to look at him through her incredible lake-blue eyes. Her blond curls floated back and he thought, suddenly, of that fantasy woman he'd dreamed up on his first day in Hunter's house. He'd gotten all the outside specifications right, but he hadn't realized how much there could be on the inside. Warmth. Humor. That refreshing honesty that was like a deep breath of air he never could seem to take.

His hand rubbed against the center of his chest.

She frowned. "Did you need something?" she asked.

"No." He couldn't say it fast enough.

"Okay. I'm going to take a bath." She headed for the stairs without another look.

Which was good, he told himself. Without her around, he could let go of the worrying and the wondering. The examining and the analyzing. Maybe he'd turn on the TV. Find ESPN. An old Western. Lauren always turned up her cute nose to those.

He could lose himself in the tube and turn off this uncharacteristic bend to his mind.

Throwing himself on the couch seemed to help. He stretched out and reached for the remote. Any moment now, he'd be thinking of nothing at all as he surfed endless waves of brain-fogging television.

Good. A rerun of the game show, *Jeopardy!*.

Bad. The first category: "Sexy Blondes."

What was his sexy blond thinking right now?

Why had she been so quiet?

Clicking off the TV, he popped up from the couch. There had to be some way of redirecting his brain from focusing on her. From focusing on *anything*. Luke Barton only gave this kind of single-minded attention to work.

Never to women.

At one end of the dining-room table, they'd dumped out the contents of box holding a thousand-piece jigsaw puzzle. Now, he fiddled with the loose pieces and started sorting all those with straight edges.

Lauren, most likely, would make fun of this orderly method. She'd want to do it the wild way, he guessed, by blindly choosing one cardboard bit and then scrambling through the 999 other choices to find it a partner.

She'd definitely want to do it the wild way.

Luke pressed the heels of his hands into his eyes, trying to dispel the images those words dealt in his mind. He didn't want to be thinking of her.

He didn't want to be thinking of what she was thinking.

Of what she was doing.

She was taking a bath, a voice inside recalled for him.

Hell. Reminded of that, how could he possibly have anything *but* her at the forefront of his mind?

And then he could think of only one logical way to shut down his busy brain.

He took the stairs two at a time.

The flowery scent of the steam curled from under the door in the master bath and yanked him forward as if a hand had grabbed him by the neck of his shirt. Beneath his fingers, the knob turned without a sound.

At the sight that greeted him on the other side of the door he got exactly what he wanted...a sight that knocked everything out of his head.

Lauren in nothing but gleaming skin and soap bubbles.

Her head whipped around to face him. Her forearm crossed over her breasts. The warm-temperature flush on her face deepened. "Is everything all right?"

"No." He stalked closer. "I need..."

Her eyebrows drew together. "What?"

What was he talking about? Luke didn't need anything. Except mindlessness. Except sex, which would drive away all that he'd suffered today.

You're good for me.

Of course I'm not in love with Trevor.

If he knew the first wasn't true, how could he possibly believe the second?

"What do you need?" she asked, drawing back against the side of the tub as he came even closer.

His nostrils flared as he took in another breath of the scented water. He could almost taste her skin on his tongue.

He *had* to taste her skin on his tongue.

His fingers snagged the nearby towel, and he stretched it between his two hands. "Hop out now."

Her gaze jumped to his and *phttt,* a match struck and lit that ever-ready fuse between them. He saw Lauren swallow hard, but he didn't retreat at that sign of nerves. It was too important that they get body-to-body right now so that he could turn off his mind.

You're good for me.

Of course I'm not in love with Trevor.

One of her hands gripped the side of the tub and she pushed herself to her feet. Rivulets of water ran down her sides. Clusters of bubbles the size of cotton balls dotted her pink, naked skin.

Luke watched, fascinated, as one group skated down her belly to pause in the wet curls of her sex. She was blond and pink there, too, and so tantalizing that hunger gnawed at him. He had to have her.

As if he was pulling her on a string, she lifted one leg and stepped out of the tub, giving him a quick glimpse of the heaven between her legs before she was hidden behind the huge bath towel.

He wrapped his arms around her, encasing her in terry cloth. She looked up at him, a faint frown on her face. "I wanted some time alone to think."

"Oh, baby, bad idea."

"You wouldn't go away if I asked you to?"

He inhaled her sweet, sweet scent. "Are you asking me to?"

The answer was in her eyes, in the flare of the flame rising between them as that fuse continued to burn. Wrapped in the towel, she was easy to pick up and carry toward the bed.

She was easy to unwrap there, too, the damp ends of her hair making dark trails against the pale pillowcase. He stared down at all her bath-flushed skin and her scent rose around him as if he was rolling in a rain-dampened, flower-strewn field. It filled his head so that he was thinking only of Lauren, of her luscious skin, of the heat that he could feel radiating from her flesh as he crawled between her legs.

"You're still dressed," she whispered.

"You're not." He licked across her belly button.

Her stomach muscles jittered and he saw her pupils start to dilate. "I think—"

"Don't," he admonished, sipping a stray drop of water that was poised on one of her ribs. "Don't think."

No thinking. This was time for touching, caressing, tasting. This was time for easy, breezy sex.

His palms found her breasts. Her tight nipples poked against them as his mouth opened on the side of her neck. She made a little sound—protest and plea both at once—and he knew exactly how she felt. He sensed everything she was feeling through her shivers and her moans. Through the way her body twisted toward his mouth and twisted into his touch.

He sensed every unspoken word.

Her hips were lifting against his as the silent words clamored in his ears. She was rubbing against his jeans, probably abrading that delicate skin just inside her hipbones and, to spare her hurt, he lifted away despite another sweet yet muffled sound of desire. He calmed her by kissing down her belly and, yes, finding the redness where denim had scraped her delicate skin. With his tongue, he took a moment to soothe the marks and then drew lower, found her center, opened wide her satiny thighs.

She was blushing here, too, all pink and swollen and so inviting that his heart slammed against his chest, knocking loudly to make sure that Luke knew it was time to open this door.

He had to have her here, too.

She gasped at the first touch of his tongue. Her fingers twisted in his hair, but he could hardly feel it, overwhelmed as he was by the sweet, creamy taste of her in his mouth. Heat poured off her skin as he held her open to his feast and his mind spun away as her tension twisted higher. He could feel it through his hands, hear it in her breathless pleas, urge it on with the insistent *bam-bam-bam* rhythm of his heart.

He gave himself up to serving her desire, let it take control of him so that nothing else could intrude. There were no bothersome thoughts, no nagging worries, nothing but Lauren, her skin, her passion, the sound of her crying out in orgasm as his tongue stroked her to paradise.

Still shaking with the aftereffects, she pulled him up to her, her hands insistent now as she yanked at his shirt and pulled at the buttons of his fly. He shoved aside what was necessary, fumbled with a condom, then slid inside all her soft, clutching heat. His eyes closed and he threw back his head at the exquisite goodness of it.

As he began to move, again there were no thoughts, no recriminations, no wondering about feelings or future. Yes. Yes. There was only this sensation. The sensation of Lauren in his arms. Being in Lauren. A puzzle piece and its partner.

When he didn't think he'd survive the flaming pleasure of her body a second longer, she tilted her hips and took him even deeper. Made him helpless to the rocking rhythm they'd begun. Then, with one sharp jolt of bliss, pleasure sank like fangs and dragged him under.

He hoped he'd drown in her.

Somehow though, minutes later, he discovered he'd survived. Lauren was cuddled against his chest, her body as boneless as his seemed to be.

One of her fingers could still move, however, and she was using the tip to draw idle yet intricate patterns on his chest. A maze, he decided, and he let himself get lost in it, his brain still unengaged, just as he'd intended.

"Why did Hunter do it?" Lauren asked, her breath tickling the sensitive flesh at his collarbone.

Luke rubbed his chin against the top of her head. "Hmm?"

"Why did Hunter set up these month-long visits for the Samurai?"

Luke didn't plan his answer ahead of time. He still wasn't thinking. He still didn't want to think. "Because we're now in our thirties? Maybe he figured we'd need something at this time in our lives."

She stacked her hands on top of his beating heart and studied his face. "Well? *Did* you need something?"

"Yeah," he heard himself answer. "I needed you."

And those weren't thinking words. They were just the truth.

Hell.

Nine

It was dawn and Luke couldn't sleep. It was just like the old days—the days before he'd come to Lake Tahoe, when he was constantly revved. Then, he'd always been energized about his work, about making a buck, about proving himself to be a success without needing anyone or anything to back him up.

Now, and all during the night, his mind had flitted between two separate subjects, first picking up one, then the other, figuratively fingering each like pieces of that jigsaw puzzle. His brother, Matt. His lover, Lauren.

Leaving the second focus of his thoughts asleep in bed, he retrieved the box of college photos from the wine cellar and carted them into the kitchen. With the overhead light switched on and the coffee starting to drip, he took a breath and flipped open the cardboard flaps.

His own face stared back up at him. Times two. Lauren had dismantled her collage on the corkboard after he'd told her about the situation between himself and his twin. The photos of Matt and Luke were on top of all the others.

He drew a fistful out and fanned them on the table like a large hand of cards.

When partnered with Matt, he'd always come up a winner.

That's what he saw in the images caught on Hunter's film. Twins, identical enough that he couldn't pick himself out in most of the shots. Each face smiling, triumphant in good health, good spirits, in…brotherhood.

Had it been Hunter's magic that had brought them together during those years? Or a genuine feeling of kinship?

If it had been authentic, how could their father's will have destroyed it?

But the stipulation in their father's will hadn't destroyed it. Matt had. Matt had double-crossed Luke in order to make that first million.

Your father raised you brothers to win, and neither of you would be satisfied to achieve victory through some sort of dirty trick.

Lauren's words. Lauren.

Now he stared at the photos on the table, unseeing, his thoughts shifting to the woman sleeping upstairs in his bed. Without the request in Hunter's will, he wouldn't have taken a weekend, let alone a month, away from work. Yes, he dated when someone striking passed through his world, and he could find willing bed partners when that urge struck as well, but he'd never taken the time to really get familiar with a woman.

To know her favorite kind of movie. How she liked her morning coffee and how that was different than how she liked her evening coffee. The silly grin she wore when she caught him staring at her.

He'd never before found himself interested in the how and the why a woman wound up with three former fiancés and zero wedding bands.

He sat back in his chair, his mind turning things again, trying to understand how the pieces fit. Lauren. Matt.

Matt. Lauren.

A knock on the kitchen door jerked him from his reverie. He looked up from the photos and out the mullioned windows of the Dutch door. His reflection peered back at him.

Startled, Luke jumped, then his surprise ebbed away as the door handle turned and he realized it was Matt, not his own ghost, who was walking into the kitchen.

"Bro," his brother said. "Long time no see."

Luke shot to his feet and leaned against the table, using the shield of his body to hide the old photos from his twin. The last thing he needed was Matt supposing he was sentimental. When it came to his brother, he wasn't going to be stupid enough to reveal any weakness like that. "What the hell are you doing here?"

His twin sauntered over to the counter where he helped himself to a mug of coffee. "I thought I'd check in. See if you needed anything." His gaze circled the room, brushing along the granite countertops and the gleaming stainless-steel appliances. "Hunter did it up right, if the outside of the place and the inside of this kitchen are anything to judge by."

Luke crossed his arms over his chest. "You'll be comfortable enough when it's your month. Now go away until then."

Matt leaned against the counter, mimicking Luke's pose against the table. His head tilted. "You're looking fine, too. Rested."

"There's not much to do here but rest."

"It's more than that," Matt said. "I can't quite put my finger on it, but…"

"But I suppose your assessment of my appearance can be excused from your usual razor-sharpness due to the fact that we haven't seen each other in—how long?"

"Well, we did run into each other last year in that parking garage by the opera house. We both had tickets to…"

"Wagner," they said as one.

"God spare me," came out in tandem as well.

And then they were grinning at each other.

Their smiles clicked off at the same moment, too, as if simultaneously recalling their long-standing enmity.

Matt looked away. "Your date was stunning," he offered.

"Yours, too," Luke replied. "The woman I was with—"

He halted, as he suddenly thought of the woman he was with right now. The woman upstairs, sleeping like an angel in his bed.

Matt's fiancée, Lauren.

Matt and Lauren, two pieces of a puzzle that he definitely didn't want to link up today.

Setting his jaw, he pushed away from the table and headed for the kitchen door. "While it's been so much fun catching up," he said, "now it's time for you to go."

But his brother's gaze had caught on the photographs that Luke had been concealing. His mug firmly in hand, Matt walked toward the table instead of to the door that Luke was pointedly pulling open.

His brother lifted one of the snapshots off the table to study it. "Where'd all that go?" he murmured, turning the photo Luke's way. "You and me laughing together?"

"It went to hell, exactly where I'm wishing you right now," Luke answered, narrowing his eyes at the man who had promised to marry *his* Lauren. He couldn't get it out of his head, the image of her walking down the aisle and into the arms of the one man who always snatched away what Luke wanted. Their father's approval. The family wealth. The woman sleeping upstairs. "Time to leave, Matt."

"Lunkhead, for the last time, I didn't do a single damn thing to you, all right? I know you believe I somehow messed with your chances to win the Barton holdings, but I didn't. And it was *you* who refused your half later."

Luke didn't have time to get into this. There was a tick-tick-tick clicking away in the back of his brain, reminding him that any second Lauren could awaken, smell the coffee and head downstairs to find some…and him.

Two of him.

"Get out, Matt."

His brother appeared to grow roots that sunk into the slick surface of the kitchen floor. "Not until we get to the bottom of this. I'm damn sick of your false accusations and your bitter recriminations hanging over my head."

Anger tightened Luke's chest. False? Bitter? How could his brother dismiss his grievances like that? Still, it wasn't the time—there wasn't time—to hash it out with Matt. His fingers curled into fists and he jerked his head toward the open doorway. "I'm asking you to go."

Matt was shaking his head as a female voice floated down the stairs. "I woke up to an empty bed. Is my favorite man in all the world already up and making my favorite beverage in all the universe?"

Oh, God. Every muscle in Luke's body cramped to charley-horse tightness. *No. Not now.*

He remembered wanting to watch his brother's face when Matt realized Luke had Lauren first. He remembered rationalizing how fitting that would be, how it wouldn't be hurting anyone, not really, except the bastard who had delivered Luke that body blow by cheating him all those years ago.

But he'd never imagined the look on Lauren's face when she found out what he'd done. And he didn't want to see it now. Not until he figured out a way he could explain it to her that made sense—and made him look less like the villain he was suddenly feeling himself to be.

Frozen by his own body and seconds away from disaster, a desperate Luke sent an unspoken message to his twin. It had worked in the old days. The good old days, when they were a team. Real brothers. Maybe it would work now, as long as Matt hadn't recognized Lauren's voice.

Please God Matt hadn't recognized Lauren's voice. *Do what I ask, bro,* Luke silently urged his brother. He managed to jerk his head once more toward the door. *Please.*

Apparently Matt didn't realize who the woman in the house was—and apparently he still had some decency left. It surprised the hell out of Luke, but with a quick nod, his brother set down his mug then strode toward the door.

Luke released the breath he was holding as his twin, with a two-fingered salute, stepped over the threshold.

All right. Crisis averted.

Then Lauren's voice sounded again. Louder. Closer. "Matthias? Are you in the kitchen?"

Luke's brother stilled.

In a slow move, he turned around just as Lauren entered the room.

She stopped up short, her gaze jumping between their two faces. If she sensed the catastrophe in the offing, her expression didn't immediately show it. Instead, her hands tightened the sash of her robe, then she moved forward, her hand stretching for Matt's.

"Good morning," she said, her voice and smile warm.

Yeah, Luke thought, his body still in that frozen state. The looming catastrophe had yet to chill her air.

"It seems you've caught us," Lauren finished.

Oh, hell. She didn't have a clue.

Matt's hand stayed at his side and he just stared at her for a long, tense moment, taking in her short robe and the glimpse of thin nightgown underneath. Then his gaze shifted to Luke, wearing nothing but his pajama bottoms.

Finally, Matt laughed, a mirthless sound sharp enough to cut glass. "I guess I did catch you, didn't I? How long has this been going on? You and my brother, behind my back, f—"

"*No.*" Before that ugliness could make it into the room, Luke's paralysis evaporated and he surged forward to slug his twin in the face. At the blow, his brother reeled back, Lauren shrieked, and the red tide rising in Luke's vision threatened to swamp him. He caught Matt by the shirt before he hit his head on the upper cabinets.

"Don't say that word," he snapped out, holding his brother steady. "That word is not what Lauren and I are about."

Matt's left eye was already swelling, though it didn't hinder its ferocious glitter. "That's not the way I see it," he said. "If there really is a 'Lauren and you,' then I've been royally—"

"Leave Lauren out of this," Luke broke in again, his voice harsh. "She didn't—she doesn't know it was me."

"What…what do you mean?" Lauren's voice. Lauren.

Luke watched his fists tighten on his brother's shirt. He couldn't turn his head and look at her. He couldn't speak another word.

"Damn it, lunkhead," Matt said, stepping back so he broke free of Luke's grasp. "What the hell have you done?"

What the hell *had* he done? It hit Luke, it hit him one brick at a time. Pretending to be his brother. For days and days. Making love to Lauren while she thought he was Matt. Time and time again.

Even with the engagement off the table, even when she'd said "can't we just be two people," it was still the most underhanded, ugly thing Luke had ever done in his life.

A something that, now, in the cold light of this morning, couldn't be excused, no matter what underhanded and ugly thing Matt had done or was trying to do to Luke's business.

Yes, Luke was the villain here. That destructive wolf he'd once imagined himself to be.

Swallowing hard, he forced himself to swing around, his gaze finding Goldilocks, her face pale and her blue eyes shadowed by growing suspicion.

"Lunkhead?" she echoed. "You—you said I didn't know it was you. What didn't I know? What's going on?"

And he had to put the pieces of the puzzle together for her—there were really three pieces, he realized now—as much as he wished they didn't fit. Three pieces: Matt, Lauren and himself.

"I'm Luke," he confessed. "I got a call, Matt wanted me take his month and, then…"

Lauren's hand rose to her throat. "He wanted you to take his fiancée, too?"

"Keep me out of this," Matt said, as he turned to pull a bag of frozen peas from the freezer. He winced as he placed it over his eye. "I was as much in the dark about my twin's little deception as you."

Lauren glanced over at Matt, then returned her gaze to Luke, horror overtaking the confusion on her face. "You…you were…"

A dozen excuses came to mind. Phrases that might, somehow, save the situation. Explanations that might, with luck or with charm or with both, absolve him. But his mouth refused to utter them. His lips would only form three words. "I was wrong."

They were the same three that sent her flying away from him.

In the master bedroom, Lauren worked at erasing her presence from Hunter's house. Maybe, just maybe, if she made it as if she'd never been here, then the past days would be like a dream—a nightmare—that she could wake from.

It didn't mean the monster wouldn't find her one last time, however. Though she'd hoped Matthias—no, *Luke*—would stay well clear of her after what he'd confessed in the kitchen, when she felt a little tingle at the base of her spine, she looked over to find the man who'd tricked her leaning against the doorjamb. Wrenching her gaze away from him, she continued stripping the sheets from the mattress.

"What are you doing?" he asked quietly.

With the bathroom towels in a pile on the floor and the pillowcases already on top of them, she thought he could figure it out. "Don't worry, I'll remake the bed," she said.

The tension in the room leaped higher and when she glanced over at him, she saw the new hard-set to his jaw. "Lauren…" he started, but then gusted out a sigh and stalked off.

She released her breath and rubbed her damp palms on her jeans. Maintaining her dignity while in his proximity was paramount—though next to impossible.

However, she wasn't going to leave until she completed this cathartic little process.

Or stall tactic. Maybe that's what it was. Because though she knew that Luke had betrayed her, it hadn't sunk in quite yet. At the moment she was almost numb…and she liked it that way.

The bottom sheet joined the pile of dirty linens. Then she turned toward the hallway to find clean ones but instead found him barring her exit from the bedroom, his arms full of what she was after.

"I'll take those," she said, sweeping them away.

Her gaze avoided his naked chest, even as the back of her hands tingled from where they'd rubbed against his. Without a word, he disappeared into the walk-in closet, but he was back too soon, now dressed in jeans and a T-shirt.

The Game Palace, it read. Where Guys Go To Get Game.

He'd played her, all right.

The thought jabbed through her anesthetized emotions and made a direct hit at her heart. Ducking her head, she reached deep for calm as she smoothed the bottom sheet along the mattress. It stretched away from her hands and she looked over to see Matthias— *Luke*—pulling it up to reach the opposite corner.

"I can do it myself," she hissed, then felt herself flush, embarrassed at the slip in her composure. *Find the numbness again,* she told herself. *Let him think it meant nothing to you. Let him think you don't care that you went to bed with the wrong man.*

Then how come it had felt so right?

She bit down hard on her bottom lip as she continued making up the bed. What was the big surprise that she'd messed up again? She'd been wrong three times before. The fourth should have been a given. It *had* been a given! She'd come here to Lake Tahoe to break it off, then she'd met Luke and he'd messed up her plans.

Her hands shook as she picked up a pillow. Then she found herself staring at him, across the width of the bed where they'd slept together so many nights. "Why did you do it?"

He shrugged, staring down at the fresh sheet before he looked up to meet her gaze again. "I told you once. I was tired of my brother having everything I want."

He hadn't wanted *her,* though. Not really. He'd merely wanted something of his brother's. She could see that now. "Were you laughing at me?"

His eyes closed. "No. Never." Then they opened, a faint smile trying to quirk the corners of his mouth. "Okay, sometimes, when you cried at those tragic movies."

"That's not funny, Matthias." She groaned at her own mistake, even as she felt hot tears sting the corner of her eyes. "Luke. *Luke.*"

She sank to the edge of the bed and rubbed her forehead with her hand. "Funny, in my mind I started thinking of you as the bad twin. I guess I was right."

"I guess you were," he agreed. "Because I can see now that my reasons—"

"You actually think you have an explanation for this?" Flabbergasted, she stared at him, then wiggled her fingers in a little go-ahead gesture. "I can't *wait* to hear it."

He scraped his hand over his face. "I told you about what happened with our father's will, how Matt cheated a supplier to make his million first."

"That's what you say happened."

"It's happening again now. I've been in talks with a company in Germany over the last few months, putting together something that's make-or-break for my company, Eagle Wireless. Everything seemed to be proceeding fine and dandy and when my brother asked me to do him the favor of taking his month at Hunter's house, I agreed. But then I found out the second day I was here that Matt was in Stuttgart, talking to my guy and trying to take over *my* deal."

And for a man like Luke who hated to lose... She knew all he didn't say, and it amazed her that he'd been able to hide his anger and frustration over the past few days. No wonder he'd found it so difficult to relax. Every minute with her here meant another minute jeopardizing the success of his company.

"But you have to see that this—" he continued, gesturing toward the half-made bed, "—you have to know that this was never something I did to hurt you."

"Well, you could never hurt me," she scoffed. She was numb, remember? Anesthetized. Thank God, because his brother's actions didn't excuse the way he'd used her. "I'm not hurt."

"The engagement—"

"I took that off the table, remember? *I* already broke up with *you*, if you'll recall. I'm not wearing your ring, right?" Then she looked down at her bare hand and laughed. "Oh, but that was Matthias's ring."

It struck her as funny now. So funny that she heard

herself laughing again as she thought of breaking up with Luke who wasn't Matthias. Of going to bed with the wrong brother who had felt so right. Of taking off Matthias's ring so Luke wouldn't feel bad about breaking his promise to her.

Of how she felt about the fiancé who wasn't her fiancé after all. Still laughing, she dropped her face to her hands and gave up any pretense of dignity. It was all too funny for that.

"Lauren?" Luke hurried around the bed and sat down beside her. "Are you okay?"

Her cheeks were wet with tears. "Don't you find it hysterical?" she managed to get out.

"What?" He lifted his hand as if he was going to touch her face, but then it fell to his thigh. "What's making you cry?"

"I'm laughing," she corrected him. It continued to bubble inside of her and she had to hold her palm over her stomach to hold it down. "I'm laughing, because for the first time in my failed career as a fiancée, I fell in love with the man who put a ring on my finger, only to find out he was still the wrong man after all."

She wiped her cheeks with the back of her hands. "Just like everyone else, you never really cared about me."

Too late she heard all that she'd revealed to him.

Too late she realized all the dignity she'd lost.

Too late she recalled almost the very first words he'd ever said to her: *Never show me your weakness, I'll use it against you.*

Luke found his brother in the kitchen, making another pot of coffee. Well, not making the coffee exactly. He had the ingredients at hand but he was frowning at the coffeemaker. The coffeemaker that had been perfectly fine earlier that morning but now had a malfunctioning readout that was blinking an angry red like a malevolent animal.

He shouldered Matt aside. "Let someone with tech savvy take over."

"Kendall always makes the coffee."

"Who?"

Matt dropped into a chair at the kitchen table. "Kendall, my assistant. She brings it to me, too."

Luke rolled his eyes. His assistant, Elaine, would throw the stapler at his head if he asked her to make him a coffee. His brother's actually delivered beverages. "One in a million," he murmured.

A kabillion.

His gut churned with bile. *A kabillion.* He remembered Lauren saying that, saying it was what they could make on their bottled sexual chemistry. Closing his eyes, he gripped the countertop and hung his head, waiting for the nausea to pass.

"So, where's my fiancée?" Matt asked, his voice casual.

His head whipped toward his brother. "She took off your ring."

Matt stretched his legs out in front of him. "When she thought you were me. I can understand that."

"Damn it, she came here to break off the engagement!"

Matt stifled a yawn behind his hand. "You didn't answer the question. Where's my fiancée?"

"She left, all right? She left—"

"You. She left you."

Luke was standing by the counter and the coffee-maker one minute. The next, he was jerking his brother out of his seat, holding him by fistfuls of his starched shirt. "She never wanted to marry you in the first place."

"What are you going to do about it, lunkhead? Give me another black eye? Is that the way you're solving your problems these days?"

Luke shoved Matt back in his chair. His brother's shiner was puffy and red and he didn't feel an ounce of guilt over it. "This is all your fault," he said. "Damn it, Matt, if you hadn't cheated me—"

"Aren't you sick of that song?" Matt rose from the chair, his voice tight. "I told you I didn't cheat you then, I told it to you earlier this morning, but I'm not going to tell you again. Damn it, I'm done with my part of this little tune."

He stalked toward the door, then paused for a long moment. With a tired shrug, he turned back around. "I came here to do the right thing. You took my place in the house as a favor. Do you need me to move in now so you can get back to work?"

I came here to do the right thing. Luke stared at his brother and then Lauren's voice sounded in his head— would he always hear her? *Neither of you would be satisfied to achieve victory through some sort of dirty trick.*

"Well?" Matt prompted. "Are you heading back to work?"

Work. Eagle Wireless. Luke ran his hand over his face. Back at the helm of his company, things would make sense again. There would be meetings, conference calls, engineers who need a butt kick in order to jump-start their latent skills in speaking non-tech English. Best of all, he could immediately board a plane for Stuttgart and do whatever it took to salvage his deal with Ernst.

With all that on his plate, he'd forget about his time here. He'd forget about Lauren. He'd forget about Matt's betrayal.

Neither of you would be satisfied to achieve victory through some sort of dirty trick.

His gaze lasered in on his brother. "Where've you been?"

"I told you when we spoke last week. Germany."

"Stuttgart? Ernst?"

His twin's good eye narrowed. "You know Ernst?"

Luke laughed. So much for brotherhood. "He's *my* guy, as if you didn't know."

A strange expression crossed Matt's face. "What?"

"You must know I've been working on him to make a deal with Eagle Wireless. So I'm guessing you have a spy in my company. Somebody else you're paying off to your advantage."

"I don't have anyone I'm paying off in your company," Matt retorted, but then his voice slowed. "That I know of."

Luke laughed again. But as that odd expression once more crossed his brother's face, he swallowed his scorn.

Neither of you would be satisfied to achieve victory through some sort of dirty trick.

Luke shoved his hand through his hair. "Look, I've been in contact with Ernst since last fall. When did you hear about him?"

"*Fall?* I've only been talking to Ernst this last month." Matt looked off, his jaw tightening just as Luke's did when he was angry. "Hell."

"Damn it, Matt," Luke said. "Tell me you didn't cheat me seven years ago."

His brother's one-eyed gaze jerked back to his face. "I've told you and told you."

"Just tell me again." Luke grabbed up a few of the photos spread on the table, his gut churning once more as he felt poised on the brink of something big. Something really, really big.

"Here in Hunter's house, swear on the brothers we used to be." He held out the evidence toward his twin.

Matt reached out for the photos, but he didn't look away from Luke's face. "I'd rather chew off my own arm than admit this, Luke, but what you said about Ernst means I have to investigate what's going on. Someone I've trusted may have conned us both out of quite a lot. Believe me, though, on the memory of our good friend Hunter Palmer, on the memory of the kind of brothers we used to be, I didn't knowingly cheat you. I swear."

In a decisive strike, those last two words blew a hole in Luke's defensive wall of bitter anger. Emotions long-dammed up released, pouring relief, sadness and a weird kind of elation into his bloodstream. His brother hadn't cheated him.

He had his brother back.

"Matt." Though he felt dizzy with the revelation, he could breathe easier, he found. After all these years, he could finally take a deep breath. "I believe you, Matt."

A faint smile turned up his brother's mouth. "Say 'I believe you, meathead.'"

Meathead and lunkhead. The names from their childhood when the enemy had been each other.

"He still wouldn't be sorry for what he did to us," Luke said.

Matt knew exactly who he was talking about. Exactly what he was talking about. "Dear old Dad and those destructive games he made us play."

"I hope we can get past him, and them, again." Luke looked at the photos his brother still held. "We did in college."

"You slept with my fiancée."

Lauren. Oh, God, Lauren.

With the emotional dam that had been inside of him now destroyed, there was no longer any protection against the guilt and remorse now coursing through him like a flood. He'd hurt Lauren.

Lauren, who was in love with him.

Lauren, who'd said, *Just like everyone else, you never really cared about me.*

But Luke did care about her. Luke cared a whole hell of a lot, and he couldn't let her go on with her life thinking he was yet another failed fiancé. Except that failed fiancé would be Matt, wouldn't it?

And that made him feel better, even as it struck him again what an arrogant, unfeeling bastard he'd been, using Lauren to get back at his brother.

I'm in love with you. She'd said that.

And he'd broken her heart.

But it would be all right, wouldn't it? Give her a

couple of days and she'd realize his sorry soul wasn't worth her smiles, her laughter, her touch, her heart.

Hell.

He couldn't live with that.

"You're staying here at the house," he told his brother, making a swift decision. "I have somewhere I've got to be."

"Some*one* you've got to *see?*" Matt asked, lifting the bag of frozen peas to his face again.

"You don't love her." As a twin, he knew he was speaking the truth.

"I don't love her," Matt admitted, removing the plastic to gaze at him with both eyes. "But I was talking about Ernst."

"Ernst?" Already Luke had forgotten about flying to Germany. He waved the man's name away. "It's Lauren I'm thinking about." Lauren, who he'd betrayed.

Matt shook his head and replaced the bag of peas. "What makes you think she's going to be happy to see you?"

Luke refused to be defeated by the idea. "I'll make it right with her," he told his brother. He had to. "No matter what. It's the Barton family motto, remember? Assume success, deny failure."

Matt shrugged. "All right. Maybe it'll be okay. Maybe you just need to get your foot in the door."

Luke's shoulders sagged. She wouldn't let him get his foot in the door, would she? By the time she drove home, he was certain she would have convinced herself she never wanted to see him again.

If Luke showed up she wouldn't let him get within twenty feet.

But what if…?

He looked at his brother. "There's something else you have to do for me," he said to Matt. "And I think you're going to like it."

Ten

Dinner hour, *casa* Conover. Lauren looked around the table at her little sister, her mother and then her father who had just seated himself after making them wait while he finished a phone call. Though she'd only been back in the family house a mere twenty-four hours, it was as if she'd never left.

"That bumbling Bilbray," her father muttered as their housekeeper, June, set his steaming plate of chicken Kiev in front of him. "It's as if he doesn't understand the law of supply and demand. Didn't he go to business school? Hasn't he been working for me for more than fifteen years? Do I have to teach him to tie his shoes as well as read a spreadsheet?"

Lauren turned to her sister, raising her voice over her father's continued annoyed ramblings. "What were you saying, Kaitlyn? That Mr. Beall wants to you to design the drama department's page on the school Web site?"

Without waiting for an answer, she swiveled toward her father. "Dad, did you hear that? Kaitlyn's drama teacher is going to be paying her real money for Web site design."

At the word *money* her father paused in his brainless Bilbray-litany and glanced in his younger daughter's direction. "We could use the extra cash now that Lauren's broken it off with Matthias Barton. Though maybe I can do something about that. Maybe I can give that young man a call and—"

"Dad," Lauren interrupted. "I don't want to marry Matthias Barton."

"He'll probably give you another chance, you know. He's as eager to be aligned with Conover Industries as we are eager to be aligned with him, and—"

"Dad, I'm not going to marry Matthias Barton."

Lauren's mother looked up from her chicken Kiev, a spark lighting in her eyes. "Ralph, do you really think you can persuade Matthias to reconsider Lauren? Despite her rash response to another of her Bad Ideas? I haven't had a chance to cancel the reservations for the reception yet—"

"What?" Lauren stared at her mother. "You didn't tell me you'd booked a venue for the reception. We hadn't even started talking about that yet."

Carole Conover waved her manicured fingers. "I've had my eye on this particular Napa winery for years. You could have the wedding there, too, if you'd like, though maybe Matthias would prefer a church service instead."

Lauren shook her head in disbelief. "By all means, let's consult Matthias," she muttered to herself.

Kaitlyn's voice piped up from across the table. "There *was* that pretty junior bridesmaid's dress. I could live with the blue one with the ribbon sash."

Lauren's gaze jumped toward her sister. *"Et tu?"*

Their mother beamed at Kaitlyn. "I think you're right. Definitely the blue one with the sash."

Lauren wanted to scream. She wanted to rent her clothes. She wanted to find a completely unsuitable groom and elope to Lithuania. Ha, she thought. *Maybe Trevor can be convinced to leave his ski-heiress for me. Then* her parents would be sorry.

Which was exactly why she'd agreed to marry Trevor the first time, she realized. And why she'd said yes to her father's mechanic. And why it had almost been oui with Jean-Paul on the top of the Eiffel Tower. Luke had suggested that to her, hadn't he? And now she saw it, too. All her previous fiancés had been perfect-perfect paragons of parental rebellion.

Oh God. Had she really tried standing up to her overbearing mother and father by marrying the wrong man time and again?

And again?

Good God. If that was true, bumbling Bilbray was way more on the ball than Lauren.

"How shall you handle this, Ralph?" her mother was saying. "Maybe keep it simple and tell Matthias Barton that Lauren was just suffering a little case of cold feet?"

During which she'd slept with your brother and fallen in love with the jerk, Lauren finished for her mother. Not that she'd shared with her parents that part of her Tahoe visit. Maybe they'd been right all along. Maybe she had no business deciding what to do with her own life because she just kept on botching it up.

"I've always thought September weddings were special," her mother said with a sigh. "It's a lovely time of year for a honeymoon."

Lauren grimaced. No matter what, no matter who, it wasn't happening in September. "I'm committed to a conference for the publishing house that month, Mom. There's not room for anything else on my calendar then."

Her father waved away her objection with his fork. "Nonsense. You can just quit that silly job if it gets in the way of your wedding."

"Silly job?" Lauren echoed, even as her father went back to his meal. "Dad, I make a good living as a translator. I could even take my skills and help you out at Conover if you'd let me."

"Help me out how?"

"Translating, Dad. You know, what I've been trained for? What I've been doing for several years now. I even have a hefty bank balance to prove it. Other companies besides the publisher pay me tidy sums for my work involving technological and business matters. It's not easy to find people who can not only translate, but translate techno-speak as well."

Her father started to bluster. "We have a company on retainer—"

"Linguanotics. I know them. I know Jeremy Cloud, who does most of their work for you. I'm better. And I'd like to put together a presentation that will show you just how and why you should hire me as a consultant instead. I guarantee you won't be sorry."

Her entire family was staring at her in surprise. Lauren herself felt energized, focused, her senses as honed as when she competed against her arch-nemesis, Luke. This was what it felt like to tackle things head-on with an intention to win, she realized.

And she liked it. It was the one good thing she could lay at Luke's door—that he'd taught her the power there was in assuming success and denying failure.

"Well...I—I—" Her father sputtered, looking over at her mother for help.

"I'm sure your father will give you time for a presentation," Carole said smoothly. "But why don't you wait until after the honeymoon, all right?"

It was straightforward straight talk time once again. Lauren's heart sped up as she gripped the edge of the table and leaned toward her mother. "Mom, you need to listen to me. I'm not going to marry that man. There isn't going to be a wedding in September. Cancel the winery, call off the dressmaker, rip up any other plans you've been hatching behind my back."

"Lauren—"

"There's going to be no wedding," Lauren interjected, her voice firm. "I'm not going to marry Matthias and he certainly doesn't want to marry me."

The sound of a throat clearing had everyone swiveling in their seat. June stood on the threshold to the dining room, clutching the skirt of her apron in her hands. Her face was flushed. "Um...there's someone here."

"Someone who?" her father demanded, his gaze

flicking to the grandfather clock in the corner of the room.

"Mr. Matthias Barton."

Lauren groaned as her mother shot her a triumphant look.

Luke was practically choking thanks to his Matt-tight tie as he was shown into the Conover dining room by the pink-cheeked housekeeper. The first person his gaze landed on was a young girl—Kaitlyn, of course—and he sent her a little grin as she reacted to his face with a wince.

Then *he* winced a little, too, because the smile hurt like hell.

"Barton!" Ralph Conover stood up from his place at the table and reached out his hand. "Have you had dinner?"

Luke hadn't seen the older man in years, but even if he hadn't already recognized him he would have known him by the Lauren-blue of his eyes. "I'm fine, sir, no dinner for me. I'm sorry to disturb you, but I came to see if I might have a word with your older daughter."

He sent her a sidelong glance, but she was staring down at her plate, as if mesmerized by her asparagus.

"Lauren?" her mother prompted. "Why don't you and Matthias go have a nice long chat in the library?"

A moment passed, then, with a resigned nod, the younger woman pushed back her chair. As they exited the room, Kaitlyn called out, "Don't forget the blue dress, Lauren. It's really pretty."

In the library, she shut the double doors behind them, then spoke without facing him. "I left the engagement ring on the dresser in the master bedroom," she said. "I should have told you that before I left. Now, if there's nothing else…"

Luke stared as she started turning the double door-knobs again. She was leaving the room? Leaving his life? "Wait…wait…"

She spun to face him. "What? What is it you want, Matthias?"

He was stupid. He'd had hours with which to figure out what to say right now, and he'd thought of nothing beyond finding a way to be alone with her again. "About my brother…"

"That's quite a shiner he gave you."

"Yeah." Matt hadn't been as reluctant as Luke might have wished to give him a matching punch to the face. But he'd realized he deserved it and more for what he'd done. Most important, he'd been certain that Lauren wouldn't have agreed to see him as himself, Luke.

So he'd gone for the ole twin switcheroo again. Maybe he should feel more guilt over that, but at the moment there was only desperation in his heart.

"Look," he started, still hoping for inspiration to strike. "My brother, he's really sorry—"

"About being as stupid as I was in agreeing to marry a near-perfect stranger?"

"He can be a little single-minded about business, too, and he thought—" Luke broke off, realizing what she'd said. Realizing that she'd seen through the switcheroo. "So you know."

"Fool me once, shame on you," she said, her face expressionless. "Fool me twice, shame on me. What are you out for now, Luke? More revenge?"

His face ached like a hammered thumb and it was all for nothing, damn it. And the pain was making it hard to think. "I wanted to try again to explain what happened."

She crossed her arms over her chest. "Your brother stole something from you and you wanted to steal something from him. I get that."

Luke shook his head. "That thing with Matt…we don't know what happened exactly, only that it was something shady, but I now know he didn't do it to me."

For a moment her stony face softened. "Oh, Luke. You have your twin again."

"Yeah. Maybe. I'm hopeful." His hand went to the egg on the back of his skull. "Though he's gained a powerful punch over the last few years. When he hit me I fell back and cracked my head on the table. I was seeing double from my one good eye until noon, which is why it took me an extra day to get here."

If he thought she might respond to the sympathy card, he was wrong. Her face was cold again and that's how he felt, too, cold with…with…hell, he had to admit it. Cold with fear.

What if he couldn't get through to her?

"But someone robbed something from me, after all," he blurted out.

"I told you where the ring is."

"That's Matt's, and you know I'm not interested in a damn piece of jewelry." The cold inside of him was as icy as the blue of her eyes, and it was slowing his heartbeat to a death knell.

How could he go on without her beside him? Who would he have to watch sappy movies with? Who would give him a pinch when he was getting too competitive?

After Hunter had died, there had been no one to show him the wider, brighter world until Lauren. Even if Matt had his back, who would be at his side?

It had to be Lauren. He only wanted Lauren.

He was in love with Lauren.

The thought ran like a flame through cold snow. Until this moment, he'd never allowed himself to even silently form the words, now he was consumed by them. He was in love with his Goldilocks, with her humor and her sweet disposition. With her knack for relaxing and the way the air heated when they were in a room together.

He was in love with her blond hair and her curvy body, from her short nose to her short toes, and every inch of creamy skin in between. He loved her full breasts and her pink nipples. He loved the almost transparent color of the curls that did little to protect her sex from his gaze. He loved the little sounds she made when he touched her there and found her already wet and her little bud—

"*Luke.*"

From her annoyed expression and flushed cheeks, he figured she'd read just about all of that on his face.

"Luke, why did you come here?"

He squashed his panic at her cold, angry tone. She wasn't just falling into his arms as he might have hoped, but that didn't mean he'd give up. Bartons never gave up, and he sent out a silent prayer of thanks to his father for that. Amazing, that loving Lauren could even give him a new appreciation of Samuel Sullivan Barton.

"Luke—"

"You did take something of mine." The words tumbled out.

Her brows came together in a frown. "What?"

Here it was. Time to hand over the power. In business, he'd taught himself to always hold back, to keep some of his cards to himself, but now…now if he really wanted her he would have to lay it all on the table. He'd never had much faith in loyalty, but now he was going to have to take the risk and believe that this woman would give him hers.

"I don't want back what you took, though," he said, stalling. "You can keep it. You can have it forever."

Her frown deepened. "Well, what is it?"

Here goes. "My heart."

Lauren remembered the time she'd told Luke he looked as if she'd hit him with a cartoon frying pan, and she was certain that was the same expression she wore now. It certainly felt as if something had struck her, knocking the breath straight out of her lungs. "Wh-what?"

"I don't know if you took my heart or if I gave it or when it happened or how I could get so lucky. Maybe it's like Kaitlyn's rule and that true…true beauty only comes upon us by surprise. I wasn't expecting this, Lauren, but with you I see things so much clearer. I have a perspective that I've been missing nearly all my life. With you, I can think about breathing instead of about winning. With you, I can forget about my business and the constant hustle to make the next buck."

It was the longest speech she'd ever heard him make.

His voice, a little hoarse, a little breathless, rang with sincerity. Shaking her head, she flattened her hands against the creamy white paint of the doors and stared at him, trying to understand. Luke's eyes were serious, their expression intent.

Again, sincere.

But…but…

"You…your brother…you always want what he has," she reminded them both. "Now you're only trying to get back at him for that Stuttgart thing."

"This isn't about Matt anymore, Lauren," Luke said. "Please, please believe me, though I know I don't deserve your trust."

He *didn't* deserve her trust! "You seduced me under false pretences."

"Yes."

"You came here today, doing the same all over again."

He grimaced. "Yes. And I'm sorry, so sorry. Not so much about today, though. I needed to do whatever it took to see you again. To try to explain—"

"You shouldn't have bothered," Lauren said, bitterness giving bite to her words. "While it might be difficult for me to forgive you, believe me, I understand. I'm Ralph Conover's daughter, remember? I'm accustomed to the lengths a man will go for his business."

Her father's single-mindedness had been something she'd always half-joked about, but it had rankled her entire life. Even more as she grew older and saw how it affected Kaitlyn. The whole family had lost out on so much during his ruthless drive for the all-mighty dollar.

After the way Luke was raised, it was no surprise he was filled with the same competitive, cold-hearted zeal.

"So go away," she said, turning her face so she could avoid his. "Get on the first flight to Stuttgart and beat out your brother that way."

There was a long moment of silence, then Luke spoke again. "Lauren." It sounded strained. "Lauren, please look at me."

That was a mistake. Because despite his competitive, cold-hearted zeal, he had the appearance of a man who was more worried about losing than consumed with winning.

"I could *be* in Stuttgart right now if that's what was important to me," he said. "Matt's at Hunter's house to fulfill the stipulation of the will and if I wanted I could be in Europe, working on Ernst. *Without* a hell of a shiner, I might add, and without a bump on the back of my head bigger than a baseball. I didn't go to Stuttgart. I came to you."

Her heart jolted, one hard thump against her ribs. For the second time her breath was knocked right out of her.

Luke hadn't gone to Stuttgart.

He hadn't left Hunter's house at the first instant he could to shore up his business deal.

How could this be? How could competitive, cut-throat, cold-hearted Luke have abandoned the most important thing to him in the world?

She said it out loud, just to be sure. "You didn't go to Stuttgart." Her voice came out a whisper.

"I haven't given Germany another thought since you walked out on me," he replied. "I didn't go to Stuttgart because I wanted to be with you. I want to be with you because when we're together I actually enjoy the life that Hunter is no longer here to share. I finally figured out why he arranged that situation for the Samurai—or at least why he arranged it for me. I needed to reconnect with people again, Lauren. I needed to realize that I'm actually one myself, a person with emotions, and needs, and fears…and…and love. I'm so in love with you."

He was in love with her! Lauren felt her stomach fall toward her knees. He was in love with her? Before, he'd said she had his heart, but she'd still been trying to convince herself he didn't have one. But to say this, to say he was in love with her. And to give up his important business deal so that he could…

It was true. It must be true.

Oh, Luke.

She took a slow step forward. He froze, just watching her with those serious, worried eyes, as if afraid to believe what he was seeing.

She remembered dozens of sweet hours in his arms. Dozens of conversations about movies, travel, nothing at all. It hadn't mattered one wit what he called himself. It was the man, and not the name, she'd fallen for. Taking another forward step, she remembered again the exact moment she'd realized it, when he'd been angry, for her, at Trevor.

Her forward movement halted, her feet digging into the carpet.

Luke must have read the renewed reluctance on her face. For a second his eyes closed as if he experienced a sharp pain. Then they opened, and she could see that pain in his eyes.

Tears stung hers.

"What is it, Goldilocks? What's coming between you and my arms?" The tightness of his voice showed his strain. "I love you. Don't you believe me? Don't you believe that the man who was with you at Hunter's house, whether his name was Matt or Luke, was a man who fell in love with you?"

She shook her head, mute. That Luke hadn't hurried off to Stuttgart proved the strength of his feelings. The problem, at the moment, wasn't him.

"What can I do?" he asked, hoarser now. "What can I do to make you mine? I want to marry you, Lauren."

"I'm afraid," she said. Thinking of Trevor had opened the door to it. "I've been engaged three times before. Each time the decision was wrong."

"Make that four times, sweetheart." Luke grimaced. "Remember? I'm not Matt."

Her eyes widened and she felt them sting again. "You're right. Four mistakes. Luke…"

His hands fisted at his sides. She could see him holding himself back. Luke would always be one who reacted with action, whose first instinct would be to take matters into his own hands and force the results he wanted. But here he was, letting her come to her own conclusions. It made her love him more…feel even more unsure of what she should do about it.

"Lauren, sweetheart." He blew out a breath. "Trust yourself."

"*Myself?* Trust *myself?* What kind of reasoning is that? I'm the one who picked Trevor and Joe and Jean-Paul."

"You know what I think about them? I think you picked those three with your parents in mind, and if

that's the case, then they were exactly the wrong men—
which was exactly right for what you were after at the
time."

Oh, God. That was true. Hadn't she acknowledged
it during dinner? They'd been perfect men for her
perfect parental rebellion. Luke knew her so well. And
yet still loved her. How could she turn away from that?
Four fiancés should have taught her *something*.

"This time, Goldilocks, if I might make a suggestion,
why don't you pick the man who is just right for you."

Lauren loved the library. As a little girl, she used to
tuck herself away behind one of the leather wing chairs
and pour over old atlases that listed exotically named
countries such as Persia and Wallachia and Travan-
core. She dreamed of the people who lived there and
the sounds of their spoken languages.

Later, she dreamed of visiting those places with a
man who would share her curiosity and who would
make her spin with dizzy happiness—like the globe
sitting on the table in front of the mullioned windows.

Of course, she'd never imagined she'd be cradling
her love's head on her lap while applying a bag of
petite white corn kernels to his battered face—but she
crooned sympathetically to him in French and Spanish
as a way of making up for it.

He opened his good eye. "Did you just call me a little
toad?"

"Only because of all these new lumps on your skull,"
she said, trying not to laugh. Laughter jostled her legs
which in turn put pressure on the bump on the back of
his head. "Are you sure you shouldn't see a doctor?"

"Your mother won't let me out of the house, not now that we've convinced her *our* engagement isn't a big hoax to get back at her for not taking your career seriously."

"Thank you for making that point to her when she started going off on a September wedding date again. I'm determined to manage her in just such a straightforward manner from now on." Lauren leaned down to press her mouth lightly to his.

When he tried to take the kiss deeper, she pulled back. "No. You're supposed to be resting."

His eye closed and his lips curved up in a smile. "We'll go back to Hunter's house tomorrow and rest up for the remainder of my month."

"I'm a little afraid to let you go to sleep, though," Lauren said. Her gaze traveled over the face that had become the map to her happiness. "What if, thanks to that bump on your head, when you wake up you don't remember me?"

He opened his good eye again and the expression she read there made the love inside of her expand until there wasn't room for breath.

"Then we'll become acquainted all over again, Goldilocks, because the Big Bad Wolf has finally caught the pretty girl—and he isn't ever letting her go."

Lauren and Luke were making a final walk-through of Hunter's house before they left it for the last time. She peered under the bed and spotted a penny on the carpet in the very middle—too far to reach even if she got down on her hands and knees.

With a little smile to herself, she left it where it lay.

Maybe the coin would bring the next Samurai the same good luck Luke swore he'd found here.

On her last sweep of the master bathroom, she discovered a note taped to the mirror. Luke's handwriting was as dark and aggressive as he was, and, no surprise, he didn't waste time with greetings or goodbyes. It only read:

Dev: Remember the talk we had about women on New Year's Eve our senior year? We were wrong, man. So wrong. We didn't have a clue.

Luke came up behind her as she read over the words. She looked up to meet his gaze in the glass. "Well?" she asked.

His lips twitched. "Well, what?"

"What's it mean? What didn't you two have a clue about?"

Tenderness replaced amusement in his eyes. He twirled a curl of her hair around his finger. "You'll meet Devlin Campbell someday very soon, Goldilocks. And then you can ask him."

* * * * *

BOUND BY THE BABY

BY
SUSAN CROSBY

Susan Crosby believes in the value of setting goals, but also in the magic of making wishes. A long-time reader of romance novels, Susan earned a BA in English while raising her sons. She lives in the central valley of California, the land of wine grapes, asparagus and almonds. Her checkered past includes jobs as a synchronized swimming instructor, personnel interviewer at a toy factory and trucking company manager, but her current occupation as a writer is her all-time favorite.

Susan enjoys writing about people who take a chance on love, sometimes against all odds. She loves warm, strong heroes; good-hearted, self-reliant heroines…and happy endings.

Susan loves to hear from readers. You can visit her at her website, www.susancrosby.com.

For the Gilroy connection—
a great place to write a book. Thanks so much.

For Elizabeth Bevarly, Maureen Child, Anna DePalo,
Susan Mallery and Christie Ridgway—five
talented and generous women.

Prologue

Devlin Campbell had been taking up space at a blackjack table for two hours. By rights he should be down thousands of dollars, since his head wasn't in the game but on a letter he'd jammed into his inside coat pocket that morning. It took a lot to shake Dev up, but the one-page document typed on a California law firm's letterhead had shaken him to the core, the repercussions still resonating. It was impossible to forget the letter, so he'd settled instead on ignoring it as best he could.

He swigged his fourth Scotch and water, then glanced at the woman standing at his shoulder, observing him silently. Even before he'd gotten himself semidrunk, she'd been easy on the eyes. Her hair was long, light brown and shiny, her body curvy and tempting, but her smile didn't reach her beautiful blue eyes. Oddly, her sadness drew him as much as the physical attraction. He didn't know her name, only that she'd brought him luck since he'd first laid eyes on her more than an hour ago.

He'd been in the hole a few hundred dollars when he'd spotted her walking toward his table. He had gone on full alert, everything about her appealing to him, calling to him. She'd stopped to talk to a passing employee, who had pointed toward someplace in the distance. She'd glanced in that direction then straight at him and seemed to freeze in place. Her eyes widened. For long, increasingly fascinating seconds, neither looked away. The dealer drew him back into the game, and he won the hand.

When he looked toward her again, she was gone, only to pass by him at that very moment, within reach.

"Wait," he said, his hand on her arm, the contact sizzling. "You're my good luck charm."

Amazingly, she waited. When she tried to walk away several times over the next hour, he implored her to stay, although more with his eyes than his words. He dubbed her Ms. Fortune, hoping to make her laugh, but the sadness in her eyes only deepened.

And yet she stayed, even as a small crowd gathered, curious, as his winning streak continued and his bets became more daring. A pit boss watched. Security people milled.

They scrutinized Dev's every move, but he wasn't cheating. Wasn't counting cards, either, although he was proficient at it. He and numbers had a remarkable affinity. However, no one could count cards at the big casinos anymore, their systems too refined for cheaters to prosper. But this time he didn't care whether he won or lost, didn't have the mental wherewithal to do anything more than play the game.

Yet all he did was win.

Dev jiggled the ice cubes in his otherwise empty glass, then set it down as the next hand was dealt. He lifted the corners—a jack and a five—the kind of hand any sensible person would've stayed on, letting the dealer's hand determine the outcome, but Dev took a hit. Odds were he would be dealt a face card, putting him well over twenty-one.

He drew a six. Twenty-one. It was that kind of night.

As conversation buzzed around him, Ms. Fortune leaned close. "I really have to go," she said. "Congratulations."

He turned his head. Their noses almost touched. "Have dinner with me."

She pulled back. "I can't," she said quietly.

She left. He would've had to stop her by force, something he was tempted to do, but instead he watched her disappear into the crowd, wondering what her story was, wishing he could get his hands on that incredible body.

The thrill of the game gone for him, he scooped up his winnings, was accompanied to the cashier and cashed out. Now what? He couldn't drive home to Philadelphia, not with four Scotch and waters in him.

He could get a room, order room service and face the contents of the letter, and the memories....

He hesitated, a rarity for him. He usually dealt with situations head-on and quickly. But this was going to require some soul searching, and he wasn't comfortable with that. *Damn you, Hunter.*

Dev found the front desk, got himself a room on the twenty-fifth floor and headed to the elevator banks. When a bell pinged he moved to stand in front of the arriving elevator. The doors opened. Ms. Fortune stood there.

More than a coincidence, he thought. *Fate.*

She didn't make a move to exit. He entered, pushed the button for his floor. The doors closed behind him.

A tight, hot ball formed inside his chest at the pain he saw in her eyes. "Who broke your heart?" he asked.

Her eyes filled instantly with tears.

"Let me fix it," he said softly.

Wordlessly he moved closer, put his arms around her and gently pulled her close. She resisted, then she pressed her face into his shoulder and slid her arms around him, squeezing tight, a small sob escaping. He brushed his lips to her temple.

All too soon the doors opened.

"Come with me," he said into her ear. "Stay with me tonight."

After a moment she nodded then stepped away.

He reached for her hand. "What's your name?" he asked, holding the door, preventing it from closing.

"Nicole."

"I'm Devlin."

Hand in hand, they walked down the hall.

One

May 1, Sterling Palace Hotel and Casino,
Stateline, Nevada

Where was Ms. Fortune when he needed her?

Devlin Campbell studied his surroundings, his equilibrium challenged by the garish neon lights and incessant slot-machine noise. This time he couldn't win at the blackjack table, not one hand. He wasn't superstitious, wasn't blaming his losses on his former lucky charm not being at his side. He knew it was, instead, that sly culprit, jet lag.

And so instead of focusing on the cards, he found himself watching the people milling around, even though there was no reason to continually search the casino for *her*...Ms. Fortune. Nicole. After all, he'd met her on the other side of the country, ships passing in the night—or more appropriately in this case, ports in a storm, finding comfort and refuge in each other's arms for reasons neither of them had confided. He hadn't experienced another night like it, before or since, although he'd gone back twice, hoping…

Yeah, jet lag. With the three-hour time difference in Philadelphia, he'd already put in a full day. Not to mention the fourteen-hour days he'd been working the past month in preparation for this trip.

Dev watched the dealer dispense the cards, then turn up a king for himself. Dev looked at his hand—seven and five.

He didn't know why he'd come to the casino in the first place. The refrigerator at the lodge where he was supposed to stay had been stocked by an attractive, efficient young woman named Mary, who'd met him with a key dangling off an ornate keychain. He could've heated up one of the meals from a local restaurant she'd thoughtfully provided, then gone to bed. Instead he hadn't even unpacked, hadn't taken time to tour the spectacular log house.

"Hit or stay, sir?" the dealer asked, awaiting Dev's decision.

He signaled for a hit. A queen landed on his cards. Twenty-two. *Loser.* It wasn't a word associated with the name Devlin Campbell. Ever.

Dev scooped up his few remaining chips and left the table, in need of food. He'd spotted a sports bar earlier where he could order from the bar. He would eat something quick and simple, then go back to the lodge and sleep for at least twelve hours.

The televisions were tuned to a baseball game between his beloved Phillies and the San Francisco Giants. He ordered a beer and checked out the menu, deciding on a burger and fries. He lifted the frosty glass set before him and scanned the room. A woman walked past the entrance. A woman wearing a Sterling Palace uniform. A woman who reminded him of—

Beer sloshed over his hand as he thumped his glass onto the bar, then rushed out. He could see her maybe twenty feet ahead, moving at a quick, steady pace. The same long, shiny, light-brown hair, this time braided neatly. Killer body. Sexy legs that had wrapped around him and held tight.

"Nicole!" he called.

She turned, looked straight at him, hesitated, then picked up speed. What the hell? She was trying to get away? Why? He posed no threat. He hadn't even learned her last name. Not that it mattered, since he hadn't been on a second date or spent a second night with a woman in the past couple of years, no matter how beautiful or sexy.

Except…he'd wanted to have a second night with Nicole, who had been one passionate handful, as intense as he, assertive and demanding in a way that had made him forget everything else that night.

Even the letter.

He caught up with her, cupped her elbow. She had no choice but to stop.

"Are you in training for a marathon?" he asked. His gaze slid to her name badge: Nicole, Sacramento, California. He'd had no idea she was an employee of the Palace. She hadn't been wearing a uniform when they met, but jeans, a dark sweater and boots with heels high enough to bring her close to his height. He'd tugged them off her, then her jeans, exposing knock-out legs…

"Oh, hi," she said. "Um…"

"Devlin," he supplied, surprised. She'd *forgotten?* "January? Atlantic City?"

She tugged her jacket together, freeing herself of his grip at the same time. She was even more voluptuous than he recalled. His memory hadn't failed him. And he definitely wanted a repeat of their night in Atlantic City.

"I remember," she said, finally smiling a little but, like the first time they'd met, the smile not reaching her eyes.

"You work here," he said, looking again at her name badge.

"I'm an assistant manager for the hotel."

"Were you employed by the Palace in when we met in January?"

"Yes, for the hotel, as head reservations clerk. I wasn't on duty when we…that night. I transferred here to Tahoe…two months ago."

She gave the information reluctantly and barely made eye contact.

Both intrigued and irritated, he said, "Have dinner with me."

"I'm working." She glanced around, as if seeking someone to come to her rescue, a bit of panic in her eyes.

Surely she wasn't afraid of him, not after the night they'd shared. "When do you get off?"

She finally looked him in the eyes, perhaps concluding he wouldn't back down, although nothing in her demeanor indicated she was backing down, either. "At nine."

Less than an hour. His jet lag vanished at the anticipation. "I'll wait for you."

"Please, don't." She took a step back. "Please. I have to go."

Dev let her leave. He returned to the bar just as his food was being set on the counter.

There was something to be said for timing. Food first, then Nicole.

She wouldn't get far.

He knew where to find her.

Nicole didn't know for sure that Devlin hadn't trailed her until she slipped behind the front desk and turned around. Holding her breath, she scanned the crowd. He hadn't followed.

She slipped into an empty office and shut the door, leaning against the wall beside it, one hand pressed to her mouth, one to her stomach. Light-headed, she made her way to a chair and dropped into it.

What was *he* doing here?

What was she going to do?

Nicole stared into space until the room came into focus. After a minute she typed his name into the computer on the desk, accessing the reservations data base. No Devlin Campbell. So…he wasn't a guest. Not yet, anyway. Why was he here? Where was he staying?

For how long?

One of the front-desk clerks, Ann-Marie, came up to the window and made a face. Nicole tried to smile. The clerk opened the door and leaned in.

"Are you okay, Nic?"

I am far from okay. I am worried. And I am scared. "I'm fine, thanks."

"You look like you've seen a ghost."

Devlin Campbell was a vision, all right, but completely earthbound. Tall, dark and handsome. High-society born and old-money rich—things she'd learned about him after their night together.

"Did you need something, Ann-Marie?" Nicole saw her recoil. She moved toward the twenty-three-year-old trainee.

"I didn't mean to be so abrupt. I guess I don't really feel well, after all."

"Maybe you should just go home."

Nicole was proud that she hadn't missed even an hour of work and had no intention of starting now. Anyway, she couldn't. She was filling in for someone who'd needed to come to work an hour late. She could manage another forty-five minutes.

Under normal circumstances, she would've been gone by now, would not have run into Devlin. Once again the hands of fate had grabbed hold of her and not let go. It was too soon. She wasn't ready—

"Nic?"

She smiled at Ann-Marie. "I'll be okay until the end of the shift."

The bubbly blonde smiled back and returned to the desk. Nicole followed. It was Tuesday night. The chances of there being a rush on rooms was slim, although the possibility that Devlin might want one kept her milling around the desk, waiting.

A few minutes before nine, he approached, pointing toward a place where they could talk without being over-heard. "If not dinner, then a drink?" he asked.

She shook her head, made herself smile.

"I'll be here every night until you say yes."

Every night? Just how long— "Are you here on business?"

"I'm not sure how to answer that. It's supposed to be pleasure, but it's someone else's definition of pleasure. I'll be here for a month."

A month! She gripped the counter. Everything would be different in a month. Now what? What should she tell him? And when? She needed to figure out what to say.

But not tonight. Not tonight. Tomorrow would be soon enough. Nothing would change in that time.

"Do you need a ride home?" he asked.

"I have my own car, thanks."

"I'll walk you to it." His tone was more order than offer.

She'd never responded well to orders. "I have something to do first. I'm sure we'll cross paths another time." Take a hint, Mr. Campbell. You are dismissed. She turned away, took a few steps.

"What are you afraid of, Nicole?" he asked, his voice carrying enough that Ann-Marie looked in their direction.

She stalked back to him. "Why are you pressuring me?" she whispered harshly.

"That was a helluva night we spent together."

So. He was looking for an encore. What had she expected? Love at first sight? "That was then. Good night." She walked away, taking refuge in the office again and watching the lobby through the window. Seconds later she saw him head toward the parking lot exit.

Someone waved a hand up and down in front of the window then stepped into view. She focused abruptly on the man standing on the other side of the door, grinning.

She grinned back. Who could resist? Juan Torres was the sweetest man on the face of the earth. She opened the door.

"Thanks so much for staying the extra hour," Juan said as he pinned his assistant manager badge onto his jacket. "I owe you."

"I'm sure I'll be calling in the marker." She handed him a sheet listing the problems that had arisen during her shift, then pointed to one in particular. "The guest in 1015 has changed rooms three times since he got here at six o'clock."

"What's his problem?"

"Room's too close to the elevators. View's lousy. Noisy neighbors."

"Ah. The usual. Trying to get us to comp him."

She started to answer, then saw Mr. Room 1015 approaching the desk, his stare steely, his stride determined, obviously back for round four. "Saved by the time clock," Nicole murmured with relief. "See you tomorrow, Juan."

Nicole grabbed her purse and called a good-night to the front-desk personnel, glad to be on her way home. She needed to be alone, to think. To come up with the right words to say to Devlin Campbell.

"Wait," Ann-Marie said, hurrying to catch up, then matching her stride. "I want to make sure you get to your car okay."

Nicole couldn't help but smile. Ann-Marie was five years younger, yet she was mothering Nicole. "I'm fine." She set a hand on her belly, emphasizing her point. "*We're* fine."

"Humor me. I'm headed your way, anyway."

A few seconds later they reached the exit door to the parking lot. Devlin stepped in front of her, startling her, blocking the exit. His green eyes cold and hard, he stared into hers, then dropped his gaze to her belly.

"Um, you…go ahead," she said to Ann-Marie, who looked back and forth between Nicole and Devlin.

"Are you sure? I mean—"

"It's fine. I'll see you tomorrow." Nicole motioned Ann-Marie toward the door, then waited for Devlin to speak, aiming for calm, but failing. Fate. She couldn't seem to escape this man.

He moved closer. "Is it mine?"

Two

Dev waited for her response, then waited some more. If her answer was yes, it should've come instantly. He took a longer look at her, surprised that he hadn't noticed right away. But a minute ago when she'd curved her hand over a bump that hadn't been there when they'd made love in January, he'd calculated the time gap. Four months. His older sister was five months pregnant, her condition a little more visible. Still, every pregnancy was different—and every woman—or so Dev'd heard his sister say.

Maybe it wasn't his. Maybe his assumption was wrong. Had she turned down his invitation for dinner or a drink because she carried another man's baby? Had she cheated on that man in January? She'd never told him her last name. Maybe because—

"Were you spying on me?" she asked, shock, or maybe anger, coating her words.

"I was looking out for you. Making sure you made it to your car safely."

"I get myself safely to my car five nights a week."

"You're avoiding the question."

She crossed her arms. "Of course it's yours."

Of course? The casino sights and sounds faded as the shock of her acknowledgment ripped through him. Could he believe her?

"You took a long time to answer. Too long," he said, mimicking her posture.

"Not because I was lying."

"It's not looking like that to me, Nicole."

She finally softened a bit, losing a little of her defensive posture. "I didn't want to tell you here, among all these people and the noise."

"You should have told me months ago."

"I know. Devlin, please. This is where I work. Several coworkers have already walked by and stared."

"Fine. Let's go." He cupped her elbow, propelling her forward, but she broke away.

"I'm not going anywhere with you."

No surprise there. "We apparently have a lot to talk about."

"I agree. But not tonight. I'll meet you tomorrow."

He didn't want to give her time to fine-tune her story. He wanted the raw, uncut version. Otherwise, how could be believe her? "Why didn't you tell me? You had access to the guest data. I'm sure you found out my name and address."

"I'll give you all the details…tomorrow."

Short of kidnapping her, he couldn't make her come with him. Security would be all over him. "You won't skip town?"

"I promise."

"Like that's supposed to mean something?"

"You know where I work. How can I avoid you?"

"What's your last name?"

"Price."

Ah, the irony. There was going to be a Price to pay for falling into bed with a stranger, and then, like an idiot, not using protection. He pulled out a business card and pen, wrote down the address and phone number of the lodge, then passed it to her. "Here's where I'm staying. Do you need directions?"

She shook her head. "Every local knows about that lodge. Is it yours?"

"No. What time should I expect you?"

"I have to be at work at noon, so how about eleven o'clock?"

"Ten-thirty."

"All right. I'll see you then."

He opened the door for her, then followed her out.

"I don't need an escort." The words came through gritted teeth.

"Tough."

She stayed silent until they reached her car, a Subaru that looked to be a few years old.

"Four-wheel drive?" he asked.

"Of course. I live in snow country." She unlocked the door and climbed in.

He waited until she started the engine, then he signaled for her to roll down her window. Her expression reflected her annoyance at being delayed even longer. "Are you seeing someone?" he asked.

Her brows rose. "You mean, dating?"

He nodded.

"No."

"*Were* you seeing someone?"

"In January?"

Was she being deliberately obtuse? Probably. She probably wanted to irritate him. She'd succeeded. If he was the father of her child, and she'd known his name and where he lived, and then had decided not to tell him about the pregnancy, he had reason to be irritated. And furious. He could see no justification for her keeping it a secret from him.

He didn't answer her question about the month but gave her a look he figured she could interpret.

"I was not dating anyone then," she said, looking straight out the windshield, a white-knuckled grip on the steering wheel. "And no one since, either."

Again, no eye contact. He didn't trust someone who wouldn't look him in the eyes. In the banking business you learned to trust your instincts about people. Body language spoke loudly. He didn't like what hers was saying.

He took a step back. "See you tomorrow."

She didn't even roll up her window against the chill but backed out of the parking space and sped off.

He watched her go. He'd come to Lake Tahoe as part of a deal he'd made ten years ago. He'd come with a plan to change his life, giving himself the month to work it out, since he was stuck here, anyway.

Now his life was being changed for him.

It wasn't a good start.

At midnight Nicole wrapped herself in a quilt and stepped onto her porch. She glanced at the thermometer tacked to the porch post—thirty-eight degrees. The roads would probably be icy by morning.

Her breath puffed white in front of her, but the fresh air felt good. Since she'd moved to the area two months ago, she'd come to crave the crisp coldness of Lake Tahoe the way some people yearned for the heat of her hometown, Sacramento. She wouldn't miss the hundred-degree summers a bit, nor the humidity of Atlantic City, which she'd called home for ten years.

Nicole sat on her porch swing and eased it back and forth, the chains groaning quietly against the overhead hooks, the motion calming.

It wasn't as if she hadn't known this day would come. She'd planned to tell Devlin—just probably not until the baby was born and DNA testing could be done, because she knew he would require that.

She couldn't blame him for not trusting her. They'd been strangers, without reasons to trust each other. All he knew of her was that she'd fallen into bed with him without knowing him, without any prelude at all. The sex had been like nothing she'd thought herself capable of—anonymous, all-consuming and with little tenderness—exactly what she'd needed that night. And even without the reminder growing inside her, she would've remembered everything about those hours with Devlin. She'd cried in his arms more than once. He'd never asked her why but had simply held her, then made love to her—*with* her—again. And again. And again.

In the morning, she hadn't sneaked out, but woke him up to tell him thank you, kissing him goodbye. That was supposed to be the end of it. No regrets.

Surprise!

Nicole closed her eyes, keeping the swing moving, remembering the exact moment two months after that incredible night when she'd realized that it wasn't lingering grief making her feel so miserable, but pregnancy. Now in her second trimester, the morning sickness gone, she felt healthy and strong and capable of dealing with Devlin.

She shivered, but whether from the cold or the anticipation of contending with Devlin, she wasn't sure. She needed sleep, would try again and hope for better results than the past hour of tossing and turning.

As she stood she saw headlights coming up the road. The vehicle slowed at her driveway, stopped for a few seconds, then turned in and eased up the twenty feet to her house. Not recognizing the big black SUV, she sat again, grateful she'd turned off the porch light.

The car door opened and a man got out. Devlin. She held her breath. What was he doing? How had he found her? Did he plan to bang on the door and wake her from what should've been a sound sleep?

Apparently not. He just stood there looking around. After a minute he walked around the side of the house, out of sight, then reappeared shortly.

She wondered about his reaction. She loved her little cabin. It was only seven hundred square feet, but cozy and comfortable and hers—or in twenty-nine years and eleven months it would be hers. She'd always rented before.

Dead leaves and pine needles crunched under Devlin's shoes as he came close again, this time veering toward the porch. His hands tucked into his jacket pockets, he put a foot on the lowest step but went no farther.

"Looking for someone?" she asked, figuring he would spot her soon enough.

He swore, which made her smile. She liked that she'd been the one to do the startling this time.

"What are you doing out here?" he asked, coming up the remaining stairs. "It's freezing."

Vanity had her wishing she wasn't in a robe, flannel pajamas and fuzzy slippers, and free of makeup. "How'd you find me?"

"Typed your name into the White Pages on the Internet. I wasn't going to knock. I just wanted to see where you live." Without invitation he sat next to her on the swing. His breath billowed in front of him, as hers did. "You couldn't sleep, either?"

She shook her head. She was cold to the bone now, but she wasn't about to let him know that. And her entire body reacted to being so close to his. Memories invaded, warming her, arousing—

"Invite me in," he said, leaning toward her slightly.

Apparently the word *please* wasn't in his vocabulary. "We'll talk tomorrow, as scheduled," she said.

"You're not sleeping. I'm not sleeping. Why not talk now?"

"Because we're both overtired. One of us is bound to misspeak."

"I don't misspeak."

"Then you must be immortalized in some comic book with those other superhumans."

"You're shivering," he said, ignoring her remark. "It can't be good for the baby."

"I don't do anything to put this child at risk." What was she doing? Acting like an idiot just to prove a point—that she was doing fine without him and would continue? She'd already been headed into the house when he'd shown up. She was twenty-eight years old and acting like a teenager. "Want some hot chocolate?" she asked.

To his credit he didn't look smug but stood and held out a hand to her. He'd kept his in his pockets, so they were warm compared to hers. She let go as soon as she was standing, then led the way into the house.

Nicole had almost finished decorating. She had combined

yard-sale finds with consignment-shop treasures, had reuphol-
stered, painted and sewed, with only the baby's room to go.

The living room, dining nook and kitchen were visible
from the front entry. She laid her quilt over a chair, tightened
the sash on her robe and headed into the kitchen. She pulled
out a saucepan, milk and cocoa mix.

"Mind if I look around?" Devlin asked, tossing his jacket
atop her quilt.

"Go ahead." She was glad to have him wander off for a
minute. Her bedding was jumbled, but what did it matter?
She'd gone to bed, tried to sleep. He would know that. On
the other hand, the place was so small he would be back
before the milk had even gotten warm.

"Do you own or rent?" he asked, returning and leaning
against the refrigerator, watching her.

"Own."

"It's small…to raise a child."

"How much room does a child need?" she countered.

"More than this."

"I disagree."

He seemed about to argue but didn't. "It's rustic," he
offered after a moment.

She shook her head, amused. He was skirting around saying
what he really wanted to, apparently trying to keep the peace
between them for the moment. Obviously he wanted something.

"What do you expect, Devlin? It's a cabin in the woods.
Rustic fits the environment," she said, getting down two
mugs. "The roads are plowed in the winter, and I've got the
fireplace and a generator if the power goes out. It's perfect."
It's mine. She poured the hot chocolate into the mugs and
passed him one, then cupped hers in both hands, treasuring

the warmth. She was sorry she'd let him come in, was too tired to deal with him, just as she'd said.

"Did you know who I was?" he asked.

"I looked you up in the database." She watched him over the rim of her mug as she took a tentative sip, testing its heat.

"When?"

"In the morning, after I left your suite."

"Not before?"

She frowned. "Before, I was standing at the blackjack table with you. Before that I was passing through the casino on my way to my boss's office when I stopped to talk to a friend, a fellow employee. You caught my attention, and I stayed to watch for a minute. Then you wouldn't let me leave."

"You were my good luck charm."

"So you said." She gestured toward her sofa, which faced the unlit fireplace. "Are you asking if I recognized you or something? Stalked you?"

"Did you?" he asked as they sat at opposite ends.

"The answer is no, to both questions. How could I know who you are? You're not a celebrity, are you? And even if I'd recognized your name from the reservations—which I wouldn't have—you didn't get a room until after I left the table." She was working up a little righteous anger at his ego. "And how could I accidentally run into you in the elevator? There were twelve banks of elevators. What were the chances the one I was in would stop on the right floor at the right time to run into you again?"

"I—"

"I understand you don't want to believe this baby is yours," she said, "but you seem to be an intelligent man, a logical one. Nothing was preconceived," she added, trying to lighten the mood.

He didn't smile even a little bit at her joke, hadn't smiled once since he'd asked if it was his. "It wouldn't be the first time a woman falsely claimed a child's paternity."

Nicole's attempt at patience evaporated. "DNA testing has taken care of that problem. It makes it impossible to lie."

"So why didn't you tell me?" He set his untouched mug on the coffee table. "If you knew you could prove it, why keep it from me?"

"I did try to tell you. I even went to your house."

"When?"

"The day after I found out. The day before I was set to move here."

"I wasn't at home?"

"You pulled up to your house moments after I got there." She'd parked in front of his Society Hill town house, the beautiful building confirming her fears—that he came from wealth and status. "But you weren't alone."

The woman on his arm had worn a short, sexy black dress and very high heels. He'd slipped his coat jacket around her, then kissed her before they'd climbed the stairs arm in arm and disappeared into the house. Soon after, a light had gone on upstairs. He'd stood silhouetted in the shade-drawn window for a long moment and undone his tie, then he'd moved out of sight.

"I waited for hours," she said. "Eventually I decided it was fate that you weren't available, because as I sat there I came to the conclusion that you would think I was shaking you down for money. I figured I should wait until… Well, I thought you had a girlfriend. It sure looked like it. I decided to wait until I was settled in here."

"You've been here for two months."

She nodded. What could she say? She'd been stalling. Who wouldn't?

He leaned forward, his arms resting on his thighs, his gaze on the fireplace, even though it wasn't lit. "What do you want from me?"

She sat back. He hadn't disputed having a girlfriend. "Nothing."

"I don't believe that."

"To quote you from earlier—tough." Annoyed, she stood. She was too tired to argue with him. "You need to leave now."

He hadn't taken even one sip of his drink, but he headed to the door, grabbing his coat along the way. He hesitated, his hand on the doorknob. "Why'd you do it, Nicole?"

"Be specific."

"Go to my room with me that night. You were upset about something, enough to cry."

She closed her eyes for a moment, memories slamming into her, then made eye contact. "Yes, I was hurting, and you offered a kind of comfort. But you were upset about something that night, too."

He nodded slightly. "I'm usually scrupulous about using condoms. And I assumed you were on the Pill. I should've asked."

"I can't tolerate the Pill, and I should've said so. I don't know why I didn't, except that I was a mess that night. But you need to know that I'm not sorry." She curved her hands over the child she already loved and wanted. Not that she'd accepted her situation instantly, but it had taken a surprisingly short amount of time to do so. "I really don't expect anything from you."

Hope was another matter altogether, however. She'd felt something powerful that night, a connection she couldn't even describe. Yes, she *hoped*.

"A decent man doesn't abandon a woman pregnant with his child," he said.

"We'll come to some agreement, Devlin. But not tonight, please. I'm exhausted."

He nodded. "I'll see you at ten-thirty." He shut the door behind him.

As his car pulled away she poured his cocoa down the drain then leaned against the sink to sip hers. He was a cool one—unemotional and practical—so different from their night at the hotel, when he'd bombarded her with emotion in the form of incredible sex, intense and challenging and satisfying. Tonight she'd seen the businessman. She'd looked him up on the Internet and learned his family's business was banking, with several branches in the Philadelphia area.

Old money. Old values, too, she guessed. The privileged son of such a family wouldn't get involved with a strictly middle-class someone like her—except for a night of anonymous sex.

She wondered how he was going to explain it to his family. *If* he was going to, that is. Maybe he'd offer her a payoff to keep quiet about the child's paternity. Wasn't that the usual way of things in *his* world?

Just how much was her uncomplicated world about to change?

Three

At exactly ten-thirty the next morning, Nicole pulled into the driveway leading to the grand entrance of the lodge where Devlin was staying. She'd fallen asleep easily after he left and slept well, not waking until almost nine. She felt ready to face him.

Like everyone else in the community, she'd been dying to see inside the lodge, situated outside the small community called Hunter's Landing. The locals had been abuzz about the house—a 9,000-square-foot, multilevel, log-and-stone structure that had taken almost a year to complete. She'd climbed the path to peer inside at the end of construction, amazed by the number of fireplaces and the majestic staircases. Building permits had been issued to a nonprofit corporation in Los Angeles, the Hunter Palmer Foundation, information deemed newsworthy enough for the local paper. But beyond that, details had been stingy. Curiosity had died when the house was completed and nothing happened, except that a man had stayed there in March, then a different one in April.

And now Devlin, who said he would also be staying there for a month.

What had he called his trip? Not business, but someone else's idea of pleasure? What could that possibly mean? It must somehow tie in with the other solo occupants who'd lived there for only a month. She wondered what the connection was.

Nicole approached the tall oak entry doors flanked by stone columns. She reached to ring the bell but the doors opened and Devlin stood framed there, looking very much like the lord of the manor in his jeans, boots and plaid shirt, the sleeves rolled up. It wasn't his clothing that labeled him, but his posture and inborn confidence.

She wanted to walk into his arms, as she had in the elevator that night. "Good morning," she said instead.

"Did you sleep okay?" he asked, stepping aside, giving her room to enter.

"Yes, fine." She faced an enormous staircase that split into two different directions at the top. "Did you?"

"No." They moved side by side up the stairs, then up another flight. "Have you eaten?" he asked when they reached the top of the staircase. "Would you like some coffee?"

"I've eaten, thanks, and I stopped drinking coffee."

"Then we'll go into the great room instead of the kitchen."

Could she ask for a tour? Maybe she should ask now, in case she never got another chance. But then she saw the view from the great room and stopped to stare. The sight of Lake Tahoe rimmed by trees never got tired, and this particular view was stunning. Boats were already cruising, specks on the lake, including the paddle-wheeler sightseeing boats that ran year-round. She kept promising herself she would take one of the tours but hadn't gotten around to it.

"Have a seat," he said.

He'd lit a fire in the immense stone fireplace. She sat in a burgundy leather chair next to it. He didn't sit but stood, his arms crossed, staring at the fire. She waited, getting more nervous by the second. Which was the real Devlin? Was it the caring, perceptive, sexy man she'd known in Atlantic City or this stern-faced one who seemed to have a steel backbone?

"I'm sorry you didn't sleep well," she said into the long silence. She locked her fingers together in her lap. Her waistband cut into her. If she could just unbutton her skirt.... She slipped her hands under her jacket, behind her back, trying to unobtrusively unfasten—

"What's wrong?" he asked, looking at her intently.

"Nothing."

He raised his brows.

She stopped short of sighing. "My skirt is too tight. I'm trying to unbutton it. Okay? Satisfied?"

"You're cutting off your circulation, which is bad for the baby."

"Oh, for heaven's sake. I'm not endangering the baby. And I'm getting some maternity uniforms today. I seemed to expand all of a sudden."

His gaze slid down her body. She automatically folded her arms in front of her.

"I'll be right back," he said, then left the room.

She let out a long, slow breath, not realizing she hadn't been breathing normally until she did. Why was she letting him intimidate her? It wasn't like her at all. He was just a man, flesh and blood.

And what great flesh...

She'd dreamed about him for weeks after their night together, had hunted for him among the blackjack players, hoping he would return. She remembered every detail. How he'd looked naked. The feel and scent of his skin. His amazing hands. The incredible way he used his mouth—everywhere. He'd bombarded her senses, and she'd become someone she'd never known she could be. The night had been all about pleasing—and forgetting. She'd gotten the sense that it had been the same for him.

Nicole decided not to be sitting when he returned. If he was going to stand, so would she. The small, internal rebellion giving her a bit of satisfaction, she wandered closer to the floor-to-ceiling windows. Snow still frosted the mountain peaks but had melted from the ground. The lake was too cold for swimming, but from where she stood, the blue depths looked inviting.

Devlin came up beside her and passed her a piece of paper. "I need you to fill this out."

There was no heading, just a questionnaire with spaces for her answers: name, address, birth date, social security number and other personal information. Like a credit application or something.

"What's this for?" she asked.

"My lawyer wants to run a background check."

"On me?"

"Yes."

"Oh, your *lawyer* wants it." She almost laughed at the absurdity. While she had no doubt his lawyer had provided the form, Devlin wanted it. Wanted her to sign on the bottom line giving him permission to delve into her private life—which he would undoubtedly do with or without her permission. It was just tidier with her permission.

"If we're going to be married," he said, "I need to know who you are."

The words on the page blurred. She lifted her head. His jaw flexed, his eyes bored into her. She wished she knew him well enough to interpret his expression. Accusation? Anger? She wasn't sure.

"Who said *anything* about marriage?"

"No child of mine will be born out of wedlock."

"So you believe the child is yours?"

He barely hesitated. "Yes."

"Why?"

"For the same reason I slept with you that night."

"What reason was that?" she asked, intent.

"Damned if I know. Instinct." He paused. "Look, Nicole, DNA testing will prove paternity. Anyway, I'm laying the groundwork for our union so there will be no delays later."

How romantic. The thought stung. Just the kind of marriage proposal every woman hopes for. "This isn't the Dark Ages."

He smiled slightly, coolly. "Feels like it to me."

Well, she hadn't expected him to be thrilled, after all. "I expect you to fill out one of these forms, too," she said just as coolly. "For *my* lawyer."

His mouth quirked. In appreciation? Admiration? Irritation? She didn't know, couldn't tell if he was laughing or mocking.

"That's fair," he said.

"I'll bring your form back to you tomorrow. I expect yours to be ready then, too."

"I'll stop by the hotel when you get off work, and we can exchange papers."

"Mine won't be ready by then. I'll do it at home tonight, after work."

"You have a lunch break, don't you?"

"I eat on my lunch break. And put up my feet. And relax. It's good for the baby." Ha! He couldn't argue that point.

He crossed his arms. "I also want your doctor's name and number. When is your next appointment?"

"In three weeks. I was just there last week."

"Make an appointment for us to see him together this week."

"Her. My obstetrician is a she." No wonder she hadn't told him yet about the baby. Subconsciously she'd known he was sexist and paternal and accustomed to having someone jump at the snap of his fingers. Well, not *this* someone. "When things are more settled with us, I'll make that appointment."

"Then I'll go without you. I have questions."

"Which she won't answer without my permission."

"A reasonable person wouldn't have any problem sharing the information I need as the father of this child."

What was left of her patience went up in smoke. So now she was witless? She'd tried to be understanding, she really had. "I'll drop off the paperwork tomorrow on my way to work," she said, then walked past him a few feet before stopping and turning back.

"Here's a hint to getting to know me, Devlin. Try talking to me. *With* me." She went down the stairs and out of the house. It would take thirty minutes to drive to the Sterling. Time enough to calm down before starting work.

He just needed time, too. She'd been able to come to terms with the baby and all the changes it would entail. So would he.

She hoped.

Dev watched her drive off. She didn't burn rubber to get away, didn't even speed, but he knew she was angry. He didn't blame her.

While no one would accuse him of being easygoing, he wasn't usually a jerk. He'd also never been responsible for a pregnancy before. But he was now—to a woman he knew only sexually.

He shoved his fingers through his hair, clasped his hands at his nape and blew out a slow breath. Exhaustion was too mild a word for what he was feeling. He hadn't slept a minute last night.

He'd made this trip—this forced trip—with the intention of firming up a plan to redirect his career. He'd reached a point where he could afford to take some risks, was willing to risk what he'd earned. He planned to get out of the family business, where he'd been stagnating, a realization brought home to him when he received the letter in January that would send him to Lake Tahoe for the month of May.

He needed to be his own boss. He had achieved huge success for the bank, beyond what his father or grandfather had done before him. Now he wanted individual success, not just financially but personally. He'd been aiming toward it all his adult life. But how could he take that risk now, with a child to provide for?

And a wife.

That much he'd decided during the night. Nicole would marry him, period—even though his lawyer had tried to talk him into waiting until the child was born.

Maybe he was being a fool. Maybe it was old-fashioned and inflexible, but some values were ingrained too deeply to be ignored, like not wanting his child born out of wedlock.

Sometimes Dev felt constrained by the conservative label he lived with, personally and professionally. But when people entrusted you with their money, they expected someone who might take a few risks, but only calculated ones. Losing someone else's money was a direct path to career suicide.

His expertise was in commercial real estate investments, and he had a reputation for having the Midas touch, even with his hands tied by the bank's board of directors some of the time. Another reason for him to go off on his own.

Dev climbed two flights of stairs to the loft. When he'd wandered through the house during his sleepless night, he'd come upon the well-equipped office on the top floor. He'd also discovered a corkboard on the wall onto which photographs were tacked, all reminders of a time when his life had been carefree. During college he'd been required to have good grades and establish lifelong contacts. Beyond that, his parents asked little. Until he graduated. Then everything changed.

Dev hadn't looked too closely at the photos last night, having too much on his mind to clutter it with the past. But as he glanced at them now, he realized he didn't know much about any of the men portrayed anymore. He remembered a remarkable camaraderie, but he couldn't pick out one as a best friend at the time, except Hunter. Maybe Ryan…

He turned his back on the past and put himself squarely in the present again by sending an e-mail to his lawyer asking him to fill out the form for Nicole and fax it back, then he grabbed a cup of coffee and headed onto one of the decks overlooking the lake. The direct heat of the sun turned the chilly air bearable. He sat on a lounge chair and watched the boats make their way across the expanse of water.

As exiles went, Lake Tahoe was more than palatable. He'd intended to spend some of his time setting up his career move and some exploring the region, maybe throw in a little gambling now and then.

He hadn't counted on…Nicole. In the past few months he'd wished for more information to go on to find her, but she had seemed to be a tourist, like him. A couple of times during their night together he could've sneaked a look at her wallet and learned more about her, but he'd resisted. They'd had a tacit agreement that they would share that night only, each of them easing an unspoken need.

But she had dropped into his mind since then, memories of her lush body tantalizing, her lips soft and hungry. She hadn't hesitated, hadn't just taken, but had given in ways he'd dreamed about since. A true partner, physically.

He'd wondered why she cried but figured she would tell him if she wanted to. She didn't. Nor had she yet.

What could have been so horrific that she would forget she should've insisted on using birth control? She was obviously intelligent.

He could say the same thing about himself, of course. It was stupid not to have taken care of the protection. Stupid. Which only proved how much Hunter's letter had affected him that day.

He should've just stayed home and gotten drunk instead.

Four

A couple of minutes before eight that evening, Nicole glanced across the lobby and saw Devlin leaning against a column, watching her. Although seeing him so suddenly startled her, she wasn't really surprised, having anticipated his showing up at some point.

When she clocked out she didn't try to avoid him but walked over to where he stood. "Did you get some sleep?" she asked.

"Yes. How are you feeling?"

"I'm fine. I guess you're here to walk me to my car again."

"You guessed right."

"And follow me home." She didn't know why that comforted her, but it did. She'd calmed down significantly since she'd left him earlier in the day. They were both stuck in the same pool of quicksand. It was up to them to help each other out of it.

Plus she'd decided it was kind of nice not to be figuring things out alone anymore.

"I want to pick you up and drive you to work and back from now on."

Temptation reared its hopeful little head. They could spend time together…. "There's no need," she said.

"I know. But I think you'd like it, too."

How did he see inside her like that? He'd done so from the beginning, from that moment in the elevator. "We'll talk about it later."

"How about dessert somewhere?" he asked, switching gears easily.

"I'm not hungry, thanks."

"Then keep me company while I eat."

"What's this about, Devlin?"

"Conversation. Getting to know you."

She studied his bland expression, catching the barest twinkle in his eyes. Since she was the one to suggest it, she couldn't very well turn him down—and he knew it. "Okay. But not here."

"Name the place."

"There's a coffee bar in another casino where they also serve dessert."

"We'll take my car and come back for yours later."

"Actually, we can walk. It's less than a block away."

He took her down jacket and held it for her, lifting her braid out of the way then letting it fall against her back. She felt his nearness all the way down her back as if he'd spooned with her, just like in Atlantic City during the brief time they'd slept. Back then she'd felt safe in his arms. Comforted.

It wasn't what she felt this time.

He made small talk as they walked, asking about her

day, listening to her stories. Something unusual happened most days.

"Do you gamble?" he asked.

"Nope."

"Not allowed to?"

"It's an unspoken rule. It wouldn't be good, whether we won *or* lost."

"How did you end up in Atlantic City?"

They both had their hands stuffed into their pockets against the cold. She was grateful he wasn't pushing a physical connection.

Liar. You want that more than anything.

She ignored the honest voice in her head. "My best friend from high school and I decided to take the summer after graduation to see the country. We ran out of money in Atlantic City, found jobs, then stayed. I stayed, that is. She saved enough to get herself home and off to college. I had no college plans."

"Wouldn't your parents have sent you the money to get home?" he asked.

The surprise in his voice told her a lot about him. "I was being independent."

"I see."

"Anyway, I liked the city. My job was okay, and I found an apartment to share with two other girls. After a couple of years, the Sterling hired me. They've been good to me. And good *for* me. I'd been very sheltered at home."

"Were your parents disappointed you didn't go to college?"

"I imagine so. They never said so, not directly. How about you? Where did you go?"

"Harvard."

Harvard. Of course. The divide between them cracked wider. The only thing they had in common was the child they'd created.

Don't forget sexual compatibility. The words didn't whisper but yelled in her head. Since they'd bumped into each other last night she'd been remembering even more of the details of that night in Atlantic City. But sexual compatibility wasn't enough to make a relationship work beyond the short term.

"Why did you come to Tahoe?" she asked, as he held the casino door open. She pointed in the direction of the coffee bar.

"To honor a pact I made during college."

The casino noise prevented easy conversation. They reached the coffee bar and examined the desserts in the display case. A mile-high decadent chocolate cake called her name, but she resisted, determined to keep her pregnancy weight under control. "I'd like a hot chocolate," she said to the clerk.

"Coffee and a piece of that," he said when it was his turn, pointing to the slice of heaven Nicole had been coveting.

Great. Now she was going to have to sit across from him while he indulged himself. It blackened her mood.

They sat at a table tucked in a corner. As soon as they were settled he produced two forks, giving one to her. He smiled slightly as if daring her to argue that she didn't want any.

She supposed she could manage a bite or two. After all, how bad could it be if they shared? A quarter of a piece wouldn't hurt anything.

Well, maybe half, she amended after one bite.

She glanced at Devlin. His expression was just short of smug.

"It's good," he said, toasting her with his cake-laden fork. "Reminds me of the cake we had in Atlantic City."

She'd forgotten about it. During the middle of the night he'd called room service and ordered a couple of sandwiches and a piece of chocolate cake, her absolute favorite dessert. She'd devoured most of it, making orgasmic sounds of appreciation, which he'd commented on. He'd scooped frosting onto his finger and dragged it between her breasts and down her abdomen, then licked it off....

She met his gaze—direct and bold. He remembered, too, and had no doubt ordered the cake to make her remember.

She picked up her mug. "What kind of pact did you make?"

His eyes sparkled at her change of subject. "During my freshman year I met a fellow freshman named Hunter Palmer. He was charismatic, the kind of guy who could get you to break rules and take adventure to a whole new level. He accumulated friends, of which I was one. Because of that association I also made friends with five other freshmen he'd brought into his circle."

He sipped his coffee, his eyes unfocused, as if living that time again.

"He sounds special," Nicole said.

"Yeah. I'd had good friends before, but nothing like that— a group of guys I could count on. Eventually we called ourselves the Seven Samurai. One night we'd been partying enough to have covered our dining table with empty beer bottles, and we pledged to build a lodge on the shores of Lake Tahoe ten years after graduation. Each of us promised to spend a month there, then we would all gather after the last month for a get-together, to celebrate our friendship and successes. Hunter probably chose Hunter's Landing as his idea of a joke."

"Why spend a whole month?"

"We thought that a decade later would be a good time to examine where we'd been and where we should be going. A month seemed like the right amount of time. We were twenty-two. What did we know?"

"So you're supposed to be assessing your life while you're here?"

"Pretty much."

"And you all own the lodge?"

"No. In fact I'd forgotten about it. I've had very little contact with the guys since graduation."

"There's a story there."

"Hunter died."

He said it matter-of-factly, but his grip tightened on his mug and his jaw hardened. "Suddenly?" she asked.

"He had melanoma, but it wasn't caught until it was too late. He died right before graduation."

"It devastated you."

He nodded.

"So how did the lodge come about?"

"Hunter left instructions in his will. He created a foundation to have the lodge built in time for our pact to be carried out, then at the end of the six months, the lodge will become a respite house for cancer survivors and patients, plus twenty million dollars will be disbursed to charity. The only requirement is that the six remaining Samurai each stay here a month, as we all promised."

Amazing. Twenty million dollars given away, just like that. And the lodge must have cost millions. "That's a lot of money."

"Hunter's family is in pharmaceuticals and personal-care products. You'd recognize the brands."

It felt nice having a regular conversation with him, Nicole

thought, leaning back, sated with cake and cocoa. "Why didn't you all remain friends? I would think that would bind you even further."

"I don't think we knew how to deal with it. No one expects a twenty-two-year-old to die like that. Plus we all graduated immediately after and went our separate ways, onto lives and careers. We exchanged Christmas cards for a few years, but even those stopped."

"Are you looking forward to seeing them again?"

"In some ways. It seems like taking a step back instead of forward."

"So, you don't know if they're married or have children or how their careers have gone?"

"After I got my letter from Hunter's estate lawyer in January I checked them out on the Internet. Everyone is successful."

Awareness clicked on a light of understanding in her head. "You got your letter in January?"

"Yeah."

"I'll take a wild guess and say it was the day we met."

He laid a hand on top of hers. "About that night...I think—"

"Hi!"

Intent on Devlin, Nicole hadn't noticed Ann-Marie come up to the table.

The young woman stuck out a hand toward Devlin. "I'm Ann-Marie. Nicole and I work together."

He released Nicole's hand to stand and shake Ann-Marie's. "I remember seeing you last night."

Nicole noticed he didn't introduce himself. She glanced at her watch. "Oh, look at the time. We need to get going," she said to Devlin, standing up. "See you tomorrow, Ann-Marie."

"Are you embarrassed to be seen with me?" Devlin asked as they exited the casino.

The temperature had dropped a few degrees more and the wind had picked up. Nicole tugged her collar up around her neck. "I'm not embarrassed, just…private. Ann-Marie probably assumes you're the father of my baby. Nobody knows much about me here."

"Why not?"

She tucked her chin inside her collar and wished she'd brought the woolen cap she kept in her car. Her ears were freezing. "I've lived here for only two months, and I spend most of my days off with my father. Which hasn't left me much time to develop any friendships, just work associations, and that's not easy, either, unless you work in different departments. I'm only an assistant manager, but it does mean I have to maintain a different relationship with the people who work under my supervision." She really missed her girlfriends in Atlantic City.

"Where does your father live?"

"In Sacramento. It's where I grew up." A gust of icy wind blasted her.

"Think it'll snow?" Devlin asked after a while, looking at the sky.

"I didn't hear the forecast today. I gather it's not unheard of in May."

"I checked it out on the Internet. An average of four inches. Are you a skier?"

"No. Are you?"

"Snowboarder."

Nicole found herself tensing, waiting for the other shoe to drop. He was being too nice. Too conversational. Was he lulling her into complacency before he dropped a bomb she wasn't going to like? It made her hesitate, even as she wanted to get to know him better. He was the father of her child. They would be connected forever. But that didn't make him the boss.

"Where'd you go?" he asked as they reached her car in the Sterling parking lot.

"What do you mean?" But she knew what he meant. Everything about him set her on edge, even when he was being nice. Especially then.

"You checked out of the conversation as soon as Ann-Marie showed up."

"Did I?" She unlocked her car, anxious to get inside and fire up the heater. "I'm just cold."

Which was a stupid thing to say, since they'd been indoors when Ann-Marie had come over.

He didn't call her on her glaring error in logic, which probably meant he had more to say on the subject but knew he shouldn't keep her standing in the cold. Stuck between a rock and a hard place. She almost smiled.

"Don't leave until I pull up behind you," he said.

"I want to let the car warm up, anyway." She shut the car door, silencing the discussion.

Less than fifteen minutes later they pulled into her driveway. She parked in front of the garage. By the time she walked to her front door, he was there waiting for her.

"Safe and sound," she said. "Good night."

"Invite me in."

"We just had a really nice…" She hesitated, not knowing what to call it.

"Date. We had a date."

"Did we? Okay. Anyway, it was nice. Why ruin it?" She stuck her key in the lock.

"Do you really want to have this conversation out here?" He pointed to her thermometer. "It's thirty-three degrees."

"No, I don't want to have this conversation out here—or anywhere. I want you to go."

"Invite me in."

"Why?"

He reached in front of her and turned the key, then opened the door.

She didn't move. "Intimidation is a real turnoff for me."

"You're shivering."

Truthfully, she wanted him to come in, because she wanted to know what he'd been about to say when Ann-Marie showed up. *About that night,* he'd said. What about that night?

But she also didn't want to back down after she'd said no.

From behind her he set his hands at her waist and propelled her gently into the house. She could barely feel his hands through her thick jacket, but she remembered how his palms had felt against her skin, and the way his fingers had explored and coaxed and teased. She wondered how many other women he'd been with since then....

"I'll light a fire," he said, "while you change into something more comfortable."

She'd been about to do that. She had fleece pants and a top that were cozy but not pajamaish. Because he'd suggested it, however, she would stay dressed as she was. She took off her jacket and hung it on a hook by the front door, then reached for his to hang next to hers. "I'm comfortable, thank you. I'm wearing my new maternity skirt."

He eyed her with the barest of smiles. She was getting to know that look well, one that seemed indulgent and paternal at the same time.

Nicole bumped up her thermostat so that the rest of the house would get up to a comfortable temperature, then sat on the sofa while he got a fire going. She rarely lit one herself, because it meant a lot of ash in the house, plus having to buy wood and clean out the fireplace. Devlin's lighting of it seemed to imply he would be staying a while.

She didn't mind sitting and watching him work, however, all hunkered down, the lean lines of his body a pleasure to observe.

"Your answering machine is blinking," he said.

"I noticed. It can wait."

"Hiding something, Nicole?"

Startled, she focused on the back of his head instead of his body. "You think I'm hiding something because I don't want to listen to my messages in front of you? That's a leap, don't you think?"

"If the hurdle fits…"

Nicole couldn't decide if he was joking or serious, since he hadn't yet joked with her. She *didn't* have anything to hide, but should she prove it?

The debate went on in her head, then she finally decided it was more important that he learn to take her at her word, and for that, she needed to prove herself. For a while, anyway.

She went to the kitchen counter and punched the message button.

"Hi, Nicki. Thought you'd be home by now. Give me a call when you get in, okay? You know how I worry. Bye."

The call had come in at 8:30 p.m., a time when she was almost always home from work. "There," she said to Devlin. "Satisfied?"

"Who is he?"

None of your damn business. "Mark. An old friend."

"Boyfriend?"

"When we were teenagers. The boy next door, but just friends now. Just friends since I moved away ten years ago." She sat on the couch again and watched him baby the flame to get it going.

"How did you hook up again?"

"What does it matter? And before you ask, no, he doesn't have feelings for me, either, except as a friend."

Devlin was quiet for a few seconds. "In a pocket inside my jacket," he said finally, glancing over his shoulder, "you'll find the form you wanted me to fill out. Why don't you have a look."

She heaved herself up with a sigh and retrieved the form. Devlin Gilmore Campbell. "Gilmore?" she queried.

"Mother's maiden name."

He would be thirty-two on his next birthday, which was September twenty third. She looked up, her breath catching a little. "The baby is due on your birthday."

"I figured it would be close." The tinder had caught. He added a few larger sticks. "Poor kid. I hope he's either early or late. It's no fun to share a birthday."

"He?"

He grinned at her—finally. She'd begun to wonder if he remembered how to smile.

"Speaking in general terms," he said. "I've learned we can find out the gender for sure when you have an ultrasound, which I gather can be sometime in the next few weeks."

"I don't want to know the gender."

"Why not?"

"I want to be surprised. Besides, ultrasounds aren't always accurate. I don't want to be prepared for one sex then have it be the other."

He got quiet again, which probably meant it was something they would discuss later. She went back to reading the form. His medical history pronounced him in good health, as was his financial condition. He owned a town house valued at two million dollars and other property totaling more. A whole lot more. She swallowed. She'd known he had to be well-off, but she hadn't expected the staggering amount. It made her very, very uncomfortable. Everything she discovered about him widened the gap between them.

"Why do you own so much property?" she asked finally.

"As a hedge against inflation. It's a quick way to build a portfolio. I have good instincts for choosing the right property."

"A quick way if you have the money," she said.

"Or are willing to take the risk."

Flames licked at the small log he added, enough that he could set the screen in front of it and join her on the couch.

"Tell your lawyer he can contact mine, if he has questions," he said.

"She."

He smiled. "Figures."

"Does it?" She smiled back, wanting to keep things as tension free as possible.

"You'll need to sign a prenup. The lawyers can hash out the details."

The other shoe had finally dropped. "I want you to be involved in your child's life, and I will accept some financial assistance, because I know it will make life easier. I like knowing that I wouldn't have to take a second job. But we both know that marriage is out of the question."

"Marriage is the only answer."

She could remind him forever that there was little stigma

attached to a child being born out of wedlock these days, but he would just counter it again with something about how things were done in *his* world.

"You have nothing to say about that?" he asked.

"I've said it already. And you've said your piece, as well. We're at a stalemate."

Silence echoed in the room, not one of those comfortable moments between people who liked being together, but a now-what? uncomfortable tension. She sensed he had a lot more to say but was holding back.

"Before Ann-Marie came up to the table," she said, "you started to say something about that night."

His hesitation created a heaviness in the room. "I don't remember what I was going to say."

She didn't believe him for a second. He'd been in the right frame of mind then to confide something, but that mood was gone. Disappointment weighed on her.

"Have you lined up a nanny yet?" he asked.

Laughter rose at the very thought. He *really* needed a reality check. While she hadn't grown up in poverty, it was nothing like how Devlin was raised, in a world where children had nannies, not babysitters or day care centers.

"Why is that funny, Nicole?"

"There's plenty of time for lining up child care," she said. "I'd like to show you where I grew up, if you're interested. I have Sundays and Mondays off and I usually go see my dad on Sundays. How would you like to come along?" It was time she told her father about the baby, anyway. And maybe her father's reaction would be tempered some by Devlin being there. She could hope, anyway.

"What about your mother?"

Nicole's throat tightened instantly. "She passed away.

Two days before Christmas." She watched him digest that information.

"So, when we met…"

"I had just returned from her funeral."

"We were quite a pair that night," he said quietly.

She nodded. She hadn't been herself at all but a shell of her normal self, hurting deeply, desperate for anything to assuage the pain. Devlin had done so.

She couldn't sit still with the memories bombarding her. She walked to a low table to check the soil of her houseplants, hoping they needed water. None of them did.

After a few seconds he joined her. "You have a green thumb."

"Not usually. Most of these are too new for me to know whether they'll live or die. I generally kill plants just by looking at them—except this one." She fingered a blooming African violet. "My mom brought it with her the first time she visited me in Atlantic City. A reminder of home. Of her. It needs repotting, and I'm scared to disturb it. She always did it for me when she came to visit."

"You're afraid it will die."

"Yes. It's fragile."

"And a reminder of her in a different way now."

She nodded.

After a long silence he said, "So, you'll fill out the form and have it ready tomorrow?"

"I said I would."

"Have you made that appointment with your doctor for me yet?"

"No."

He stared at her for a long moment, long enough that she wanted to squirm, so she moved away instead, intending to see him to the door.

Wordlessly he left the room, heading toward her bedroom. After a few seconds he walked past the doorway and into the nursery.

"What are you doing?" she asked.

"Checking that the windows are locked."

"I'm not an imbecile."

"Humor me."

"Trust me," she said.

"Can't happen overnight. I doubt you trust me yet, either."

He was wrong. She did trust him. Completely. That kind of blind faith was probably unknown to him. The word *trustworthy* was probably encoded into his DNA, it was so apparent.

When he seemed satisfied that her cabin was locked as tight as Fort Knox, he came to the front door, where she was waiting impatiently for him to leave so that she could finally let down.

He snagged his jacket and slipped into it, his eyes searching hers the whole time, then he moved close to her.

"Pregnancy becomes you," he said.

Flustered by the compliment and his nearness, she said nothing.

He brushed his fingers across her cheek. "You do have that glow that I've always heard about. And your breasts—" his gaze never left hers "—are even fuller. Do you plan to breastfeed?"

She nodded. He finally looked down, easing even closer as he did. She could barely breathe. Memories assaulted her. She jumped as he laid a hand on her abdomen, then dragged his wide palm and long fingers over and down the taut, rounded flesh.

"Have you felt him move yet?"

"Her."

He smiled. "Have you felt *the baby* move yet?"

"No."

He explored her belly with feather-light touches. "Have you been well?"

"I had some morning sickness. It's gone—" Her breath caught as his fingertips grazed low. She grabbed his wrist. "What are you doing?" She barely got the words out.

"I want to know what it feels like. What you feel like. I didn't even notice when I first saw you… Was it only last night?"

Heat and longing coursed through her at his touch. She hated that he could do that to her so easily. "Good night."

He didn't smirk. She almost wished he had, so that she could be even more ticked off. But instead he just seemed reluctant to go. His gaze landed on her answering machine, then returned to her.

"He's a friend," she said. "Honest."

She shut the door behind him and leaned against it, waiting until the car was gone before curving her hands over her belly, as he had.

She didn't want to let herself hope. Like most girls, she'd dreamed of marrying her Prince Charming and living happily ever after. And Devlin Campbell seemed to be some kind of American prince.

Which meant he and his family had power.

Nicole went still as the implications sank in. Power and money knocked out roadblocks standing in the way of goals—and she could be considered a roadblock.

She shook her head. No. There wasn't any reason to worry. He couldn't take the baby from her.

No amount of money could make that happen.

She decided to return Mark's call, since he would probably

panic if he didn't hear from her, maybe even alert her father and get him all upset for nothing.

She dialed his home number and got his answering machine. "Hi, it's me, checking in. Don't call me back, because I'm going to bed. I hope everything's going okay with you. Talk to you later."

Nicole could've called his cell phone, which he always had with him, but she really didn't want to talk to him. She needed to think about Devlin and his family and his place in the world.

And where she fit in.

Five

Dev glanced toward the passenger seat in his rented Lincoln Navigator as he drove from Tahoe to Sacramento four days later. The SUV rode so smoothly that Nicole had fallen asleep, her head bobbing gently, her hand resting on her abdomen. It was the first time he'd seen her out of uniform; she was wearing black pants and a loose, long-sleeved pink blouse. She hadn't braided her hair, and it flowed around her face and over her shoulders, shiny and tempting. He lifted a strand carefully and rubbed it with his fingers, was tempted to draw it to his nose to take in the fresh floral scent he remembered from their night in Atlantic City.

She stirred slightly, so he dropped the silky strand and glanced at the map he'd printed before they'd headed out, glad he wouldn't have to disturb her sleep to ask for directions.

They'd left Tahoe at 10:00 a.m., had been on the road for

two hours. The next exit was her father's. As Dev let the car slow on the off ramp, Nicole opened her eyes. He'd hoped to ask questions during the drive, but she'd fallen asleep not long after they got on the road. On purpose, to avoid talking to him? He didn't know. They'd spent a couple of hours together each night after she got off work, making tentative progress in getting to know each other, but he'd been frustrated by how little she revealed and how much she kept him at bay.

She hadn't allowed him physically close since the night he'd touched her belly. Any time he moved toward her, she stepped back or aside.

He should be trusting her more by now. Instead he found himself questioning everything about her.

"We're already here?" she asked, sitting up and readjusting her seat belt. "I've been sleeping all this time? I'm so sorry!"

"Why?"

"I didn't keep you company."

"It's not important."

"Turn left at the signal." She pulled a brush from her purse and ran it through her hair, then put on a little shiny lip stuff.

"Did you tell your father you were bringing me today?"

"No."

"Why not?"

"The surprise element seems to work best with him."

"Does he know you're pregnant?"

"No. Turn right at the stop sign."

Dev wondered what he was walking into. A father who would point a shotgun at him? Although that would solve Dev's problems if her father would force her to marry him. "So, we're telling him together today?" he asked.

"Yes." She pointed ahead. "There's the house. The one with the big blue pickup... Shoot."

"What's wrong?"

"That's Mark's truck."

Dev didn't pull up in front of her father's house but the next-door neighbor's, out of direct sight. A sign on the truck advertised Moore's Tire and Brake.

He turned off the ignition and angled toward Nicole. "Why would he be here?"

She shrugged, but Dev figured she knew the answer. Mark was more than a friend—or wanted to be, anyway. Maybe Nicole felt the same way, but felt stuck because of the pregnancy. Dev wouldn't know until he saw for himself.

"Are you afraid of your father, Nicole?" he asked instead.

"Just of what his reaction will be."

"Why? What do you think he will do?"

"Yell. Show his disappointment."

A parent yelling was beyond Dev's experience. His parents never even raised their voices. Civility was the norm, and also was expected of him and his two sisters. Not that the siblings hadn't argued out of range of their parents, but never in front of them. Emotion was heard of, not seen.

"Won't he support you?" Dev asked.

"After he calms down."

"If he causes you any stress, we're leaving." He opened his car door.

"Wait." She touched his arm. "I don't want to tell Dad while Mark is there."

"I couldn't agree more." He strode around the car to help her out. She'd initially protested what he considered good manners by opening her car door for her, but she'd learned to wait for him.

"Do you think Dad will notice on his own?" she asked as they walked up to the front door.

He glanced to where she rested a hand on her abdomen, then raised his gaze to her breasts. Images of those breasts had been waking him up at night. She had nipples that seemed to stay hard—like now. A memory flashed of her on top of him, leaning forward and grabbing the headboard so that he could fill his hands with her firm flesh and draw her nipples into his mouth.

"It's obvious to me, now that I know," he said, forcing himself to look away. "I doubt your father looks at you in the same way that I do. Your friend, on the other hand, could notice."

Nicole opened the door without knocking, something Dev hadn't done at his parents' house since he'd left for college.

"I'm here, Dad," she called out.

"In the kitchen, honey."

Dev looked around the tidy living room they'd entered. The decor was probably called country, the furnishings comfortable and unpretentious. Homey. He pictured Nicole playing there as a child, or in the backyard, visible through sliding glass doors, another well-tended spot. Several pots of African violets sat on a kind of plant ladder, each of them in full bloom.

A man who couldn't possibly be her father stepped into the kitchen doorway. The smile on his face faded when he spotted Dev, who sized him up in an instant. *Just friends, my ass.* The black-haired man was competition. He was a couple inches shorter than Dev and probably twenty pounds heavier, all brawn. He couldn't hide the green monster of jealousy fast enough for Dev not to see how he felt.

"Hi, Mark," Nicole said, an edge to her voice.

He stepped back, letting Nicole and Dev into the kitchen, where her father was piling deli meats onto a tray. He was tall, slight and almost bald. Nicole had inherited his bright-blue eyes.

"You're early," he said to Nicole, then shifted his gaze to Dev.

"No traffic," Dev said, deciding it wouldn't be wise to admit he'd been testing the speed limits while Nicole slept. "I'm Devlin Campbell." He extended his hand toward the man, who quickly wiped his off on a towel before shaking hands.

"Rob Price," he replied, looking curiously between Nicole and Dev. "You're a friend of Nicki's?"

You might say that. Dev discarded the flippant remark. "Yes."

"And this is my old friend, Mark Moore," Nicole said.

Mark's handshake was brief and hard.

"No hug?" Mark said to Nicole.

Dev watched the man bury his face into her hair and tighten his arms around her for longer than was usual for "just friends." Dev also saw Nicole try to free herself several seconds before the guy actually let go.

"You didn't say you were bringing someone along," Rob said to his daughter.

"It was last minute." She had the grace not to look at Dev as she lied. "I didn't know Mark was going to be here, either. What can I do to help, Dad?"

"Mark brought everything—sandwich fixings and salads."

"And chocolate cake," Mark added. "Your favorite."

How many more of her "favorite" things did Mark know? Dev wondered, annoyed that Mark had that kind of intimacy with her.

"Table's set. Let's sit down," Rob said abruptly, carrying the tray to the kitchen table, where the rest of the food was already in place.

"So, Devlin, is it?" he asked heartily. "Do you live in Tahoe?"

"Philadelphia."

"We met when I was working in Atlantic City, Dad."

"You never mentioned him. What are you doing out here?" Rob asked.

"Mixing business and pleasure." He smiled at Nicole, who gave him a nervous smile in return.

"Nicki and I went steady in high school," Mark said, out of the blue.

Dev had never dealt with a jealous man before. It would be a simple task to get a rise out of the man. All Dev had to do was touch Nicole in a way that implied intimacy. Although the fact that she'd brought him home to meet her father spoke loudly enough. "Nicole told me," Dev replied.

"Did she tell you we had our first kiss together?"

"Yes." Dev sensed Nicole's reaction to his lie, but she didn't contradict him. "I was amused by her story of puppy love."

"How are you doing, Dad?" Nicole inserted. She didn't exactly elbow Dev, but her tone said it all. She wanted the conversation between him and Mark over.

"Oh, you know. Okay."

"Are you sleeping better?"

"A little, I think. So, what do you do for a living?" he asked, shifting the conversation back to Devlin, who sensed Nicole's deep sigh even though she didn't make a sound.

"I'm in banking."

"I own my own tire-and-brake business," Mark said. "Been in business for five years."

And so the one-upmanship had begun. "I'm vice president of Campbell Bank. We've been in business for two hundred years."

The silence was like the aftermath of cannon fire.

"What could you two possibly have in common?" Mark asked, not hiding his disdain.

"A baby, for one thing."

Nicole groaned.

Her father paled. "Is that true, Nicki? You're pregnant?"

"Yes." She'd turned as bright as he was pale.

"When?"

"I'm due late September."

"Are you married?"

"Not yet," Dev replied, sliding his arm around Nicole's shoulder.

"Do you have a date set?"

"Not yet."

"Why not?" Mark asked, fury in his voice.

Dev looked at Mark. "This discussion doesn't concern you."

"This is my home," Rob said, tossing down his fork. "I decide that."

"Then we're leaving." Dev set down his napkin. "Nicole—"

"Stop it!" she shouted. "Just stop it. All of you. What a bunch of Neanderthals you are. Especially you," she threw out at Dev, then pushed back her chair and fled the room, leaving the men alone.

Nicole looked at her watch. She'd been hiding in her old bedroom for fifteen minutes. She hadn't heard any shouting or gunshots, so it was probably okay to go back out there, but she was so angry at Devlin for announcing her pregnancy like that, especially since he'd agreed they would wait until they were alone with her father.

At least Mark was gone. She'd heard his truck pull away less than a minute after she'd locked herself in her room to escape the explosion of testosterone that had made it hard to breathe, much less think.

She sat up on her bed and looked around the familiar space—the lace curtains and handmade wedding-ring quilt, the maple dresser and oval mirror. There were photos on the wall from proms and sporting events, where she'd been a cheerleader.

She wished her mother was there to give her a hug and tell her everything would be okay. Her mom would've been disappointed, too, but she would've tried to help find solutions.

All Nicole wanted was the same unequivocal love and devotion her parents had shared. She didn't want to marry someone who didn't absolutely adore her, who wouldn't willingly abide by the vows spoken in the marriage ceremony.

Well, she had to face the music sometime. She left her bedroom and walked down the hallway. Devlin and her father had moved from the kitchen to the living room. Devlin stood in front of the fireplace looking at a photo he'd taken down from the mantel. Her father sat in his recliner, his fingers gripping the arms.

"That's Sherry, my wife," her father said.

"Nicole looks very much like her."

"Peas in a pod. Opposite in personality, though."

"In what way?"

"Sherry was as quiet and gentle as they come—" Rob stopped, as if he'd started something he realized he shouldn't finish.

"Nicole isn't?"

"I'm not what?" Nicole asked, making her presence known.

Both men looked at her but said nothing. Devlin's gaze drilled her.

"I'm fine," she said, hoping it would answer all unasked questions.

He replaced the photograph, then took her hand and made her sit on the sofa.

"I imagine you have questions," Dev said to her father.

He leaned toward them. "I expect you're going to make an honest woman out of my daughter."

"Yes."

"Hold on," Nicole said. "I'm pregnant, not dishonest."

"In my day, Nicki, people who were expecting got married."

She rolled her eyes. "Your day was the sixties, Dad. In San Francisco, no less. Your generation defined free love and women's liberation and all those free-choice kinds of things."

Rob smiled for the first time, although crookedly, a little sheepish. "So, when did you say my grandchild is due?"

"The end of September."

"And what exactly is your problem with marrying the father of your child?"

Before Nicole could answer him honestly, Dev wrapped a hand around one of hers. "Nicole and I are making decisions together. We will keep you in the loop."

Rob's brows rose at being put in his place. "What about your family? Have you told them?"

"No."

"Why not?"

"Because I haven't had the chance yet. Be assured I am looking out for Nicole and the baby."

"And apparently you can support my daughter just fine."

"No dowry is necessary."

Silence settled between them.

"Did you need help with your bills or anything?" Nicole asked her father.

"I've finally got them figured out," he said. "I appreciate all you did to help, but everything's under control now."

Nicole was sorry she'd asked. He seemed embarrassed at Devlin's knowing he'd been leaning on her. The lack of conversation allowed for the sound of children playing in the street outside, and traffic noise and a siren that stopped nearby.

"Is it against the rules to ask how you met?" Rob asked. "You said it was in Atlantic City, but how? It doesn't seem like your paths would cross."

"At the casino," Nicole said.

"She was my good luck charm," Dev added.

"In what way?"

"I'd been losing at blackjack until she came along, then I wouldn't let her leave. Won a lot of money that night, too."

"You're a gambler?"

"Occasionally. Recreationally." He squeezed Nicole's hand. "You need to finish your lunch."

"I'll wrap it up and take it with me. Did you eat?"

He nodded. She guessed his appetite wasn't bothered by emotional upheaval the way hers was.

"We should be going," she said to Dev, who knew how to take a cue. He stood.

"So soon?" her father asked, although he also looked relieved. "I'll get your lunch."

Nicole tugged her hand free of Devlin's. "Please wait here for a minute." She followed her father into the kitchen.

"Are you disappointed in me, Dad?" she asked as he tucked her lunch into a paper bag.

"Only if you don't do the right thing."

"The right thing isn't necessarily marriage." She held up a hand when he started to protest. "I don't want a marriage that will end in divorce. I need to know it will last. Surely you understand that. You were married to the love of your life. You don't want anything less for me, do you?"

"Of course not. But you slept with the man. Made a baby together. You cared about him enough to do that."

Since she would never share the details of how she and Devlin had gotten together, there wasn't much she could say in answer. "Give us time to get things figured out." She hugged him. Tears sprang to her eyes at how familiar and comforting he felt. "I love you, Dad."

"Love you, too, honey."

They walked together to the living room. He held out a hand to Dev. "Take care of my baby."

"Count on it."

"You never told me what happened to your mother," Dev said to Nicole as they got on the freeway headed back to Tahoe.

"She had a stroke the day before Christmas. I caught the first flight out, but I didn't get to the hospital before— I never got to say goodbye."

"I'm sorry."

She nodded. "It was just so unexpected. She'd always been in such good health and had taken care of herself. And I hadn't talked to her for a couple of weeks. I don't know why. I'd just been…busy. I was supposed to fly home the day after Christmas and was going to stay until New Year's, so I hadn't worried about…talking to her or anything."

"Guilt is useless, Nicole."

It took her a moment to react. "I suppose you have no regrets about anything?"

"I examine where and how something went wrong, but then I put it out of my head."

"How nice for you."

"It doesn't mean I don't feel anything."

"You seem part robot."

If that was true, his father would be one proud man. Dev had been trained by the best. Particularly in banking, one had to be rational. Money and emotion didn't belong in the same sentence.

Nicole wasn't the first to allude to his inability to fill a woman's emotional needs, complicated as they were. His familial duty had been made clear, however—find an acceptable wife who could provide the next generation of Campbells. Ever since that edict had come down two years ago from his father, he'd taken to dating perfectly suitable young women, but his interest never lasted beyond the first date. Since it wasn't something he was in a hurry to do, it hadn't mattered. Nicole had been the only woman he'd wanted to see again.

And look how that turned out.

Dev merged into the middle lane. Hunter had to be laughing. Years ago, he had called Dev a rebel in conformist's clothing, had challenged him not to go directly from college to the bank but to set off on his own, saying that the confines of that business and his family would turn Dev into an old man before his time.

Dev had even been considering it. Then Hunter died, and Dev had no interest in causing a rift with his family. He'd graduated on a Thursday and reported to work on Monday.

The recent events were strikingly similar. Thanks to the letter from Hunter's estate, Dev had come to Lake Tahoe with a plan in mind for his future, one where he would take the big step away from his family—then, wham, he found out Nicole was pregnant and he would have to put her and the baby's needs ahead of his own.

He could write a book about his life: *The Dutiful Man*.

"I'm sorry," Nicole said, breaking into his thoughts. "I shouldn't have said you are part robot. I barely know you."

"Yeah. Let's change that."

"What do you mean?"

"Move into the lodge with me. Today."

"No," she answered, just as unequivocally.

"You would have your own bedroom."

"I already have my own bedroom. It's comfortable. I like it. All my stuff is there."

"How much stuff do you need? We're talking a few weeks, and you can swing by and pick up anything you need, anytime." He glanced at her. "It's my right to be involved, Nicole."

"In the pregnancy?"

"More than that. This is a lifelong connection."

She took a long while to answer. "I'll agree to stay with you," she said finally, "if you agree to one thing. That you don't pressure me about marriage. We get to know each other, period."

"Agreed." A wise man knew which battles to choose.

She settled back again. "Have you ever been married?"

"If I had gotten married, I would still be married."

"Meaning what?"

"I will marry once, and only once."

"Have you ever lived with a woman before?"

Was that tightness in her voice jealousy? He eyed her, but she looked straight out the windshield. "No, I've never lived with a woman."

"Why not?"

"My father and grandfather wouldn't have approved, for one. As a bank officer I have to uphold certain moral and ethical standards, which may seem strange in this day and time, but it's a fact of my life."

"So you're going to be in trouble because of me…and the baby?"

He smiled slightly. "It's not something that matters to me. Anyway, the most important reason is that I never met a woman I wanted to live with. If I had, I would've married her. How about you?"

"I've lived with women, lots of women." She grinned when he raised his brows at her. "No, I haven't been married or shacked up, either. These past couple of months have been the first time I've lived alone. I love my cabin and my privacy."

"I understand that. The last three years of college I rented a house with my six friends. It was great, but I was ready to be on my own."

"I'm guessing that Hunter was one of those friends?"

"The ringleader. He found the house in Cambridge, signed the lease, then took us all there. No one had a choice."

"Was there something else you wanted to do? Live in a fraternity house or something?"

"No. We just became a kind of fraternity ourselves. We initially came together as a group when Hunter convinced us to nail the Hall's rec-room furniture to the ceiling."

The way he smiled at the memory said a lot to Nicole. She'd missed out on that kind of experience, since she'd never gone to college. She'd had a series of roommates, some good, some not, but since she'd left Atlantic City, even the good friendships were fading. "Did you get in trouble?"

"Yeah, but Hunter got us get-out-of-expulsion-free cards with an oratory defending the action as an engineering experiment. You'd have to know Hunter to understand his charisma. If he'd lived, he would've been president some day. I'm sure of that."

Devlin made a quick lane change to avoid a huge pickup about to move into the same lane without enough clearance.

Devlin didn't swear, didn't exhibit any impatience at the un-observant driver. Nicole probably would've been shaking her fist.

"Do you like to cook or should we stop to eat before we get to the lodge?" he asked, deftly changing the subject.

Nicole had dated a lot, having had several steady boy-friends over the years, so she was accustomed to men not wanting to discuss anything remotely emotional. She also wanted not only to keep the peace with him but to find a way for them to learn about each other without a lot of friction. She wondered if that was going to be possible.

"I like to cook *and* I like to go out," she answered, allowing the change of subject.

He nodded. She would be glad to get home and out of the car, the intimacy of the confined space getting to her. She had closed her eyes on the trip to Sacramento to avoid talking to him, but had fallen asleep almost instantly. She'd slept so long that she wasn't tired now. What safe topics could she bring up for the rest of the trip?

"You mentioned once that you had sisters," she said.

"I do. Older sister, Joan, younger sister, Isabel. Joan's thirty-four. She's five months pregnant with her third. Izzy's twenty-four and finishing at Wharton next week."

"Finishing?"

"She'll have her MBA."

"Will she join the bank?"

"She's been politicking for that."

"Why does she have to campaign for a job in her own family's business?"

"She's female."

"Women aren't employed by your bank?"

"Not Campbell women."

"How sexist."

"Izzy's the first Campbell woman to express an interest in joining the bank. She's been talking to my mother and our grandmother, trying to get them to campaign for her."

"Do you get along with your sisters?"

"Joan and I are close. Izzy's eight years younger and very…strong willed."

She pictured him as a brother, wondered if they'd fought like most siblings. He was always so polite. Did he ever let loose? And how?

"Did you work while you were in college?"

"At the bank, during the summers. It was my internship, so that when I graduated, I went into management right away."

"You told my dad you are the vice president." Which was utterly intimidating to her. Being his wife would require social skills she didn't have.

"I've held that position for the past four years."

She thought about his beautiful town house she'd seen that one time from the street, a public symbol of his success. She never would have met him in his normal life. And now they'd not only met but had a lifelong connection ahead of them, as he'd termed it.

But she needed to be honest with herself, too, about the fact she was hopeful that the relationship could become something more than being the parents of the same child. Girlhood dreams didn't die easily. She wanted the happy-ever-after ending.

What was wrong with loving the father of your child, anyway? She knew it was probably just a fantasy that they could be a real family. Could she risk falling in love with him in hopes that he would fall for her, too? In hopes that he would be proud enough of her to take her home to meet his family?

It was just that she kept remembering that night in January, and how emotional he'd been and yet attuned to her needs and desires, how he hadn't asked questions but had recognized she was hurting about something, too. There'd been nothing robotic about him then.

Of course *then* he hadn't been stuck with an unplanned pregnancy, either. That changed everything.

The question again was, who was the real Devlin Campbell?

She wanted to know more of the Devlin she'd met in January. The Devlin she'd met since was more difficult. More dictatorial. Less flexible.

She wanted to *know* him. That's what it came down to. There wouldn't be a better time to discover each other and make decisions about the future.

Now, how would they do that without falling into bed together? Because she was just as attracted to him now as she'd been that night. And from the looks she caught him sending her way, he felt the same.

It seemed that they'd just lit a long fuse on a powerful stick of dynamite.

Six

Nicole surveyed the kitchen, cupboard by cupboard, getting the lay of the land. Night was upon them.

"This is quite a kitchen," she said, admiring the interesting combination of contemporary stainless-steel appliances and Tuscan-look antiqued walls and decor. "I think my whole house could fit in here."

The space easily accommodated fifteen for eating, suiting the huge expanse of the lodge well.

"I put your things in the guest room," Devlin said. "I'll show you to the room so you can unpack."

"Okay, thanks."

They hadn't spoken much in the past hour or two. In the car he'd finally put in a Coldplay CD to cover the silence, and she'd sung along now and then. He'd tapped his fingers against the steering wheel. It hadn't been completely awkward, just strange and new being with him.

Now they headed upstairs. They hadn't gone halfway when she turned around, catching him lifting his gaze in a hurry.

"These stairs are wide enough for three, maybe four people, side-by-side," she said, challenging him to deny he'd been following her to stare at her rear.

"But the view from here is spectacular," he said, then climbed two stairs to meet her. "Attraction isn't an issue between us, Nicole, I think you'll agree. The only question is what we do about it."

"I'm as aware of that as you are," she said. "What would you like to do?"

"Are you sure you want an honest answer to that?"

"We can't afford less than honesty."

"Okay." He held her gaze as he moved closer, then put his hands on the banister behind her, trapping her. "I'd like to know if your ass is as firm as I remember."

Very little space separated their bodies. He held her gaze, his expression intent, his breath a whisper of warmth on her face.

Nicole didn't want to be known as a tease, but she also craved his touch. A slow roll of arousal made its way through her. Her body felt heavy and hot.

"No response?" he asked. "Honesty, Nicole."

"I guess I don't know how firm you remember it to be."

"Very."

It wasn't the word but the way he said it. She moved his hands to her rear. He took it from there, cupping her flesh with his long fingers and broad palms and squeezing.

"Yeah," he whispered. "Exactly." He inched closer, tucking her close against his abdomen.

Nicole felt him, hard and thick. She'd wondered at the accuracy of her own memories. They were true. All true.

"You don't have to stay in the guest room," he said, his mouth close enough that they were almost kissing.

She touched her tongue to her lips, nervous and excited. "It would confuse the issue," she replied.

"I think it would help settle it."

"As you said, sex is easy for us. It's the rest that's going to take time."

He pressed her into the banister and moved against her. "Remember how good it was?" he whispered, his lips grazing hers.

How could she forget the most memorable night of her life? Her best sexual experience ever? His body was perfect—lean but well muscled, with barely any chest hair, but still a line that had tapered down his abdomen, inviting fingers and tongue to follow it. He'd filled her hands, her mouth, her very core. Once they'd undressed, she hadn't felt any shyness. Nothing but appreciation and satisfaction in a long night of exploration.

She wanted that again. Now. She wanted him. Now.

"Come to my room," he urged. "Be mine again."

His words stunned her into awareness. Be his? She wasn't his. Sex *would* only confuse things, distort problems that they needed to deal with.

"We need to have our own rooms, Devlin."

He pulled back slowly, then slipped his hands in his pockets, his expression blank. "The offer will remain on the table," he said, then he started up the stairs, leaving her to follow.

Nicole realized she could make a big deal of his attitude—or not. She decided to ignore it, determined to find a connection with him beyond the baby.

She didn't rush to catch up but followed at her own pace. She saw a door open to what must be the master suite, dominated by another stone fireplace and an enormous sleigh bed.

She entered the guest room—suite, she amended, a large space with views and its own bathroom. "What, no fireplace?" she asked, smiling.

His shoulders relaxed. "Guests should be accommodated but not made so comfortable they won't leave."

"Oh, is that the way your people treat company?" She opened her suitcase and began to pull out items. He'd hung up the clothes she'd brought that were already on hangers.

He laughed, a very nice sound. "My people?"

"If the label fits." She grabbed a handful of lingerie and slipped it into a drawer as casually as possible, although she noted his interest in the stack of silk and lace.

"You dropped something," he said, then dangled a purple lace thong in front of her face.

She snatched it out of his hand and shoved it among the rest of her things.

"So, you haven't switched to granny panties yet."

"Never." She planned to be sexy at nine months. "This is another beautiful room," she commented as he sat in a chair, apparently in no hurry to leave. "I've never seen paneling like this. It's more like planks, isn't it? Are all the other bedrooms decorated like this one?"

"There are six suites, but only two are decorated, although the walls are like these, yes. I'm assuming the others will be furnished by the time it's turned over to the foundation."

She carried her toiletries into the roomy bathroom.

"Are you hungry?" he called out.

"A little. Are you?"

"Yeah." He came up to the open bathroom door. "I'll fix a tray of something for us."

"Would you mind if I peeked into the master suite?"

"Go ahead." He left.

After a moment she wandered down the hall and into his room, enormous and elegantly rustic. She went into the bathroom, which showcased a huge whirlpool tub with a fireplace in the wall beside it and a large separate shower. She still couldn't imagine having the money to build such a place.

Nicole could hear him in the kitchen. She started downstairs then changed her mind and went up a different flight instead, encountering an office space with a balcony overlooking the room below. The desk had a full-size computer that was shoved to the back and turned off, a laptop in its place in front. All the other necessary equipment was there—fax, printer, scanner. A bulletin board covered with photographs drew her. It didn't take long to determine that these were the Seven Samurai from his college days. She singled out Devlin. His hair was slightly longer, and in all the pictures he was smiling, even grinning broadly. He was ten years younger then, of course, and more carefree than now.

Now he was going to be a father—and not by choice.

"Quite a crew," he said from behind her.

She jumped. His hand came down on her shoulder, steadying her.

"Not a mediocre one in the bunch," she agreed. Indeed, they were all very good-looking men. "And twins," she said, angling closer to one photo.

"Luke and Matt Barton. Luke was here last month. He left me a note."

"What'd it say?"

"It was cryptic. I haven't figured it out yet. Requires digging into my memory."

"Who put up the photos?"

"I don't have a clue. Maybe it was part of Hunter's plan. I can't picture either Nathan—who was the first of us to come here—or Luke having kept all those photos, much less bringing them along."

"Why?"

"I think only Hunter would've been called sentimental. Plus everyone's busy with their careers. Luke owns a wireless technology firm, and Nathan's president of the Barrister Hotel."

"Just your ordinary working men," she said, with a grin.

He tugged on a hank of hair.

"Who were you closest to, aside from Hunter?"

"Ryan, probably." He pointed to the picture of the brown-haired, brown-eyed man, as tall and handsome as the rest of the group. "We didn't have so much in common as we just… clicked. Both of us were pretty serious. Hunter changed that. Ryan's scheduled to come here next."

"For the month of June?"

"Yes. Food's ready."

"Peanut butter and jelly?"

"I did a little better than that, I think."

He'd done a lot better, having prepared a tray of antipasto items—three kinds of olives, artichoke hearts, salami, two cheeses and pepper crackers. He'd poured her some apple cider in a wineglass that matched his. The fire he'd started in the great room made the huge space seem cozy. Only one lamp was on, and that on low. Light jazz came from the many speakers. Outside, the sky was inky black, except for the infinite expanse of stars.

They sat side by side on the sofa so that they could share the plate of food. She had an urge to feed him, and smiled at the thought.

"What?" he asked.

"I'm just relaxed. It feels good."

"It wasn't an easy day for you, with your father finding out about the baby."

"I'm glad that's over." She lifted her glass, then stopped. "I really miss my mom."

Devlin eyed her steadily. "You were close?"

"She was my best friend, as well as my mother."

"I can't imagine that. A parent being a friend." He popped a large green olive in his mouth and chewed, his expression thoughtful. "I respect my parents, but I don't confide in them."

"Who do you confide in?"

He frowned, not answering right away. "I talk to my sister Joan the most about non-work-related issues. I can't say I've felt much need to confide. Not my style."

"It's been hard for me since I moved here and didn't know anyone and with my mom gone. And being pregnant." She set down her glass and faced him, folding her hands in her lap. "I need to know if you have a girlfriend."

His brows rose slightly. She tried not to squirm at his direct look. She had a right to know if some woman was going to come after her for stealing Devlin away with a surprise pregnancy.

"No."

That was it. *No.* Short, simple, definite.

"Have you ever been in love?" she asked.

"No. Have you?"

"If you can call what I felt for Mark as a teenager love."

"*Is* that what you call it?"

"At the time I would've said so."

"Yet you took off for the summer then never returned. No regrets for leaving him behind?"

She tried to remember. "We'd been next-door neighbors

since we were kids. Friends who started dating. It seemed easy and natural."

"Too easy?"

"What do you mean?"

"No passion?"

"There was passion."

"Did you sleep together?"

"That's none of your business, Devlin."

"You won't answer the question?"

"I don't see how knowing whether Mark and I slept together is important."

"He's still in your life. It affects me."

"No."

"No, you didn't sleep together?"

"No, it really doesn't affect you, too." Nicole decided he seemed a little jealous, which she found interesting. Or maybe just possessive, not quite the same thing as jealousy.

He swigged the remainder of his wine. "I'm going to assume you did."

"Assume away."

"So much for getting to know each other." He poured himself another glass of wine, then moved to look out the windows at the night sky.

"Some things are going to take time and trust." Nicole joined him, sorry he was upset, but unwilling to give him everything he wanted when she knew he wouldn't be opening up and sharing with her in return. She wanted a partner in this relationship, a balance. She would meet him halfway, if and when he decided to do that, too.

"You asked me if I had a girlfriend," he said. "I answered."

She figured he was used to having control, and this was outside his control in many ways. She had a certain sympathy for him in that sense. "Mark isn't my boyfriend. He hasn't been for ten years. I did already tell you that I wasn't seeing anyone when we met, nor have I been since."

He angled toward her and met her gaze. "Tell me honestly how you feel about having a baby."

She didn't hesitate. "It's not about having *a* baby. It's about having *this* baby, which I consider a gift sent to fill the emptiness of my mother being gone. I'm grateful. It wasn't anything I sought, but I'm happy about it. I know you're not."

He said nothing. She didn't know how to react to his silence. Her throat burned. She was afraid she would cry.

"It's been a long day, Devlin. I'll say good-night now."

He didn't stop her. Normally she would've put the food away and washed the dishes, but she walked past them, leaving them for him, not caring.

In her room she sat on the bed and fought tears. Her dreams of marriage to a man who loved her passionately and infinitely weren't going to come true. If he resented her, or resented the baby that was changing his life, it didn't bode well for his being a good father. He didn't seem to have had much of a role model, either, which made it doubly hard.

After a while Nicole heard the music shut off. She had no idea whether he stayed up late or was an early riser, and didn't hear him climb the stairs if and when he did.

She changed into a pink-flowered cotton nightgown, which clung to her in ways it hadn't before she was pregnant. She loved the changes in her body, except that she was warm all the time, a byproduct of pregnancy, and Devlin seemed to like a warm house.

Nicole climbed into bed and turned out the bedside light. She'd left the curtains open so that she would see the sunrise in the morning.

Morning. A fresh start. A new beginning. She always looked forward to the new day. Maybe tomorrow would be a better day.

She rubbed a soft woolen blanket between her fingers as sleep eluded her. Refusing to let him take the joy out of her pregnancy, she vowed to be more patient, to understand what a shock it was to him, and to lower her expectations.

It was good to have a plan.

Dev glanced at Nicole's bedroom door as he headed to his room. While he'd enjoyed the beauty of the surrounding country, he hadn't enjoyed the vast spaciousness of the lodge itself—one person living in 9,000 square feet seemed ridiculous—yet having Nicole there made it all seem…too small. Closed in. As if there wasn't enough space at all. Everything seemed more personal now. Intimate.

Intimate.

He didn't even like the word. Sex, yes. That was easy. Intimacy? Nothing he aspired to.

Neither, apparently, did Nicole. She didn't want to answer personal questions? Okay. No big deal.

Dev peeled his shirt over his head and tossed it on the closet floor, his designated hamper. He sat on a chair and yanked off his boots, lobbing them toward the open closet door, as well. Socks. Jeans. Those he wadded up and heaved. Stripped down to his boxer-briefs, he shoved his fingers through his hair then slumped in the chair.

Why wouldn't she answer his question about Mark? She denied having feelings for him beyond friendship. And what the hell kind of thing was that, anyway? Everyone knew that men and women couldn't be friends. Did she not see that her faithful Fido, Mark, was her self-appointed sentry? Her love slave? Hell, all she would have to do was crook a finger and he'd be kneeling in front of her, awaiting any command.

Dev had no respect for a man who gave himself up to a woman like that.

However, Mark wasn't someone to dismiss easily. He had an inside track with Nicole—longevity and first love. Dev didn't want Nicole confiding in him. No man wanted his woman confiding in another man. He knew how that game was played—be a little sympathetic and she fell right into your arms. Worked every time.

Dev shoved the quilt off the foot of the bed and slid under the covers. It was early for him to try to sleep. He'd been up late every night since he'd arrived, working on his plan to break away from the bank—his family, really. The early numbers he'd put together seemed to indicate he could pull it off—enter the world of venture capitalism through real-estate investment. His father and grandfather would be furious, especially since he'd brought more to the bank's coffers—and therefore to the Campbell family bank accounts—in the past ten years than had been made in the previous twenty. And family was loyal to family. In some ways he would become their competitor, except that they would turn down deals he would take.

There was a lot more money to be made, but not within the bank's conservative constraints. He was ready to take more risks, *had* taken more risks with his personal wealth, and was about to take even more.

He tucked his hands behind his head and stared at the ceiling. He figured he needed about five years before he would feel financially secure. He hadn't expected to marry for another few years, would've put off having children for a few more....

Had Nicole and Mark slept together?

Dev snapped off the bedside lamp, socked a fist into his pillow and laid his head in the indentation. Like he could sleep. Right.

He sat up on the side of the bed. Restless, he left the room. He would work for a while, until he was tired enough to close his eyes without visions of Nicole kissing the lumbering old boyfriend.

In the kitchen he found Nicole standing at the sink drinking a glass of water. She wore a sleeveless midthigh-length nightgown made out of T-shirt fabric that conformed to her body.

"I was…thirsty," she said, crossing her arms, her gaze slipping down his body. "All that…salty food."

"Yeah. Me, too."

He walked toward the refrigerator, aware of her watching him. He should've put on his robe, but the house was warm. Anyway, she'd seen him in less.

The only light in the room came from a small pendant lamp above the sink. "I didn't know you were up," he said after the ice cubes had landed in his glass, which he then pressed against the water lever. "Not sleepy?"

"I'm tired, but my mind doesn't want to slow down."

He nodded.

"You, too?" she asked.

"It's early for me. Thought I'd do some work. Aren't you cold?"

She shook her head. "Pregnancy stokes up the internal temperature." She gestured toward him. "What's your excuse?"

"I didn't expect your…presence. And I upped the heat intentionally so that you wouldn't get cold. I'll turn it down a little." He put the counter between them, leaning his elbows on the granite.

"I've got a couple of books on pregnancy you might like to read," she said.

He'd done some research online already, had even seen pictures of how large the baby would be at this point. Five inches long and weighing seven ounces. He'd held out his hand, trying to picture it. "I'll ask questions as we go along."

"Okay." She set her empty glass in the sink. "Good night again."

"Nicole?"

She stopped next to him, her eyes wary. "What?"

"I don't want you having any contact with Mark."

Her lips stretched thin. "Dictating to me doesn't win you any points, Devlin."

"You're carrying my child. I don't need any more points than that." He talked over her sputtering reaction, saying, "If you want to give us a chance to figure out where we're going, we'll need as few outside influences as possible."

"We don't need to make changes for each other. We need to adjust to each other's lives as they are."

She had a point. When it came down to it, the only thing Dev wanted different was Mark gone from her life. And for her to quit her job. And for her to marry him.

He decided not to bring up those other issues yet.

Nicole patted his arm and smiled sweetly as she continued on. He didn't like her having the upper hand, so he wrapped his fingers around her arm, stopping her. He hadn't kissed her on the stairs earlier—close, but no real contact. He'd been trying not to upset her, but he couldn't keep the peace at the cost of losing control. He would do what he needed to do to get what he wanted.

He cupped the back of her head and drew her close, not

letting her have a say in the matter. He'd let her earlier, on the staircase. Not now. Maybe not ever again. She was his now.

He captured her lips with his, pressed them open, slipped his tongue into her mouth. When she tried to pull back, he didn't let her. She stopped resisting. Started responding. Came at him.

Her belly was hard against him, a reminder. He gentled the kiss then, enjoyed her soft, throaty moans and the feel of her tongue tangling with his, exploring. She dragged her hands down his chest, his abdomen, and stopped at the elastic waistband. He sucked in a breath as just her fingertips slipped under the band.

His turn to moan, to attack her mouth with a new frenzy of need. He moved his hands to her breasts, full and firm. Her fingertips pressed into his flesh, but she didn't move her hands lower, just that tantalizing nearness. He remembered how wet and hot her mouth had been on him there....

Dev thumbed her nipples, circled them, brushed them back and forth. He fisted her nightgown, dragged it up—

"Stop," she said, pulling back. "We have to stop."

He slid his mouth along her jaw. "Why?"

"We just do." She moved farther back.

He lifted his head, her nightgown still crushed in his hands. It wouldn't take anything to peel it up and off her, to toss it aside, to lay his hands and mouth on her naked body. He knew he could convince her after that.

Then he looked into her eyes, bright with desire and... fear? Of him?

He released her. Without a word she left. He heard her jog up the staircase, then close her bedroom door with a ring of finality echoing through the house.

Seven

The following Sunday Nicole stood at the stove, making breakfast—eggs over easy, ham and English muffins, a simple meal. Since the previous Sunday when she'd moved in with him, they'd established a routine, avoided talking about the future and never got below the surface of each other's thoughts. Nicole wanted to share more, but she was afraid to give him ammunition—for lack of a better word—since he never opened up to her emotionally. She felt as if she was a business deal he was waiting to close.

Except he also wanted to sleep with the client.

She knew enough about business to know that was a big mistake. So she resisted as much as she could and hadn't let things get out of hand as they had that first night in the kitchen. But he'd asserted his rights as the father of the baby to touch her belly, to leave his hand there as they talked in the evening in front of the fire or watched television.

Did he know how much that simple gesture aroused her? Not just the contact, but the possessiveness of it, which she liked a lot more than she probably should. He said he was waiting for the baby to move, wanted to feel it the first time when she did, even though she'd read to him from a book that stated that she would feel movement internally before anyone could feel it externally.

"First time for everything," he'd said.

She'd learned he liked his coffee strong and black, and that he didn't talk much until he'd downed the first cup while also watching the business news on television. He took short showers and long hikes. He could work at his computer for hours straight, forgetting the time. His phone calls were all business—succinct and numbers oriented. He wrote notes on yellow legal pads and never doodled. If he made contact with anyone other than for business, she never heard it.

What an insular life he led, she decided, one dedicated to financial pursuit and gain, driven by a need she didn't understand. He shared little of his work, only that he was in the process of making a big change. How it affected *her* she didn't know.

All she knew for sure was that they had about two and a half weeks until his month was up.

Nicole dished up their meal, then called up the stairs toward his bedroom that breakfast was ready. They should get on the road soon to go to her father's house for the day. She hadn't heard from Mark, but then she hadn't given him Devlin's phone number, either, and the only time she turned her cell phone on was when she wanted to make a call. She knew she should have called him from work sometime to try to patch things up, but she'd been dragging her heels about it.

She missed having a close girlfriend now more than ever. There was no one to confide in, to help her sort out her feelings. She was so afraid she would fall in love with Devlin and that love wouldn't be returned.

He strode into the kitchen. "Morning." He took the plates from her and set them on the table, then held out her chair for her. "How'd you sleep?"

"Good." She had a full eight hours. "How about you? What time did you go to bed?"

"Couple hours after you." He sliced into the ham. "Need a shot of whiskey before facing your father again?"

She caught the twinkle in his eyes. "I think the worst is over. What more can he say?"

"He's your father. He probably has plenty to say, now that he's had a week to think about it."

"You may be right. So. What are you working on that's keeping you up so late at night?"

"I've got six deals in the works. Takes a lot of research and analysis."

"Real-estate deals?"

"Commercial ones."

"Big deals?"

"About eighty million."

She held her fork midair. "Dollars?"

"Poker chips."

She didn't know if she was more surprised by the eighty million or the fact that he'd made a little joke. "How big a gamble are you taking?"

"Big. But I won't do all six deals. Three of them, maybe. I haven't decided which ones for sure—*if* I'm doing any of them. Some other things have to fall into place first." He got up to fill his mug. "I'm going to fly home tomorrow for my sister's graduation, so I'll meet with a few people while I'm there. Get some answers in person. I need the face time."

Nicole was stuck on the fact that he was leaving tomorrow but hadn't told her until now.

"I just decided this morning," he said, sitting down again.

She smiled. "Was I that transparent?"

He smiled back.

"What about Hunter's will? How will you get around the rule that says you have to stay put for a month?"

"I'll be gone less than twenty-four hours. I chartered a jet." He cocked his head. "Will you miss me?"

The phone rang.

"Saved by the bell," he murmured, humor in his voice as he picked up the portable from the counter and said hello. "Yes, sir. How are you?" He listened for a second. "Sure. Hold on, please."

He covered the mouthpiece as he held the phone out to Nicole. "Your father."

She sat up a little straighter. "Hi, Dad."

"Hi, honey. How're you feeling?"

"Fine. No problems. We'll be heading down to Sacramento in about fifteen minutes."

"Um, that's why I'm calling. I just got an invitation to do something I'd like to. Can we skip today?"

Was that all there was to it—another invitation? Or was he avoiding her? "Sure we can skip today. What's happening?" She noted Devlin's curiosity and shrugged at him.

"A picnic with some people I know. Next week, okay?"

"I guess—"

"Bye, honey."

At the immediate click, Nicole lowered the phone and stared at it, then finally hit the off button. "We're uninvited for the day. He's going on a picnic."

"That's unusual, I gather?"

She set the phone on the table. "Unheard of."

"So, what would you like to do instead today? Go to a movie or something?"

It seemed like such a normal, mundane thing to do—go to a movie. And their week had been filled with a kind of manufactured normalcy. It could've been an exciting time, filled with sex and revelations.

"A movie would be good," she said finally.

"That was a long, tough decision for you?"

"Well, I—"

He laid a hand over hers, stopping her words. "We're doing a lot of tiptoeing, aren't we? Trying to guess the motivations behind everything. It's just a movie and dinner."

Which was all it did turn out to be, except that he held her hand, as if they were on a real date, and at dinner was attentive in a new way, a more focused way, instead of seeming as if most of his thoughts were on crunching numbers, calculating risk and profit.

And instead of kissing her good-night at her bedroom door, he held her for a long time.

"I'll be up and out of here by four," he said, stepping back, his hands still cupping her shoulders.

"Come tell me goodbye before you go."

"I think you should just sleep."

"Either you come say goodbye or I'll get up to tell you goodbye."

"When you put it that way…"

"Good."

"How're you going to spend your day off tomorrow?"

"I'm going to my cabin to work on the nursery."

A tense silence settled, then he released her. "Why?"

"There's nothing for me to do here."

"Read a book."

"Why does it bother you?"

"The task is unnecessary."

She didn't want him to leave with an argument between them, but she also didn't want him to think everything was resolved. "Nothing's been decided."

"*Everything* was decided on January second, Nicole."

It struck her how much she wished everything was different. Wished that they'd fallen in love first, courted, got married, *then* made a baby. Establishing a relationship backward was hard, especially when trust was involved.

"I don't want to argue with you," he said.

"I can't just blindly do whatever you want me to, Devlin. How much respect for me would you have if I did? Do you want someone that easy?"

After a moment he smiled. The smile grew broader.

"Okay, okay, okay," she said, fighting a smile in return. "I was pretty easy in January. But so were you."

"Not arguing the point. Extenuating circumstances on both our parts, however. I'm assuming you don't routinely pick up men in the casino and take them to bed."

"I didn't pick you up. You picked *me* up."

"Murky point."

"Crystal-clear point, Mr. Campbell. Do you have a lot of one-night stands?"

"Yeah."

She didn't know what to say to that.

"Not women I pick up," he clarified. "I've dated a lot of women one time."

"Why?"

"Just the way things worked out."

She frowned at the vague answer.

"Mostly I've been married to my work. I knew I had a responsibility—a duty—to continue the Campbell name, but I wasn't going to worry about it for a few years, until I was successful enough to satisfy myself about the future."

"And now here I am. Someone not of your acceptable breeding."

"And pregnant, besides," he added, although not with any heat.

"Your parents aren't going to be happy." In fact, they would probably resent her. "Will you tell them while you're back there?"

"No, not until you and I have finalized our plans."

A reprieve, then. "Remember to wake me before you leave."

He nodded and slipped his hands in his pockets.

She shut her bedroom door, then waited there until she heard him walk away a few long seconds later. What was he thinking? About telling his parents he'd disappointed them? About how to introduce her to them? To his friends?

Would he thumb his nose at them? Throw caution to the wind and tell them he'd fallen madly, hopelessly in love with a strictly middle-class woman, and to hell with them all?

Well, maybe it wouldn't go that far, but every girl had a right to the dream.

Eight

Just back from Philadelphia the next night, Dev pulled into the casino parking lot. He relaxed at the sight of Nicole's car and parked next to it. He'd called the lodge on his way from the airport but hadn't gotten any answer, which worried him as it was pretty late. She'd left a message on his cell phone that said she'd traded days with Juan Torres and was working instead of having the day off.

Why was she working so late?

After a few hours with his family and a few more traipsing around properties with men and women fawningly anxious for his investment dollars, he wanted Nicole's quiet, steady company.

He'd almost confided in his sister Joan about Nicole and the baby after Joan commented on how relaxed he looked. Relaxed? That surprised him. He felt stressed almost to the breaking point. Too much was up in the air. He was task driven and accomplishment-minded, and there were too many incomplete items on his agenda at the moment. Anyway, the opportunity to talk to Joan slipped away when her three-year-old daughter fell and needed her attention.

In the end, he'd been grateful for the interruption. He needed to make his own decisions. He also didn't want his family to know all the circumstances of his personal life.

The casino noise bombarded him as he stepped inside the building. He'd read that fetuses could hear some outside sound. Could the clinks and clanks and other odd clamor imprint before birth? It was a far cry from Mozart, the recommended music of prenatal stimulation.

He headed across the gaming area toward the hotel's front desk, where only a drift of casino noise could be heard, which made him feel better about it all. Nicole didn't spend much time in the casino itself. After a couple more weeks she wouldn't be spending any time there at all....

"Hi! You're Nic's friend, right?"

The bouncy blonde with the hyphenated name—Ann something—blocked his path.

"Yes. Is she working late?"

"She's downstairs in the coffee shop."

"Thanks." He walked past her.

"Um. She's not alone."

He turned around and waited for her to continue.

"She's with some guy. Cute. Buff." A slight questioning inflection ended her words, as if asking if Dev knew who she was talking about.

Dev showed no outward reaction. "Okay." He didn't pick up speed, but everything inside him raced as he made his way down the escalator and to the coffee shop, where he'd met Nicole for lunch several times during the week, satisfying his need for her to take a real break from work. He didn't like how much she was on her feet all day.

"I'm meeting someone," Dev told the hostess as he breezed by. He spotted Nicole tucked in a quiet booth with a man whose back was to Dev, his head down, as if looking at the table. There was no doubt who it was.

Nicole's hand rested on Mark's on the table. She was speaking, her expression earnest. He finally lifted his head.

Something poker-hot twisted into Dev's gut. He didn't stop until he reached the booth, then he slid in next to Nicole, startling her. He cupped the back of her head and pulled her close. "Hi, honey, I'm home," he said evenly, then he kissed her, not thoroughly enough to embarrass her but long enough to establish possession.

"You're early," she said, her cheeks pinkening.

"Surprise." He turned to Mark, extended his hand. "How are you?"

Mark couldn't politely ignore the gesture.

"Passing through town?" Dev asked, sliding his arm along the top of the booth behind Nicole. He fingered her hair.

"I came to see my friend. You got a problem with that?"

"Maybe."

"Devlin," Nicole said low. "Please."

"The man asked a question. I answered."

"Nicki doesn't seem all that happy to see you, Campbell."

Dev studied her face, which took on a deeper, allover pink hue. "She looks happy to me. Are you unhappy, Nicole?" He was counting on her to keep their public image a united one.

"I'm glad you're back," she said, not truly an answer to his question, which upped his admiration for her a notch. There were reasons why he'd dated all those other women

only once, and why he'd gone searching for Nicole again—
reasons he'd just begun to understand.

He wanted to know who'd set up this meeting. Had Mark
called and asked if he could come? Had *she* called and invited
him, thinking Dev wouldn't be home yet? Or had Mark
ambushed her? Questions with critical answers.

"Why haven't you set a wedding date?" Mark asked, challenge in his voice, as if he knew something Dev didn't. "A
decent man would've married her long before now."

"Decent men don't pursue another man's woman," Dev
countered easily.

The thought of Nicole confiding in the hulk annoyed Dev.
He understood that women needed to talk about their issues
more than men did, but she should be talking to a girlfriend, or
him, not to an ex-boyfriend who so obviously still carried a
torch.

Dev didn't like that Mark remained an option for her. She
should've figured out by now that no other man would raise
his child.

He turned to Nicole. "Shall we go?"

Her irritation was barely restrained but obvious in the way
she set her tightly clasped hands on the table. "I'll catch up
with you by the escalator."

Again he was surprised by—and he admired—how she
didn't let him dictate to her. He nodded, ignored Mark and
left the table. The escalator was out of sight of the dining
room. Dev wouldn't see what transpired in the farewells.
Would they hug? Kiss? Look longingly at each other? Had
Nicole confided in Mark how she'd come to be pregnant
because of a one-night stand? Or perhaps just hinted at the
circumstances enough for Mark to jump to his own conclusions?

The fury that rose in Dev as he reached the escalator was something he'd never experienced before over a woman. The only thing comparable was how angry he'd been at the world when Hunter had died, a twenty-two-year-old young man of such huge potential. Without him the Samurai would've never come together, never found that bond they'd had, as evidenced by how easily the ties had broken after his death. Had Hunter lived, Dev was sure they all would've remained close friends. Hunter wouldn't have settled for less.

Dev hadn't known how much he missed that camaraderie until now, with his life in upheaval. He'd rarely doubted himself before, but where did self-confidence leave off and arrogance begin? The answer was in the eye of the beholder, he decided.

His father was arrogant. His grandfather, too. Dev hadn't recognized the trait in himself until Hunter had bluntly told Dev once to lighten up, that he was being an arrogant son of a bitch. And for the next few years, Dev had been different, more open to change and adventure.

Where had that Dev gone? He must have died along with Hunter.

Nicole caught up with him. She was alone. There wasn't happiness in her eyes, as he'd hoped for upon his return, but hurt and distance. In *her* mind he probably should've handled that situation differently, but he didn't regret anything. She was his.

"Don't," she said when he started to talk. "We'll discuss this at…the lodge."

Had she started to say *home?*

He stood a step below her on the escalator, his gaze trailing her back. He admitted to himself that he'd wanted her to be at home when he got there. Had wanted her to greet him with a hug and a warm welcome, like the sweet, sleepy goodbye she'd given him the morning when he left.

If he could just get her into bed again, everything would be different. All their problems would be solved.

In the parking lot she climbed into her car, started the engine and took off.

Oh, yeah. Furious.

It was going to be a long night.

Nicole saw Devlin pull into the driveway right behind her. She got out of her car and headed toward the door, key in hand, ignoring him, refusing to feel any kind of guilt, which he seemed to want to put on her. He didn't follow immediately, giving her time to start up the second flight of stairs before she heard the front door shut.

"I'm going to change," she said, not wanting him to follow.

"I'll start a fire."

"Whatever." Nicole loved that word, one nuanced by the tone of voice that accompanied it. *Whatever* could be an expression of disdain, annoyance, dismissal, even acceptance. Let him wonder.

That morning she'd gone defiantly to her cabin to work on the nursery, then hadn't even cut out the curtain fabric, going shopping instead for maternity clothes before going to work, her purchases including a couple of comfortable, casual long gowns to wear for times like this, sitting in front of the fire. She changed and went downstairs.

"Are you hungry?" she asked, stalling their conversation.

He glanced over his shoulder from where he was hunkered in front of the fire. She didn't know why he insisted on starting fires from kindling when there was also a gas line that made the process simple. Some latent Boy Scout genes in him, she guessed.

"I wouldn't mind a sandwich," he said.

She fixed him a ham-and-Swiss on rye, added a dill pickle and some chips, and poured a glass of beer. He was closing the fire screen when she placed the tray on the wood-plank coffee table in front of the sofa.

"You're not eating?" he asked.

"No."

"You look nice. Is that new?"

"Yes."

He didn't sigh audibly but she saw its equivalent in his body language. She didn't want to be annoyed with him. She had anticipated his return with more pleasure than she'd expected, then he'd ruined it all with his me-Tarzan, you-Jane routine. If he wanted information, he was going to have to ask the questions. She wouldn't offer anything voluntarily. He still didn't trust her. She got that. And she didn't like him much at the moment. That gave them an even playing field, as far as she was concerned.

"You're not going to make this easy, are you?" he asked, lifting his sandwich from the plate.

"No."

He sort of smiled, examined his ham-and-Swiss a moment, then took a bite. The crackle of the fire was the only sound in the room.

"I don't like Mark," he said.

"I got that, loud and clear. Is it Mark or any man?"

"I haven't seen you with another man, so I can't answer that question. Did you invite him up here?"

"He showed up right before the end of my shift."

"Uninvited?"

"Yes. He was worried. I hadn't called him since he found out about…us. The baby. I hadn't given him the number here."

"Why not?"

She shrugged.

"Why not, Nicole?"

"Avoidance, I guess."

"Shame?"

"Maybe a little. Although more embarrassment than shame, I think."

"At what?"

"Getting pregnant," she said in a tone she figured he should understand. It was stupid in this day and age to get pregnant accidentally.

"You're embarrassed about me."

She had to think that through for a minute, then finally said, "I don't know what to make of you. You say you won't tell my father about the baby in front of Mark, then you do. You barely know me, yet you claim public ownership. I spend a lot of time trying to figure you out."

"Me, too."

"Figuring yourself out or me?"

"Myself. I'm going to be a father. That's amazing. I'm not the man I was before because of that."

Since he'd given her that much, she decided to tell him everything that had happened with Mark. "Mark came because he was worried and a little irritated, too. He blames you for keeping me from him, which wasn't true, since I'd done that on my own."

"But would've been true if I'd known about it," he offered, surprising her with his honesty.

"I think he'd been hoping he and I might get back together."

Devlin laughed, short and unamused. "You think?"

"He offered to marry me if you didn't." Nicole hadn't

intended on telling Devlin that. Maybe she liked his jealousy some. What did that say about her?

He stared at the fire a few seconds, then said, "You told him that wouldn't be necessary, right?"

"You showed up at that precise moment."

"And when I left you alone later to say your goodbyes?"

"He didn't bring it up again. Neither did I."

"You don't seem like the type to tease a man, Nicole. Or give him false hopes. Maybe you're keeping him on a leash, just in case."

Maybe she was. She didn't like that about herself, but there it was. "I think he could see where things stand between us," she said toward the fireplace.

He turned her face to his. "There's never going to be another man in your life but me."

"Even if we don't love each other?"

His hesitation was brief but intense. "There's more to life than love. More to a partnership, too."

"Do your parents love each other?"

"I have no idea."

How sad. How very sad. "My parents adored each other. Their love was strong and solid and infinite. I want the same thing for myself. I don't want to settle for less."

"We don't always get what we want, Nicole. There are consequences for our actions that must be faced, must take priority. In this case, an innocent child."

"Which is why I'm here." Although that wasn't exactly the truth. She was also there because he intrigued her, as he had from the first night. There was so much more to him than he shared. What would it be like to open those floodgates?

"I have something for you." He pulled out a box from under the coffee table and presented it.

It wasn't wrapped like a present, didn't have a bow, yet from the look of expectation on his face he was presenting her with something special. A gift. His first gift.

She peeled off the tape, folded back the flaps. Bubble wrap surrounded the contents. Safe inside the protective wrapping was a beautiful white ceramic plant pot. Her throat and eyes stung as she looked at him. "Thank you. Thank you so much."

"I noticed you like white pots," he said, running a finger along the scalloped edge.

Was he nervous, waiting for her reaction? She hugged the pot to her chest. He'd remembered about her African violet, her special, important plant.

"I know you're nervous about repotting your violet. I'll help," he said.

"You garden?" The thought made her grin.

He smiled, too. "No. But I think I can manage that much. I talked to the garden expert at the nursery that my sister Joan uses."

"You got this in Philadelphia?" He'd carried it on the plane? Across country?

"Yeah."

"This is one of the nicest gifts anyone has ever given me. Thank you."

He looked pleased. It was a good moment between them, a simple, normal, everyday kind of moment. But she didn't know what to do next. She was tired, not having gone back to sleep after he'd left that morning. She'd heard every sound the lodge made, every creak of wood, every whistle of wind outdoors, every brush of tree branch against the log siding. She was tired, yes, but she didn't want to leave him yet.

"Let's enjoy the fire together for a little while before bed."
He patted the sofa cushion next to him, once again discerning exactly what she wanted.

How could she turn down that invitation? He put his arms around her and pulled her close, so that her back nestled against his chest. His hands settled on her belly.

"Relax," he murmured. "Close your eyes."

"I might fall asleep."

"Sleep is good."

She didn't know what to do with him when he was gentle, but she gave in to the moment. It had been a very long time since she'd just been held, taken care of. Independence always had a price.

He massaged her belly with sweeping circles. After a minute he angled her differently, giving himself room to rub her back. She moved catlike against him, almost purring. His chin rested on her head. She loved the smell of him, the sturdy feel of his chest, the steady rhythm of his breathing. She matched her breaths to his, slowing hers until she felt a lack of oxygen and let her breathing return to normal. She drifted along, loving his touch, wishing it never had to end.

Her body started to object to the position, cramping a little, stirring up sensations of...not numbness, but something different and hard to describe.

She opened her eyes, pressed her hand to the spot.

"What's wrong?" he asked.

"I think I feel movement." She angled her head back. "I'm not sure."

"Where?"

She grabbed his hand and moved it where the fluttering was. "It's like little ripples," she said.

"I can't feel anything. Has it gone away?"

"No." She pressed his hand harder against the spot. "Oh. It stopped." Disappointment washed over her. She wouldn't know if it was the baby until it happened again. "I'm sorry you didn't feel it."

"Yeah. Me, too."

They lay still then. The anticipation of a repeat sensation took the tiredness from her for another ten minutes or so, then her eyes closed again.

"Want to go to bed?" he asked.

She nodded.

"Want me to carry you?"

She nodded again, then adamantly shook her head.

He laughed. "Should I just grab a pillow and blankets and let you sleep here?"

"On you?" she asked, sleepily, rubbing her cheek against his chest.

"If you like. Or you can just come to bed with me."

He moved her hand down him, until she blanketed the placket of his jeans, finding him aroused.

She curved her hand over him, remembered how his skin had felt, how hot and hard he'd gotten. She'd made him shudder. She remembered that distinctly, because she'd never made a man shudder before.

And he'd given her three orgasms in a row just with his mouth....

She sat up, intending to sit on his lap, wanting him, but before she made a move, his cell phone rang, jarring her out of her fantasy.

Wake-up call. She pulled back. He squeezed her shoulder, keeping her close as he dug the phone out of his pocket and glanced at the screen.

"My sister Izzy," he said, surprise in his voice. He flipped it open. "How's the graduate?" He looked quickly at Nicole. "This really isn't a good time, Iz…. What? Now? Here? Hold on a sec."

He covered the mouthpiece. "My sister decided to pay me a surprise visit. She's about fifteen minutes away."

"Do you want me to leave?" *Please say no. Please say no.*

"No. You okay with her coming here?"

"It's up to you. Is she staying overnight?"

"I assume so."

"Where? There's only one guest room with furniture, and all my stuff is in there."

He stared at her a few seconds more then spoke into the phone again. "I'll leave the lights on…. You've got directions?… Yeah, the Internet is amazing. See you soon."

He snapped the phone shut, then stood. "I'll transfer your stuff into my room. You might want to change into something less comfortable."

"I can't sleep with you." She said the words with panicked conviction.

"Do you want my sister to know we don't share a room?"

She hated that he was being logical. She accepted his help to stand. "Good thing I changed the sheets this morning," she muttered, then headed toward the stairs. "Is she going to like me?"

"I don't have a clue."

"Great."

"Nicole?" He caught up with her. "It doesn't matter."

"It doesn't matter if your sister likes me? What planet do you live on?"

"We also need to look like we're…together. A couple. It's important, Nicole. If she notices that things aren't quite right with us—"

"I got it," she interrupted. And she did. He wouldn't like losing control.

After ten minutes of frenzied activity, they headed down the stairs just as the beam of car headlights swept across the great room.

Nicole straightened her shoulders. *Showtime*.

Nine

Nicole stood at the top of the stairs, just out of view of the staircase, her hands clasped, her heart pounding. She could hear the conversation between brother and sister but couldn't see them.

"What are you doing here?" Devlin asked.

"I'm meeting Ashley in San Francisco day after tomorrow for a few days. I've never seen Lake Tahoe. One plus one equals—"

"Why didn't you tell me you were coming?"

The volume of their voices rose as they climbed the stairs.

"I was going to surprise you on the plane. I figured you were on the company jet, but you didn't show, so I asked Father if I could take it. How'd you get here?"

"I'd hired my own plane. You should've talked to me about it, Iz."

"I didn't think you'd mind. I mean, you don't have a woman stashed or—"

She came to a quick halt as she spotted Nicole.

"Actually," Devlin said, humor lacing the word. "Nicole Price, this is my impulsive sister, Isabel."

Nicole had changed into one of her new maternity outfits, a deep-purple, washable-wool pants and top. She'd added a chunky necklace, hoping to draw Isabel's gaze upward, but she fixated on Nicole's slightly rounded belly right away.

"It's nice to meet you," Nicole said. Isabel had the same green eyes as Devlin, but auburn hair in a straight, shaggy, chin-length cut, stark and contemporary. She was maybe an inch taller than Nicole's five-seven, but probably thirty pounds lighter, her facial features angular but attractive. She wore pencil-leg jeans, a forest-green pullover and boots that probably cost more than Nicole made in a week. An air of sophistication surrounded her, for all that she was only twenty-four.

"You're… She's…" Isabel turned to her brother, her brows arched high. "Apparently you neglected to tell the family something important at my graduation."

"Which is the point—it was *your* graduation. But, yes, Nicole and I are having a baby in September. I'm asking you not to tell Mother and Father."

"Why didn't *you?*"

"When I'm ready I will."

Sensing a rising tension between the siblings, Nicole interrupted. "Would you like something to eat or drink, Isabel?"

"A glass of Merlot, thanks."

Devlin set her suitcase at the bottom of the next staircase. Thank goodness he didn't take it on up to the guest room and leave Nicole alone with his sister.

Nicole escaped to the kitchen. She hadn't missed the up-and-down look Isabel had given her. It was important not to alienate Devlin's sister, but Nicole had a bad feeling about her. According to Devlin, Isabel wanted to join the bank, a first among the Campbell women—which meant she was ambitious. And that assessing once-over she'd given Nicole hadn't been a friendly one, not by a long stretch, rather one that seemed…calculating?

Nicole returned to the great room with the wine and also a tray of grapes, cheese and crackers, even though Devlin had already eaten. She wondered if Isabel ate such high-calorie foods.

Devlin moved to help Nicole with the tray. She smiled her thanks, then caught Isabel looking back and forth between them intently.

Nicole had no appetite, so she sat in a chair by the fireplace, leaving the sofa for the siblings to share the tray on the coffee table.

"Congratulations on your graduation," Nicole said. "I imagine it feels really good to be done."

"Like the prison doors just opened up."

"Are you going to take some time off?"

"That depends on Devvie."

"Devvie?" Nicole repeated, fighting a smile.

Devlin eyed his sister. "Payback for 'Izzy.' Which is actually short for Dizzy. When she was little, she would spin around and around until she got dizzy and fell." He grabbed a stem of red grapes. "Why does your time off depend on me?"

"I'm counting on you to convince Father and Grandfather to hire me. You'd think an MBA in finance from Wharton would have earned me the right for at least a trial run. I have exactly the same credentials as that Brett Allen they hired last year. I'm even more qualified than *you* were, brother dearest."

Devlin had told Nicole that he hadn't gone on for an MBA

because his job was already secure for life, so what was the need for more? And after his friend Hunter had died, more college was the last thing Devlin was interested in.

"Why would they listen to me, sister dearest?"

"Because you're the golden child, and you know it. I could be, too, if they'd give me a chance."

"You didn't apply anywhere else?"

"Why should I? I belong at Campbell Bank." She clasped her hands. "We had a bit of an argument about it."

"Ah. So *that's* why you left town in such a hurry. I'm surprised he let you use the jet."

"He wanted me gone as much as I wanted to *be* gone."

Their discussion went on until Nicole couldn't keep her eyes open any longer. She stifled a yawn. "I'm sorry to duck out on you, but I really need to get to bed." She stood, as did Devlin. "You don't mind, do you?" she asked him. "It'll give you two a chance to catch up."

"We'll have tomorrow while you're at work. I'll come with you."

"Where do you work?" Isabel asked.

"At the Sterling Palace."

"The casino?"

"I'm an assistant manager at the hotel. Really, Devlin, stay and talk with Isabel."

"It's been a very long day for me. I'm ready for bed." He slid an arm around Nicole's waist, then looked at his sister. "You're welcome to stay down here and enjoy the fire, but let me show you your room first."

"I'll go to bed, too."

Nicole moved to pick up the tray. "I'll take care of this."

"I'll come back down and do it," Devlin said. He urged her along, and Isabel followed. She'd gone quiet, and

Nicole wondered what she was thinking. She must have a ton of questions.

"Good night," Nicole said when they reached the top of the stairs, then she headed into the master suite. She shut the doors quietly and slumped against them. She would make a friend of Isabel, Nicole vowed. Devlin had thought about Nicole while he was gone. Had bought her the pot. Had said he would help her transplant her precious flower.

For his sake, for her own sake, she would find a way to be friends with his sister.

Nicole wasn't anywhere near sleep when Devlin slipped under the covers beside her fifteen minutes later. "Are you awake?" he asked.

She was being cowardly, not answering, afraid to start something she wasn't ready for, at least not with his sister there.

He went silent and still. She didn't move from her spot on the far edge of the bed, wondering if he would continue to talk to her in the dark.

The bed was enormous. Several feet of empty space stretched between them. She thought it would feel strange sleeping in the same bed, but it didn't. Of course, they'd shared a bed before, but the circumstances were so different that she couldn't compare them to this time.

At midnight she still hadn't relaxed enough to sleep and needed to go to the bathroom. She crept out of bed and returned just as quietly. While she was gone, he'd moved to the middle of the bed. Suspicious, she brooded over what to do. If he'd fallen asleep, he was the most silent, least fidgety person she'd ever known, because he hadn't made a sound, hadn't even rolled over—until she'd left.

Which led her to believe he was still awake, since she'd

done exactly the same thing. She glanced around the room, searching for an alternative, but although the overstuffed chairs looked comfortable to sit in, sleeping wouldn't be easy. Plus there was the issue of his ridiculing her....

She got in bed and rolled onto her side, facing away from him, and closed her eyes. The ripples she'd felt earlier returned, in exactly the same spot. So it *was* baby movement, she decided, happy about it, wanting to tell Devlin that it hadn't been some fluke.

"You're thinking too much," he said from behind her, sleep in his voice.

"I feel the ripples again."

"Yeah?"

She backed up until she was right next to him. He tucked his legs behind hers and wrapped an arm around her. She pressed his hand to the spot. "I think we have a night owl," she said.

"I don't feel anything."

Nicole relaxed, enjoying the feel of his body against hers. His heat soaked into her, more than she needed with her internal temperature already high, but she didn't want him to move away, either.

"Maybe the fabric gets in the way," he said, not waiting for her to agree but tugging her nightgown up high enough that he could easily touch her belly. "Do you still feel it?"

"Yes." Her voice came out a little breathless. "It just shifted more toward the middle." She moved his hand, holding hers over his and pressing down. "Feel that?"

"No." Frustration layered the word.

"It'll happen soon, I'm sure."

After a while he said, "You haven't slept."

"No. Have you?"

"With you finally where I've wanted you? No."

Her heart fluttered at his words, but she had to ignore them. "Do you think your sister will keep quiet about us? The baby?"

"Yeah."

"What makes you so sure?"

"I asked her to."

Since Nicole didn't have siblings, she didn't understand his conviction, but she hoped he was right. Nicole got the impression that Isabel would do whatever was necessary to get what she wanted—which was a job at Campbell Bank. If she could discredit Devlin somehow, maybe her loyalty would somehow be rewarded. Nicole didn't know exactly how that kind of thing worked in their world. Her only experience with their social level had come from television and movies, hardly accurate sources. But didn't art imitate life? Of course, it also exaggerated life.

Fitting into Devlin's world wouldn't be easy.

Sleep finally wouldn't wait any longer. As she drifted, she wriggled against him, getting more comfortable. His hand went lax against her belly, indicating he was fading, too.

The little ache that had throbbed between her legs settled now that his hand wasn't making the same kind of contact—until he adjusted his position a little. His hand flattened against her stomach then slid up and curved around her breast.

"Nice," he murmured.

"Big," she said, smiling.

"Yeah."

His tone of voice told her everything. He liked the changes in her body. "I've gone up two cup sizes."

"I noticed."

"I guess you're a breast man."

"And legs. Yours are exceptional."

She loved listening to him talk, his voice low and sexy.

"Every part of you is exceptional, though," he added.

"I can say the same about *you*."

"Yeah? What's your favorite?" He tucked himself closer, until she could feel he was aroused—and naked.

"That part's high on my list," she said.

He made a low, growly sound. "You feel very warm."

She was more than warm. She was on fire. "Your heat added to mine creates a furnace."

"Why don't you take off the nightgown? That'd help." At her hesitation he said, "Nothing will happen unless you want it to, Nicole."

Nothing had changed. She didn't want to be intimate with him again while they had company. He probably wouldn't understand that, but it kept her from allowing things to get out of hand.

"What are you afraid of?" he asked.

Giving in. Giving up any semblance of control over my own life. Falling in love with someone who won't love me in return. So many things....

Although sex would be nice. Very nice.

"We have a lot to work out first," she said, staying stronger than she thought she could.

"You'll let me know when we've reached that point?" he asked drily.

She grinned. "You'll be the first."

She thought she felt his lips brush against her hair, then he said good-night.

She finally let herself sleep.

Dev heard the shower come on. He opened his eyes and glanced at the clock—8:43. They'd slept in.

The shower in the master bathroom was enclosed by crystal-clear glass. He had a choice—invade her privacy or leave her alone. He'd bet anything she was trying to take the fastest shower of her life.

He tucked his hands behind his head and contemplated his situation. Things were happening one step at a time. He'd gotten her in his bed, thanks to Izzy. A natural progression would follow.

Izzy had peppered him with questions. He'd put her off. The hardest question to fend off was why they weren't married. No one in his family would understand that. He didn't know how much longer he could wait for Nicole to come around to the fact they had to get married as soon as possible. It was an issue not open to debate. He'd been more tolerant with her than with anyone in his life, but he couldn't let her dictate their relationship, not when appearances mattered so much.

He felt as if he was losing control of this relationship. He needed to rethink how he was handling it.

To hell with it. He got out of bed and walked straight into the bathroom. She was rinsing her hair in the shower, her eyes closed, head tipped back. Shampoo bubbles trailed down her magnificent breasts and rounded abdomen.

He didn't hesitate, but opened the door and stepped inside with her. She reacted in the most female way, trying to cover herself with her arms.

"Don't," he said quietly. "You're beautiful." *And you're mine.*

He watched her gaze drift down his body, too, his need for her evident. "How'd you sleep?" he asked.

"Like a baby." She smiled hesitantly. "How about you?"

"Incredibly well. I like having you in my bed."

She swallowed, obviously nervous.

"Need soap?" he asked, reaching for it.

He lathered his hands then placed them on her shoulders. He worked his way down her body, slowly, teasingly. Whenever he looked at her face, her eyes were closed, her head angled back slightly. He slid his hand lower, felt her body jerk in reaction, then teased her, taking her to the brink, then leaving her there. He handed her the bar of soap and turned his back to her.

She didn't curse him out loud, but he figured she was reading him the riot act in her head. Maybe she wouldn't return the favor? But after a long moment he felt her hands glide slickly along his back, over his rear, down his legs. He turned around. She started at his shoulders, made her way down his abdomen, then skipped to his legs, her face level with his hips. She stood. With her gaze locked on his, she soaped her hands then grasped the last remaining spot to be cleansed.

"It may require two washings," he said. "Possibly three."

"I could be mean and do what you did."

"You could be."

"I think one washing will probably take care of it," she said finally, her eyes sparkling.

"You could be right about—" What she was doing with her hands stole speech from him. He saw the small, triumphant smile on her face as he gave in to the sensations, concentrated and intense, a reward for his very long wait, until his body stiffened as release came in a long, satisfying explosion of completion.

He didn't let her bask in her triumph but went to his knees and pressed his mouth to her, enjoying her with long strokes of his tongue, then settling on her. She didn't protest. As with himself, it didn't take long to bring her to climax. He wasn't satisfied. He wanted to be inside her, to feel her surround him, to bury himself deep and then take and take until they both were exhausted.

"Let's go back to bed," he said, kissing her.

"We have company."

"Who cares?"

"I do, Devlin."

The serious tone in her voice made him lift his head.

"There'll be time for more after she's gone," Nicole said.

"That's not until tomorrow."

"I know." She turned off the water.

At least she'd stopped hiding her body from him. She let him towel her dry and then dressed in front of him, which stirred him up again. She laughed as he tried to zip up his jeans, giving him a little pat as she returned to the bathroom to dry her hair.

"I'll go play host," he said, deciding to shave later. Or maybe not to shave at all. He couldn't remember a day since he'd graduated that he hadn't shaved.

She came back, put her hands on his face and kissed him. "You look a little dangerous."

Yeah. Maybe he wouldn't shave for a few days.

He found his sister in the kitchen, scarfing down a bowl of cereal.

"You've gone soft, sleeping in like that," she said, then focused on his unshaven face. "And lazy."

He started making coffee.

"I've already been for a run," she added. "You used to get up early to do that, too. And I've never seen you with a beard."

"I run after Nicole goes to work. She works the noon-to-eight shift. As for not shaving—it's none of your business, is it?"

"Nope." She cocked her head. "You look happier this morning than you did last night."

"I was tired last night."

"Uh-huh. So, will you answer questions this morning?"

"Like?"

"Like how you came to be an expectant father? And why you aren't married yet? And why you haven't told Mother and Father?"

He flipped the On switch to let the coffee start brewing. "I came to be an expectant father in the usual way. You did learn about the birds and the bees, didn't you?"

She stuck out her tongue.

"Takes more than that," he said, making her laugh. He *was* happier this morning. Lighter. He had hope for a smooth transition into marriage. "We're not married yet because we haven't had a wedding."

She groaned.

"And I haven't told Mother and Father because it has nothing to do with them."

Her brows arched. "Does that mean you're not inviting them to your wedding? That would never be tolerated. They would resent Nicole, you know. It would start things off on the wrong foot."

"It's my life. Mine and Nicole's."

"You have obligations, Dev."

"I know."

She rinsed out her cereal bowl, then leaned against the counter. "What's going on with you? You seem really different. More relaxed and yet more tense at the same time."

"I've got a lot on my plate."

"Are you going to help convince Father and Grandfather to take me on at the bank? It's time for you to move up the ladder, too. Maybe I could take over for you."

"You can't step into my job. You have to prove yourself."

"I've got a portfolio," she said. "I tried to show it to Father, but he brushed it off. I know it'll impress the hell out of them."

"Have you got it with you?"

"Yes."

"Show me after Nicole leaves. We'll see."

A few minutes later they were standing on the balcony overlooking Lake Tahoe, sipping coffee and enjoying the view, when Nicole appeared, her hair braided, makeup on and dressed for work. Dev made room for her in the shaft of sunlight warming the deck.

"I hope you slept well," she said to Izzy.

"I did. And you?"

"The same," Nicole said.

Dev slipped an arm around Nicole's waist and was pleased when she relaxed into him. "How about I fix breakfast?" he asked.

She looked at her watch. "I don't have much time. I wanted to stop by my cabin and pick up my violet to repot."

"I'll do that when I take Iz on a tour later."

"Really? That would be great, thanks."

"Iz? Breakfast?"

"The cereal I had was plenty, thanks."

"I'll leave you two to get to know each other," Dev said, a little worried about what Izzy would ask and what Nicole would answer....

Ten

Nicole tried not to panic. She didn't know what she was allowed to say. How much of the truth could she reveal to this sister of his, whom he trusted to keep his secrets?

"Dev hasn't been very generous with details about you," Isabel said. "Is he protecting you or himself?"

"Only he can answer that question. What would you like to know?"

"How you met."

"In Atlantic City. I used to work at the Sterling there."

"Your eyes met across a crowded casino floor and it was love at first sight?"

The memory made Nicole smile. "Exactly."

"Really?"

Nicole nodded. "Fate."

"You do realize you are completely different from the women he usually dates. Dated."

"He told me." He'd dated a lot of women…once. Women his parents would have deemed acceptable as his wife. "But he chose me."

"Did he? Or did the pregnancy?"

The blunt question caught Nicole off guard. She hadn't expected Isabel to be rude. Nicole didn't know what to say.

"I figured he's waiting for the birth to be sure it's his," Isabel said. "That's why he hasn't married you."

Her arrogant expression made Nicole want to retreat, but she didn't. "I assure you, this child is his."

"Something you planned, I imagine. The Campbell money must look awfully good to someone of your background."

"Money doesn't equal class."

Isabel's lips pursed, then she nodded slightly. "Touché."

Nicole switched subjects, wary of the other questions Isabel had. "Who is the girlfriend in San Francisco you're going to see?"

"Ashley and I roomed together through high school."

"High school?"

"We attended the same academy."

Ah, yes, a different life, indeed. She wondered if Devlin would expect their child to go away to school at a young age. She would never agree to that. Never.

"Ashley wants me to look for a job in San Francisco," Isabel added, "so that we could room together again."

"Why don't you? Wouldn't it be better to be hired by a company that really wants you than to force yourself somewhere you're not welcome?"

"You wouldn't understand."

"Why wouldn't I?"

"It has to do with entitlement. And tradition."

"And those are words I don't understand? I may have

been raised differently, but I have a sense of what you're talking about."

"You couldn't possibly, or you wouldn't need to ask the questions."

Maybe Isabel was right about that. Nicole had been trying to forge a relationship with a woman who would, at the very least, be an aunt to her child. Perhaps it was an impossible wish that they could become friends, too.

"I've worked hard for this," Isabel said, her voice harsh, revealing her emotions. "Harder than Golden Boy ever did. All he had to do was show up. He even got to spend his summers working at the bank. But I knew I had to prove myself."

"How could you stand working for someone who is so antifemale?" Nicole really didn't understand that need at all. Nor had she experienced that kind of ambition.

"It's *my* heritage as much as any man's in my family." She angled closer to Nicole and kept her voice low. "He's not going to marry you, you know. Or if he does, it'll only be temporary, for appearances. He knows his responsibility to the family. We all do. And it isn't marrying beneath him."

"You've come to a lot of conclusions about me, I see." She looked through the window, making sure Devlin wasn't near. "Your brother trusts you, you know. Please don't hurt him."

"My relationship with my brother is not something we're going to discuss," Isabel said. "I'll be gone by the time you get home from work. If I'd known Dev had company, I wouldn't have crashed his party. Ashley won't mind if I'm a day early. And I don't want to interrupt your...interlude."

Nicole chose not to sink to her level. "You're welcome here, Isabel."

"Your words are gracious, but your eyes tell a different story. Perhaps we'll meet again. Perhaps not."

Nicole had doubts now, too. She hated that the trust she'd been building with Devlin could be so easily shattered by a few words. And Devlin would think Nicole chased his sister off somehow. "I think you'll get what you set your mind to, Isabel."

"Are you saying I'm ruthless?"

"Your word. But a good one."

Isabel merely smiled.

"Breakfast is ready," Devlin said from behind them.

Nicole made sure her expression didn't reveal any emotional upheaval before she turned to face him. Isabel made the transition easily, smiling brightly.

His gaze slid from one woman to the other. "Everything okay?"

Isabel didn't let Nicole answer but looped her arm through Nicole's. "I've had a nice time getting to know my future sister-in-law."

Oh, she was a sly one, all right, and definitely capable of backstabbing her way to the top. Was Devlin blind to his sister's take-no-prisoners ambition?

Nicole was grateful she could escape to work. Even if Devlin accused her of saying something to scare off Isabel, Nicole would be glad to see the manipulative woman leave.

And Nicole could act just as innocent as Isabel.

A few hours later Dev watched his sister drive off, then he took a walk around the property. He hadn't been surprised that she'd left a day early, especially when she hinted that Nicole hadn't made her feel welcome. Something had transpired between the women that morning, but neither of them was owning up to it.

He wasn't sorry Izzy left. Things were too tenuous with

Nicole to have someone intruding, altering the path of discovery they were on, but if Nicole had somehow forced Iz to leave, it was a side of Nicole he hadn't seen. And wouldn't like. In his world, the game was always played. Civility and courtesy were expected. She'd told him stories about irate hotel guests and how'd she'd soothed them, so she certainly had the skills for keeping the peace with his family.

Giving up on understanding the female mind, Dev stopped to watch the activity on the lake, all the sailboats, speed boats, and the large paddleboats that carried tourists around the huge expanse and into the exquisite Emerald Bay, its green water shimmering in the sun. He'd traveled a lot, had visited some incredible places in the world, but the simplicity of the Tahoe area appealed to him in a different way, a straightforward, undemanding way. The scent of pine wrapped around him. No hustle and bustle, except in the casinos. Maybe that was part of what drew him there sometimes. He hadn't fully adapted to a slow and peaceful way of life.

He should get back to work, had taken a long break, considering he'd slipped away yesterday, too. Instead he let the memory of his shower with Nicole that morning play in his head.

Everything would be different now. He could start making wedding plans. The hotel had a nice wedding chapel. They would invite only a few people, closest friends and family. She could give a two-week notice at work, then at the end of his month, they would be free to move back home to Philadelphia. Perfect timing.

He pulled out his cell phone and called Nicole at work as he hiked back to the lodge.

"Is everything okay?" she asked.

"Yeah. I just wanted to let you know that Izzy left."

He couldn't interpret her long silence.

"That's too bad," she said at last.

"I can't say I minded."

"Okay."

Okay? What *had* they talked about? "I had a look at her portfolio."

"And?"

"It's not bad. There's potential."

"Will you talk her up to your father?"

"Yeah."

"I'll bet she was thrilled."

Was that sarcasm in her voice? "I didn't tell her. Didn't want to get her hopes up. I'll see you in a few hours."

When Dev let himself into her cabin later he stood just inside the door and studied the space she'd made her own, looking for clues about her. He didn't think there was a new piece of furniture in the place, but there was a certain charm to what she'd put together, although it was a far cry from the sharp, contemporary lines of his town house furnishings. He wondered what her reaction to it was going to be. She would look like a daisy in a steel planter.

He wasn't sure it was the right setting for her.

He found the potting soil under her sink, where she'd directed him, then grabbed the flower pot. As he headed back to the front door, he noticed the message light on her answering machine was blinking. He rubbed his fingers against his still-unshaven cheeks, contemplating the flashing red light.

He pressed the message button. Four messages in a row were from Mark, asking her to call him, each message a little more frantic. Then the last message, obviously left last night or today, after Dev had found them together.

"We left things up in the air, Nicki," Mark said. "My offer will be there forever, no matter what else happens. Please just

stay in touch with me. I just want to know what's happening. I don't like him. I don't think he's good to you. You know I would be good to you. Call me, please."

If Mark didn't mean anything to her, why hadn't she deleted the messages from the previous week?

Dev focused on the photographs on her mantel, pictures of her mom and dad, a couple with girlfriends, but no photos of Mark. That should've pleased Dev, but a man on a mission like Mark could break down barriers. It might take only one misstep from Dev to send her running.

It looked as if he was going to have to take matters into his own hands regarding Mark, make sure he understood that he needed to back away, not just for now but forever. No lovesick hulk was going to play knight in shining armor for his wife.

Dev decided to go to the casino and play a little blackjack, but he was in a foul mood by the time he reached the Sterling a half hour before Nicole's shift was up. He needed to hide the mood from her. Things were changing between them. He didn't want to damage what they were building. So a little playtime was in order, to get his mind off Mark, and Izzy's early departure. He wanted the night to be free of problems when he and Nicole got into bed later.

Tonight he would seal the deal with her. They would make love *and* a wedding date. She wouldn't consider Mark an option ever again.

He headed to the front desk first to let Nicole know he was there and where she could find him when she was ready. Since she'd never agreed to let him drive her to and from work, he'd occasionally used blackjack as an excuse to show up now and then. She didn't seem suspicious that he was really showing up so that he could make sure she made the half-hour trip home safely.

The bubbly Ann-Marie gave him a wave but continued talking with a guest. He didn't see Nicole, not even behind the glass door of the assistant manager's office.

"She's upstairs dealing with a guest," Ann-Marie told him as soon as she was free.

"Thanks. When she gets back, would you tell her I'm here? I'm going to try my luck at the blackjack table until she's ready."

"Sure. Maybe I should warn you, though." Ann-Marie looked around, then whispered. "She's on the warpath about something."

He couldn't imagine what Nicole looked like "on the warpath." He winked, as if it were all a joke. "I know how to take care of that."

She grinned. "I'll just bet you do."

He walked away, wondering what had happened to upset her. He found a table, bought himself some chips, played a few hands, lost a couple of hundred dollars.

Nicole approached the table a few minutes after eight.

"You're just in time, Ms. Fortune. I'm in need of a little luck."

She leaned close. "Your luck has run out."

He looked at her sharply. She was on the warpath because of *him?*

He played out the last hand, betting everything he had left, then not just winning but also recouping his losses. "It seems you were wrong," he said coolly to Nicole. "You're still my lucky charm."

She waited until they got to her car before she let him have it with both barrels. "The next time you invade my privacy will be the last time."

"What'd I do?"

"You listened to my phone messages."

Caught. "What makes you say that?"

"Don't give me that innocent look. No one else has a key to my place. I called to check messages, and the machine said there were no new messages, yet there were five saved, not the four that were there yesterday. So I listened to them all, and what do you know? There was a message I hadn't heard before, yet apparently I had. It came at nine o'clock this morning. From Mark."

"Did you intend to keep it a secret?" he asked.

"Don't you dare deflect this onto me, Devlin Campbell. You had no business listening. You would be furious if I did that to you."

"I have no secrets from you."

"Bull."

He gave her a complacent look. "You may not like or understand any message you might overhear, but I wouldn't care if you heard them."

"Bull."

"You seem to have some trust issues, Nicole."

"I have— I seem to have trust issues? If you trusted me, you wouldn't have listened to my messages."

"If I hadn't listened to them, I wouldn't have known that Mark continues to call you *and* that you don't erase his messages. That speaks volumes to me. I don't trust you yet. Why should I? You haven't made a commitment to me."

"My making a commitment would make you trust me?"

"It would go a long way toward it."

Dev figured his anticipated night of sex was shot to hell now. He'd never worked so hard at a relationship before, yet he got nowhere, it seemed.

She used her remote to unlock her car. He opened her door.

"That's another thing," she said, gesturing broadly toward the car. "I'm perfectly capable of getting myself in and out of cars."

"That's part of being polite, Nicole. I was raised that way," he said, exasperated. "I hold coats and chairs and doors. I say please and thank you. I write thank-you notes. I don't like a woman to pay for any part of a date."

"You're a relic."

"And proud of it."

She got in her car and took off. It took him a few blocks to catch up. At the lodge she beat him to the front door and was halfway up the stairs by the time he'd gotten the potting soil and plant from the back of his car. She didn't stop at the great room but kept going up one more level, marching straight into the master bedroom. He was on her tail.

When she flung open a dresser drawer and grabbed an armful of lingerie, he understood that she was moving back to the guest room.

No way.

"Put that back," he said, low and steady.

"Make me."

They faced each other, two strong-willed people, both believing they were right. All the progress he'd made was about to disappear if he didn't do something different, didn't defuse the tension now.

"Make me," she said again, but with less heat.

"Nicole," he said softly, seeing something in her eyes that told him she didn't want to fight, either. He cupped her face, waited a second, then kissed her. He felt her let go of the lingerie, felt it land on his feet, a tempting heap of silk and lace.

She came at him hungrily, the heat of the argument transforming into passion.

"You can't move out of my bedroom," he said against her lips. "Ever. Please. Unless one of us is out of town, we will be sharing a bed for the rest of our lives."

Her eyes went bright. "Why are you making this so hard?" she asked, the words a rasp of sound.

"I'm not trying to. I'm trying to make this as easy on you as possible. Why can't *you* see that?"

"We're too different, Devlin."

He brushed her hair with his fingertips and tried to lighten the moment. "You don't have to be so formal, you know. Dev's fine. Or darling. Even, Hey, you."

She flattened her hands against his chest and leaned her forehead against him.

"So, we're different," he said. "What does it matter?" He was making light of it, but he knew she was right, to a degree. If he married a woman who shared his upbringing, it would be easier in some ways. They would have the same expectations, the same experiences. But he had no doubt that Nicole would figure out how to fit into his world. She was bright and competent and, well, friendly. She'd do fine.

The question was, could he fit into hers?

Nicole showered, unbraided her hair and changed into one of her new comfortable gowns. He'd finally left her alone after she assured him she wouldn't move her clothes out of the room.

Which didn't mean she still wouldn't move herself out, she thought rebelliously. What was it about him that made her want to do the opposite of everything he said?

She didn't like when he got possessive and bossy—and yet she did like it, too. No one had taken care of her since the day she'd hit the road after graduation. She'd always done the caring for, even in her other relationships. She'd given and given, not ever receiving the equivalent in return. Even her job was all about service. Why couldn't she just enjoy the things he wanted to do for her?

Because it meant giving up control. And giving up control meant giving up a piece of herself. She would only give up a piece of herself when she knew she could fill the vacant spot with a piece of him, one that he gave her freely.

She padded down the stairs and into the great room, following the strains of quiet jazz and a crackling fire. She kept going into the kitchen, stopping as soon as she saw him. He'd spread a towel on the counter. On top of it was her African violet, the bag of potting mix and the new pot, only slightly larger than her old one. He'd changed into sweatpants and a T-shirt and was barefoot, as was she.

"Shall we do it?" he asked.

"Do it?" She felt heat rise in her face.

He laughed low. "I guess there are two meanings to that question, but I'm referring to the plant."

They worked side by side. He recited the instructions given by the nurseryman, and the job was done. She carried it to the bottom of the staircase and placed it on a pedestal where sunlight was diffused, perfect for the plant.

"Thank you," she said, hugging him.

He held her close, without turning it into something seductive, and she appreciated that he knew it was an emotional moment for her, that it was a memory of her mother. After a while they headed back up the stairs, hand in hand.

"We didn't get a chance to talk about your trip home," she said. So much had happened since he returned. It'd seemed like a week instead of a day. "I heard you talking about a party for Isabel's graduation?"

"We went to dinner, just the family and one of her oldest girlfriends."

"Does she have a boyfriend?"

"If so, he wasn't there. I don't stay in touch with Iz like I do Joan. Joan e-mails and sends photos of the kids and calls."

"Did you tell Joan about me? The baby?"

They settled on the sofa. The fire was perfect.

"There wasn't time or privacy."

Nicole wondered about that. You could always find time and a place if you really wanted to. "Is that why you didn't tell your parents, either?"

"As I said to Izzy last night, it was her party. Not the place to bring up my own news and steal away the attention. I'll let you know as soon as I break the news," he said, tugging on her hair a little.

Which meant she should drop the subject. "What about the business you were taking care of? The face time you needed?"

"I decided against one deal. Have to make up my mind about the others soon, before someone else grabs them."

"What's taking you so long to make a decision? You seem like the decisive type."

"Everything will fall into place soon." He gathered her to him. "You always smell good," he said, threading his fingers through her hair, nuzzling her. "Let's go upstairs. It can only help," he added softly.

Could it? Last night she'd been ready, so what was holding her back now?

Isabel, she decided. His sister had stolen whatever confidence Nicole had found, as well as her hope for a true, long lasting marriage.

But, oh, how she wanted him. And she was so tired of

denying her needs. She just didn't know what price she would pay...

"Devlin," she said tentatively.

"Nicole," he said, conveying his need in the single word.

She knew he was waiting for her to say yes.

Nicole sat up. She looked him in the eyes.

"No more waiting," he said.

The freedom in his taking the decision out of her hands set her in motion. She straddled him, kissed him deeply, thoroughly, their mouths merging into one flaming entity. Down low she felt him, hard and strong, pressing against her own burning need.

Nicole tugged his shirt up and off him, then tossed it aside. She dragged her tongue down his neck and across his chest, sliding her fingers along the same path. A breath of air cooled her rising heat as he peeled off her gown, lobbing it on top of his shirt, then he maneuvered his sweatpants off. Face to face, skin to skin, they both paused. Looked. Enjoyed. Settled.

She arched her back and moaned as he sucked a nipple into his mouth.

"This is what I remembered about you," he said against her flesh. "How good you taste. How hard your nipples are. How perfect your body is."

"You really did go back to find me?"

"Oh, yeah." He met her gaze. "If I'd known you were an employee, I would've haunted the place."

"And broken your one-date rule?" She waited, almost breathless, for his answer, which mattered a lot to her.

"Yeah."

"But only for sex."

"The best sex I could remember."

It was a start, Nicole decided. A very good start. The fact that he'd admitted it pleased her, as well. "Me, too. I did things I'd never done before."

"I remember them all." His jaw tightened, his gaze burned into her, then his hands got into the action, stroking her first with long sweeps, then searching lower and lower. She raised herself up on her knees a little, giving him access. He slid a hand to the juncture of her thighs, caressed her tenderly, thoroughly, then slipped a finger inside her, leaving his thumb to rest where the ache had intensified.

"I remembered this, too," he said, his words like sandpaper.

Her breath had caught in her throat. "Remembered what?"

"How wet you get, how tight you are, how good you feel when I'm inside you."

"So, get inside, why don't you?" She gripped his shoulders to steady herself. "I don't think I can wait any longer."

He helped position her over him, to slide down him. "Don't move," he said harshly. "Don't move for a second."

She didn't, but she couldn't help but squeeze him tight. He made a long, low sound of ecstasy.

The sensations may have started where they were joined, but they shot like liquid fire everywhere, fast and overwhelming. It wasn't going to be one of those slow rolling climaxes but one that hit hard and didn't relent. Her own voice echoed in the vast room, not words but sounds she had no control over. She became aware of his helping her slide up and down on him, then his rising to meet her. Their mating was mutual, intense and primal, obliterating anything that had gone before. Waves rolled through her long after they'd collapsed against each other.

"Better than I remembered," she breathed against his shoulder.

"Yeah."

After a minute her legs cramped. He helped her shift onto the couch and rubbed her thighs until she could feel sensation again, then he laid his hands on her belly. She opened her eyes.

"Nicole."

She waited.

"Anytime you're in the mood, you don't hesitate to let me know. Don't hold back."

"You're pretty good at reading my mind." *Seeing into my soul.*

"I don't want to guess."

"Okay, it's a deal, provided you do the same."

"You turn me loose like that, and the only time you'll be dressed is when you're at work. I can't get enough of you."

She ran her thumb along his lower lip, let it dip inside. "There's something to be said for anticipation."

He bit her thumb lightly. "I've been anticipating too long already."

"Patience is a virtue."

"Patience is wasted energy."

She grinned.

"Were you comfortable enough?" he asked.

"Until the end when I couldn't move my legs."

"We'll have to get creative." He helped her up. "Let's go to bed."

"Perchance to sleep?" she asked.

"Perchance."

Eventually they did.

Eleven

The week passed, the routine of their days merely a way of killing time until the nights, in Dev's opinion. The ripples Nicole had felt in her abdomen turned into what she called tiny flutters instead, distinctly different but still too light for Dev to feel, frustrating him.

His month was winding down. Decisions about their future together couldn't be put off much longer, especially since she was approaching her fifth month. The wedding needed to happen *now*. Plus she would need to give notice at work. And put her cabin on the market. He wanted to take care of that for her, take the responsibility off her shoulders. She might not be able to fly much until after the baby was born, so he would fly her father to see her as often as they liked. That should help ease her concerns about leaving him.

Dev hoped he'd thought of everything. They had an appointment to see her obstetrician in a few days for a consultation and ultrasound. Joan had shoved ultrasound photos in his face for all three of her children, including the one still tucked safely inside her, so he knew what to expect.

Nicole was still asleep on this Sunday morning, but Dev was wound tight. He'd awakened early, watched her sleep for a little while, then eased out of bed. While waiting for the coffee to finish brewing, he jogged up to the office to study the photos of the Samurai. Because he'd been looking at them every day, he'd started to feel a connection to them again. Memories of their time together came back in bits and pieces. He looked forward to the mass reunion in October, when they'd all served their time, as he'd begun to think of it.

"Well, Hunter, are you satisfied?" he asked, focusing on the man with the biggest smile and broadest gestures. "You wanted us to reassess our lives during our stays in the wilderness." There was very little he hadn't reassessed, personally and professionally.

The plans were set, he thought just as his cell phone rang. He saw on the screen that it was his father, the first call he'd made to Dev all month. Dev had always called *him*.

"Hello, Son."

"Morning, Father." He rubbed his cheeks, unshaven for days. He could only imagine how his father would feel about that.

"I understand you have news."

Dev's heart slammed into his chest. Since Izzy was the only one who could've told anyone—

"Ed Maguire says you're close to a deal," his father went on to say. "Yet you haven't even presented the property to the board. You don't have the authority to make the deal on your own."

Dev let go of the satisfying image of wringing Izzy's neck, although the way his father had chastised him didn't sit well, either. Had he always spoken to Dev in that paternal, dicta-torial voice, even after all these years of his doing his job beyond anyone's expectations?

"I'm not close to a deal with Maguire, Father. That's just wishful thinking on his part."

"He said you checked out the property when you were home last week."

Dev had already denied the claim, yet his father contin-ued to push? "I did. I decided it was a bad risk."

"Fred Hayden and Ron Allister said you took meetings with them, too."

Cold, hard accusation coated the words. Dev shouldn't have been surprised that the men had spread the word to his father.

"What are you up to, Devlin?"

He sat in the desk chair, ready to explain. "I—"

"Before you answer with a lie or a half truth, you should know that your sister told your mother and me about a woman you apparently impregnated. Someone who works for a casino." The last word was said with disdain, as if that were worse than Dev getting a woman pregnant out of wedlock.

He would wring Izzy's neck, after all. What had she hoped to gain by violating his confidence?

"You have nothing to say?" his father asked.

"I have plenty to say."

Nicole appeared in the doorway, her hair mussed, her smile sleepy. She wore a flannel shirt of his that came to the tops of her thighs. He held out an arm to her, inviting her in.

"Well?" his father said impatiently.

Nicole took his hand and placed it on her belly. Apparently she was feeling kicks, but he felt nothing.

Dev had paid closer attention to his parents while he was home last week, trying to figure out what kind of relationship they had. He couldn't imagine his father ever anxiously awaiting his children's first kicks. He and his mother had never once touched during the hours Dev had spent with them. Had they ever been hungry for each other, as he and Nicole were?

"I'm still waiting," came the stern voice on the other end.

Dev kept his gaze locked to Nicole's as he spoke into the phone. "I am going to be a father in September. My fiancée's name is Nicole. She doesn't work at a casino but a hotel. You'll meet her soon."

Nicole had jerked back when he'd called her his fiancée. He tightened his hold.

"I tolerated your taking a month off from work since you've been able to work from there, but I won't tolerate your marrying a woman I don't approve of. You'll bring her home tomorrow so that your mother and I can meet her."

"That won't be possible."

"If you value your position—"

"Don't threaten, Father," Dev said mildly. It felt freeing to take control of the conversation.

"I can't believe you let yourself get taken in by the oldest trick in the—"

Dev snapped his phone shut and set it aside. He pulled Nicole to stand between his thighs. "Good morning."

"Fiancée?"

"Just because you don't have a ring yet doesn't make it any less true."

"There's been no asking and answering that I know of."

"It's going to happen, Nicole. You know it and I know it."

"You don't allow a girl any fantasies, do you?" she asked. She moved away. He didn't understand what she meant, and after the difficult conversation with his father, he didn't want to pursue why she was upset with him now, too.

"I want to go see my dad on my own today," she said.

"Why?"

"Because I'd like a little time alone with him. He's been acting strangely every time we've talked. I need to settle things with him."

He wanted to offer to drive her, even if only to drop her off and pick her up later, but he knew her by now. It wouldn't sit well with her, so he didn't even suggest it.

"You've got to start trusting me sometime, Devlin," she said, interpreting his silence incorrectly. "I'm not going to see Mark."

"Mark may come to see you."

"I can't stop him from doing that, since it's my father's house. Trust me. Please."

"I do." He just didn't trust Mark. Dev knew how men thought; Nicole didn't.

"Thank you." She gestured to his phone. "You told your father."

"Izzy did."

Nicole's face paled.

"I'm calling her the same names as you are in your head," he said. "I can't believe she did that. I can't imagine what she thought she might gain from it."

"To discredit you with your parents."

"Why?"

She hesitated. "You know, I hardly know her. This is between you and her."

"You have an opinion. I'd like to hear it."

"I'm angry. Very angry. It's bad enough when a friend plays you false. For a sibling to be disloyal is unforgivable. I mean, I don't have any siblings but..."

So she was championing him? "Thank you for your allegiance," he said.

"I believe in loyalty," she said, then she kissed him, surprising him with her intensity.

He slipped his hands under the shirt, curved his hands over her rear and drew her close, the discussion well and truly over. "You weren't planning to leave soon, were you?"

She smiled seductively. "I have time to let you have your way with me."

He stripped her shirt off, sat her in the desk chair and did, indeed, have his way with her, giving her a memory to take to Sacramento with her.

Nicole got an early start, arriving twenty minutes before her usual time. A strange car was parked in the driveway as she approached, a small red sedan. Just then her father and a woman came into view, walking arm in arm up the pathway from the house. The woman was as round as he was slender, and was younger, maybe by ten years. She looked up at him and smiled; he bent to give her a quick kiss.

Stunned, Nicole pulled over, blocking the driveway. She stared through the window until they noticed her. Nicole rolled down the window.

"Dad?" she asked, stunned.

He looked mildly uncomfortable but held tight to the woman's hand. "You're early," he said to Nicole. "This is Liz. Liz, my daughter, Nicole."

"What's going on?" Nicole asked, her voice raw. Her gaze drilled her father, then Liz.

"We'll talk in the house, Nicki."

"I was just leaving," Liz said quietly, then with a quick, sad look at Rob, she got in her car.

After a moment Nicole pulled out of the way and parked the car, not getting out until the red sedan was gone. Her father met her on the sidewalk, but she didn't look at him. Couldn't look at him. Hurt and bewilderment tumbled around her in an avalanche of emotion as they walked into the house and straight into the living room.

"Who is she?" Nicole asked hoarsely as her father sat in his big blue recliner.

"I met Liz a few weeks ago at the grocery store. She helped me pick out some…cantaloupe." His voice faded. "I was just standing there, staring at the bin, not knowing what to look for. I missed your mother so much, and I was mad at her, too, for putting me in that predicament. She always did the shopping."

"I know," Nicole said. "But it's too soon."

"By whose timetable? I'm lonely. Sometimes I'm lost. Liz helps."

"Are you sleeping with her?"

"That's none of your business."

He was right, of course. She'd just blurted it out, not even wanting to know if it was true. "It's only been five months," she said aloud finally, her voice shaking, tears burning her eyes.

"I'm sorry you're hurt, honey. But I like her. You would, too, if you gave her a chance."

"I can't, Dad."

"You're moving forward. I need to, too."

"There's a big difference. I'm having a baby. And you were married to Mom for thirty-five years."

"I know you won't understand this, but I'm honoring her. She wouldn't like that I've been sitting at home mourning rather than living. You know she wouldn't."

Nicole finally sat. "I know she would want you to keep living, Dad. But dating so soon?"

"I'm not saying I'm going to marry Liz. But she's a kind, cheerful, undemanding woman, and for now it's nice to have company. She's widowed, too, so she understands. And she has a lot of family and friends. She keeps me busy. She keeps me from thinking too much. She likes to cook."

And he didn't. Nicole knew that. He'd been relying on frozen dinners and whatever she made on Sundays, which she made in quantity to freeze extra portions for him.

"You can't take care of me forever, Nicki. You've got your own life. I imagine you'll be moving to Philadelphia."

It was one of the things Nicole had stuck her head in the sand about—moving. Moving meant giving up her cabin. Her job. Her proximity to her father. It meant cutting all ties and starting over, knowing only Devlin, becoming part of a family who would probably start off resenting her for "tricking" their son into marriage.

"I'm not asking you to accept Liz as anything other than a new friend in my life," her father said.

"I miss Mom." The ache that stayed with her day by day, hour by hour, became white-hot. She missed her mother like she never thought she could miss anyone. Nothing could ever replace her. It was a black hole of emptiness.

"I know, honey. I know." He pulled her out of her chair and into his arms. They cried together. Nicole wished she'd found it healing, but she felt even emptier, maybe because everything with Devlin was so complicated, too.

"Have you made wedding plans?" her father asked a little while later as they headed into the kitchen to make lunch.

"No."

His brows rose. "What's the holdup?"

"Time. Trust. Love." There it was, the biggest reason. She'd spent the past three weeks falling in love—may~

because she wanted to so much. Devlin had rarely given any indication she was much more than the woman he got pregnant, who was now his responsibility. The woman he lusted after, yes, but loved? No. He could be tender at times, and kind, and even funny on occasion.

"Do you believe in love at first sight, Dad?"

"Yes, I do. I also believe love can grow out of a deep and abiding friendship to become something even better." He gave her a fatherly look. "*Mark* loves you."

Nicole laughed a little. "Dad, please."

"Well, he does."

"Do you seriously think Devlin would let another man raise his child? Besides, I don't love Mark."

"You love Devlin?"

"Yes." Yes, she did. Stupidly and wonderfully loved him. Maybe she'd let it happen because she carried his baby and they had a future because of that baby. But maybe she'd fallen for him that first night.

"But?" her father asked.

She needed to tell someone, talk to someone, so she opened up. "Do you know what it's like loving someone who doesn't love you in return?"

He shook his head.

"It's lonely. It's painful. You start to feel used, even though it's your own choice to give so much, *too* much. I've been through it in a much less harrowing way before, and I decided I wouldn't ever get myself into that position again. Yet here I am, in an even worse position, because I'm pregnant and my choices are limited."

"You're welcome to come live with me. I'll help raise the baby."

Nicole reached for his hand. "Thank you. I appreciate the

offer, Dad. But there's no way Devlin is going to let anyone else raise his child, not even just me. He's in my child's life—my life—forever. I just have to figure out what I can live with." She straightened her shoulders. "And that's enough about me. I'm ready for lunch."

She discovered a refrigerator full of food, and the bills paid and organized. He didn't need her anymore, not the way he had. Her life continued to change.

Nicole was tired enough to take a nap before she left for home, but she didn't want to stay at her father's house any longer. She needed time alone to think about him with a woman other than her mother, and to think about Devlin and where they would go from here. Her expectations had probably been too high when she'd agreed to spend the month with him. A month wasn't enough time, and she was fairly certain he wouldn't stay beyond the month. He seemed anxious to get on with his plan, whatever it was.

Instead of driving home right away, she took a sentimental journey around Sacramento. It had been a great place to grow up, a big city, an important one politically as the state capital, yet with a small-town atmosphere and lots of trees; in fact its nickname was "City of Trees."

She drove to Land Park. How many times had she visited the zoo and Fairytale Town? Nostalgia swept over her in agonizing waves. Reminders of her mother were everywhere here—picnics and summer escapes and fun. Mom would pack the car with kids and spend the day like a recreation director. Everyone would go home tired and dirty and satisfied.

What was Philadelphia like? Aside from being home to the Liberty Bell, she really didn't know much about the city, except that it was more sophisticated, probably, and historical. How easy would it be to make friends? Would Devlin's friends accept her? Would she find places to take her child where they would make the kind of memories she had?

Nicole realized she couldn't wait any longer to decide her future. It was make-or-break time. Tell him yes or no. She would either marry Devlin and move to Philadelphia, and find a way to make a good life with him—and hope he would come to love her…

Or she would move back to her cabin and find a way to fit him into her life without benefit of marriage. She had rights, too. Emotional, as well as legal.

By the time she got to the lodge she would have made her decision. She would tell him tonight.

Twelve

Pacing, Dev glared at his watch again. Why wasn't she home yet? He'd talked to her father, learned she'd left almost four hours ago. Dev wouldn't wait too much longer before he contacted the California Highway Patrol to see if there'd been any accidents.

His cell phone rang. He grabbed it, ground out a hello.

"You called?" Izzy asked leisurely.

Dev moved to stare out the window, where he could see the driveway. Anxiety over Nicole grabbed him by the throat, but it didn't stop the anger directed at his sister. "I trusted you, Iz. I can't believe you told Mother and Father about Nicole."

"It just slipped out."

"In what context?"

"I asked Father if you'd talked to him about me. He said no. Then it just slipped out."

Not a slip at all, but retaliation for his not acting fast

enough for her. "I had every intention of talking to him, Iz, but I wanted to do it in person and show him your portfolio, which would've earned you points."

A long pause, then, "I assumed since you hadn't said anything…"

"One of the first rules of business—don't assume. That little slip cost you. It cost you big-time."

"Why?" She sounded haughty and defensive. When had she turned into their father?

"Because now you're on your own, without my support. Second rule of business, Iz—trust matters. I don't trust you anymore."

"But, Dev—"

"I'm done." He ended the call. He couldn't deal with her and her ambitions right now.

He was about to dial 4ll to get the highway patrol's number when Nicole pulled into the driveway. Anger dynamited its way through relief as he hurried down the stairs and flung open the door.

"Where the hell have you been?" He shouted the words. Having never shouted at anyone before, he amazed himself that he was even capable of it.

She stopped in her tracks. "You know where I was."

"You left your father's house more than four hours ago. Four hours." He came within a foot of her, examining her, then her car. No damage that he could see.

"My father is dating…."

He almost couldn't make out her barely spoken words. "So?"

Her eyes went bright. "So, my mother has only been gone for five months."

"That's what made you late? That's why you didn't call

to say you'd be delayed? You scared the—" He stopped ranting when he saw her recoil. "What exactly took you so long?"

She walked past him and entered the house. "You wouldn't understand."

"Try me." He followed her upstairs and into the great room then on into the kitchen, where she dumped her purse on the counter, grabbed a glass and pressed it to the cold water lever in the refrigerator door.

"I needed some time alone," she said, eyeing him directly, then taking a long drink.

"Why?"

"To think. To remember my mother."

She'd put him through hell because she'd needed to *think*? He'd been scared to death something had happened to her or the baby. "Did you even once consider I might be worried when you didn't come home within a reasonable time frame?"

"Don't yell at me."

No apology? "You don't have a clue what you put me through."

"I needed time, Devlin. I needed—"

"Stop. Just stop. I'm through being patient. Here's what's going to happen." He watched her set down her water glass, her body going rigid. Where was the sexy woman he'd taken back to bed that very morning? The even-tempered woman he'd come to enjoy sharing space with? He should've taken charge weeks ago.

Control. He needed control back. Something had gone haywire today. He couldn't let that happen again. Couldn't be afraid like that again.

"First, I'll drive you to the Sterling tonight so that you can give notice that you're leaving your job. It won't be a considerate two-week notice, but they'll have to manage. Second, we'll contact a real estate agent tomorrow to put your cabin on the market."

He saw her retreat, mentally and physically, but it didn't slow him down any. "Third, we'll get married at the Sterling's wedding chapel on Saturday. Invite as many people as you want, except your *friend,* Mark. Fourth, I'll hire a moving company to pack up your things and have them shipped to Philadelphia, although you won't need to take much. Your furnishings won't fit in my house anywhere. Fifth—"

"What an interesting way to win me over," Nicole interrupted, ice dripping from her words.

She grabbed her purse and walked away, taking long, slow strides, as if time was infinite. He started to follow, but she left the house without packing her things, so he knew she would be back after she cooled down. Surely she would be able to see how reasonable he was being. There weren't any options other than the ones he'd cited.

When she returned, they would have a reasonable discussion. She would apologize for putting him through hell while he waited for her to get home, and he would apologize for yelling.

To kill time Dev opened a bottle of beer, grabbed a bag of pretzels and turned on the television, catching a ballgame between the Giants and the Oakland A's. Night fell. Why wasn't she back? Surely she'd calmed down by now.

He called her cell phone. Turned off, as usual.

Needing to do something, Dev decided to go looking. He grabbed his keys, headed down the staircase. At the bottom he saw the pedestal. Empty. She'd taken her African violet. Her only possession that mattered.

He approached the pedestal slowly, placed his hand on the

empty stand. It said more than any words she could've thrown at him before she left.

Still, he needed to know where she was. That she was all right. He wouldn't think about anything else until he knew she was safe.

Dev didn't see her car along the route to the Sterling, or in the parking lot, so he drove to the only other place he figured she might be—her cabin. All the lights were out. Her car wasn't in the driveway. Then he saw a curtain move inside.

He stopped, got out, headed to her front door. He changed his mind, continuing on until he reached the detached garage. He pulled open the door a crack, saw her car inside.

He closed his eyes for a few seconds, then headed to her door. The crunch of leaves and pine needles on the dirt-and-rock path to her house reminded him of the first time he'd come, the night he'd found out she was pregnant—a lifetime ago yet not even three weeks. The air had warmed up considerably since then, when she'd been sitting on her porch swing watching him without alerting him she was there until he'd almost tripped over her.

She wasn't on the porch now. He would bet his stock portfolio that she wouldn't answer the door, but he knocked anyway. Waited. Knocked again and called her name. Waited.

"I know you're in there, Nicole," he said, hoping his voice wouldn't drift to the nearest cabin, about fifty yards away. "Your car is in your garage."

He laid a hand on the door frame. "You're being childish."

A soft thump hit the door. He pictured her throwing a pillow, which made him smile, even as he was torn by her leaving. He couldn't picture his mother ever tossing a pillow at his father. Nicole was certainly the liveliest woman he'd…

dated? He couldn't exactly define their relationship in those terms, but he didn't know what else to call it.

"Come on, Nicole. Open up. Let's talk." Women always wanted to talk to clear the air.

"Okay," he said. "I'll just sleep on your swing tonight. If I freeze to death, it'll be on your conscience."

He underestimated her, however. She didn't open the door, not then, not an hour later. The temperatures may have warmed during the month, but it was still only forty degrees.

He had a choice—go home or try to force her hand. She was too kindhearted to leave him there to freeze…wasn't she?

She took her violet.

Another hour passed and she still didn't open her door to him. He used his cell phone to call and talk to her answering machine.

"I don't know why you won't talk to me," he said after the beep. "Maybe I owe you an apology. I know you owe *me* one. But this kind of behavior accomplishes nothing but to keep us at an impasse." He paused, then added, "I'm going to miss you sleeping next to me. Good night, Ms. Fortune."

He waited a few seconds, hoping to hear the lock turn. He would come back early in the morning with breakfast, since he knew she had no food in the house. He'd be damned if she'd deny his child sustenance.

With that plan in mind he went home to his big, empty bed.

Nicole listened to his car fade into the night. What could have been a night of celebration when she told him she had decided to marry him and move to Philadelphia had been shattered by his chauvinistic attitude. Okay, maybe she'd been wrong not letting him know she would be late. That wasn't an excuse for his tirade. No excuse at all.

She was not going to give up her good job, her first home and her proximity to her father for a man who didn't even care enough about her to involve her in critical decisions. Her feelings for him had shifted during the seismic eruption of orders he'd inflicted on her. Obviously he had no idea what it meant to be a partner.

A tear slid down her cheek. She swiped hard at it, angry that he'd affected her enough to cry. She'd had such hopes, had truly thought they could make a go of it, even with the strikes against them of coming at the relationship backwards, of hardly knowing each other, and expecting a baby, and coming from two different worlds.

She realized how crazy she sounded. Why *had* she been hopeful? She'd been the one doing all the compromising, after all. He'd gotten his way about everything.

How could she have thought for even a second that she could marry him without his loving her, adoring her? Impossible.

Nicole moved from the sofa to her bedroom and climbed under the covers. Even though the bed was much smaller than the one she'd shared with Devlin, it had way too much empty space.

She would have to learn to live with it.

Thirteen

After an almost sleepless night, Nicole scanned her refrigerator the next morning. The contents included ketchup, mustard, pickle relish, salad dressing and three kinds of jam. The only item in the freezer was ice. She'd taken everything else to the lodge weeks ago.

The cupboards weren't much better, but at least there was soup. She poured a can of chicken noodle into a bowl and put it in the microwave, then sat at the kitchen table with a pad of paper. She needed a plan. She needed to present Devlin with orders of her own.

Nicole held the pen poised over the paper, but no words would come. The microwave beeped that the soup was done. Still she didn't move. After a few minutes she laid her arms on the table and put her head down.

She wanted a father for her baby. She wanted a husband for herself.

She wanted love.

As much as she'd proclaimed that it wouldn't bother her to be a single, unmarried mother, it did bother her. A lot.

But if she let him get his way about everything now, would she ever get her way about anything in the future—or even compromises? Would they ever have a meeting of the minds, find a way to be partners? Maybe he was used to a household where parents didn't show affection, but she wasn't. She hadn't known how deprived of touch she was until the past couple of weeks, when he'd been within touching range all the time. She'd only had to reach out. It had been wonderful.

But it had been all about sex for him. And being in charge.

The microwave continued to beep every so often. She grabbed a spoon and opened the microwave door, then heard a car approach. Already? It was only 7:30, and Devlin was already starting in on her? But when she moved to the window to peek out from behind the curtain, she saw instead a minivan with the words Lakeside Diner painted on the side.

A teenage boy hopped out and ran around to the back. She could see into the van, where he opened a hot pack and pulled out a white foam plastic container, then slammed the door shut and raced to her door, banging on it.

"Delivery!" he called out.

She tightened her robe sash and opened the door.

He shoved the box into her hands. "Morning."

"I didn't order—"

He snagged a piece of paper from his shirt pocket and looked at it. "Nicole Price?"

"Yes, but—"

"Breakfast is served." He grinned, then hopped down the stairs.

"Wait. I'll get a tip."

"Taken care of," he said with a wave, then he was gone.

Nicole set the package on the table as if it might contain explosives. The smell of something wonderful wafted up. Her stomach rumbled. She lifted the lid. Inside was a blueberry muffin, still warm, a bacon-and-avocado omelet, and a beautiful orange, peeled, sliced and sprinkled with powdered sugar. A note wrapped in plastic was tucked into the lid.

"Good morning," it read. "I've been jogging past this little diner almost daily without ever going inside. For some reason, today I did. Guess what I learned? The mayor of Hunter's Landing, whose family owns this place, married one of the Samurai—Nathan. Amazing coincidence. They're in Barbados at the moment, but apparently they are in and out of Hunter's Landing a lot. I'll try to catch him—or meet her. Figured you would be out of food. Dev."

Nicole stared at the note. No pressure. No demands.

What was he up to?

She devoured the food, made a shopping list instead of a game plan, then went to the grocery store. At least it was her day off, so she had time to get her cabin in order again. Everything needed dusting. Then she would start on the nursery curtains. Plus, somehow, she needed to get her clothes and toiletries from the lodge.

But later, as she carried her grocery sacks from her car into the cabin, two cars pulled into her driveway, Devlin's and a sleek black Cadillac with a rental agency sticker on the bumper. Nicole couldn't retreat into the house and shut the door because two more bags of perishable food were still in her trunk, including ice cream, so she just kept moving, ignoring them.

"Need some help?" Devlin asked, coming up to her.

"I've got it. Thanks." Out of the corner of her eye, she saw a slender, elegant man get out of the Cadillac, reach inside it, then head toward them, a black leather briefcase in his hand. Another man, big and burly, climbed out of the driver's side and followed.

Everything about the thin man screamed *lawyer*. The bearer of the prenuptial agreement, she decided. Why it took two men to deliver one little document she didn't know, unless the big guy was supposed to strong-arm her into signing.

Nicole tried to grab the two remaining bags from her car at the same time, but she couldn't manage both at once. She heard Devlin pick up the other bag, then close her trunk. He followed her. She set her bag inside the house then turned and reached for his. Then she shut the door in his face.

"Thank you," she called from inside.

"Nicole." His tone of voice was patient, even indulgent.

"Thank you for breakfast, too." She put her ice cream in the freezer, along with the frozen vegetables. Milk into the refrigerator. Fruit. Salad fixings. Chicken breasts. All the while she was aware of Devlin right outside her door.

If only he would say he was sorry. If only he would say he loved her....

An anvil dropped on her chest, making it hard to breathe.

"I just want to show you something," he said through the door.

"What?"

"Open the door for a minute. Please."

"I'm not signing anything."

"I'm not asking you to. I just want to show you something."

She took her time washing her hands, then moved to the living room window and looked out. When he didn't spot her, she tapped on the glass.

"What do you think I'm going to do, kidnap you?" he asked, his earlier patience apparently being tested.

"You wanted to show me something?"

He gestured to the men waiting at the bottom of the steps, who joined Devlin. The attorney held up the briefcase and opened the lid.

"This is Mr. Sokoloff, who has been kind enough to fly in from Philadelphia so that you can choose from his selections."

The case held a display of probably fifty engagement rings, mostly with diamonds, but a few sapphires and other stones she couldn't name. So, the big guy was a bodyguard? She couldn't begin to imagine the total value of the rings.

"What do you like?" Devlin asked.

A hot lump formed in her throat. *I'd like to be proposed to. I'd like to hear you pledge your life to me.*

She didn't care about a ring, although her eye was drawn to a square-cut diamond with sapphire petals surrounding it. "It doesn't matter."

Mr. Sokoloff didn't even blink, yet he surely couldn't be accustomed to balky, belligerent recipients of his fine jewelry.

"It doesn't matter?" Devlin repeated. "So, *I* should choose?" When she didn't reply, he seemed to mull over the case, stroking his chin. He still hadn't shaved, and the last time she'd touched his face, his beard had finally gone from scratchy to soft.

"Personally, I like this one," he said, pulling out an enormous diamond in an intricate setting.

"Excellent choice, sir," Mr. Sokoloff said. "Five carats. Platinum setting. Perfect quality."

"Five carats? Are you crazy?" she asked. "I don't want five carats. It's…gaudy. It isn't me."

She caught Devlin smiling then, just a little satisfied smile. He'd gotten a rise out of her, which was apparently what he wanted.

"Tell me what appeals to you, Nicole."

"If you knew me at all, you wouldn't have to ask that." She yanked the curtains shut.

Nicole knew she was being a brat, but he was a conservative man, with old-fashioned values and actions. Why couldn't he see that she needed roses and candlelight as much as any woman did, maybe even more so because she was pregnant and they'd gone about everything backward. She didn't want to choose her own ring—at least not until after he'd proposed and she'd accepted.

A few minutes later she peeked through a crack in the curtains as the men left the porch and walked to the Cadillac. When Devlin glanced toward the house, she took a step back, out of sight. Then she heard a car start. The jeweler was leaving. Devlin, however, climbed the stairs, sat on the porch swing and stayed. Every time she peeked, he was there, sometimes making the swing move slowly, sometimes resting his head, his eyes closed, as if asleep.

Her neighbor's golden retriever, Alamo, came crashing up her stairs, waking him up, and the two played fetch with some twigs for a long time. Of course, Alamo liked everyone....

Around five o'clock Devlin had a pizza delivered, which made her laugh. Why had he all of a sudden become funny? Maybe he hadn't been much fun—or funny—because of their situation. Come to think of it, she hadn't been much fun, either. How could she expect him to love her when she'd never shown him the true Nicole?

Later he seemed to be playing a video game on his cell

phone, was putting his whole body into it and shouting at success or loss. Eventually he knocked on her door.

"Can I use your bathroom?" he asked.

She opened the door and let him in. He gave her a nod, went directly into the bathroom, came out a few minutes later, gave her another nod, then he went directly outside, shutting the door behind him.

Guilt grabbed her and shook hard.

By the time night settled, she'd accomplished nothing, had spent the whole day sneaking peeks of him, had constantly stopped herself from going out and sitting in his lap.

He finally knocked on her door, said good-night and left. Twenty minutes later her phone rang.

"I had a good time today, did you?" he asked.

She smiled. "It was different." She waited but he didn't say anything. "You didn't get any work done."

"I phoned my computer and told it I was taking a sick day."

"I bet you'll be up all night catching up."

"Maybe. Nicole?"

"Yes?"

"Are we going to be able to resolve this?"

"I hope so."

"You don't sound mad at me. I don't understand why you're not here trying to work things out."

His confusion gave her strength. He needed time without her. If they were together, they would be making love, and he would be focusing on what wasn't a problem between them—sex. She hoped he would miss her as much as she missed him.

"I'm sorry you don't understand," she said, twisting a tassel on one of her sofa pillows. "Sleep well."

His long silence seemed to shout at her. "You took your

plant," he said finally, sounding defeated by that action. Without hope. "Good night, Ms. Fortune."

Tears filled her eyes when she hung up. Was she being too hard on him? On them? On their future? Didn't she have a right to expect more than she'd gotten?

Because she was exhausted, she finally slept, then the next day he didn't show up in the morning, nor did he join her for lunch at work later. When she drove home after her shift, her driveway was empty.

The day after was the same. She didn't know what to do. Had something happened to him? She didn't want to call, so she drove to the lodge. The lights were on. She saw someone moving around the great room and assumed it was him. She kept going until she found a place to turn around.

At least he was okay.

The next day when she arrived for her appointment with her obstetrician, he was there, already seated. He came to the counter while she checked in, then took a seat next to her. He'd been thumbing through a parenting magazine but had put it aside. He didn't pick it up again.

She smiled at him, glad to see him but unsure. *Why did you disappear for two days?* "Hi."

"How are you feeling?" he asked.

She couldn't tell anything by his tone of voice. "Good. Fine. You?"

"Fine."

Was he angry? Had he given up? *Please don't give up.*

The inner door opened and a close-to-her-due-date woman came into the reception area. She led with her belly, one hand pressed against her lower back. A toddler held her other hand.

"Ain't life grand?" she said to Nicole, flashing a smile, seeming to mean her words.

Nicole smiled back. That would be her in a few months—well, minus the toddler. Would Devlin find her attractive then?

He looked at her just then, and she wondered if that was what was going through his mind, too. Would he resent her when the physical connection had to be put on hold?

"Nicole?" The doctor's assistant, Jennie, held the door for her to enter. Devlin followed.

Nicole stepped on the scale, and Jennie cheerfully announced her weight aloud as she recorded it, then directed Nicole to sit on the exam table to have her blood pressure taken.

"Slip off your skirt and put the drape over you. The doctor will be with you in a few minutes."

"Is that true?" Devlin asked after the door closed.

"Is what true?" Nicole climbed off the table, handed him the drape, kicked off her shoes and stepped out of her skirt. She was wearing the purple thong that he'd held up the first night she'd stayed at the lodge. She'd worn it on purpose, hoping he would be there, would see it and be reminded.

"Is your doctor prompt?" His slowness in responding made her look at him.

She caught him eyeing her legs and took her time getting back onto the table. "She's generally prompt. Would you hand me the drape, please?"

He stood and opened the paper fold by fold, then he laid it over her lap. He rested his hands on either side of her.

"You shaved," she said, realizing why he looked different.

"Yeah."

"Why?"

"It was time."

"Because it's time to go home and back to work?"

"Because the experiment is over."

The door opened then and the doctor entered. "You must be the dad," she said, extending her hand. "I'm Dr. Saxon."

"Dev Campbell."

They shook hands, then she sat on a stool and opened Nicole's file. "Your weight's good. Blood pressure is excellent. Any problems?"

My baby's father doesn't love me. "None."

They went through the usual routine of stethoscope listening and abdomen measuring. Devlin seemed fascinated, not speaking, hardly even blinking. Dr. Saxon got out the fetal heartbeat implements, and the sound soon resonated in the room, swooshing and beating, fast and furious. Devlin's face paled a little. He grasped Nicole's hand.

"Awesome, isn't it?" Dr. Saxon said. "I never get tired of hearing it." She tugged a different machine closer, shoved Nicole's drape out of the way then squirted some gel on her abdomen. "Watch the monitor."

"We don't want to know the baby's sex," Nicole said in a hurry.

"Speak for yourself," Devlin said.

"Uh-oh. I hear this all the time," the doctor said. "Should I leave the room and let you duke it out?"

Nicole made eye contact. After a moment he said, "No. We'll do it her way."

It seemed like a huge victory to Nicole.

"Okay. I can't guarantee you won't see something to give the secret away, you understand, but I'll do my best."

She put the device on Nicole's abdomen and slowly moved it around, pressing down every so often and taking a picture. Nicole saw blurs followed by things she could almost pick out, then blurs again. Devlin seemed hypnotized. He crushed Nicole's hand in his, his gaze on the screen.

"Have you felt movement?" the doctor asked.

"Yes. Flutters."

Dr. Saxon looked at Devlin. "Can you feel them yet?"

He shook his head.

"It may be a little while still. Firsts are sometimes more difficult to feel. Okay." She put away the wand, handed Nicole some cloths to wipe off the gel. "Here's your Broadway premiere."

She showed the pictures then, pointing out all the body parts. Fingers and toes. The spinal column. A beautiful little head. Arms and legs all tucked up close. The life-sustaining umbilical cord. Nicole's eyes welled, which made her mad. She wanted to see everything.

"He looks perfect," Devlin said.

"She," Nicole countered, wiping her eyes.

The doctor just laughed, then handed Devlin a piece of paper printed with four different photos, copies of the ones in which she'd pointed out the details. "Take good care of them, Papa. I'll see you in a month."

The door shut. Quiet settled in the room. He seemed as in awe as she was. She held out her hand. "Can I see those again?"

Nicole traced all the tiny features with her fingers. "Look," she said. "She has your nose."

He didn't laugh at her teasing. Instead he stared into her eyes for a long time. "I have to go," he said finally.

She called his name. He kept going. She climbed off the table, the drape clutched to her, the page of ultrasound photos clenched in her hand, totally bewildered. And maybe a little scared, too.

It seemed like a now-or-never moment. Like his leaving meant something huge and important. He hadn't been unpredictable before. She had no idea what his actions meant.

Nicole dressed, made her next appointment and then drove to work.

"If it's just you and me, kid," she said to the photographs, a lump in her throat, "we might as well start getting used to it."

Fourteen

Nicole woke from a sound sleep to banging coming from her front door. She looked at the clock, saw it was almost midnight. She was scared to get out of bed to such a ruckus. Then she heard him call her name. Devlin.

The pounding continued.

She slipped into her robe as she hurried into the living room, turned the lock with shaking fingers, then opened the door.

"What are you doing?" she asked, tempted to grab his arm and pull him in. He looked awful. His eyes were red and his hair uncombed. Once again he looked as if he hadn't shaved in the two days since she'd seen him at the doctor's office. Two long, devastating, horrible, crushing days when she'd felt lost and lonely. A look into her future, she feared. She'd cursed him, cried over him. She'd dialed all but the last digit of his number, then hung up, several times. She didn't think she could take much more, and now here he was, looking as miserable as she felt.

"Are you drunk?" she asked, studying him. She wished she could hug him and make whatever was hurting him go away. She wanted him to hug her back.

"Maybe a little."

"How little?"

"I've had a few. Not enough to leave me incapacitated."

"And you *drove* here?"

"I took a cab."

Which meant she had to deal with him. It was too cold to leave him outdoors. "Come in." She was still stunned by—and hopeful about—how horrible he looked. "Why were you drinking?"

He lifted a hand toward her hair then dropped it. "Because I ran out of other ideas."

"I think we'd better sit down." She tugged him along with her, was amazed how he let her take control. "What's going on?"

He sat bonelessly, his knees spread, his hands resting on his thighs. "I told my father I quit."

"Wow. I'm sure that came as a shock."

He snorted. This Devlin was so different from the one she'd known until now that she could hardly believe he was the same man.

"Yeah, which is why I let him rant for a while."

"About what?"

"Tradition. Responsibility. Obligation. Duty."

He said the word *duty* as if it were an obscenity.

"I had to hang up on him."

"Of course you did."

"He called back a couple hours later. Told me the board had decided to make me president of a new commercial real estate division. I'd have a lot more autonomy and authority."

"Good." When he glared at her she said, "Not good?"

"I have never worked anywhere other than my family's bank. I'm good, Nicole. I'm damn good. I want to prove it to myself and everyone else. I want to sink or swim on my own."

"Looks like you're going to do that." She patted his arm. "So, getting a little drunk was supposed to help you get ideas for the new job?"

"No. You. I ran out of ideas about *you*."

She shook her head, still not understanding.

"I don't know what else I can do. I don't want my child born out of wedlock. I told you I believe he's mine—"

"She," she said automatically.

He didn't crack a smile. "I wanted you to choose a ring. I've told you I would take care of you forever. I even stayed away, giving you the space you seemed to want." He dragged his hands down his face. "Then I saw the ultrasound. It made it so real, you know?"

"Real?"

"I see the changes in your body. I've felt them. I knew there was a child growing inside you. But when I heard the heartbeat and saw the images, saw his arms and legs moving, it was suddenly *real*. I wanted to protect him and love him and be a completely different kind of father than mine."

He looked straight at her. "And I realized I'd fallen in love with you. I didn't recognize it was love until it was walking away. *You* were walking away. And I don't know what else I can do to convince you to marry me beyond what I've already offered."

Joy swept through her like nothing she'd known. She could barely see him through her tears that began to well. "I fell in love with you in Atlantic City."

"Did you?" He reached out tentatively to touch her face.

"I think I did, too. All I knew was I'd never wanted a second date with anyone until you. And now I want a lifetime."

She tried to breathe. Words poured out of her. "You want a prenup, sweetheart, I'll sign a prenup. You want to live in Philadelphia, we'll live in Philadelphia. I'd like to keep this cabin, however. Maybe we could vacation here occasionally. Maybe my dad would like to use—"

He crushed her in his arms, emotion flowing from him like a palpable thing. He'd probably been storing it up for a lifetime but had never felt he could let his guard down with anyone before.

"I told you I will marry only once," he said close to her ear. "No prenup necessary for that. And if you want to stay on here, we can do that. I can work from anywhere. Except—" he leaned back "—we have to build another home. This is too—"

"Small. I know." She cupped his face, welcoming a kiss, his beard scratchy, but what did it matter? "We can live anywhere, Devlin. Sweetheart. Anywhere."

She pulled his hand to where their baby had started to kick.

"I feel him," he said quietly, then he smiled. "Her."

"*Him* is okay."

After the movement stopped, he dug into a pocket and pulled out a jeweler's box. "I've been carrying this around with me."

Before she could open the lid, he slid to a knee on the floor and faced her. "I love you, Nicole. You are my lucky charm. I want to have more children with you. I want to take care of you. I want to be your partner forever. Please, marry me."

After a proposal like that, she would never again think he married her because of the baby. She was his choice, even if they *had* gone about things backward. "I love you, Devlin. Yes, I'll marry you."

He pushed the lever to open the box. The ring she'd admired winked at her, a sparkly sapphire-and-diamond flower. She put a hand to her mouth. "How did you know?"

"It was the one I'd picked. The others were window dressing." He plucked the ring from the box and slid it onto her finger.

"It's beautiful."

"It had to match the setting, the very beautiful woman I love."

She barely recognized this gentle, besotted man, but she liked him. She also liked his old self-confidence as much as his new devotion. She hoped the two sides of him would merge and mingle.

"The wedding?" she asked.

"I don't think we should delay, do you? Can you put it together in a week? Next Saturday at the Sterling's wedding chapel?"

"I wouldn't have to do anything but make decisions. The wedding planners do all the work." Her head started to spin. "I want two of my girlfriends from Atlantic City to be my attendants. We'll have to figure out how to get their dresses. And my dress."

"Whatever you want."

"Hey, you're lucking out," she said, framing his face. "I only have a week to be a bridezilla, then it's over. Some women drag that out for months. You'll only have a week to worry if you made a mistake."

He smiled. "I haven't made a mistake."

She squeezed his hands when another thought struck her. "Your parents…"

"Will be invited."

"What if they don't come?"

"It doesn't matter who else is there, Ms. Fortune. You show up, and it's fine with me. I'm sure my sister Joan will come, and her husband, and their two and two-thirds off-spring. You can even invite *Mark*."

She brushed his unruly hair, then linked her fingers at the back of his neck. "Rubbing it in, huh?"

"Maybe."

"I never slept with him," she said, then kissed him.

He didn't say anything, but she could tell he was glad.

"Would you like to go to bed?" she asked.

"Yeah." One word, but layered with so much meaning. "I missed you."

The words were music to her ears. "Let's go make up for lost time."

Dev lifted the frosty glass of ice-cold beer the bartender had just set in front of him. He scanned the casino's sports bar in time to see a man stride into the room. Beer sloshed onto Dev's hand in a déjà vu moment as he thumped the glass onto the bar. A grin stretched his mouth as the dark-haired, dark-eyed man approached, then stopped in front of Dev.

"I don't see a ball and chain," the man said. "But I hear you've got one."

Dev laughed, extended his hand, then pulled Ryan Sperling into a quick, hearty hug. "Man, you haven't changed a bit, Ryan. Not a bit."

"You have." He took the seat next to Dev's and ordered a beer. "What's that fuzz on your face?"

"It's coming off for the wedding. But I'm leaving it on until my father gets here tomorrow."

Ryan laughed, low. "I hear you."

One of the ties that had bound Dev and Ryan was their difficult relationships with their fathers. Apparently, that hadn't changed for Ryan, either. "Thanks for being my best man."

"I'm honored. When do I get to meet the miracle worker?"

"Nicole's working her last shift. She'll be done in an hour. Hey, we moved out of the lodge and into her cabin, but the caretaker, Mary, says I can't hand the keys over to you tonight. She'll clean the place in the morning and get the keys to you."

"No problem. Coming in a day early, I figured I'd get a room here anyway."

"Nicole got you a suite. It's on us."

"Yeah? Thanks."

"I hope you enjoy the lodge—the Love Shack—as much as I did. And Luke and Nathan, for that matter. You did hear they both got married, right?"

Ryan shuddered. "Yeah. Not me, though. No wedding. No hooking up. No *permanently* hooking up."

"Good luck with that. The lodge is magic. And, hey, if you find you do need a best man, after all, I'll be happy to return the favor."

"Bite your tongue."

Dev spied Nicole heading their way. The past few days had been a whirlwind as they prepared for the quick wedding. She hadn't even come close to a being a bridezilla, but a glowing woman who showed her love at every opportunity. He knew she was worried about meeting his parents. He tried to assure her that his first loyalty would always be to her, that *they* were a family now. It was something he was going to have to show her, not just tell her.

"Here's my beautiful bride." Dev introduced them.

"Are you sure you want to marry this guy?" Ryan asked her. "Do you have full disclosure about him? Maybe I should tell you about—"

Dev slapped his arm around Ryan's shoulders. "I think Nicole has to get back to work now."

"Not really. I—"

"Yeah. You do." He kissed her soundly, ending the discussion.

"So that's how you stop a woman from talking," Ryan said. "I'll have to remember that."

Nicole grinned, taking the kidding well. "Here's the key to your suite," she said. "It's got a view you won't believe. My bridesmaids, Lisa and DeeDee, are in the next room. They're both single," she added with a wink before she left.

"So," Ryan said, taking his seat again and lifting his glass in a toast. "You're going to be a father."

"A different kind from mine, Ryan. Completely different."

"Good."

Dev reached into his pocket and pulled out a piece of paper he'd been carrying around since his first night at the lodge, a note that had been taped to the bathroom mirror. He opened it, placed it on the bar and slid it in front of Ryan. "Luke left me this."

Ryan read it aloud. "'Remember the talk we had about women on New Year's Eve our senior year? We were wrong, man. So wrong. We didn't have a clue.'" Ryan frowned. "I'm not recalling that."

"Took me all month to figure it out myself. Remember the list we came up with? The universal truths about women?"

Ryan rapped the note with his fist. "Oh, yeah. They tie you down."

Dev grinned. "They cut off your freedom."

"Right! And they won't let you ever do anything dangerous again."

"Yeah." He hesitated. "Like what? What do you suppose we meant?"

"Like… Hell, I don't know. Become a Navy SEAL."

"Right," Dev said, trying not to smile, then adding another from their list. "Sex gets boring."

"The worst of all, man. Boring sex." Ryan took a long swig of his beer, then set the glass down carefully, contemplating Luke's note. "I don't get it. Why does he say we were wrong? All those things are true."

"Because we were talking about women. Plural. In general. Not a woman in particular. Maybe it is all true—except the boring sex part. I refuse to believe that one. But when it's the right woman, we want to be with her. We want to be there for a lifetime. None of the rest matters. Except the boring sex."

"Shoot, man. You're hopeless." Ryan tempered it with a grin, then clinked his glass to Dev's.

Dev nodded, but he knew the truth. He wasn't hopeless at all. He was the most hopeful he'd ever been in his life. The universal truth he'd learned was that love changed everything.

He studied Ryan, who'd turned his attention to the Giants game on the television, just as Dev had been doing a month ago. Before his life changed for good.

For *good*.

* * * * *

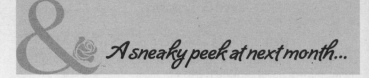

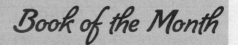

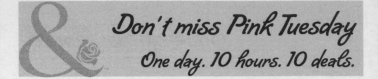

Don't miss Pink Tuesday
One day. 10 hours. 10 deals.

PINK TUESDAY IS COMING!

10 hours...10 unmissable deals!

This Valentine's Day we will be bringing you fantastic offers across a range of our titles—each hour, on the hour!

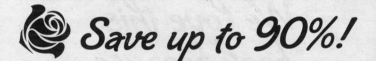

Save up to 90%!

Pink Tuesday starts
9am Tuesday 14th February

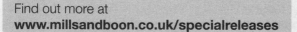